Enemies within these Shores

OTHER TITLES BY DEBBIE TERRANOVA

The Scarlet Key

Baby Farm

Mowbray Brothers

Enemies within these Shores

A Novel

DEBBIE TERRANOVA

This is a work of fiction. Names, characters, organizations, places, incidents and dialogue are either the product of the author's imagination or used fictitiously. Certain historical figures feature in this book and some of the events did take place, however these are depicted as characters, settings, and scenes as imagined or dramatized by the author and are not intended to represent actual persons, living or dead, or to be factual accounts.

First published 2018 by Terranova Publications
PO Box 4144, St Lucia South, Queensland 4067 Australia
Email: terranovapublications@gmail.com
Website: www.terranovapublications.com

ISBN-13: 978 0 9941700 2 6 (paperback)

Cover design by Elise Terranova
Website: www.eliseterranova.com

For Sam, Elise, and Adam.

In memory of Luigi

Author's Note

What is real and what is imagined? Often, in a historical novel such as this, it comes down to perspective. While the characters and story of *Enemies within these Shores* are essentially creations of my imagination, the settings and events associated with Australia during World War Two are either real or have been reconstructed from research and documentary evidence.

Sometimes it is hard to draw a distinction between truth, propaganda, and imagination. Indeed, in reading newspaper articles of the war years it is apparent that creative licence or straight out propaganda was used to influence nations.

The *Brisbane Line* is one example, in my opinion. In the event of invasion by the island-hopping Japanese, the alleged plan was for the Australian Military Forces to abandon the northern part of Australia and defend only the southern states.

The actual position of the *Brisbane Line* varies from source to source. Some say it was near Rockhampton, others say it was not far from Brisbane's northern outskirts, while others place it even further south.

On a recent visit to the Tenterfield district of New South Wales, I discovered 'relics' in the form of timber tank-traps and concrete pyramids called 'dragon teeth' installed in bushland gullies and across a creek. How a few flimsy barriers might have stopped the Japanese Imperial Army is beyond my imagination. Was the real purpose of such measures simply to make citizens feel more secure?

That aside, the historical events that drive the various storylines of *Enemies within these Shores* are largely true. The locations of Cairns, Brisbane, Loveday, and country towns with wartime associations such as

Barmera and Hay, are real. While Wooranoora does not exist per se, it is representative of a typical sugar town in far north Queensland.

All of the characters are creations of my imagination. Some are representative of historical figures, for example US General Douglas MacArthur who was the Supreme Commander of the campaign against the Japanese in the southwest Pacific, and Justice Philp who was a judge of the Supreme Court in Brisbane. In order to bring the stories to life, I have used artistic licence to recreate how they might have behaved, what they might have said, and how they might have felt. In so doing, I have not sought to draw any character as purely good or evil.

The story of Luigi is a reconstruction of a real person's life whose details were pieced together through painstaking research. The character Luigi Innocenti is based on my father-in-law, a cane farmer who was interned for no reason other than his Italian origin. I never had the privilege of meeting him. He died in 1963.

In the early 1920s, my father-in-law and four of his brothers came to far north Queensland to escape turmoil and poverty in Sicily and to make a better life for the families they intended to have. Two brothers returned within a few years but three remained for a lifetime. While clearing land shortly after he arrived, Luigi suffered a debilitating accident. Unable to do heavy work for a time, he became the cook for a boarding house.

Later he worked alongside his two brothers on a cane farm they bought in partnership at Happy Valley near Babinda. Throughout the Great Depression they prospered. When Italy declared war on Great Britain in 1940, everything they'd achieved was dashed away. One by one, the three brothers were 'captured' by the local police and imprisoned like common criminals. In Brisbane, their appeals were dismissed and they were banished to the Loveday Internment Camps in South Australia where they remained for the duration of the war.

Today, little remains of the internment camps apart from a few footings, crumbling walls here and there, and a large building near Thiele Road that incorporates part of the recreation facilities of General Headquarters.

A character based on the internee leader of Camp 9, Prince Alfonso del Drago, a member of the royal family of Rome, features in the story.

Another character is based on the camp commandant, Lieutenant-Colonel Edwin Thayer Dean, a visionary leader who treated the internees with dignity and respect. On 4 December 1945, *The Advertiser* (an Adelaide newspaper) described the Loveday Internment Camps as 'a story of vision and enterprise'.

When certain essential items such as vegetable seed, morphine and insecticide became unobtainable due to the war, the Loveday camps came to the fore. A total of 46,000 lbs of vegetable seed was produced, mainly tomato, bean, beetroot, lettuce and cabbage. In the 1944-45 season alone, 35 tons of opium poppies were harvested and 10 tons of pyrethrum flowers were cut to make insecticides. About 25 acres of guayule, a Mexican shrub with a rubber-like sap, were planted but the project did not proceed beyond the experimental stage.

In just two years, the Loveday poultry project produced 291,300 eggs and 2,800 birds for meat. Paid internee labour was used to repair tents, horse rugs and web equipment for the army.

Nothing was wasted.

The 1,250 bacon pigs produced by the piggery were reared largely on scrap food. Surplus fats from the camps were converted into 110,000 lbs of soap and distributed to the army.

Despite these successes, the day-to-day operations of the Loveday camps were not all plain sailing. Stories such as the escape attempt by German internees and the murder of Francesco Fantin are based on actual events.

The characters Edith Zucchero, William Delahunty, and Ted Long are entirely fictional. That said, their stories reflect the lives and times of ordinary Australians during the period 1939 to 1945.

Through these characters, readers will come to appreciate what it was like to be a young mother who must manage a cane farm alone; or a state Member of Parliament who must accommodate a *friendly invasion* of American servicemen, half of whom do not comply with the White Australia Policy; or a military guard who must control thousands of Italian, German and Japanese internees with conflicting political alignments, religious beliefs, customs, and languages.

In creating or recreating these stories, I have imagined how events might have played out and interactions that might have occurred between characters. I have attempted to portray names found on documents as rounded characters with talents, feelings, and flaws.

If, in the creative process, I have misrepresented a person who once lived, or presented inaccuracies or unintentionally caused offence, I hereby apologise.

Hardcopy records held in various government archives in Brisbane, Canberra, and Adelaide, digitised records and photographs on the website of the National Archives of Australia, and digitised newspapers on the National Library of Australia website have been valuable sources of information and inspiration in piecing this narrative together. Publications used for reference are listed at the end of the book.

Also invaluable was the assistance of regional historical societies, in particular the Cairns Historical Society, the MacArthur Museum Brisbane, the Barmera Information Centre, the Cobdogla Irrigation Museum, and the many volunteers who live and breathe local history.

A special thank you goes to the late Max Scholz, Barmera historian and author who spent an entire afternoon showing me memorabilia and recounting experiences of his boyhood, when he delivered milk from his grandparents' dairy farm to the Loveday Internment Camps.

Family members, friends, and acquaintances have also provided much of the background material for the novel.

However, the primary source of information about daily life in far north Queensland, cane farming, tractors, Italian dialects, Sicilian superstitions and mannerisms, and Luigi's life story (remembered from childhood) was my darling husband, Sam.

Troubles in the West

One

Brisbane, 24 May 1939

In his office in Parliament House, William James Delahunty, Labor representative of the far north Queensland electorate of Endeavour, combed his brillantined hair and slipped on his suit jacket. At today's Cabinet meeting, the main topic of discussion would be the coming war.

Aged in his late forties, Delahunty was not unfamiliar with war. As a youth, he'd enlisted and served his nation for two full years during the Great War. In 1916, while his unit was dug-in at the Somme and operating under the vilest conditions imaginable, a stray shard of shrapnel had caught his left thigh. He was evacuated to hospital in London, where he remained unfit for active duty and was later redeployed to Communications Operations until the armistice was signed.

After two decades of hard-won peace, there were rumblings that Europe was about to explode again. Earlier in the week a so-called *Pact of Steel* had been signed between Adolph Hitler and Benito Mussolini, which formalised a political and military alliance and supported the expansionist ambitions of both dictators.

This was most disconcerting indeed.

Armed with *The Courier-Mail* and a copy of some federal legislation enacted for the previous war, Delahunty strode into the Cabinet room.

Most of the chairs around the boardroom table were empty. Apparently, an upcoming by-election and an early 'flu epidemic had decimated the number of Members who could attend. Despite this, at nine o'clock sharp the Premier declared the meeting open.

Three items were foremost on the agenda: stemming the flood of undesirable immigrants into the state from nations such as southern Italy; securing a supply of suitable rural workers while continuing to uphold the

3

White Australia Policy; and ensuring the safety and security of Queensland in the event of a major conflict between the powers of Europe and Britain.

As the elected representative of a large sugar-growing district, Delahunty was one of the most vocal on all counts. 'If this turbulence comes to war, we should take the opportunity to rid ourselves of troublemakers and illiterates who have no right to be in this country. We, of the far north, are fairly drowning in immigrants who refuse to learn the language or assimilate into our way of life. These *peasants*, these wretched *curs*, are blights on our society. They fill our towns, live off the smell of an oily rag, and send all their earnings—*black money*, I might add—south or out of the country. On top of that, they work for less than the award and undermine the union movement. This state receives no benefits whatsoever. In fact, we are being milked for all we are worth! No-one in the Federal government has the intestinal fortitude to turn the situation around. Well, if Prime Minister Menzies can't do his job, then we should take matters into our own hands and run this State the way we see fit.'

For this little homily, he received a few hear-hears and hearty applause.

The Premier said, 'I am sure those in this room are well aware of the problems, Mr Delahunty. Can you offer any solutions?'

This was the prompt he was hoping for. On cue, he placed his two exhibits on the table.

'Here, gentlemen, is my solution. Exhibit one: according to the press, war is inevitable. It may not happen next week or next month. But, mark my words, it will happen before next year. Exhibit two: in 1914, federal legislation was passed to allow enemies of Britain to be interned as a pre-emptive measure. This was most effective in forcibly removing undesirables from the community and preventing attack from enemies within these shores. I propose that we make representations to Canberra for similar legislation to be passed immediately. Furthermore, I propose that we draft parallel and enabling legislation for the state.'

'What say all of you?' said the Premier. 'Is it *yea*?'

The five men present raised their hands in support.

'Thank you Mr Delahunty,' said the Premier. 'I shall instruct my staff to make this a top priority.'

When the meeting broke up for lunch, Delahunty put on his hat and exited the building to George Street. In the botanical gardens opposite, the lofty palm trees and spotted crotons took his mind to the tropical north. For three months he'd been living out of a suitcase. He missed his home in Cairns and he missed his wife, although from all observations she showed few signs of missing him. She seldom wrote and, whenever he was in town, she avoided all forms of physical contact. He felt like a leper and an impotent one at that.

'Frigid' was the term his physician had used when Delahunty consulted him—in Margaret's absence—about the delicate subject of sex.

'How old is your wife?' the physician had said.

'Forty-seven.'

'Sometimes it happens with the change of life.'

'Is the condition permanent?' Delahunty asked warily.

'I'm afraid patience is the recommended cure.'

Patience! He was a politician for Heaven's sake. There was not a patient bone in his body.

Instead of descending the stairs into the botanical gardens, he turned left and wandered along George Street, past the Bellevue Hotel with two layers of white iron-lace and the red-brick Mansions. Opposite the sandstone Treasury Building was the equally-imposing Bank of New South Wales. More for something to do than any other reason, he crossed the street and entered the cavernous foyer.

Marble columns towered over a patterned terrazzo floor. Behind the polished-timber counter was a row of tellers dressed in white shirts and red ties. Only one did not wear a tie: a young woman, the sole representative of the fairer sex. She was slim and shapely and in her mid-twenties. Her chestnut hair was coiled into a snood, the latest *look* in New York, according to the women's pages of *The Courier-Mail*. Her lipstick was strawberry red.

Customers were queueing for service. Loitering in a bank was a sure way to attract attention of the wrong kind. He ought to join a queue or else leave. Although he didn't actually need any cash, Delahunty found himself in the line for the female teller.

In his jacket was his bank passbook, accidentally left there after withdrawing two pounds for dinner at the Queensland Club the day before. He fumbled the grey booklet to the current page and presented it through the grille to the woman. She accepted it with a smile so alluring that he couldn't think of anything but kissing those sweet luscious lips.

'Please complete the withdrawal slip and sign it.' She pushed back the passbook, along with a pink form.

Blood rushed to his head. On thousands of occasions he had withdrawn money, but this time his mind had gone blank. He was behaving like that nervy pimple-faced youth he once was, before losing his virginity in a whorehouse in Calais.

'It's okay, Mr Delahunty. I can help you fill it out.'

5

He gazed into her bottomless green eyes. 'How did you know my name, Miss?'

'Why, it says so right here in your passbook.' She smothered an amused grin.

He took the pen, dipped the nib into the inkwell and completed the task as instructed. The amount he'd written was one hundred pounds.

'Cash or cheque, Mr Delahunty?'

'Cash please. I'm feeling lucky.'

Her perfect eyebrows lifted slightly. 'Sorry sir, but a large amount like this will take a few minutes to process. Please take a seat and I'll call you when it's ready.'

He retreated to the waiting area while she turned to the next customer.

Ten minutes later she waved him up. His palms were sweating. She pushed the passbook with the banknotes towards him. As he reached for it, their fingertips accidentally touched.

It was now or never. As inexpertly as a schoolboy, he gripped her fingers and whispered, 'If you're not busy after work, would you like to meet me for a drink?'

Oh God, he hadn't done that in years. What was he thinking? What if she slapped his face? Worse, what if she screamed or called her supervisor? He could see the headlines now. 'Senior Politician Arrested for Indecent Proposal.'

Her response was a complete surprise. 'The Grosvenor, private bar, five-thirty.'

'Thank you, Miss.'

'The name's Amy.'

He removed his hand and with it the passbook and the money. Some of the cash he stashed in his wallet, which was now too fat to close. The rest he folded into the fob pocket of his trousers. That he'd emptied his entire savings account on a whim weighed lightly on his conscience. What Margaret didn't know wouldn't hurt her. By the time he returned north, he would have returned the money to its rightful place and his wife would be none the wiser.

Shortly before the appointed time, Delahunty entered the dimly-lit private bar of the Grosvenor. The carpet was rich burgundy, patterned with golden swirls. The walls were covered in plush wallpaper; chandeliers hung from the ceiling.

He scanned the room for her. Several tables were occupied by young chaps in suits. Law clerks, most probably. The Supreme Court was less than twenty yards away. Huddled in a corner booth, three shopgirls in MacDonnell and East uniforms were whispering behind their hands. Giggles suggested that the topic of conversation was the menfolk at the next table.

After ascertaining that he was definitely the first to arrive, Delahunty ordered a whisky on the rocks and took it to a booth at the rear of the bar. From there he could observe the comings and goings of customers and hopefully spot the delightful bank teller called Amy as soon as she arrived. He prayed that she wouldn't change her mind.

He checked his fob watch. Five-forty.

Damn, she was going to stand him up; he could feel it in his bones. Then he'd need a bit of extra fortitude to accompany him to the hotel where he was staying and get him through yet another long, lonely night. To think that a pretty young thing would find him attractive was downright delusional. He was nothing but an old fool.

Five minutes later he finished the whisky and went to the bar to order another. Suddenly a soft voice was caressing his ear. 'Sorry I'm late, Mr Delahunty. Trouble balancing the books. Can you get me a gin and tonic?'

He turned to face her, then took her hand and pressed it to his lips. 'Please, call me William.' She was all pearly teeth and cute dimples. Utterly mesmerising. 'I thought you weren't coming. My apologies for being forward at the bank. I'm not normally like that with women, but how could I resist? My dear, you quite take my breath away.'

The drinks arrived and they moved to the booth that he'd claimed earlier. He swirled the spirits around the ice, took a sip. The whisky lit the fire in his loins.

'I don't normally accept over-the-counter invitations from customers,' she quipped.

'What made you accept this one?'

She smiled coyly. 'I know who you are, William Delahunty. I've seen you outside Parliament House. You're the Member for Endeavour and your *marriage* as well as your drink is on the rocks. Am I right?'

'Got it in one. Let's make a toast.' He raised his glass. 'To the start of a beautiful friendship.'

Two

On the back porch of the farmhouse, Luigi Innocenti shivered and rolled the first cigarette of the day. Dense fog had blanketed the valley, muffling the sounds of the early morning. The birds were hushed and moisture dripped silently from the milky pine tree.

Although the outside privy was just twenty steps away, its outline was not visible. Nor were the sixty acres of cane fields that rolled down to the creek, nor the deep blue mountains beyond. Thick fog like this was rare in the far north. It had the character of a miasma, tainted with the stench of death. His mother would have warned him to remain indoors out of the noxious 'bad air', lest he contract some life-threatening disease. But he didn't believe in her old superstitions, so he unhooked the sugarbag from its peg, covered his head, and took a bold step out into the moist air.

He headed for the chook pen. It was late and the poor creatures hadn't been fed. Angelo was usually up and at work long before the sun rose. His beloved hens took precedence over humans. But Angelo had gone back to Sicily to see their family, so all the farm chores fell to him.

The gate creaked open. Squawking and squabbling, the hens scurried around his legs. After doling out the feed and refilling the water trough, he went to the laying boxes to collect the eggs. The first was empty and so was the second. In the third was just one lonely egg.

'*Mamma mia!*' Grimly he shook his head. Whenever the hens went off the lay, something out-of-the-ordinary was up. He hoped it had nothing to do with Angelo. Four months had passed since he'd left and he had not sent one letter. Typical!

Luigi should have gone instead. By now their business in Sicily would have been settled and he certainly wouldn't have kept his brother on a knife-edge, waiting for a letter that never came.

In the kitchen, Luigi cracked the fresh egg into a china bowl and added two from the previous day. He put the cast-iron frypan on the stove, added a slurp of oil, chopped capsicum, chilli, and garlic from the plait by the door. While the mixture sizzled and spat, he whistled tunelessly. A few minutes later he added the eggs. Meanwhile, the tea was brewing in the enamel pot.

Deep in thought, he ate the meal without tasting it. The unseasonal fog, the off-the-lay chooks, the long silence from Italy. It must be an omen.

His fingers wandered across the table to the worn leather pouch. In it was a relic of San Filippo, patron saint of his town. The relic had the power to ward off the evil eye, but today he used it to send a prayer.

It was Friday, the day he collected the rent from the manager of the boarding house. After breakfast, he went down to the tank stand to shave. His wavy hair—once jet black—was silvering at the temples; his skin was as tanned as cowhide.

Afterwards, he dressed in his one and only suit and waded through the fog to where the Terraplane pickup was parked. As he kicked the block of wood from beneath the front wheel, a pain shot through his gut. He rubbed the scar, souvenir of his scrub-clearing days. Cane growing was heavy work but until Angelo returned he must continue to run the farm on his own.

Luigi turned on the ignition and gave the crank-handle a few turns. After one lame splutter, the engine fired. He settled into the driver's seat, shifted the gearstick into first. The vehicle rolled down the incline and onto the dirt track that meandered between the cane farms of the Cassowary Valley.

With care, he navigated the potholes and washouts, tiptoed the wheels through the creek crossing where fast-running water had polished the stones into smooth ovals. Sunlight filtered through the fog, steam curled from the earth. Although it was just six miles to town, the deplorable state of the track made it seem like sixteen. He lit a smoke, rested an elbow on the window sill and breathed in the cool air.

After all the years in the tropics, he still found it hard to call the mid-year season 'winter'. Winter in the old country was wicked. Frosts froze the wheat fields and their stone house on the mountainside was as cold as an icebox. In Australia, summer was the killer. Even through the hottest months, the brothers toiled in the paddocks. Rain, hail, or shine, the cane quota had to be grown, cut, and delivered to the mill for crushing.

Last season Angelo had gone down with heatstroke, so they'd done a deal with two of the boarders. Non-unionists of course. Accommodation and full board in exchange for labour. Lucky neither the union nor *the Mob* found out, otherwise they would have all been in trouble. Other farmers had been blacklisted by the union or had their crops torched by *the Mob*. One fellow who'd refused to pay the extortion money had lost an ear to a cane-knife.

Nearer town, Luigi drove between paddocks of *badila* cane, the purple stalks bulging with juice. The pickup rounded the final bend. At the crossroads, he turned left to Wooranoora. Compared to the track from the farm, the main road was broad and smooth. It ran parallel to the Great Northern railway line, one thousand miles of narrow-gauge track from Cairns all the way down to Brisbane. Four months before, Angelo had caught the train south before boarding the steamer to Italy.

Surely a letter would be waiting at the post office. Perhaps he should go there first. He swung left into Sugarmill Street, stopped halfway along the strip of shops.

Tony Zucchero, his accountant and friend, was loitering outside the post office.

'*Buon giorno*, Luigi!' They gripped hands. '*Madonna!* What a morning!' He was smiling but his palms were sticky with sweat.

'What's happened?' said Luigi.

'Father-in-law problems … again. That man is bloody impossible.' Tony balled his fists and shoved them in his pockets. 'For God's sake, don't mention this to my wife,' he was quick to add.

'Of course not. Is there anything I can do to help?'

'No, thanks anyway. Either it'll work itself out or I'll be excommunicated from Edith's family. Either way, I don't really care.' He slapped Luigi on the shoulder. 'Better get myself to work. The tax office waits for no man. *Ciao.*'

Luigi opened their post office box. Three bills but no letters from Italy. His blood pressure rose a notch. Again, he cursed Angelo for his thoughtlessness.

Returning to the pickup, he drove east across the train tracks towards the boarding house. To the locals, the two-storey building near the railway station was known as the *Italian Boarding House*. Wide verandas and white balustrades hugged a central timber core. Workers who blew into town knew the place by reputation: a clean bed and hearty meals for a modest weekly rate. They came not just from Italy but from all parts of Europe: Albania, Malta, Finland, Yugoslavia, Russia, Spain. The common language was a hybrid of dialects and bumbling English. Britishers steered clear of the place, preferring to stay at the newer State Hotel down the street which was also licensed to serve grog.

Luigi climbed the two front steps and walked across the verandah. The manager, Mrs Ross—five-foot tall and almost as round—came waddling towards him. A mischievous grin played about the creases of her face.

'Come into the dining room, luv,' she puffed. 'There's a lovely surprise.'

She hung back while he followed the scent of fresh-baked cake down the hall. The over-furnished dining room contained three large tables and about twenty mismatched chairs. Against the wall was an enormous sideboard, stacked to the brim with china and glass. Lightbulbs hung from the pressed-metal ceiling. Although the furniture was old, it was solid and serviceable and the brothers saw no reason to replace it.

At the middle table sat a stocky man in a suit. His back was to the door but his identity was unmistakable.

'Angelo!'

'*Ciao,* brother!' The other man spun around and grabbed Luigi in a hug.

Luigi pulled up a chair and said in Sicilian, 'But you weren't due back until August!'

Mrs Ross brought in a tray with a plate of cake and a teapot. 'I'll leave you to it, my dears. Rent money's in the calico bag under the counter. Everyone's paid in full.'

'Thanks, *Mississa* Ross,' said Angelo in unsteady English.

'No trouble at all, luv.' She smiled, her teeth a collection of ivory that was far too big for her mouth. 'Nice to have you back.' She cut the cake into generous wedges and exited the room.

Luigi took a piece. It was warm and buttery. Mrs Ross certainly knew how to cook.

'So, what happened?'

Angelo groaned. 'What a complete and utter disaster!' He dropped his head into his hands. 'Fourteen days! That's the entire time I was there. From the minute I disembarked until the minute I left. There was no time to get anything done.'

'Why did you have to leave so fast?'

'If I didn't, they would've put me in the army.'

'*Porca miseria!*'

Luigi poured the tea, added three spoons of sugar and a dash of milk. 'I take it we're no closer to finalising our father's estate.'

Angelo shook his head.

'How's the family then?'

'Mamma's health isn't too good. Our brother Tano and his brood have moved in to help. As you know, the house was bequeathed to me but possession is nine-tenths of the law. What could I do?' He turned up his palms and shrugged.

'Hmmm. What about the land Papa bought for us?'

'Same. The other brothers are sitting on it. They grow wheat and run goats. There's a roof over their heads but they don't make much of a living.' He rubbed his thumb and fingers together. '*U pizzu*. If you don't oil the right palms …'

'You don't have to spell it out. That was one of the reasons we left.' Full well he knew that some of *the Mob* had migrated to Australia. Thankfully most were based in the sugar towns a long way to the south.

Luigi pressed on. 'I don't suppose you found a nice woman then.'

'*Mamma mia!* I'm not Rudolph Valentino! I was there only a few days.'

Later at the farmhouse, Angelo rummaged through his travel port. Amongst his clothes were a few souvenirs: a snow-dome of Mount Etna, the three-legged flag of Sicily, picture postcards of Messina.

He unrolled a singlet and uncovered a hunting-knife with a six-inch blade and a carved bone handle. 'Remember this?'

Luigi turned the blade in his palm. 'It was Tano's pride and joy.'

'He gave it to me on loan, only until he gets here. He's determined to come back to Australia, you know.'

Luigi ran his finger over the steel. 'He would've been here two years ago if it wasn't for that bloody Sergeant Pitt.' Although he spoke in Sicilian, he always swore in English. Australia had the best swear-words in the world. 'We should put in another application to sponsor him out.'

Returning to the port, Angelo removed a bulging grey sock. 'This is for you.'

Inside was Papa's silver cigarette case, only ever used on special occasions. The etching on the front was of the King of Italy, Vittorio Emanuele III, a distinguished-looking man with a handlebar moustache.

Luigi flipped the clasp and the little case sprang open. He closed his eyes and inhaled the intoxicating smell of old tobacco. It took him back to the *terrazza* of the family home in Agira. Life then was simple. Work, eat, sleep, work. The small memento was better than a chest of treasures.

From the bottom of the port Angelo took the last of his booty. Three books and a few leaflets in Italian. He fanned them out on the table.

Luigi picked one up. *Parla il Duce* (Mussolini Speaks). According to the blurb, it presented a blueprint for Italy's future, penned by the great leader himself.

Luigi frowned. 'Why did you buy these?'

Angelo shrugged. 'I didn't. People were giving them away. As you know, politics doesn't interest me but in Italy big things are happening. Mussolini is pulling the country out of a hole. He's building new railway lines, bridges, highways, houses. He's creating opportunities so that ordinary people can put food on the table and give their kids an education.'

'You say he's doing *good* for the country?' Luigi was sceptical. 'People here say he's *pazzo* (mad).'

'Who knows? I brought the books back for you. If you don't want them, I'll take them to the boarding house.'

'Leave them on the dresser. I'll look at them later. Now, let's eat. *Spaghetti con zucchini*. I'm cooking.'

'Mmmm.' Angelo rubbed his belly. 'Six weeks of awful English food on the ship then three days of sandwiches on the train. It's a wonder I survived.'

'It'd take more than that to kill *you*.' Luigi grinned as he lit the fire. He filled the pasta pot with water, chopped the zucchini and put the garlic in the pan to fry. Despite their occasional differences of opinion, it was good to have his brother home again.

Three

Wooranoora, 3 September 1939

The battle of the morning was over a wine cork. It began when Edith Zucchero tried to remove the offending item from her toddler's mouth. Goodness knew where Bella had found it, for the kitchen floor was normally spotless. But found it she had and, like everything else within reach, into her mouth it went.

Edith tried cajoling the two-year-old but she wasn't about to give it up without a fight. While the cork remained intact, it was probably not dangerous but already little bits were crumbling off. She was terrified that her daughter would choke.

In a last-ditch attempt Edith resorted to the distraction method, a tickle-and-snatch manoeuvre that resulted in the successful recovery of the cork. For a moment Bella looked a bit surprised, then without warning she sank her teeth into her mother's calf. Her little jaws had the grip of a rabbit trap; her teeth were razor-sharp.

'Bella! Let go!'

With a defiant frown, the infant eyed her.

'Let go, I said!' What she did next went against Edith's ideals of modern parenting but there seemed to be no other option. She raised her hand and slapped her palm down on her daughter's thigh.

The deed took a split second to register. Bella opened her mouth, sucked in air, then let rip an ear-piercing scream.

The horror-show proceeded to unfold. Yelling at the top of her lungs, Bella threw herself down and thrashed about like a wounded pup. With hands and feet, she pounded the floor. Her face went as red as an overripe tomato. In an uncontrolled state of fury, she worked her way across the room, leaving a snail-trail of tears, dribble, and snot on the green lino.

14

Edith slumped into a chair. What had she done to deserve this? If moving to a desolate shack in the wilderness wasn't enough, now her beautiful baby had turned feral. She had no-one to turn to, no-one to help her. Tony was out working on the farm. Her mother was a thousand miles south in Brisbane. Her nearest neighbour lived down a rough dirt track, way beyond shouting distance. Tears of self-pity rolled down her cheeks. Meanwhile her offspring continued to convulse in the most spectacular demonstration of temper that she'd ever seen.

Three years ago, Miss Edith Allenby had been the English mistress of a large secondary school. Her passions were literature and the theatre; occasionally she turned her hand to writing poetry. Until Tony Zucchero came along, her life had hovered in a stratosphere where conversations were about art, music, and politics. Her father was a stockbroker. Her family home was a sprawling Californian bungalow in the affluent suburb of Clayfield.

The day after she married, she lost her teaching job. That was the law. No married women were allowed to work for the State. Disappointing but necessary, she supposed. The dire state of the economy and high unemployment made drastic measures necessary.

Like a good wife, she accompanied her new husband to his farm near Wooranoora. Her father was not happy but, for the first time in her life, Edith tasted freedom.

She unpacked her city clothes in the bedroom of a timber-and-tin shack that Tony cheekily called *The Manor*. Surrounded by paddocks of nodding sugar cane and an unpredictable creek that frequently overran its banks, she attempted the impossible: to turn a rough shelter into a proper home.

In the early days, beggars and itinerants—victims of the Great Depression—came knocking on their door, asking for food in exchange for odd jobs. How they found their way to *The Manor*, so far removed from the road and the railway line, was beyond her imagination. To her, poverty was a novelty, an experience to add to her expanding knowledge of life outside the cosseted world of privilege. Those poor fellows, hungry and dressed in rags, touched a soft spot in her heart. She'd give them a bit of tucker or old clothing from Tony's wardrobe and send them on their way.

At last Bella's tantrum blew itself out. The sodden child lay hiccupping on the floor.

With a tea towel Edith wiped her own tears and picked up the toddler, who seemed to be leaking from every orifice. Thumb in mouth, Bella clung to her like a koala.

Hic, hic, hic. *Hiccup!*

'Let's clean you up.'

Edith lay the baby on the bed and removed the cloth nappy. With a flannel she sponged her off and finished with a dusting of baby powder. The child looked utterly spent, her eyelids were fluttering closed. Edith pinned up the fresh nappy and put her down to sleep in the metal cot by their double bed.

Perhaps she ought to have a kip herself. Goodness, she was tired enough.

Being a mother was far tougher than teaching other people's kids. The hours of darkness were the worst, for Bella was not an easy sleeper. Edith woke to every sniffle, every whimper. To allow Tony a good night's rest, she'd take the baby out to the rocking chair on the verandah. If she managed four hours sleep, she considered herself lucky.

Sometime later, Edith woke with a start.

Voices outside floated in through the casement window. Tony and another man were speaking in Italian. Italian was her husband's first language; his birthplace was a village near Bassano del Grappa at the foot of the Italian Alps. When he was three, his family emigrated. His father, a man of vision, encouraged his children to speak English at home. 'To be successful in this country, you must speak as good as the Britishers and you must work twice as hard.'

As a result, all four brothers went to university, entered the professions, and married women of British descent. One became a lawyer, one a chemist, another was training to be a doctor. Tony was an accountant. But he also owned a cane farm which was his passion.

When the conversation ended, Tony climbed the front stairs of the house. Before entering, he removed his sandshoes and left them on the verandah with his cane knife.

'Where's my best girl?' he called to Edith from the door. 'What's for lunch?'

Edith straightened her hair and raced into the kitchen. It was nearly noon and she hadn't begun to prepare the meal. 'I'm so sorry, darling. I must have fallen asleep.'

Tony gave her a hug and kissed her forehead. 'You look upset, *amore.*'

'Bella has been a handful.' She leant into him, breathed his reassuring odour of sugar-cane and sweat. 'Is a sandwich okay?

'Anything is okay, as long as it's food.'

She cut thick slices of white bread, smeared them with butter and yellow pickles, added slabs of cold corned beef. 'Who were you talking to?'

'Renzo, the cane cutting contractor. This year we got an Italian gang. Best news I've had in ages. They work hard and don't get drunk or make trouble. They start in a week. After lunch we'll go and check out the barracks. Perhaps you could give them a clean. Oh, before I forget, Renzo said we should listen to the midday news.'

Tony switched on the wireless which reigned over the room from atop a dresser made out of kerosene boxes. The distinctive orchestral fanfare, prelude to the ABC broadcast, blasted the kitchen.

'Good afternoon, ladies and gentlemen.' The announcer's voice sounded sombre. 'Stand by for an important announcement from the Prime Minister of Australia.'

A moment later, the plummy voice of Mr Menzies came over the airwaves.

Fellow Australians,

It is my melancholy duty to inform you officially that in consequence of persistence by Germany in her invasion of Poland, Great Britain has declared war upon her and that, as a result, Australia is also at war.

Edith's heart leapt into her mouth. Australia was at war with Germany! Again! She was too young to remember much about the Great War, but she'd seen what it had done to her parents. Her father, who'd enlisted and had served in France as an officer, returned to find solace in the bottle. Although he was a partner in the stockbroking firm, he spent more time at the pub than he did at the office. His behaviour sometimes became aggressive and erratic. Late at night, she and her mother would hide when his boots came stumbling up the stairs.

Tony was chewing his lip. 'Last time they had conscription.'

Edith threw her arms around his neck. 'I couldn't bear for you to be sent away.'

She choked back tears. What would she do, abandoned beyond the periphery of civilisation, with a farm to run and a young child to rear? What if he came back like her father or didn't come back at all?

Reason crept in. Germany, still reeling from the Great War, would be weak against the combined military might of Great Britain and all the other nations of the British Empire. Australia, New Zealand, Canada, India. This war would surely be over in a matter of weeks.

She brightened. 'Let's worry about it if it happens. Until then ... Bella's fast asleep.' She kissed him full on the lips and tweaked his nether cheek.

'*Amore*, I don't need a written invitation.' He swept her into his arms, carried her to the sleepout, and quietly closed the door.

The evening before Renzo's gang was due to begin, Tony and their neighbour, Mr Sampson, took flaming torches to the westernmost cane field. Firing the cane prevented Weil's Disease, a deadly illness spread by rats. As well as rats, the fire repelled snakes and other vermin that lived amongst the cane trash. Although firing marginally affected the sugar content of the cane, it made cutting far less hazardous.

From the back verandah, Edith watched the spectacle. The tinder-dry cane trash went up like orange fireworks against the darkening sky. Flames leapt thirty feet into the air; the glow reflected off low-hanging cloud. Everywhere was a scent like burnt toffee. Embers swirled like a million fireflies. As the breeze came up, flakes of sticky black ash swirled toward the house. Abandoning the light show, Edith raced to shut the windows before her nice new curtains were ruined.

Monday morning, the air was thick with a burnt-syrup odour. Renzo and the Italian gang had arrived before dawn. After stowing their belongings in the barracks, they took cane knives, food and waterbags and set off for the cane paddocks. One of the gang, the nominated cook, remained in the barracks to prepare the midday meal. Hard work made for healthy appetites. The talent of the cook could make or break a gang.

Normally the farmers kept away from the barracks. The gang boss and the union rep were the intermediaries who dealt with complaints and resolved disputes about accommodation, pay, or working conditions.

Apart from cleaning the rooms before and after occupation, Edith never set foot in the place. The barracks was the realm of working men and she respected that. Even after the long, low building was vacated she felt like an intruder in a world she neither knew nor understood.

This time, however, was different.

Like a moth to a lantern she found herself drawn towards the rudimentary timber structure, one hundred yards distant from the house. It was a wild-west sort of place: four small rooms, each with sufficient space for two single beds and little else, and a verandah across the front. At one end was the cookhouse, a rustic affair with a wood combustion stove, a meat safe, a refectory table and bench seats.

Someone in the cookhouse was singing. Not a sea shanty or dirty ditty like the previous cook, but an aria from Puccini's *Tosca*. For a tenor, the voice was a little high but its strength and quality were superb.

With Bella on her hip, Edith drifted towards the citrus grove that screened the barracks from the house. The last of the green-skinned oranges clung to the trees. Bella was struggling in her arms, reaching out toward the branches. With her ears tuned to the opera singer, Edith leant in and allowed the child to pick the fruit. One by one, the oranges snapped off and dropped to the ground. The little girl giggled; it was all another game.

Mid-verse, the aria stopped. Edith froze. Should she rush back to the house or introduce herself to the marvellous vocalist?

Between the branches she glimpsed a shortish, stoutish figure in a grey canecutter's singlet walking towards her. Edith took a step backwards.

The woollen singlet barely covered a pair of large and pendulous breasts!

'*Buon giorno, Mississa.*' The female voice lilted with a soft Italian accent.

'Hello. Sorry to disturb you. I was enjoying the performance.'

The woman was of indeterminate age. Amongst her dark wavy hair were threads of silver. Her face, the colour of milk tea, was dancing with vigour.

'I glad you like my song.'

'Your voice is ... how do you say ... *bellissimo.*'

The cook flashed a smile. 'When I am young, I am singing in *La Scala*. You know, opera house in Milano. Now, I cook for my 'usband and 'is mates.'

'But I thought women weren't allowed to. Union rules.'

'Shhhh! Doan tell. We all get in trouble.'

Bella reached out her little arms to the woman, who took her without hesitation.

'*Ciao bella.*' She tickled the infant under the chin.

'How did you know her name?' said Edith.

'All little girls are *bella*. You know, means beautiful.' She smiled and the dimples on her face danced. 'My name is Rosa.'

'Pleased to meet you, Rosa. I'm Edith.' Normally she insisted that farm workers call her Mrs Zucchero, but any thought of formality had vanished from her mind. Female company was hard enough to find in this rough world of men.

'If there's anything you need ...' Edith continued.

'Thanks, but I all right.' She handed Bella back to her mother. 'Gotta go cook. *Ciao*.' She turned on her heel and retreated to the cookhouse. A minute later, to the clank of a spoon against a pot, the impromptu recital continued.

Days passed. Mornings and afternoons the cane train, laden with blackened stalks of cane, chugged along the permanent tracks outside *The Manor*, bound for the mill on the northern outskirts of town. From the kitchen window, Edith could see the distant plume of smoke billowing from the mill's chimneys as their precious crop went through the process that converted charred plant matter into crystals of gold.

On the fourth day of the harvest, a black sedan drew up outside the house. Three bulky men got out and lumbered up the stairs. Beneath his breath, Tony muttered 'bloody union thugs' as he thundered to the door. Edith took Bella to the bedroom where she could hear and not be seen. Somehow it gave her comfort that, should things turn bad, she was within running distance of the barracks. Her newfound friend, Rosa, seemed like a capable woman who'd know what to do.

One of the newcomers opened with an accusation. 'Our members tell us that Renzo's gang has a woman cook. You know that's against the rules.'

Tony said, 'Look, I engage them to do a job. How it gets done is up to the overseer. Whether the cook is male, female, black, white or brindle is no concern of mine.'

A second man spoke with the authority of a bulldozer. 'A sheila's got no right to take a man's job. Either she goes or yer farm gets blacklisted. Then you'll have no-one to cut yer cane.'

'You need to talk to Renzo. But first, have you confirmed the allegation?' said Tony.

That seemed to have them stumped.

Tony reframed the question. 'Do you know for sure that the cook is a woman?'

In the bedroom, Edith glanced out the window at the barracks. There was a flurry of activity about the cookhouse. Perhaps word had spread that the union was on the prowl. A pair of bare legs, struggling beneath an enormous bundle of clothes, beetled toward the house.

Edith put Bella down in the cot and ran out the back door and down the stairs.

Somewhere beneath the load was Rosa. 'Quick, Edith. Can I use your laundry?'

'Of course.' Edith relieved her of some the burden, which she took under the house and dumped into a concrete washtub.

The union men were on the move. The trio marched straight past the washerwomen without even a nod of acknowledgement. At the barracks, they pounded on the door and demanded to see Renzo.

'Not here,' was the reply from one of the canecutters.

'He won't mind if we take a look around then.'

'Don't take too long. I gotta cook lunch,' said the canecutter.

In the laundry Rosa whispered, 'He my 'usband. Today we swap places. Today he is cook. You understand?'

From the barracks came the sound of doors being slammed, furniture being moved, and a goodly amount of cursing.

Rosa grinned. 'They won't find nothin' o' mine. All my stuff is in 'ere.' She opened a pillowcase to reveal a bra, underwear, a pair of ladies' shoes, and a floral frock for special occasions.

'You clever thing! I think you've done this before.'

'We gotta make a living.' Rosa shrugged and opened her hands. 'Now I must wash for real.' She sorted the clothes into two bundles. Into one tub went the woollen work shirts for soaking, and into the other went cotton shorts and sheets for boiling in the copper. She turned on the brass tap and water gushed from the tank into the tub of woollens. Edith gave her a box of Lux soapflakes, which she sprinkled on top.

'Now, you go look after your *bambina*.' Rosa kissed Edith's cheeks. 'And thank you, my friend.'

Four

Brisbane, January 1940

For William Delahunty the declaration of war on Germany was validation of his insight into international affairs and his ability to predict the behaviour of nations' leaders. What he'd achieved due to these personal qualities was deserving of a hearty pat on the back. Not only had he convinced his Cabinet to draft pre-emptive State legislation to stop the influx of undesirable immigrants from southern Italy and to control the movement of aliens in general, but he'd also been instrumental in influencing the Federal government to delegate additional policing powers to the states.

The *National Security Act* had been passed in September 1939, a few days after Prime Minister Menzies announced that Australia would stand with Great Britain. The legislation authorised any member of the police force of the Commonwealth *or of a State*—when Delahunty read the last four words he glowed with self-satisfaction, for he took full credit for the new law—to take any action with respect to enemy aliens and also to naturalized persons. The term 'enemy aliens' was defined in the Act as people who were not British subjects and whose country was involved in 'the present war between His Majesty the King and Germany'.

With the stroke of a pen, the definitions were later expanded to cover 'any war in which His Majesty is or may be engaged', and to apply to any aspect of an enemy alien's or naturalized person's life, including their property, their trade or business, and their civil rights and obligations. These amendments were made on the strength of Delahunty's meeting with a Queensland Senator (a United Australia Party member at that) who, he was assured at the time, would insist on the revision.

In a flurry of meetings that went well into the night, the Queensland government passed its own legislation that boosted State police powers and imposed restrictions on all citizens in the name of public safety. As reward for his foresight and intervention, Delahunty's portfolio was expanded to encompass police and state security.

Although it was not intended that every element of the Act would apply straight away, the legislation was written so that any future changes necessitated by the war could be made swiftly and with a minimum of fuss. In the case of enemy aliens—regardless of their nationality or political persuasion—the instruction to police was to arrest first and obtain evidence later.

Now Delahunty had the teeth, as well as the will, to stamp out undesirable elements from the far north of the state. For decades he'd promised his electorate that he'd stop the outflow of cash and put an end to the enclaves of blood-sucking foreign interlopers who were there to make their fortunes and didn't give a damn about anyone else. Now the opportunity had arrived, thanks to a militant German leader with a huge ego and a ridiculous moustache.

Back home in Cairns for the summer break, Delahunty suggested to Margaret that they take a well-earned vacation together. They were sitting at the rosewood table in the parlour, a steaming teapot between them. Today Margaret looked more gaunt and haggard than usual, an illusion perhaps, exacerbated by the depressing mauve of the housedress she'd chosen to wear.

It bothered him that, since his return, she'd behaved with more indifference than ever before. No, she was not indifferent towards him; she was downright frosty.

Recalling the previous conversation with his doctor about women of a certain age, he applied no pressure in the bedroom department, hoping that she'd eventually come around. She hadn't. He also wondered if any of the local gossips had been chewing her ear about his extra-curricular activities in Brisbane. A holiday might crack the ice in more ways than one.

'But where would we go?' said Margaret doubtfully.

'I've heard there's a nice place to stay on Green Island.'

'You know I don't like the seaside.'

'What about the mountains? Kuranda perhaps.'

'Too many snakes.'

'The Tablelands? Lush fields, rolling hills, crystal clear lakes. So pretty and green it'll remind you of England.'

Tears sprang to Margaret's eyes. 'Nothing in this country could be as beautiful as Cumbria. I want to go home, Will. I'm sick of the heat and the humidity and the glare and the mosquitoes. Not to mention the people! Not an ounce of culture between them. When you're away I have no-one to talk to. Please, William, take me home.'

Delahunty's jaw dropped slightly. 'You've never said you were homesick before.'

'You never asked me. Twenty-five years I've endured this miserable existence. Twenty-five years! That's nearly half my lifetime.' She dropped her head and sobbed into her open palms like a child.

Totally out of his depth, he dipped into his pocket for a handkerchief. 'There, there, my dear. It can't be as bad as all that.' He attempted to blot away her tears, but she pushed him away.

Only once had he seen her weep. That was when her pet terrier, Scottie, met an untimely end after a valiant battle with a taipan.

'We can't go to England now, my dear. There's a war,' he said weakly.

'All the more reason to go *now*. Before it gets any worse.' She sniffled and wiped her eyes on a dainty handkerchief that magically appeared from the inside of her bodice.

Delahunty stood up and strode to the sideboard, where he poured himself two fingers of whisky from the crystal decanter. 'Would you like a drink, my dear? It might calm you down.'

'Yes, thanks. I'll have whatever you're having.'

That was when he realised she was serious. Margaret never drank hard spirits, and never did a drop of alcohol pass her lips before noon. By the grandfather clock, it was half past ten. This was shaping up to be one long day.

In silence they drank their whiskies. One shot and then another. As the sun moved higher in the sky, the atmosphere heated up like a sauna. Delahunty said they ought to get a plate of sandwiches and go outside, maybe sit beneath the poinciana tree in the backyard where it was cooler.

Margaret eased out of the upholstered armchair and wandered into the kitchen. She seemed a bit unsteady on her feet. Ten minutes later she called out that everything was ready. Her voice sounded normal, no hint of malice or grief. Perhaps she'd come to her senses and realised the foolishness of her request.

Delahunty was feeling mellow. He congratulated himself for averting yet another domestic disaster, thanks to the medicinal qualities of whisky.

Outside in the deep shade, it was indeed more comfortable. A breeze whispered in from the east, bringing with it the squawk of seagulls and the brackish perfume of the sea. A tray of sandwiches, cut into neat triangles, and a jug of orange cordial arrived at the table, along with his wife. He dropped his corpulent body into a cane chair and reached for a sandwich. Lightly-pickled cucumber on de-crusted white bread. How very English! Was this a hint or a statement of intent? Perhaps she had been dropping hints all along and he'd been too consumed with his own concerns to notice.

She took a bread-and-cucumber triangle and nibbled at the edge.

'Do you want to talk?' he ventured.

'Remember our wedding day?'

He nodded. 'As if it were yesterday, my dear.'

'Remember what you said?'

'That I'd love, cherish, and honour you until death us do part.'

'Yes. But what about afterwards, when I told you that I'd miss home? You begged me to give Cairns a chance. Because I was in love, I agreed. Then you said, "if you still don't like it here in five years' time, we'll go back to England together." Those were your exact words. Well, it's been *twenty-five* years, William. And I *still* don't like it here. I want to go home and I want to go now.'

'My dear, we can't simply pack up and leave. I'm the Member for Endeavour for goodness sake! I have to live in my electorate or else relinquish my seat in Parliament. My political career is finally taking off. I've been given a new portfolio. There's an enormous amount of responsibility in holding the state together during a time of war. Please, Margaret, walk in my shoes and see this from my perspective.'

'If you won't honour my wishes, then I'll go on my own.'

'Margaret, be reasonable! How could you possibly travel all the way to England alone when we're in the midst of a war?'

She shot him a look that would have slain a lesser man. 'All right then, have it your way. If I can't go to England, Brisbane will do. Yes, why not? You already spend half your time there. If I moved down to Brisbane, we could keep this house in Cairns as your primary place of residence. No-one would be any the wiser.'

She was more animated than she'd been in weeks. Only a cad would refuse. Deep down, he still loved her. There was one small complication.

Amy.

They'd been seeing each other for seven months now and they took pains to be discreet. After that first liaison in the dimly-lit Grosvenor Hotel, they agreed to meet in places where no-one would see them at all. Usually that meant Amy's flat in the inner suburb of Auchenflower.

The flat was one of six, carved out of a sprawling timber house. There was one bedroom, a kitchenette with a table and chairs, and a couch. The washing and bathroom facilities were shared with the other tenants.

A short walk from the railway station, it was easy for him to get there without being noticed. To the other commuters on the peak-hour train, he would have looked like an ordinary middle-aged man going home to his wife and family in the suburbs. He could have been a businessman or a department store manager or a senior public servant. Little did they realise that his suit pocket held a hipflask of whisky and half a dozen French letters. The little deceit made his clandestine visits to Amy all the more erotic.

In August, she'd given him a key so he could come and go as he pleased. He'd made it clear that his position as a parliamentarian depended on his remaining married. He'd also emphasised that his marriage to Margaret was effectively over.

Amy seemed happy with the arrangement, and he showered her with gifts that were unobtainable for most of the population. Due to his position in politics, he was able to get scarce items such as nylon stockings with ease.

For a female office worker, stockings were an essential item. If not worn, the miscreant would be likely to be sent home. When supply failed due to the war, the strict dress code was not relaxed. Girls resorted to painting their legs a certain shade of brown. But even with a pencil line drawn down the back of the calf to imitate a seam, leg makeup was a poor cousin to the genuine article.

Amy's delight in the small but thoughtful gift far outweighed the inflated price he paid for stockings on the black market.

'What do you say to my suggestion, William?'

Margaret's sharp voice brought Delahunty back to earth.

'Yes, my dear. I suppose that might work.'

Was it possible to juggle a relationship with two different women in the same town? When Parliament resumed sitting, he'd find out.

The Pact of Steel

Five

Benito Mussolini's speech, in which he declared that Italy had joined Germany against Britain, was delivered in Rome at six o'clock on Monday evening and broadcast live. In Wooranoora, on the other side of the world, the time was three o'clock Tuesday morning. In the Italian Boarding House, everyone was asleep.

The sudden turn of events in Europe went unnoticed until breakfast time when Sergeant Pitt and Constable Moody banged on the boarding house door. Entering without a warrant, they proceeded to the dining room and arrested all the Italians in residence.

Angry objections and demands for reasons fell on deaf ears. Even if the policemen had been fluent in Italian, they couldn't have explained the urgency required by police headquarters in Brisbane to complete the roundup. Their orders were plain and simple. 'Arrest all Italians who are enemy aliens and anyone you suspect is a Fascist sympathiser.'

At nine o'clock in the morning, Constable Moody and a young constable arrived at Innocenti Brothers' farmhouse. After a cursory search of the premises and confiscation of a book brought from Italy, the policemen arrested Angelo for possessing 'subversive materials'. He was handcuffed and frog-marched to the police van.

All Luigi could do was stand helplessly on the verandah and watch him be taken away. He scratched his head, wondering why the police chose to arrest Angelo and not him. The only difference between them was that Angelo remained an Italian national while Luigi had been naturalized and was a British subject.

The books were irrelevant. Angelo, three years older, had not completed primary school due to a siege and civil upheaval in Sicily. As a result, he could not read or write.

Angelo put up no resistance at all. As with every obstacle that life threw him, he accepted his loss of freedom as a minor wrinkle that could be easily ironed out.

Later, Luigi drove into town to see what could be done. The scene at the police station was complete pandemonium. The entire district was there, howling and jabbering and arguing at once. Farmers, canecutters, wives, and screaming kids. Even the parish priest had turned up. Alone behind the desk, the young constable—not a day over nineteen and as green as a new shoot of cane—seemed to have no idea of how to control them.

From the collective opinion of the crowd, Luigi ascertained that the status of the captives had flipped overnight from 'alien' to 'enemy alien'. In the eyes of the law, Angelo and the others in the lockup were now at war with Australia. Because they were enemies of the British Empire, they were being detained.

'They did the same in the Great War,' said one old timer. 'Happened to my German neighbour in Bartle Frere. Locked 'im up for a couple of years down south. Don't know where exactly. But after the Armistice he came back none the worse for it.'

This gave Luigi little comfort. A couple of years! Angelo was not a well man. A couple of years in a cold, dark prison cell would likely be the death of him.

What a difference a piece of paper made! The certificate of naturalization, which Luigi had been granted a decade ago, had brought him freedom. At the time, his decision was made in order to buy the farm. Without naturalization papers, he could not legally purchase property. Although Luigi had no intention of ever leaving Australia, renouncing his Italian citizenship while his parents were alive had not been easy. Somehow it seemed disrespectful, not only to Mamma and Papa, but also to a long line of Sicilian ancestors that went back centuries, possibly as far as the Roman Empire. Italy had shaped who he was, what he believed in, and how he lived.

However, he'd made the decision to remain in this country and naturalization was essential for doing business. On the other hand, Angelo hadn't bothered, nor did he need to. He relied on his brother to manage his affairs and he trusted him completely.

Now the poor fellow was behind bars. How bloody unfair!

At the police station it was Luigi's turn at the desk. He removed the scowl from his face and put on his best accent. 'Why has my brother, Angelo Innocenti, been arrested?'

'National security,' said the constable.

'But he isn't a soldier.'

'Doesn't matter. He is an enemy alien. You may bring him one port of clothing and toiletries to use while he is detained.'

'How long will that be?' Luigi tried to sound calm but his rage was growing.

'As long as the war lasts.' The constable shuffled the papers on the counter. A nervous rash was rising up his pale neck.

Luigi glanced behind. At least thirty people were pushing into the tiny police station. Their agitation was palpable; things could turn nasty. Sergeant Pitt and Constable Moody were nowhere to be seen. The young constable ran his finger around the inside of his collar. In some respects, Luigi felt sorry for him. This was not his decision; he was merely carrying out orders. Alone against half the town's population, he must have been quaking in his boots.

Luigi persisted. 'Where will you keep all the prisoners?'

The constable shrugged. 'We haven't been told.' He turned away. 'Next please!'

Luigi drove the pickup east across the railway tracks to the boarding house. Mrs Ross was upstairs, bundling someone's belongings into a tea chest.

As he came into the room, she straightened up and put her hands on her hips. 'Fine pickle we're in now. Six Italian boarders gone with a snap of the fingers. Two of them owed a week's rent. Well, we can kiss that money goodbye.'

'O Dio! Six of them!' said Luigi. With a full house, she'd been turning men away this past month. Now it would be hard to fill the rooms unless a mob of eastern Europeans with cash in their pockets happened to stroll into town.

'Yep. The cops took them all to the watch house.'

'Who did they get?'

She rattled off a list of names. 'All we have left are the Finns, the mad Russian, and two Yugoslavs. I dunno who'll cut the cane this season.'

'O Dio!' said Luigi. At their farm, the cane had reached full height. The mauve feather-duster blooms that heralded the start of the crushing season had already sprouted and unfurled. Sign-on day for the canecutter

31

gangs was Monday but this dramatic turn of events would throw the process into a spin.

As it turned out, the season proceeded without mishap. The gang that Innocenti Brothers drew in the labour lottery, run jointly by the Cane Growers Association and Australian Workers Union, was British-Australian. Every one of the eight members had several years of experience swinging the cane knife. However, unlike the Italians, the going rate was non-negotiable as per the award and there was no under-the-table kick-back for taking them on.

The overseer was John Stubbs. At their first meeting, Luigi was quick to point out that the owner of the farm was a naturalized British citizen and not an enemy alien.

'Makes no difference to me, mate,' said Stubbs. 'As long as we get paid.'

'That, I can promise you.' Luigi nodded and they shook hands on the deal.

It was October 1940. More than three months had passed since Angelo had been captured. Last time Luigi had seen his brother was two days after the arrest, when the police marched the captives to the railway station and put them on the southbound train. Despite his efforts to get information about Angelo's whereabouts, nothing had been forthcoming. It was as if he had vanished into thin air.

Amongst the Italian community, there was much discussion about this dreadful state of affairs yet no-one put their hand up to take action. With a war on, a shroud of suspicion descended over the town. Trust between neighbours and countrymen evaporated. Everyone was tight-lipped and guarded. Families withdrew into themselves.

Tony Zucchero summed up the sentiment. 'Opportunists benefit from wars while everyone else suffers.'

Luigi hated wars. He was in Sicily during the Great War. When it began, he was twenty and Angelo was twenty-three. Although most of the fighting took place in the north near the Italian Alps, the country imposed conscription on male citizens between the ages of twenty and forty. Five out of the six brothers and one brother-in-law were earmarked for the army. That would leave only Papa and the youngest—a boy of seven—to grow the wheat and pick the olives. Food was scarce which made their crops valuable, even after *the Mob* had taken its commission. The family could not survive without income, so Luigi and Angelo made a pact. Family before country.

Angelo took Tano's hunting knife and they used it to make cuts on their ankles. They rubbed ash into the wounds and within days an infection blossomed. The pair duly reported for military duty but failed the medical examination. Those war years produced more income for the Innocenti family than they ever dreamed of. The army purchased all the wheat from Sicily to feed its troops.

From the state of affairs in Wooranoora, it was apparent that wars also provided opportunities to get even with foes and to dispose of troublemakers. One thing was clear: the police were on a mission to gather as much information about every enemy alien in the district. As sure as the sun rose in the east, there'd be no shortage of informants amongst the British townsfolk, whose opinion of *wogs* and *dagos* had switched from mild annoyance to outright animosity.

When Luigi walked down Sugarmill Street, the feeling against him was obvious. Doors shut, curtains flipped closed. Storekeepers put out signs that said, *Only English spoken here.*

Outside Arbuckle's Pool Rooms and Barber Shop, which was situated directly opposite Lorenzo's Continental Hair Emporium, was a sandwich board.

Get your hair cut here before the day goes.

When Luigi first read it, he smiled at the cleverness of the double meaning. However, from that day on, he avoided walking on Arbuckle's side of the road.

On Saturday afternoons, when the week's work was done, the Italian men would gather at the boarding house to play cards or *bocce* on the back lawn, or listen to the news on the shortwave wireless. Sometimes a piano accordion would come out and they'd sing songs from the old country. They'd drink tall bottles of NQ Lager, share stories and generally have a relaxing time.

Conversations ranged from cane-beetle damage or the skyrocketing price of fuel to the lamentable shortage of decent women in the district. Even *indecent* women were scarce in the off-season, for the *bordellos* operated from June until November to cash in on the seasonal workers. When the canecutters left for the fruit picking season in the south, so too did the ladies.

Occasionally *il Duce*'s name came up, but only in passing. The boarding house had an unwritten rule. On Saturday afternoons, politics was banned.

On Saturday 12 October, the main topic of conversation was the police. In the preceding week, Sergeant Pitt had raided a dozen or more

Italian properties in the district. In the name of public security, farmhouses had been ransacked, documents and photographs had been taken as 'evidence'. This, everyone agreed, was beyond a joke.

'I've lived in this country more than fifty years,' said one old timer. 'They came to my place and turned it upside down. Didn't find anything of course. My wife was terrified. How can I complain? They're the law. If I say anything, they'll treat us even worse.'

'They took my wireless set and all my books,' said another.

'That's nothing. They took my shotgun. How's a man to protect himself without a weapon? Where I am, there are wild boars and crocodiles. *Porca miseria!* I was born here! Would I be a traitor to my own country?'

O Dio! The guns! If the police were to raid the farmhouse at Cassowary Valley again, Luigi would be in terrible trouble.

Many years ago, good old Sergeant Whelby had granted him a licence to trade in firearms. Not that he was a professional dealer. No, his interest in guns was purely as a farmer. In fact, the whole buying and selling thing had started quite by accident.

Not long after he arrived in Australia, Luigi had bought a shotgun from a canecutter who was short of cash. The shotgun was the only thing of value that the man owned. It was a nice piece: well-balanced with a light kickback. Luigi used it to shoot bush turkeys for the cooking pot. Soon after, a fellow from Aloomba spotted it and offered him double what he'd paid. And on it went. Again, and again, and again. Every deal made Luigi a profit. The cash went straight into the cigar tin under his bed to be saved and sent back to Italy.

When Sergeant Whelby caught wind of the ongoing trade, he gave Luigi a warning and also some fatherly advice. 'Get a firearms licence now or else cop a hefty fine.'

Luigi handed over the fee and the sergeant wrote him a certificate.

At the farmhouse, Luigi wrapped his arsenal of three shotguns, four rifles, and one handgun in a tarpaulin and buried it twenty paces due north of the milky pine tree. The hiding place was well concealed and far enough from the creek to be spared from inundation in the wet season.

Thankfully Sergeant Pitt would have no list of the guns in his possession. Sergeant Whelby, who'd since been transferred, was never one for keeping records.

For now, Luigi was safe. But for how long would his luck hold?

Six

Wooranoora, 11 June 1940

Although Edith didn't know it at the time, the day Italy entered the war her life would change forever. The tipping point came when the telegram boy cycled out to *The Manor* with a dreaded window-faced envelope. With nervous fingers, she ripped it open.

We need to talk. Phone me. Urgent. It was from her father in Brisbane.

Her blood went cold, her chest went tight. Something must have happened to her mother. A dozen scenarios flashed through her mind, all of them equally unpleasant. She chewed a fingernail. What should she do? An only child, there was no-one else to care for her ailing mother. Here she was in the deep north, a thousand miles away from the city where she was needed. She grabbed Bella and ran down the stairs to the machinery shed where Tony was tinkering with the crawler tractor.

'Can you run me in to the post office?' Choking back tears, she handed him the telegram. 'I need to telephone my father urgently.'

Tony nodded. 'Sure, *amore*. Let's hope it's nothing serious.'

She sighed. It *had* to be serious! Her father would never send a telegram unless it was. The only other she'd received since leaving home was to inform her that her maternal grandmother had died. The old lady was eighty-three. At the time Edith was six months pregnant. After debating whether to make the two-day trek to Brisbane for the funeral, she decided in the negative. Instead, she telephoned her mother and sent letters of condolence to her aunts. On the day of the funeral she planted an orange tree in memory of her grandmother who loved nothing more than making cauldrons of orange marmalade which she bottled and gave away to her friends.

Tony wiped his hands on a rag and set off toward the house. 'Since we're going to town, I might see some clients. Have you heard this morning's news?'

'No, Bella has kept me busy.' Her husband wasn't one to discuss crimes, accidents or politics, the usual topics of the morning news.

As they walked up the stairs he said, 'Mussolini has joined up with Hitler.'

'Then he's a fool,' she snapped.

'Edith, this is terrible! Half of Wooranoora is Italian. *I'm* Italian for Christ's sake.'

'Shhh! Don't blaspheme in front of the baby.' She placed Bella on the kitchen floor, along with an enamel pot and a wooden spoon to play with. 'Anyway, you're naturalized. In the eyes of the law, you are British.'

'I'm not sure that holds when you're at war. I'll call my brother, Ben. As a lawyer, he'll have an opinion on where I stand. He was born in Australia so *he* has nothing to worry about, lucky sod.'

'I'll be ready in five minutes.' She changed into a clean frock for the trip into town.

The eastern end of Sugarmill Street was in chaos. There was a large crowd on the footpath outside the police station. Everyone was shouting in Italian but Edith's language skills weren't good enough to understand what the uproar was about.

Tony kept on driving. Outside the post office, further along the street, he stopped the truck and they both got out.

'You make the call to your father,' he said. 'I'll take this little one somewhere to play. See you in half an hour.' He gave her coins for the trunk call and swung Bella onto his shoulders.

The little girl clasped her hands around his forehead and kicked her heels into his ribs. 'Gee-up, Daddy. Gee up.'

On cue, he whinnied and trotted down the footpath in the direction of the memorial park.

Edith watched them, her heart swelling with love. Her husband and her daughter were the two most important people in the world. Despite the war and the bad news she was certain to receive, she was one lucky woman.

At the post office, she gave the operator the phone number of her parents' residence in Clayfield. A few minutes later, she picked up the receiver and heard her father's voice shouting 'hello, hello' into the other end of the phone.

'Hello Dad,' she said as calmly as she could. 'I got your telegram this morning. Is anything the matter?' While waiting for his answer, she tapped her fingernails on the telephone shelf. Waves of dread rolled over her.

'No, dear. We're both well. What about you?' Today he was sober Dad. A promising start. Sober Dad was pleasant and reasonable, a person you could talk to. As opposed to sozzled Dad, the argumentative alter ego.

'We're fine too. Look, Dad, trunk calls are expensive. Don't tell me you wanted to hear the dulcet tones of my voice.'

'Okay, I'll get to the point. Your mother and I have been talking. We don't think it's safe for you to be in a place full of ...' He faltered, as if searching for the appropriate word. 'In a place full of *foreigners*. Especially now that we are at war. We think you should to return to Brisbane immediately. In fact, we insist. There's plenty of room here for you and the baby.'

Edith chewed her lip. 'I appreciate your concern, Dad, but we have a farm to run. Despite what you might think, Tony is a good man. The best. As his wife, my place is with him. And, by the way, he's more Australian than you are.' The jibe was meant to hurt. Her father had immigrated from England as a youth; his Yorkshire accent was still as strong as ever.

'If you won't do it for yourself, then think about your daughter. Surely, she deserves a better life than running around barefoot like a savage. In case you haven't heard, we are now at war with Italy. A young child like that could be kidnapped and held to ransom to save the hide of a dirty dago who has no right to be here.'

'Enough! Neither Bella nor I are going anywhere ... and that's final!' She was acutely aware that everyone in the post office could hear the argument, or at least her end of it. Her face was burning with fury and embarrassment.

'Think about it, my girl.' With that, her father slammed down the receiver.

Her first reaction was to ring him back and tell him *exactly* what she thought. Instead she burst into tears.

'Would you like a glass of water, Mrs Zucchero?' The operator gave her a sympathetic smile.

Edith mopped her cheeks with a hanky. 'No thanks. I'd best be getting on. How much do I owe you?'

'Two and six.'

After paying for the call, Edith made a hasty exit. Blood raged like rapids through her body. She needed to calm down before Tony and Bella returned. She stormed along Sugarmill Street, past Arbuckle's Pool Rooms and Barber Shop with the curious sign outside. Past the bootmaker, the draper, the shire office, the courthouse. Her lace-up leather shoes beat a brisk tattoo on the pavement. Before she knew it, she was caught up in the riot outside the police station. In the thick of it all was a familiar Italian woman with a resonant voice.

Edith pushed her way between the jostling bodies. Some she recognised from social nights at the community hall or from doing business about town. Everyone was too engrossed in their protests to notice her petite body squeezing through.

'Rosa!' Edith waved. 'What's going on?'

The other woman turned. Her eyes were puddles of tears. 'They lock up me 'usband.'

'Gosh, Rosa. That's awful.'

'They lock up everyone in Renzo's gang. Everyone but me. They all in gaol!'

'Whatever for?'

Rosa shrugged. 'They say we the *enemy* now. But we no hurt nobody.'

'This damn war!' She gave Rosa a squeeze. 'Surely this is a mix-up. The town needs canecutters; they'll soon work it out.'

Rosa flapped her arms. '*Mamma mia!*'

Edith fought her way out of the rabble and retraced her footsteps along the footpath. Outside the post office Tony was sitting on a bench seat with Bella on his lap.

'Did you speak to your father?' he said softly. 'Is it bad?'

'Oh, it's nothing.' She waved her hand airily but her face was burning hot. 'He wanted to blow off steam.' Then she told him about Rosa and what had happened to the canecutters that morning. 'How soon can you talk to your brother?'

'I'll do it straight away.'

At home, Edith asked Tony about the telephone call to Ben. While in town she'd avoided the subject. 'The walls have ears' was a line she recalled from an old spy movie. In a small place like Wooranoora, she was sure that piece of wisdom would hold true.

They were in the farmhouse kitchen; Bella was asleep in her cot. Edith filled the coffee percolator—the upside-down variety popular in modern Italian households—and set it on the combustion stove. A cool breeze was whistling in through the floorboards. For once she was thankful of the heat generated by the wood-burning stove.

Tony took some notes from his pocket. 'According to Ben, the actions taken by the police—whilst harsh—are perfectly allowable within the law.' He read out the relevant clauses from the *National Security Act*. 'In a nutshell, this law authorises the police to arrest and imprison *anyone* who might be considered a threat. It seems they've been putting dossiers together on all aliens for some time now. I am not immune. This can apply to naturalized citizens too. All the police need is an excuse to take action.'

Edith slammed her hand on the table. 'But it goes against all our Australian principles of justice! The police can't arrest a person without any evidence of wrongdoing. Everyone is entitled to a fair go.'

'They can do anything they like now, it seems.'

'Then the law's an ass! We must fight it! Mr Delahunty, our state Member of Parliament, is a client of my father's stockbroking firm. He seems to be a reasonable man. Perhaps he can intervene and stop this insanity. I could arrange a meeting; we could drive to Cairns and see him.'

Tony drew her into his arms. 'Do you think stirring the pot would help us? Or would it be better to lie low.'

She put her head on his shoulder. 'I only wanted to help Rosa, and all the others who haven't got a mean bone in their bodies.'

'A noble sentiment, *amore*. But don't risk everything *we* have in the process.'

In the weeks that followed, the police systematically rounded up every Italian who had not been naturalized, and others who were considered troublemakers. The lockup was full to overflowing. Some had already been sent south on the train. Destination unknown.

One of them was Gianni Fiumefreddo, Rosa's husband, a fifty-year old Sicilian canecutter who'd lived and worked in this country since the beginning of the century. There seemed to be nothing that Edith or anyone else could do to get him back.

Seven

Barmera, August 1940

Many years had passed since Ted Long last wore a military uniform. Twenty-two, to be precise, but he preferred not to keep count. The last time in khaki was at the celebration of the Armistice in November 1918, when he and his unit marched in a ticker-tape parade through the streets of Adelaide. Girls rushed from the crowd to kiss them. They were hailed as heroes, yet Ted didn't feel at all heroic.

War was not a thing he cared to remember or commemorate. Too many of his mates and his only brother—young diggers sent to do the dirty work of the British—had perished or had gone missing in action, presumed dead. Every Armistice Day, he busied himself in his cabinetmaking workshop in Barmera and steeled his ears against the bugle call for silence to honour the fallen.

Lest we forget.

Forget: there was nothing he'd rather have done. Most nights he woke in a cold sweat, his mind in the treacherous trenches of Fromelles while his body was safe in bed in South Australia. A cup of tea and a nip or two of brandy—for medicinal purposes—would be required before restless sleep would find him again. Five years ago, his wife had traded their listless marriage for the bright lights of the city. Now his sole companion was Bessie, a border collie cross, who shared his modest cottage surrounded by the vineyards and orchards of the Riverland.

As an ageing second-time bachelor, Ted's entire social life centred on the Barmera Lawn Bowls Association. During his time in France, he'd developed a straight eye and a steady hand, skills that were transferrable to a game that became an obsession. On Saturdays, his team would travel to other towns in the district to compete. The previous month he'd skippered the fours in a tournament at Angaston and they'd won. His counterpart on the Angaston team was a larger-than-life character called Edwin Dean.

Afterwards, over a few schooners of lager, the two men got talking. Dean, a grazier the same vintage as Ted, had been contacted by some military big-wig in Adelaide and cajoled into re-enlisting in the army. The war in Europe was hotting up and the army needed solid leaders with battle experience to manage the home front. The government had acquired a large tract of grazing land on the plains of the Murray River. His brief was to construct a secure camp capable of holding two thousand prisoners of war.

'I know you fought in France,' Dean said. 'And you are a fine wood-worker.'

Ted nodded. He was feeling a little mellow. The beer had lubricated his lips and this chap was an easy conversationalist. But he couldn't actually recall when he'd given Dean this information.

'From what I've seen and heard, you're exactly the sort of fellow I need. Would you consider signing up again—maybe for a year or two—to work on this important project? You'd be doing your country—and me—a great service.'

'When would it start?'

'August. The site is close to Barmera. You could live at home and drive in each day.'

Ted took a swallow of beer, letting the thought slosh about in his mind. The one thing he'd missed these last few years was a purpose in life. Sometimes it was only Bessie's whining that got him out of bed of a morning.

'If I signed up, there's absolutely no chance I'd be sent overseas?'

'I guarantee that would never happen. My word as a gentleman.'

The offer was sorely tempting; Dean's obvious faith in him gave a boost to his self-esteem. As it was, his life was going nowhere. His marriage had produced no children; his closest living relative was a young sister who lived a thousand miles away in Queensland. His business was struggling and no-one had any money to pay.

Although he worked diligently in his workshop, earning enough to live on was another matter entirely. Last time he'd spoken to his bank manager, he'd received an ear-bashing about the size of his overdraft. That night he'd had four shots of brandy to steady his nerves ... and he'd continued having four shots ever since. At this rate, the grog bill alone would bring him down. As he limped past middle-age, he faced a poor and lonely existence.

A project like this would give him that sense of purpose. And a regular income wouldn't go astray either. After two more beers, he agreed. Nothing to lose, plenty to gain.

On 12 August 1940, Lieutenant Edward Long put on his new khakis and drove his delivery truck to the site of the proposed POW camp at Loveday. There he joined Colonel Dean, three other officers, and around forty veteran soldiers of various ranks from the Fourth Ground Battalion.

There was no time to be lost. The camp had to be built and provisioned ready for occupation within two months. Under the direction of Colonel Dean, the men went straight to work. Army surveyors marked out the boundaries for two separate compounds, located close enough to share common facilities for the guards, yet far enough removed so that the inmates could not band together and make trouble. The first to be built would be named *Number 9 Internment Camp*.

Mr Burr, a building contractor from Adelaide who had won the tender for the construction work, hired forty of the best men for the job. As soon as the timber was delivered, the crew commenced work. Hand tools were used, for the site initially had no electricity. By early October, Camp 9 was finished. Thirty-three sleeping huts, four mess huts, two kitchens, ablutions block and latrines within a diamond-shaped arrangement of barbed-wire fences. Power lines from nearby Berri brought electricity to the site. When the builders departed, the soldiers were left to clean up and connect the services: electricity to the huts, and water, which was pumped from the nearby River Murray, to the kitchens and ablutions blocks.

Then came the hiccup. Although the internment camp was ready on the scheduled date, the war had taken another turn and the government had changed its mind about accepting prisoners of war from Europe and North Africa.

By February of the following year, the facility was still vacant. The soldiers were idle and bored, and the project was looking like a white elephant. Not a man to be idle, Dean sent a proposal to the brass in Adelaide and it was accepted.

All but a skeleton staff were redeployed to internment camps elsewhere in Australia, including Dean himself. Of the three soldier caretakers who remained at Loveday, one was Ted Long.

Four tedious months passed. Each day Ted and his canine companion, Bessie, inspected the perimeter fence and the buildings. He tested the pumping systems and made minor repairs as necessary. Nothing much happened. Certainly, no-one made any attempt to break in or sabotage the place.

His life fell into the same monotonous rut as it had been in during the Great Depression, when he'd made inconsequential pieces of furniture—hall stands, folding chairs, hat racks, and the like—which he'd hawked from door to door.

Then, out of the blue, everything changed. Someone in the upper echelons of power signed an order for Italian civilians to be rounded up and banished to internment camps. Loveday had a new purpose.

Colonel Dean and the commanding officers arrived in May 1941, followed a week later by other military personnel who would be guards, administrators, and ancillary staff. Overnight, a total of 280 army men converged on the place.

Most of the soldiers were aged in their fifties, survivors of the Great War who'd signed on like Ted to serve their country within its shores. At meal times, they shared stories and showed their battle scars, each remembering the hell of the trenches where comrades were as likely to die of a horrible disease as of a bullet wound.

For the first time in more than twenty years Ted found himself talking about the Great War. Once he started, it was hard to stop. It felt like a good old-fashioned blood-letting. All that hatred and misery that had been festering inside, gushed out. With the poison released, there was a chance that the wounds might heal at last.

Eight

As it turned out, Margaret's decision to move to Brisbane couldn't have worked out better.

Shortly before Parliament resumed in March, she'd accompanied Delahunty down on the train. They'd stayed in a city hotel until the Queenslander he'd purchased in the leafy suburb of Ashgrove settled and they moved in. With a view over a little park, an established rose garden— an impossible dream in the tropical north—and situated two minutes' walk from the tramline that went into town, the house was exactly what she'd asked for.

Overnight, her dark mood lifted. While he was at work, she waved her feminine wand over the somewhat run-down house. Exquisite carved furniture arrived from Bell Brothers in the Valley, the walls were painted duck-egg blue, the rooms were re-curtained in the richest of brocades. Not content with interior decoration, she set to work redesigning the garden, adding trellises for sweet peas and concrete-edged flower beds for roses and annuals.

In the spring, the garden became a potpourri of perfume. Stocks, delphiniums, gardenias, gerberas. The Queenslander with soaring latticework across two white wings floated on a lake of colour.

To Delahunty's surprise, his relationship with the delectable Amy also blossomed when the warm weather came in. Until then, he didn't know it was possible to be in love with two women simultaneously. He'd worked out a schedule that allowed him to divide his time between both, yet keep them well apart. Of course, neither knew about the other and he intended to keep it that way. His life was complicated enough without problems on the home front as well.

As far as Amy was concerned, his marriage was all but over. As far as Margaret was concerned, he was a dedicated politician whose long hours at work were his priority.

The one thing that threatened to bring him unstuck was the upcoming election, which was mooted for March 1941. The Premier had announced that he would stand for office for a fourth consecutive term. All members of the Party were expected to knuckle down and secure their seats. 'Come Hell or high water' were his exact words. That meant getting out amongst the people and doing some old-fashioned electioneering. If there was one thing that Delahunty had let slide this past year, it was being out in the electorate and talking face-to-face with the constituents of Endeavour. This he must remedy at all costs, for it wouldn't do to lose his seat after all these years in Parliament.

Being in politics was the only life he knew. He'd been born into it, cut his teeth on problems like securing labour for the sugar industry and doing deals with the unions. When he was in his twenties, the baton of the Endeavour electorate had been passed to him by his father, the Honourable James Bertram (JB) Delahunty, who retired soon after the Armistice was signed in 1918. By then, JB had taught him everything about people and politics and the mechanics of winning and keeping supporters.

When it came to politics, JB waxed evangelical. 'You must walk amongst your flock,' he preached. 'Don't let the devils beat you down.' The old man, who was now seventy-nine had retired to Yorkeys Knob, a beachside settlement to the north of Cairns.

With his father's words ringing in his ears, Delahunty announced to both his women—separately—that he would be returning to his flock as soon as Parliament rose for the end-of-year break.

The electorate of Endeavour was vast. It stretched from the northernmost tip of the state, south to Cardwell, and west across the Atherton Tablelands. The crushing season was in the final stages, which meant the high tide of seasonal workers had peaked. Come the election in March and the drifters would have flowed out of the district and down the coast to the Lockyer Valley west of Brisbane or the Riverina in New South Wales for the vegetable and stone fruit harvests.

For Delahunty to visit every town in his entire electorate in a three-month period would be a mammoth task. On the train ride to Cairns, he had a brainwave. JB had never truly retired from politics and was as sprightly as ever. The old man remained a legend in the north. So much so that Delahunty constantly walked in his father's shadow. So, why not tap into all that popularity and use it for his own benefit?

As soon as he reached home, Delahunty telephoned JB with a proposition: an all-expenses-paid road-trip through the cane-growing districts in exchange for a few speeches and visits to his old mates who were doyens of the union movement.

As expected, JB leapt at the opportunity. The plan was to make their way south through the big coastal sugar-growing towns. Being the start of the wet season, the going would be slow with multiple river crossings, waterlogged roads, and possible flooding to contend with. JB's response was, 'Grab the bull by the horns I say. Get your young electoral officer to pack a camera. There's no better publicity than a photograph of an MP helping children and old ladies to safety.'

Two days later Delahunty, his electoral officer Patrick Magee, and JB set off in the black Buick. JB was in irrepressible form. From the moment he got in the car, he regaled the young Patrick with stories about his influence during the early days of the sugar industry.

'I started out as a union rep,' JB began. 'Way back when Kanaka labour was first banned. They said white men couldn't work in the tropics. Too hot, deadly diseases and the like. So they opened the door to Southern Italians. It was an experiment, you see, to test whether *white coolies* could adapt to the steamy conditions.

'Well, wasn't that a mistake! No sooner did the first shipload arrive—and at taxpayer expense I might add—than all their earnings were being sent back to the wife and kids in the old country. Not one penny did they spend. I'm telling you, laddie, those blokes could live off the smell of an oily rag. That's when I got my big break.

'The bloody dagos were undercutting our contractors, working for less than the award and giving kickbacks to the farmers for hiring them. Of course, the growers were used to cheap black labour and liked the arrangement. But we at the Union worked relentlessly to organise the British canecutters and stamp out the rogue operators. Not only that, but we also improved the safety and working conditions of our members. "United we stand" and all that. There's strength in numbers, m'lad.'

It promised to be a long and tedious trip.

First stop was Gordonvale. Tucked beneath a pyramid-shaped hill—aptly named *The Pyramid*—the Mulgrave sugar mill was pumping white clouds from its towering smokestack. Cane trams, laden with blackened stalks, lumbered along the tracks toward it. It was noon. The canecutters would be setting down their cane knives to rest and avoid the fierce blaze of the sun.

As expected, the town was bristling with pubs, their names as predictable as their clientele: the Commercial, the Great Northern, the Railway, the Central. Within fifteen minutes every establishment would be bursting with hot, thirsty men.

JB piped up. 'If we divvy up the pubs between us, we can talk and shake hands with the entire town all at once.'

Delahunty had to agree. Until then he'd regretted asking the old man along, but this practical suggestion showed he might be of use after all.

At the Great Northern, Delahunty made straight for the public bar. Cane and mill workers and old timers were gathered around the long, tiled counter, soothing parched throats with ice-cold beer. He drifted between the various groups, asked about their hopes and fears, listened to their complaints about the government, the Italians, and the war.

'Bloody dagos, we're finally rid of them,' said one gnarly-looking gent. 'You can't trust a bloke who doesn't drink.'

'They don't live like us, they don't speak the language, and they think they're above the law. As for the union, they thumb their noses at everything it stands for, and then turn around and want to be members. Good riddance to bad rubbish,' said another in a grey woollen singlet.

'As soon as this war is over the government should ship the lot back to Italy,' said the first. 'Speaking of the war, what will happen to us canecutters?'

Delahunty reassured them that if conscription was re-introduced, the sugar industry would be exempted because sugar was considered an essential item. 'As well as that, cutting cane is damn hard work.'

'Too right,' the canecutters chorused.

'Unlike factory work, it's not something women could do,' Delahunty hastened to add.

After receiving a fifteen-minute earbashing about the problems of allowing women to do men's work, Delahunty handed out his Labor Party flyers, advising how to vote in the upcoming election. He wondered how many would be read and how many would end up as dunny paper. After shaking everyone's grubby hand, he exited the bar-room. The heat outside hit him like a brick wall. Shading his eyes, he hurried across the street and ducked into the second pub on his list. There the entire performance was repeated for a different but equally engaged audience.

At two-thirty, the trio of campaigners regrouped at the car. All reported great success for minimum effort. Onward they travelled south towards Wooranoora, where a public rally had been arranged in the evening at the community hall.

Pregnant clouds bore down from the mountains. Soon it began to rain. Drops the size of grapes smashed onto the windscreen. The wipers wouldn't go fast enough to clear them away. Delahunty slowed the car, strained to make out the lie of the road. Visibility was less than three feet; runoff filled the potholes and flowed across the road. Giving up, he pulled over to the side and turned off the engine.

While they had been driving, Patrick had been working on a speech for the rally, the first of the election campaign. He passed a draft to Delahunty. 'What do you think, sir?'

While the handwriting was neat, the content was appalling.

'What a rambling tirade! Short and sharp is what we need.' Delahunty tossed the page back. 'You can do better than this.'

JB piped up. 'I've never written a speech in my life. Always knew what I wanted to say, then spoke straight from the heart. That's what country people want. A straight-shooter who says it like it is. Son, I've heard you on the wireless. If you'll pardon my French, you come across like a bloody smart-arse. You need to get in touch with your roots. Now, before it's too late.'

Delahunty's blood pressure lifted a notch but he managed to keep his temper. He should have known it'd be like this. The constant comparisons, his father always telling him that he was wrong, that he should do things better. He felt like a little kid again, strangled by resentment.

Patrick said, 'What if I jot down a few points for reference. Then you could ad-lib and not forget anything important.'

'Great idea, lad!' roared JB. 'What do you think, son?'

Delahunty swallowed his gut response, which was to tell his father exactly what he thought. While the rain hammered the roof of the car, he took a moment to consider. The suggestion had merits. In truth, public speaking terrified him. Standing in front of a crowd turned his brain into mush. That was why he'd always deferred to the written word.

'Okay,' he said at length. 'Let's give it a try.' In the rear-vision mirror, he glanced at Patrick, who was grinning from ear to ear. 'Wipe that smirk off your face and get cracking.'

'Yes, sir.'

The rain eased to a dull roar. Using his hanky, Delahunty wiped a porthole in the condensation inside the windscreen. He turned on the ignition, checked the rear-vision mirror, and pulled out. The going would be slow, for the road wore a slimy film of silt that was as treacherous as ice.

By the time they reached Wooranoora, daylight was fading. Outside the State Hotel, Delahunty parked and they all got out. Nobody was at the reception desk so Delahunty wandered the corridors, following a rabble of voices to the public bar on the western side of the building. The bar room was enormous: the ceilings soared like a cathedral, the counter was as long as a cricket pitch. It was full to capacity. Three middle-aged barmaids were pouring the beers as fast as the kegs would allow. He took a position near a beer tap and waited for one of the women to make eye contact.

'Excuse me. We have a reservation for tonight,' he said.

The barmaid, a sunbeaten specimen with a face like a sugarbag, shrugged. 'Sorry luv, we're short staffed here. Some big wig politician's in town so the girls have gone down to the hall to help set up. Can you come back in half an hour?'

'No, not really. My name is William Delahunty.'

'Look luv, I don't care if your name is King George the Sixth. If I don't keep the beer up to these jokers there'll be all hell to pay.'

'Okay, who should I ask for? I'll go down there and get them myself.'

'Mrs Maroney. Tall and skinny. You'll recognise her at once. But if you don't, just ask around. Everyone in town knows that one.'

With a face like a thundercloud, Delahunty strode from the bar room. About fifty yards along the main street was a sign announcing Wooranoora Community Hall. The front door was shut so he went around the back. Inside was a flurry of activity: folding chairs were being placed in rows; tables were being set; garlands of palm leaves and bush flowers were being pinned up to decorate the hall. In the midst of it all, a thin woman in a swivel chair was booming directions to all and sundry.

Delahunty approached. 'Mrs Maroney?'

'Yes?'

'I believe you can assist with accommodation booked in the name of Delahunty.'

Springing to her feet, she smoothed her grey skirt and made what might pass as a prim courtesy. 'Why, Mr Delahunty, I'm honoured to meet you. I thought the girls would have checked you in. Please accept my apologies.'

She led him to the front door; she was taller than him.

'Your rooms are ready. I'm so sorry to have put you out,' she flustered as they walked along the footpath towards the hotel.

'No problem.'

'Can I bring you a sandwich or a pot of tea?' By this time, they'd reached the reception desk. JB and Patrick had made themselves comfortable in a pair of armchairs. A sparrow had found its way inside and was nonchalantly pecking at crumbs on the floor.

'Thank you, Mrs Maroney. Tea would be nice.'

She completed the paperwork and gave them the keys. They were on the second floor overlooking the yard at the rear.

In his room at last, Delahunty lay down on the single bed and closed his eyes. Day one and he was already exhausted. Maybe he was too old for this. After all, he was a mere seven years younger than the Premier, who'd indicated on the quiet that he'd retire after the next election. In half an hour, he would have to make his improvised speech and he was worried. What if his mind went blank? He dug in his pocket for the paper with the important points. There were six. He read them through, committed them to memory. He must speak about each with conviction. Straight from the heart.

He needn't have worried about his presentation. Every seat in the hall was taken and the audience showed its support with applause. As he cast his eyes around the sea of faces, he realised what he'd been missing by reading off a page. These people were reacting to his every word with nods and facial expressions. It was as his father had said 'like talking to a group of friends'.

In the front row were two women dressed in neat summer frocks. One would have been around thirty and the other was somewhat older. He doubted they were mother and daughter, for the younger woman was fair while the other was dark and swarthy.

Afterwards, Delahunty mingled with the crowd. The two women were standing off to the side, waiting patiently while the menfolk pushed forward to speak their minds to a Member of Parliament. Delahunty was being grilled about the high cost of wages set by the state for semi-skilled workers. He shot an apologetic glance at the women.

The younger one smiled as if to say 'take your time, we don't mind'.

A weather-beaten cane farmer was pounding his fist into his palm. 'You and your bloody unions are sending us farmers broke. What happens then? If the sugar industry folds, it'll be Labor's fault. First you took away the Kanakas, and now you've taken away the Italians who do a decent day's work for a reasonable rate of pay. All we've got left are whinging bloody unionists who'd rather guzzle beer than cut a paddock of cane.'

JB must have overheard the slur against the union and came barging in. 'If it weren't for the union, young fella, you lot would've gone out of business years ago. Who stopped the spread of Weil's disease? Eh? Who got rid of the foreign standover merchants who'd rather chew off your ear than do a day's work? Things mightn't be perfect in this town, but they're a bloody sight better than in my day. Anyhow, mate, I'm out of politics now. Can I shout you a beer?'

'Yeah, why not?' said the farmer.

Together the two walked out of the hall and made off in the direction of the pub.

Released from an awkward situation, Delahunty turned to the women. 'Good evening, ladies. To what do I owe this pleasure?'

'The pleasure is all ours,' said the prettier one. 'My name is Edith Zucchero and this is my friend, Rosa Fiumefreddo. Could we have a word in private about a matter of great importance?'

The attendees were filing out of the hall. Patrick was talking to a group of stragglers by the door. Soon Delahunty would be free to retreat to the hotel's dining room and eat a lovely roast dinner that had been promised by Mrs Maroney.

'Would you like to talk over a cold drink?' he said.

The women exchanged a glance before agreeing.

Most of the men from the rally had congregated for the post-mortem in the public bar of the State Hotel, a place that was off-limits to women. At the rear of the building was the private bar, which was open to the ladies and had comfy wicker chairs. It was deserted. From the front bar, Delahunty ordered two shandies and pot of beer.

When they were settled, Edith began. 'Mr Delahunty, we would like to ask your assistance in relation to Rosa's husband. He is a good man and a hard worker. He has lived in this country for more than thirty years and is not, and never has been, a soldier or a Fascist supporter. Despite this, he has been arrested and sent to a prisoner of war camp. Is there any way he can get a reprieve?'

Delahunty took a mouthful of beer, which bought him a moment to think. 'I understand that the previous Minister of Police—my predecessor—ordered the arrest enemy aliens who posed a threat to public safety. The intention was to prevent associates of the enemy from doing anything subversive.'

Rosa said, 'Me 'usband, he a good man. He only cutta cane. All the time, he working, working. He never make no trouble.'

'You see, Mr Delahunty, this arrest means that Rosa has nowhere to live and cannot earn an income to support herself. For obvious reasons she can't return to Italy and she has no other relatives in Australia.'

'Where are you staying at the moment, Mrs ... ah ... *Fum-e-odo*?' His tongue baulked at the unpronounceable name. Why didn't these people have nice easy names like the British?

'Fiumefreddo,' corrected Rosa. 'You say like this: *Fume-e-fred-doh.*'

Her voice was deep, hypnotic. She gave him a little smile and dimples danced across her face. In her younger day, she would have been quite a beauty.

Returning to the question, Rosa said, 'I stay on farm of Mrs Zucchero, but she also 'ave canecutters there. All men, all British. It not good for me.'

Edith resumed the story. 'Until last year, Rosa's husband had been working with Renzo's canecutting gang and Rosa had been their cook. According to the union, having a female cook isn't legal so now she is out of a job. But this is not about Rosa, it's about Gianni Fiumefreddo who is locked up, goodness knows where. Is there any way he can prove his innocence and be released?'

Delahunty said, 'I understand that internees may appeal against their capture. I'll ask my assistant to find out how and let you know.'

Tears were rolling down the older woman's cheeks. 'Thank you. Thank you.'

'I can't make any promises,' he was quick to add.

'But surely you can promise justice?' said Edith.

He raised his palms. 'Internment of enemy aliens is a federal matter. While I can make representations, I am not in a position to make decisions.'

'Let me put it another way, Mr Delahunty. If you were locked up for no reason at all, how would your wife get money to live on?' said Edith.

'Hmmm.' Delahunty drained his glass.

The Premier had often warned his Cabinet ministers about the unintended consequences of policy decisions. 'Before you pass any legislation, read the draft in detail. Think about possible loopholes and how it might play out in the real world.'

Delahunty had heard this advice so many times that he no longer listened, yet here was an example of a hardworking man, who appeared not to pose a threat, caught up in the dragnet of paranoia. Until then he had not considered the impact on those left behind. In this case, a wife's only option was to rely on the benevolence of strangers.

He had no answers. Not then. Glancing up he saw JB and Patrick strolling towards the dining room. It was a few minutes before nine o'clock; soon the kitchen would close.

'I'll do what I can,' he said with conviction. 'Now you must excuse me, ladies.'

Edith gave him a note. 'Our names and addresses. Thank you for your time.'

'Thank *you*, Mrs *Zoo-ko* and Mrs *Fum-e-et-to*.' He bowed stiffly, proud that his stiff tongue had finally mastered the impossible surnames.

At dinner, he retold the women's story and asked Patrick to send an appropriate letter of response. Although he'd been touched, his first priority was to be re-elected. He needed the numbers and he needed policy positions that would appeal to the majority of British voters. Helping enemy aliens to be released from internment, while noble, would win him no votes at all.

He raised his glass and proposed a toast. 'To the success of this campaign.'

The Captives

Nine

On a hot Thursday in late summer, the hatchet finally fell.

Since Angelo's capture, Luigi had lived as if his neck were next on the chopping block. It was only a matter of time before he would be herded into a freight wagon and sent away to some awful place down south. Some days he wished the police would come and get him; then all the uncertainty would be over.

To prepare for this eventuality, he'd assigned a power of attorney to his accountant, Tony Zucchero, to allow him to do whatever was necessary to operate the farm. Mrs Ross would continue to manage the boarding house and deposit the rent money into the brothers' account at the ES&A Bank. He'd also withdrawn a substantial amount of cash from the bank and buried most of it in a treacle tin behind the farmhouse.

At ten o'clock that steamy Thursday morning, the paddy wagon eased up the track to the farmhouse and stopped at the back porch. Wearing work shorts and nothing else, Luigi was sitting on the steps, with a pannikin of tea in one hand and a cigarette in the other. In the space of a second, his heart leapt with relief then promptly sank to the pit of his stomach.

Behind the wheel was Constable Moody in a khaki uniform and slouch hat. His lips were pressed together in a straight red line that looked more like a slash than a mouth. He had not come alone. Beside him was a pasty new recruit who barely looked eighteen. A city boy for sure, probably talked into joining the Force by parents who thought catching criminals would be safer than defending the country on the battlefield.

Moody got out and flashed his police badge. 'We're here to search the house.'

Luigi stepped aside to let them pass. Ransacking would have been a better description of what followed. From the racket inside, they must have upended every stick of furniture and emptied every drawer. Fifteen minutes later, Moody's giant boots thundered onto the porch.

'Luigi Innocenti, you are under arrest. You are required to accompany us to the police station. You have two minutes in which to pack a port.' He checked his wristwatch. 'The time starts now.'

Several months ago, Luigi had packed in readiness. The port was stashed beneath his bed. All he had to do was slide it out. But when he entered his room, he rubbed his eyes in disbelief. The port, its contents, and everything else in the room were scattered about as if a cyclone had struck. He grabbed whatever touched his hand and stuffed it into the cardboard case. Thankfully the brown-paper lining appeared to be intact. What it concealed might be his salvation.

Outside, handcuffs were snapped on and he was pushed unceremoniously into the back of the paddy wagon. He spent the night in the lockup along with Carlo Monte, a former boarder who, for the last three months, had avoided capture by camping out in the bush. The others in the cells had been brought in from outlying properties. Some were known to him; some were newcomers.

Next morning, after a meagre breakfast of bread and jam, the captives were again manacled. This time a chain was threaded from man to man through eyes in the metal cuffs. Like a gang of dangerous felons, they marched single file along Sugarmill Street towards the railway station. It had been raining; water had pooled everywhere.

Withering with shame, Luigi set his jaw and kept his eyes on the road. His brown leather shoes were gathering mud; the hems of his trousers were wet. Steam rose from the puddles, adding moisture to the already dense air. Mosquitoes whined and dive-bombed around his ears. Lorikeets screeched like witches.

As they crossed the railway tracks, he glanced up. The white balustrades of the boarding house were directly ahead. Two Yugoslavs, single men who'd stayed on after the cutting season ended, were smoking and leaning on the rails. Luigi ducked his head into his collar so that shadow fell across his face. Never before had he felt so humiliated.

The manacles bit into his wrists. The chain clanked sadly against his thigh. In his right hand was his hurriedly-packed port. Last night in the lockup he'd checked its contents: three shirts, one pair of trousers, his winter suit, two grey woollen singlets, underwear, comb, soap. Somehow, he'd managed to throw in all the essentials within the allocated two minutes.

Carlo, immediately ahead, hawked and spat. He swore at Moody's back. *'Figlio di buttana.'* Son of a whore.

Luigi wrenched on the chain; the other man's hand flew back. 'Shhh! We're already in enough trouble.'

'Stupid prick can't understand a word we say,' said Carlo in rough Sicilian.

The Yugoslavs, now the sole inhabitants of the boarding house apart from Mrs Ross, retired to the comfy cane chairs and began to play cards.

Unable to control himself, Carlo jerked his chin at Moody and spat again. *'Bastardo!'*

Across the railway tracks trudged the line of men. On the platform in a section cordoned off with rope, several women wearing black had gathered. Young children swung around their skirts or played catch-me between the seats. On the ground were baskets of food, blanket-rolls, bundles of clothes, vessels of wine.

Sergeant Pitt marched the captives to the far end of the platform. Although the sun had just risen, its intensity promised yet another torrid day. Sweat trickled down Luigi's back; his shirt was glued to his skin. If he'd had any sense he would have worn his farm shorts and a canecutter singlet instead of his Sunday best.

The women were wailing and pleading in broken English for their spouses to be released. 'Me 'usband, he good man. He no done nothin' wrong. You letta 'im go.'

'Moody, get those troublemakers out of here!' bellowed Pitt.

Moody took a step in their direction and made shooing actions. 'You lot, clear off!'

The women continued to beg for mercy, their faces contorted with woe.

The scene reminded Luigi of the Great War, when reluctant conscripts were bundled into trains headed north to defend the Alpine provinces. The farewells were excruciating to watch. Although he'd managed to avoid all that, he was not especially proud of his actions. Some might have called him cowardly, but at the time he was being practical.

'Scat! Go home!' shouted Moody. He waved his arms, his bulk cast formidable shadows across the platform.

One by one, the women swung their children onto their hips. Weeping loudly, they slinked off the platform. The provisions they'd brought were left behind.

Moody put his hands on his hips and turned to his boss. 'What do we do with all this bloody stuff?' He kicked a food basket; a jar of black olives rolled out. 'What is this shit anyway?' With distain, he examined the contents of the jar. 'Looks like sheep turds.'

'Let the bastards have their wog food. Might keep them occupied on the train,' said Pitt.

In the distance, a plume of grey smoke came drifting over the cane fields. A flock of ibis lifted into the air. The chug and clatter of the engine grew louder as the southbound train rounded the bend. With a blast of steam, the locomotive shushed into the platform. The second-class carriages were packed: young soldiers in khaki and pretty girls in summer frocks. Everyone was smiling and chattering as if they were on a joy ride to the seaside or the mountains or a country fair.

At the rear of the train were three freight wagons. Hardwood, paint the colour of rust. One side opening, no windows. The chain connecting the prisoners was removed but the handcuffs remained.

Pitt rolled open the door of the last wagon, which was empty apart from a scant scattering of straw. Dust billowed out and Luigi began to sneeze.

Carlo exploded in a tirade of vile Sicilian. 'This shit-hole is for animals, not men!'

A ripple of dissent grew into a mighty roar. Everyone started yelling and pushing back, away from the open doorway.

Moody raised his baton. 'Get in or get a swift kick up yer arse!'

The threat was enough for the older men to make a move. A couple of the young bucks hung back, possibly to judge whether making a dash for it might be a better option.

Mentally Luigi shrugged. He was too exhausted to care. Wherever this train was going, he was likely to be reunited with his brother. That, if nothing else, was reason enough to comply. He took a step towards the wagon. From behind came a hard shove. He lost his footing; his leg slipped through the gap between the platform and the wagon. Somehow Carlo managed to catch him and haul him out. In the manoeuvre, Luigi's knees took a hard hit and his body twisted badly. He yelped in pain.

'Get a move on!' This was Pitt. *Whack!* came the blow of the truncheon.

Luigi crawled into a corner of the wagon and leant against the wall. As he brushed off the dust, his nose began to itch.

Achoo! Achoo! Aaaah-choo!

His knees were stinging. He blew his nose and looked down at his trousers. Blood was oozing through the fabric.

Finally, everyone was in. The wagon door slammed shut.

In darkness, the men pounded the walls with their fists.

'Let us out! Let us out!'

From outside came the clang of hammers. Metal striking metal.

Carlo yelled out in dismay. *'Porca miseria!* They're *nailing* us in!'

A whistle-blast drowned out their cries. The train lurched forward. Their bodies crashed together. Luigi swallowed a lump in his throat. Whatever was coming, was coming. He must do whatever it took to survive.

Sometime later Luigi woke from a restless sleep. The wagon was as dark as midnight yet he knew that outside the sun still shone. Certainly, it was hot enough. The smell of dust, sweat, and urine made him gag. He sat up, sneezed. Cursed beneath his breath.

'Keep your head, *paesano.*' The accent was old-time Sicilian, familiar and comforting. The speaker could have been his own Papa.

Garlicky breath tickled his ear. A cigarette flared. In its feeble glow, he saw the outline of a craggy face with white hair and whiskers.

'How can I keep my head in this stinking pigsty?' Luigi banged his fist on the floor. It dislodged more dust and he sneezed again.

'Calm down. Relax. Pretend you are *in vacanza.* The time will soon pass.'

Luigi dragged his hands through his hair and sighed. 'I suppose you're right.'

'At my age, you know how to survive practically anything. Want a smoke?'

Gratefully Luigi accepted. *'Grazie.* My name is Luigi Innocenti.' He rolled the meagre strands of tobacco into the paper and licked it to seal.

'Vito Vento. But everyone calls me *Vecchio* (old man). It's the truth and I don't mind … I *am* old.' They shook hands; the chains on their handcuffs jangled. 'Days like this I sure miss the old country.'

'Certo. Everyone told us we'd make our fortune here. But all we wanted was to buy a farm and help our family back home. Now look where we are!'

'You got a wife?'

'Not yet. One day I'll marry. One day, after the war. My brother Angelo and I came here in 1922. He was captured and sent away months ago … I don't know where.' Luigi took a drag of the cigarette. The oven-like environment and the nicotine set his head spinning.

'I came out in 1902. Always thought I'd go back but never got around to it.' Vecchio's voice grew thin. *'Si,* this is where I'll die.'

'Don't talk about dying. It'll bring bad luck.'

Vecchio began to cough; his lungs rattled with catarrh. When it seemed like he'd never catch his breath again, the spasm passed. He wiped his mouth with the back of his hand. 'I'm not afraid to die. San Filippo watches over me. And in case I'm not worthy of a saint's attention, I take this *medicina* for my health.' From his top pocket, he took a clove of garlic, peeled off the skin and swallowed it whole. 'Want one?'

'Later maybe.'

The train veered around a bend. The men tumbled like manikins. Salt-scented air whistled between the boards, cooling the wagon to a simmer. The afternoon sun speared in through the cracks. The walls were burnished with golden light.

'Where do you think they'll take us?' said Luigi.

Vecchio said, 'Brisbane, probably.'

'All the way to Brisbane! In this crate! *Stronzi*!' This was Carlo. In the gloom, his face loomed as menacing as a storm-cloud.

There was not much more to be said. Luigi stood and stretched. The sparse straw did nothing to protect his backside from the constant paddling dealt out by the floorboards. Saddle-sore without the horse, he rubbed the tender spots as best he could with hands that were manacled together.

He needed time to think. And, above all, he needed to keep his head.

Self-control was not a strong point amongst Sicilians and Luigi was no exception. For something to fill the time, he found his tobacco, rolled a smoke, and passed the pouch to Vecchio. They lit up from the same match. Luigi drew back and let the smoke fill his lungs. At last his brain began to tick over.

What he had said earlier was true. The main reason he'd come to this country—this Promised Land—was to make money. For nearly two decades the brothers had worked and scrimped and saved. Hundreds of pounds had been sent home, believing that it would help feed hungry mouths and also go towards buying land of their own. But now everything was falling apart. On that fateful trip in '39, Angelo was unable to finalise their father's estate, nor could he discover exactly what had happened to all the money they'd sent to Papa. Now, with a war on, returning to Sicily was out of the question and nothing further could be done to sort out the mess.

Sometimes he wondered if he ever wanted to go back at all.

Like a fool he'd fallen in love with *this* country. The over-ripe jungle, the mauve sugar-flowers, the summer downpours, the fairy-floss cloud on the mountains. He'd tried so hard to be loved in return: to be part of the community, to be a good British subject, to speak the king's English. His Certificate of Naturalization hung proudly on his bedroom wall. He'd expected that buying the farm would bring respect. But no. Then when they took over the boarding house, he'd thought acceptance might be forthcoming. Negative again. When Mussolini came to power, he'd been careful to remain noncommittal and not offend anyone about politics. Like the dog that bit its master's hand, the law turned on him. He and his *paesani* were labelled 'enemy aliens' and treated like crooks.

He'd done all he could to assimilate but it wasn't enough.

The hours crawled by. They ate the 'wog food' brought by the women and drank the home-made red wine. Someone began crooning. The lyrics of the song were in dialect, passed from generation to generation by word of mouth. Soon they were all singing. They sang until their throats were dry and afternoon became early evening.

Eventually the train stopped. The nails were wrenched out.

The door rolled open and a burly policeman ordered them onto the platform.

Somewhere along the route their numbers had swelled. Two extra freight wagons had been added to the end of the train. They were herded out of the station—a grand red-brick building with white arches—and into a square bordered by spreading Moreton Bay fig trees. Towering over them was a mighty bluff, dotted with stunted trees. The red rock monolith was all angles and bends; its flanks cascaded right into the heart of the town.

'Castle Hill. I'd know it anywhere,' said Vecchio. 'We're in Townsville.'

On the road behind the fig trees four trucks were parked.

'Get in and make it snappy!' ordered the policeman.

There were too many men and not enough space. In the tray-back they squeezed together on timber planks, their ports on their laps. A flaming sun, hovering just above the treetops, cast long shadows across the brown grass.

With a jolt, the truck took off. They motored along a graded dirt road to the outskirts of civilisation, then turned onto a bush track which ran for several miles. Ahead was a high concrete wall with rolls of barbed wire on top. They stopped outside a pair of formidable gates made of heavy-duty steel bars.

'Are they taking us to *gaol*?' said Carlo, incredulous.

Luigi shrugged. To him, they looked like the gates of Hell.

'I'll be complaining to the Red Cross if they are,' said Vecchio.

'No. We'll go straight to the top. To *il Duce* himself.' Carlo spat and ground a fist into his palm.

The gates groaned open. The trucks rumbled into an asphalt quadrangle surrounded by squat red-brick buildings. Tired and irritable, the captives climbed out, stretched their legs, gazed around the depressing barren place.

The handcuffs were removed. The roll was called. Many of the surnames were familiar. Luigi knew most of the cane workers around Wooranoora and if he didn't know the man himself, he'd know a brother or an uncle or a cousin. In far north Queensland, his countrymen had cast a wide web. That's how they operated. While the Britishers traded in cash, the Sicilians traded favours. Someone always knew someone, who in turn knew someone who would help.

When the guards were satisfied nobody had escaped, the captives were marched into an exercise yard at the rear of the main building. A wonky chain-wire fence divided the space in two. On one side, the inmates sat about in civvies. All were Italian. The men on the other side wore greyish-white cotton pants and shirts stamped with black arrowheads. Of the latter group, most were dark-skinned. Aboriginals, Islanders, Kanakas. The rest were wild-looking Caucasians, and there was also a handful of Chinamen.

Much to Luigi's relief they were directed into the section for civilians. Whoops of recognition came from the existing inmates as friends and countrymen were reunited. Luigi scanned the faces for Angelo. No such luck. From the other internees, he learnt that this was the notorious Stewart's Creek Gaol and those on the other side of the fence were murderers and madmen. The flimsy wire promised little protection.

'*Porca miseria*!' said Luigi to one of the internees. 'How do you sleep at night?'

'We don't. That lot are completely crazy; they yell out all the time. It's like being in a lunatic asylum. Daytime is as bad. My advice is don't go near that fence.'

Luigi shivered. 'How long have you been here?'

The fellow checked his wristwatch. 'Eight days, six hours, and thirty-five minutes. Not that I'm counting.'

A bell jangled; everyone lined up for food. The brew in the metal vat smelt like swamp-water and looked equally appealing. Everyone got the same serving: a chunk of white bread and a pannikin-full of cloudy brown liquid. Unidentifiable bits of decomposed matter floated on top. Luigi was so hungry that he scoffed the lot.

At seven o'clock the men on the other side were locked in the cells.

The internees remained in the open yard. In the cloudless night sky, the constellation Crux—the Southern Cross—rested sideways above the roof of the nearby cellblock; the stars on Orion's Belt glistened like diamantes. A sea breeze came in, sweeping away the dust of the day and chilling the night air. Thankfully there seemed little likelihood of rain.

No bedding was provided. Luigi made a swag from the clothes he'd brought; his port was his pillow. Before turning in, he visited the latrines: metal buckets lined up along the wall. There was no newspaper to clean himself and nowhere to wash his hands.

In the morning, breakfast consisted of grey lumpy porridge and black tea. Lunch was white bread with a thin spread of jam. Another truck-load of Italians arrived in the late afternoon and a second night was spent under the stars.

Before dawn on the third day, the internees were handcuffed and trucked back to the red-brick station in town. But instead of entering the platform, they were directed to the railway yard at the back. The train consisted of six passenger carriages at the front and six freight wagons at the rear. Luigi groaned at the thought of spending several days locked in an animal crate again. But, to his surprise and relief, the line of one hundred captives was steered toward the front of the train.

A police guard was stationed at either end of the carriage. Luigi settled into a window seat. Vecchio sat beside him. At the first blush of dawn, the locomotive eased out of the railway yard. They were on their way south. Final destination unknown.

Countless acres of unruly scrubland whizzed past. Mile after monotonous mile. They were forbidden to open the windows. With the sun blazing on the roof, the carriage heated up to more than a hundred degrees. Everyone was complaining.

Vecchio rose from his seat and went up to the guard. In excellent English he said, 'If we don't get fresh air soon, you'll have blood on your hands.'

After conferring, the two guards—who looked mighty sweaty and uncomfortable themselves—delivered the verdict. 'You can open the windows a bit, but only while the train is in motion.'

All day they travelled without a break, apart from picking up coal and water at sidings along the way. The food on offer was a choice of sandwiches: jam or peanut paste. The doughy white bread set like a rock in Luigi's stomach. What he wouldn't give for a nice bowl of pasta!

Hours passed. The train hurtled into the darkness of night. Tired to the bone, Luigi rested his head against the rattling window frame. Around midnight the temperature dropped and he fell into a deep and dreamless sleep.

Sometime later the men began to stir. In the grey light of morning, bushland became farmland. Waterbags were passed around and breakfast arrived: jam sandwiches.

The click-clack of the wheels began to slow as the sparse open spaces gave way to denser settlements. Rows of timber cottages backed onto the railway lines. There were vegetable patches, chook runs, mango trees, backyard privies, choko vines. Bitumen roads, power lines, trams.

The train passed by city buildings, clanked through a long sooty tunnel. Emerged at the other end into dazzling sunlight. At Roma Street Station, they stopped. All around were rose gardens and red geraniums in hanging baskets. Soldiers in slouch hats were in position beneath the corrugated-iron roof. The internees scrambled to their feet and grabbed their belongings, eager to get out of the confined space.

They spilled onto the platform. Roll-call.

A sergeant with a megaphone voice stumbled over their unpronounceable names. If it weren't for the circumstances, Luigi would have laughed. Instead, everyone responded politely with '*si*' or 'here' or '*presente*'. When Carlo Monte's name was called, he said '*va fanculo*', which raised a few smirks amongst the prisoners. The sergeant read on, oblivious to the crude insult.

The police guards unshackled them; the soldiers took charge. After forming two straggly lines, the captives filed out. They were driven half an hour in a fleet of army-green trucks to Gaythorne military camp on the outskirts of town. The place was vast—forty acres of rolling grassland—and fortified with high barbed wire fences. Inside the compound were four corrugated-iron Nissen huts and dozens of rows of tents. Magnificent gum trees lined the banks of a brown creek that divided the camp in two.

In the hut nearest the road, the prisoners queued before small desks that had been set up across the width of the room. Young soldiers worked through the forms, asking them their dates of birth, religions, occupations, next of kin, and questions about their families and possessions.

Whenever Luigi said *no understan'*, the soldier would repeat the exact same question, only louder.

'*Porca miseria.* I'm not deaf,' Luigi muttered.

Eventually, the soldier called for an interpreter. The necessary details were obtained and recorded in perfect copperplate script.

With the interrogations complete, their luggage was searched. Scissors, nail files, and flasks of liquor were confiscated. Luigi lowered his eyes and prayed that the stash in the lining of his port would go undiscovered. A bored-looking soldier upended it on a bench and picked through the clothing. Finding nothing of interest, he shoved the jumble back to Luigi to repack.

The third part of the humiliating process was the so-called 'health check', which was in fact a security search of every orifice of their bodies. Naked except for a smattering of insect bites, Luigi folded his hands across his paunch, conscious of the horrible scar from the accident. A crinkled patch of red.

The examiner prodded the scar with a tongue depressor. 'What happened here?'

Luigi said, 'Got hurt cutting down trees. Very bad thing. I lucky to live.'

The examiner nodded noncommittally, prescribed calamine lotion for the bites, moved on to the next man.

Finally, the captives received standard army kits—cutlery, utensils and bedding—and were allocated tents. Later, in the mess hut, they assembled for lunch. Meat stew, the smell of which reminded him of woollen singlets soaking in hot water. Luigi forced himself to eat in order to keep up his strength.

After lunch, they were dismissed and left to their own devices. Luigi and Vecchio set off for the creek. Beneath the gum trees they sat on the grassy bank. A school of silver fingerlings flashed in the shallows. A brackish odour—sediment and mangroves—oozed from the mud.

Vecchio rolled a cigarette and tossed the tobacco pouch to Luigi. He took a long drag and puffed out the smoke in rings.

Luigi said, 'Now what?'

'We should put in an appeal. There's a chance we could get out.'

For the first time in days, Luigi felt a boost of hope. Yes, his police record was unblemished. If only good old Sergeant Whelby had been still at Wooranoora, instead of that mongrel Pitt. Then Luigi would have received a glowing report, not a prison sentence. He suspected Pitt had something to gain from the arrests made under his name. A promotion perhaps, or an easier job in the city. In a short time, the new sergeant had befriended the most influential bigots in the far north, including a certain state Member of Parliament who'd made no secret of his loathing of Italians. Luigi wondered how far the tentacles extended.

'Would an appeal really work?' said Luigi.

Vecchio puffed on his smoke. 'Nah, probably not.'

Ten

Brisbane, March 1941

A statement of appeal was needed but Luigi had no idea where to begin. After consulting with others who'd been through the process, all he'd gleaned was what *not* to write. The tiny proportion of individuals whose appeals had been successful were released straight after the hearing. As a result, nobody remaining in detention had actually written a convincing argument. It was hard to know where to get proper guidance.

Approaching it in the same way as the other hot-heads was a sure-fire way to fail. Luigi wracked his brains for a different angle but came up blank. What kept him going was a thread of belief that the justice system would recognise his innocence.

'I am right and this is wrong,' he repeated to himself.

In frustration, he turned to the camp interpreter—Mr Alighieri, a former schoolteacher—who'd helped hundreds of inmates write their appeals. Surely, he would know the requirements of a strong appeal statement.

'Make it short and sweet,' Alighieri advised. 'Put your strongest arguments first.'

After agonising for another week, Luigi set out his claims as dot points in Italian, then made an appointment with the interpreter to talk it through.

Silently, Alighieri scanned Luigi's notes. Taking a fresh sheet of paper, he hand-wrote another version in English. Luigi had no alternative but to trust the man. He hoped the translation accurately represented his case, for he had no way of knowing for sure.

In Italian, he could write most things, although technical and legal terms sometimes escaped him. As a language, Italian made sense. If you knew how to pronounce the alphabet, reading was a breeze.

But English! Spoken, it was the devil to understand and slang was an artform. Although he'd bought an Oxford dictionary, most of the words used by the folk of Wooranoora were not listed.

In its written form, English was downright impossible. All those silent consonants and strange arrangements of vowels. No two spellings were pronounced the same way.

Alighieri read out his translation slowly so that Luigi could understand.

> *Dear Sir,*
>
> *I object against my internment order on the following grounds:*
>
> *that I am a British Subject by naturalization;*
>
> *that I have resided in Australia for a period of eighteen years and it has always been my intention to establish myself permanently in Australia;*
>
> *that I have never belonged to any political organisation nor have I ever been guilty of political activities;*
>
> *that I have always been a law-abiding citizen and I have never been convicted;*
>
> *that to my knowledge I have never been guilty of disloyal remarks or actions towards the British Empire;*
>
> *that I require my freedom in order to take care of my business.*

To Luigi it sounded impressive. He gave a nod of approval and smiled. Surely an honest judge with compassion and common sense would consider this letter favourably.

They shook hands. Alighieri wished him luck then gave the draft to a middle-aged woman in a navy-blue tunic to type up on the Remington. Luigi sat on the other side of the desk, mesmerised by the machine's keys clacking in quick succession against the black ribbon. He dared not breathe, which might cause her to make a mistake. His freedom depended on that single sheet of paper.

When it was done, he scanned the page. The typewriter ink exuded the heady scent of confidence. He admired the nice way she had set it out: the crisp letters, the even keystrokes, the nicely-balanced paragraphs, the dotted line where he was to sign. With a sigh, he dipped the nib in the inkwell, scribbled his signature, and kissed it for luck.

Six weeks passed. Six weeks of worrying that his appeal would go the same way as most of the others. Nights, he would lie awake on the straw palliasse, smoking and staring at the inner apex of the tent. Outside in the trees flying foxes squabbled, storm birds wailed like spirits of the dead, possums growled and hissed. The hours of darkness seemed to go on and on.

During the day, he tried to get information from anyone who'd already been through the proceedings. 'A complete waste of time' was the general verdict.

Carlo Monte, whose appeal had already been heard, advised him to ask for an interpreter. 'I tried it in English but there were too many tricky words. *Bastardi*! Everything got twisted around. The interpreter was a *cazzo* (dick) with an awful accent. I could hardly understand him.'

'What did they ask?'

'Mostly about things the police found. Letters from my family, a flick-knife, some leaflets about *il Duce*.'

Luigi had no idea what Constable Moody had taken on the day of the raid. In his mind he went through a list of items they might have regarded as suspicious. Yes, there were letters from home in Italian and booklets that Angelo had brought back from Sicily. Thankfully he'd had the sense to hide his guns so he shouldn't be penalised for that. Apart from Tano's bone-handled hunting knife, nothing dubious came to mind.

On 28 March 1941, the morning of the hearing, Luigi polished his brown leather shoes and dressed in his best white shirt and his woollen suit, vintage 1922. Although officially autumn, the day promised to be as hot as mid-summer. The army jeep, which was to take him to the Supreme Court in the city centre, was parked near the corrugated-iron hut where the captives had been processed on the first day. Four other internees were standing about, smoking or chewing their nails. At least he wouldn't have to face the ordeal alone.

One by one they climbed beneath the canvas canopy of the vehicle and took their places on hard plank seats. Luigi's stomach was churning. Too nervous to eat breakfast, he was now feeling queasy. The streetscape whizzed by as the jeep sped along a tree-lined thoroughfare. Now and then they stopped at an intersection or to wait for a tram. Shopgirls in black-and-white uniforms and factory workers wearing hairnets streamed across zebra crossings. Apart from a few young soldiers, the men on the street were either white-haired or crippled.

In the city centre, the jeep made a right-hand turn through imposing wrought-iron gates. Inside was a large courtyard with neat lawns bordered by gardens of red geraniums and *monstera deliciosa*. Down one side was a grand colonnade, exactly like the Royal Palace in Palermo. The sandstone building behind was massive: a monument to power, wealth, and permanence.

The jeep moved on. Under its weight, the gravel driveway crunched like breaking bones. They came to a stop at the foot of a stone staircase. Luigi's legs were trembling; his heart was bursting inside his chest.

Silently he repeated his mantra. 'I am right and this is wrong.'

The captives were ordered to climb down and follow the guard up the stairs. Near the entrance was a bronze statue. Themis, goddess of law and order. In her right hand were balancing scales, in her left was the sword of justice. She was blindfolded but her face was serene. Surely, in this supreme court of the state of Queensland, common sense would prevail.

After trailing through a maze of corridors, they came to the courtroom. Luigi's case was first on the list. The others waited outside, guarded by two soldiers.

Inside the small courtroom, the air was close and oppressive. Dark oak panels made it feel as if the walls were closing in. At one end was a raised platform and an oversized rosewood bench. Below were two desks, heaped with books and papers.

The attendant ordered Luigi to stand in the centre of the room. His guard was positioned directly behind, so close that he could feel warm breath on his neck.

Not a minute passed before five stony-faced men came in: three in officer uniforms and two in civilian suits.

'All rise. The court is now in session. Justice Philp presiding,' said the attendant.

A sturdy gentleman in white wig and robes entered through a rear door and took his seat at the bench. The hearing commenced with a to-and-fro of legal arguments that Luigi couldn't understand.

By now, the butterflies in his stomach felt like rhinoceros beetles. Between the unfathomable debate, the echo of voices off stone walls, the unseasonal heat and lack of sustenance, his body was threatening to shut down. He must not faint. Not now, not while there was yet a chance to save himself.

Luigi dug his fingernails into his palms, focussed his attention on the judge. He would have been around fifty. His eyes were steel-grey and his wit was sharp. Everyone bowed and nodded as if they were in awe of him.

Philp turned his eyes to Luigi.

He felt like a 'roo in the headlights. His pulse was hammering and suddenly he needed to pee.

'Is your name Luigi Innocenti?' said Philp.

'Yes, your Honour.'

'Do you wish to give evidence to the court?'

Luigi said, 'Please, I not understand English very good.'

Philp summoned one of the army officers to the bench and they spoke in whispers.

The officer nodded then spoke to Luigi in Italian. 'I am Lieutenant Spinelli, official interpreter for the Australian army. All communication in this court will be directed through me.' His accent was hard to understand and he raced through the message as if his arse was on fire.

When Luigi said *'piano, piano'* to slow him down, he sniffed and turned away.

Despite this hiccup, the preliminary questions were easy enough. Age; address; how long had he been in Australia; what was the value of his property; where did his family live?

Throughout, Philp stroked his jaw. Then he fired the first round. 'So, what do you think of Mussolini?'

Spinelli translated the question.

Luigi's mind whirled like a dust devil. He took a breath, glanced at the judge and then responded through the interpreter. 'I can't say anything about Mussolini because I don't know. I came out here in 1922.'

Philp nodded, which seemed to be a sign of encouragement.

The officer who opened the army's interrogation was Captain Robinson. He was young—perhaps in his thirties—with narrow lips and a cruel jawline. He spoke only to the interpreter. Luigi might as well have been invisible or standing in another room.

'Who does he want to win the war?' Robinson asked Spinelli.

The question was translated.

Luigi replied to Spinelli, who reported back in English. 'He says that he has been eighteen years in Australia and he likes Italy, so that it makes no difference to him.'

The judge raised an eyebrow. 'It does not make any difference to you who wins the war?' He spoke directly to Luigi in slow easy English.

'No,' replied Luigi with a touch of defiance. 'It doesn't.'

Judge and prisoner locked eyes for a moment, each sizing the other up. Philp's face was open. He seemed like an intelligent and reasonable man. Luigi wanted to believe he was also fair. But fairness didn't seem to count in a world at war.

Robinson continued. 'Is he glad or sorry that the Italians are losing the war?'

Luigi answered as best he could, but his confidence was slipping away. In his heart he knew it was a charade; the questions were as hollow as marrow bones.

Robinson dumped a folder of papers on the desk. 'I refer to the police dossier dated December 1940. The following statement was provided by Sergeant Pitt of Wooranoora Police. "I have heard him say that if we were at war with Italy, he would fight for Italy." Can the prisoner confirm this is correct?'

Through Spinelli, Luigi answered. 'How could I fight for Italy when I am here in Australia?'

Robinson rolled his eyes. 'Has he ever been to any meetings of Fascists?'

'No.'

Robinson held up three publications for the court to see: *La Tua Patria* (Your Country), *La Battiglia del Piave* (The Battle of Piave), and a copy of *Watchtower*. 'What does he say about these?'

The first two Luigi had never seen before. The third was a pamphlet given to him by Jehovah's Witnesses who'd been kind enough to visit him at the Brisbane General Hospital when he was receiving treatment after the tree-felling accident. Lonely and bored, he'd welcomed the company of the two young men, one of whom spoke a little Italian. Although he made it clear that he was Catholic, and intended to remain so, they continued to come every day.

'Those books aren't mine. I don't know who owns them.'

'Does he own a book called *Mussolini Speaks*?'

The book had been circulating in the boarding house for months. Luigi had skimmed a few pages and put it aside. In his opinion, politicians caused more problems than they solved. The winners were either born into power or wealthy enough to buy votes. Politics was a dirty game. Mussolini's slim volume had sparked many an argument amongst the firebrands, some of whom worshipped *il Duce* as Italy's shining star while others condemned him as the puppet of a madman with a toothbrush moustache.

'I'm not a Fascist. There were books at the boarding house but I did not read them,' Luigi said. It was the truth. With so much work to do, reading was a luxury he could ill afford.

Robinson took a sip of water. The next exhibit came as a complete surprise. It was the silver cigarette case that Luigi had inherited from his father. Until then, he'd thought it was safely hidden in his wardrobe at the farmhouse.

'If he is not a Fascist, why does he have a portrait of Mussolini?'

'That's not Mussolini, it's our king,' said Luigi.

'Pssht. Looks nothing at all like King George.'

Luigi felt his face getting hot. The etching was of King Vittorio Emanuele, which he wanted to say but then changed his mind. Let them think whatever they liked. The sooner this ended, the sooner he could get some fresh air.

The ceiling fan squeaked and turned listlessly. Sweat was trickling down his back; his skin was crawling. What he wouldn't give for a smoke!

'Has he got a wireless set?' Robinson asked.

'Yes.' The word slipped out without a thought. Now he'd be up to his neck in *merda* (shit). Owning a wireless was definitely against the law. The ancient beast lived in the dining room at the boarding house. Rather than dispose of it, Mrs Ross had hidden it beneath a tablecloth and a vase of paper flowers. Late at night, the men would gather and listen to international broadcasts. From time to time there'd be an announcement about events in Europe, but mostly it was tuned to music or harmless banter. Although the reception was unreliable and there was tooth-clenching static, the wireless was a lifeline to their distant homeland.

Robinson pounced. 'Is it a shortwave set then?'

'Yes, but it's broken and we didn't get it fixed.' Saved by a burnt-out valve. They had no spares and it was too risky to get a new one from the repair shop.

Robinson cleared his throat, tried a different angle. 'Has he ever worn a black shirt?'

In Italy, black was the colour of mourning. But these days, black was also the colour of Fascists. The wrong answer and he'd be labelled as one of Mussolini's Blackshirts.

'Yes, when my father died.'

The corner of Robinson's mouth lifted in a wry smile. 'And I suppose he also wore a Fascist *badge* when his father died?'

The tone of sarcasm was unmistakable.

Spinelli translated the snide comment. Verbatim.

Luigi bit his lips to prevent a response he might regret, however his rage refused to be silenced. 'No, I did not!'

Looking impatient, Justice Philp consulted his fob watch. 'Is there anything further you wish to say, Innocenti?'

This was Luigi's last chance to clear his name. He wanted to say how much he loved this country, how hard he'd worked, that he was an honest law-abiding citizen. He wanted to condemn the Fascist regime that had ripped his family apart. And he wanted to argue that being arrested and imprisoned without a trial went against the Australian ethos of a 'fair go' for all. But the homily he'd prepared slipped away.

'Well?' the judge prompted. 'We don't have all day.'

'The only thing I can think of is that somebody in Wooranoora is jealous of me.' As the words left his lips, he wished he could snatch them back. He sounded like a fool with a grudge, yet he pushed on. 'Somebody there wants to send me broke—'

Justice Philp cut him off. 'Do you know who it is? Do you have someone in mind?'

Luigi's throat contracted. Nothing he said now would change the outcome. Even if he were to name a likely suspect, it wouldn't help.

'No. I don't know.' Luigi's eyes misted as he conceded defeat.

Philp tapped his papers into a neat pile. 'That is all. A report will be made to the Minister. You will be advised in due course.' He pushed back his chair and rose.

The court stood. The hearing was over. Luigi was taken to a waiting room, away from the other appellants whose claims were yet to be heard.

One by one they joined him, their hopes similarly crushed.

On returning to the camp at Gaythorne, Luigi received his first letter. It was a one-pager from Angelo, written in an unfamiliar hand.

> *Yesterday I was sentenced to internment for the duration of the war. They did not accept my application, which I expected. Now we must resign ourselves to spend the whole period patiently and tranquilly. We must comfort ourselves in the destiny that is coming. Let us hope it will not last long and that we will be together again forever.*

The attitude was typical of Angelo. Acceptance and determination to endure whatever came his way. Others would have railed against their predicament, or blasted the politicians or the police or the army who held them with no credible evidence at all. But not Angelo. He was as calm and positive as always, and Luigi admired him for it.

Exactly two months after the court hearing, Luigi was officially advised the outcome in writing. The single sentence confirmed his fears.

'Your appeal has been dismissed, therefore you are to remain in internment.'

The paper was heavy in his hand. All hope of release was now gone. The brothers would remain in prison until the end of the war. How long would that be? Although newspapers were not allowed in the camp, rumours were spreading that the Axis forces were gaining victory over the Allies. Perhaps the end would be swift after all.

Carlo, who was in thick with the Fascist contingent, boasted that by year's end Australia would fall.

'Ha! Then the tables will be turned! English will be banned and the bloody mutton-eaters will have to speak Italian. Now *that* is justice indeed!'

Luigi was not so sure. To be honest he really didn't care what happened as long as it was over quickly. He missed the farm, he missed his freedom, and he worried about his family's safety on the far side of the world.

In the period that followed, time seemed to stand still. In the internment camp at Gaythorne there was little to do. No work, no entertainment, no diversions, no joy. Every day was as vacuous as it was long. Boredom, it seemed, was the punishment for being in the wrong country at the wrong time.

Some wrote letters to pass the time. Full well they knew that while the two countries were at war, letters to Catania or Salerno or Bari were unlikely to ever reach their destination. Paper was rationed: one sheet per man per week. Paper became a tradeable commodity, along with the weekly ration of tobacco. Those who didn't write and didn't smoke had the advantage. To a bored prisoner, both were as lifegiving as water.

Every day, Luigi whiled away the hours by the creek. Sometimes he'd sit on the bank and catch tiny fish that swam into the shallows. Sometimes he'd skip stones. As morning become noon and noon become evening, the shadows of the gum trees would creep across the grass until the empty night snatched them away.

Another day ended. Who knew how many yet to go.

Perhaps Vecchio was right. *Treat this as a vacation.* One day, when the war was over, the hard work would begin again.

Eleven

Wooranoora, 29 April 1941

Weeks after her inconclusive meeting with William Delahunty at the political rally, Edith received two formal letters from the Office of the Member for Endeavour. Both were signed by the man himself, however Edith suspected they had been drafted by a member of staff, whose job was to attend to correspondence.

The first expressed apologies that the matter of Rosa's husband was out of the jurisdiction of the State. It explained that captives who had been transferred to internment camps were no longer the responsibility of the Queensland police but of the Australian Military Forces.

The second letter, received a few days later, contained details of how a person in internment might lodge an appeal.

By the time the letters arrived, both pieces of information were obsolete. Gianni Fiumefreddo had already lodged an appeal and had subsequently attended court. The appeal had been dismissed, which meant he was destined to remain behind barbed wire until the war ended.

Meanwhile, Tony had contacted his cousin in the fruit-growing district of Stanthorpe about Rosa's predicament. By return mail, Cousin Franki announced that she was soon to become a mother again (for the fourth time) and would therefore welcome some help to grade and pack fruit. With a shortage of able-bodied men due to the war, experienced farm workers were in short supply. Rosa would receive a modest wage and could stay in the farmhand's cottage rent-free until Gianni returned from 'down south'.

Rosa jumped at the offer and caught the train a few days later.

Now there were three of them left on the farm: Tony, Edith and Bella. There might as well have been two, for Edith barely saw her husband. Most of his accountancy clients—all of the Italians, at any rate—had vanished from the district, leaving him in charge of their affairs. Although it was the slack season, his workload had trebled. As the appointed power of attorney for about twenty farmers, he had to negotiate all manner of financial deals to keep their farms operating and their machinery from either being repossessed by the bank or confiscated by the army for the war effort. Often, he visited the wives or elderly mothers who had been left alone on the family property. Mostly the women spoke no English, could not drive a vehicle, had no knowledge of how to keep a business afloat, and no idea about growing sugar cane.

'Worse than that,' Tony explained. 'They are completely terrified. Terrified for the safety of their families in Italy; terrified that their husbands will die in prison; terrified that the police will raid their homes or take their children away; and terrified that the soldiers in the district will attack and rape them.'

Edith's eyes filled with tears. But for the mercy of God, this could have been her too. A woman alone, a small child to care for. Her saving grace was that both her parents were British: a fluke of nature that gave her the right nationality and the right language.

'If I could speak Italian, I might give them some comfort. Will you teach me, Tony?'

'*Amore*, you would have to learn two hundred languages. They speak a bastardised form of Italian: a mixture of regional dialects, basic primary-school Italian, and Italo-English. The northerners can't understand the southerners, and vice versa. I'm flat out communicating most of the time.'

'Thank God I've got you, my darling. I'm an incredibly lucky woman.' She took his hands, drew him close and nuzzled his neck.

'Is our daughter asleep?' he whispered into her ear.

'Out like a light.'

He kissed her lips, softly and gently. Ran his hands down her spine.

She shivered slightly, then moved in closer. Ever since she'd been with him, she'd marvelled at how well their bodies fitted together. It was as if her curves and his muscles perfectly complemented each other.

She took his hand and led him to the daybed on the verandah.

'We really do need to move Bella's cot out of our bedroom,' he said.

'Maybe next week. Look at the wonderful view we have!' She opened her arms to the brilliant green of the cane fields and the rolling hills beyond. It was the off-season so there was nobody around for miles. Just the two of them and a sleeping child.

'It's you I'd rather look at.' He covered her with kisses.

They lay close together on the single daybed, so close it was hard to breathe. Edith didn't care; she'd gladly give up her life for him, this beautiful, generous, clever man. He unbuttoned her blouse and traced the mounds of her breasts with his tongue. As he pressed into her, she closed her eyes and arched her back. How right their love felt. How very wonderful it was to touch and hold him and to be loved in return.

The next day, the unthinkable happened.

Bella had gone down for her afternoon nap when there was a loud rapping on the front door. Edith scurried to answer it. If Bella was disturbed now, there'd be all hell to pay for the rest of the afternoon. The second molars were pushing through and she'd had her cranky pants on all week.

A man's silhouette blocked the doorway. The dazzling glare of the mid-afternoon sun cast his features into deep shade but his slouch hat told her it could be none other than Police Sergeant Pitt.

'Good afternoon, Sergeant. Do come in. What brings you here?'

Taking a step onto the veranda, he said, 'Is your husband home?' He sounded somewhat apologetic.

She looked him up and down, saw in his hand what she'd dreaded most. An envelope, window-faced, the coat of arms printed in black at the top. She'd seen them before. Tony had shown her the arrest warrants they'd served on his clients.

Usually the letter consisted of one short sentence. 'Under the provisions of the *National Security Act (1939)*, you have been identified as an enemy alien and, as such, are hereby detained by the State of Queensland'.

'Oh no!' she gasped. 'You can't be serious!'

'Sorry, Mrs Zucchero. Really I am. Orders from Brisbane Headquarters.'

Suddenly the world was spinning. She lowered herself into a chair and dropped her head into her hands. 'How can I run a farm and raise a child on my own?'

'Please, tell me where he is. I'll make it as painless as I can.'

'Paddock three, down by the creek. He's planting cane.' In utter disbelief, she shook her head. This couldn't be happening. Tony would never incite treachery against his country. Somebody must have made a mistake.

Sergeant Pitt turned to leave.

'Wait!' She sprang out of the chair. 'Why are you arresting him?'

'We received information that he is involved in a Fascist network. Witnesses have seen him visiting various Italian farms in the district to gather intelligence about the movement of British troops.'

She snorted. 'What poppycock! Who told you this?'

'I can't say any more.' Halfway down the stairs, Pitt halted. 'Mrs Zucchero?'

'Yes?'

'You should pack a port for him. It's likely he'll be detained for quite some time.'

They said their farewells through the bars of the police lockup.

'You're a strong woman, *amore*,' Tony said. 'I know you'll find a way to manage. But *Madonna*, I'll miss you.' He squeezed her hand. 'When you look at the stars at night, think of me. And I will think of you.'

Her tears fell in torrents.

He tucked a stray lock behind her ear. 'Promise you'll take good care of yourself and Bella?'

'I promise. Look after yourself too, my darling.'

When the constable said it was time for Edith to go, they kissed through the bars. Her head was spinning; it felt like a delirium. Without looking back, she walked out of the lockup and into the gathering darkness. In the garden bed outside, she threw up.

The next morning, Edith arranged for their Australian neighbour, Mrs Sampson, to mind Bella in order to spare her the distress of seeing her father go. When the child was settled, Edith drove herself to town in the Ford farm truck. What a nerve-wracking trip! The roads were a bog and she never felt confident driving the wily old beast. With every gear change, she had to double declutch. Not only did this require muscles of steel but also precision timing. More often than not the gears bucked and grated like the devil. It was all she could do to steer the wretched machine and keep its wheels on the slippery track.

Down by the river was the half-planted paddock where Tony had been captured by Sergeant Pitt. Twenty acres of empty drills rolled out like dark-brown corduroy. In a few weeks' time, part of it would be a lush carpet of fresh-sprouted cane and the rest would be a forest of weeds. She'd never planted cane before but it didn't look difficult. Perhaps she'd manage the rest herself. That way they would have an income, which would keep the bank off their back. It was anyone's guess how long this dreadful war would last, and how long it would be until she got her Tony back.

In drenching rain, Edith stood on the platform of Wooranoora railway station and watched her shackled husband scramble like a captured animal into the prisoners' wagon. Her eyes were dry—she even managed a smile—and a fire burned in her belly.

The decision to banish her husband hadn't come out of thin air. Someone in town must have made a complaint. That someone must have known about the responsibilities he'd taken on at the behest of his Italian clients. Other accountants would have done the same, regardless of race or nationality. It was not uncommon for a trusted professional—a lawyer, accountant, or even the family doctor—to be given power of attorney over clients' affairs. But this was wartime. What had previously been considered normal had been turned on its head.

According to the police report, Tony was akin to a Fascist spy. If the charge weren't so serious, she might have laughed.

Instead she made a vow. If it took the rest of her life, she'd find out who was behind this atrocity. And then she'd make him pay.

Later, Edith inspected the paddock by the creek. It was plain to see how the planting was done. Full stalks of cane had been placed in the drills, then chopped into short lengths and covered with soil. In the stand of mature cane set aside for planting, she took a few practice swings with the cane knife. It would be backbreaking work for a city girl who struggled lifting the weekly wash out of the copper. Bella, now three, who'd accompanied her to the paddock was running along the muddy drills, chasing lizards. Although the morning sun was still low to the horizon, its strong rays were turning the humidity into a sauna.

Edith took off her hat and wiped sweat beads from her brow. She was wasting her time. This was definitely men's work. Either she employed someone to finish the job or they would have to survive on the proceeds of a reduced harvest. She understood enough about cane farming to know that their contract with the sugar mill bound them to a quota but she didn't know what would happen if they were unable to deliver. Was there some kind of penalty imposed or would the mill cancel their contract? Either would crush them financially.

'Come on, Bella,' she called. 'Back to the truck.'

The little girl came running. 'Look, Mummy. Lizzies!' She held out a grubby fist with two squashed skinks dangling out. 'I catched 'em by myself.'

'*Caught*, darling. You *caught* them.'

'Aren't I clebber, Mummy?'

81

'Yes, dear. You're indeed *clever*. Now, put those poor lizards back where you found them and we'll get ourselves cleaned up.'

Dressed in her Sunday best, Edith bundled Bella into the old Ford and drove to town. She had no idea of how to hire men to plant cane. Hiring and firing were always tasks handled by Tony. Where should she go and whom should she ask?

She suspected many of the arrangements were made in the public bar of the State Hotel. But because she was a woman, that avenue was out of bounds.

As she rounded the final bend to Cairns Road, she spotted the Italian Boarding House. Once this would have been a good place to hire workers. Now there'd probably be no-one left in residence.

Outside, a short plump woman was sweeping the path. The manager-cum-caretaker. Edith had met her at Mass. Perhaps she could help.

Edith parked the truck and cut the engine. 'Good afternoon, Mrs Ross.'

Mrs Ross waddled toward the vehicle. 'Good afternoon, Mrs Zucchero. If you'll forgive me, I couldn't help but notice what happened to your husband. How very dreadful! When will this bloody war end?' She shook her head. 'Fancy a cuppa?'

'Bella's with me.'

'Then bring her in! She's a little darling, that one.'

Edith climbed down from the driver's seat and lifted the child to the ground. 'Say hello to Mrs Ross.'

Bella held out her skirts and curtseyed like a princess.

'Now that deserves a big glass of lemonade, don't you think?' Mrs Ross led them into the dining room. 'Make yourself comfortable and I'll put the kettle on.' She disappeared into the cookhouse and returned a few minutes later with a tray containing a teapot, lemonade, and a plate of ginger biscuits.

The brew was good and strong: exactly what Edith needed. A little milk and a spoonful of sugar and it was perfect. When her nerves had settled, she said, 'You've been around farmers and canecutters for a long time. Any advice on how to get the right men to run a farm would be most welcome.'

Mrs Ross's eyes lit up. 'Well, you've come to the right place. As it so happens, I have four Yugoslavs currently in residence. All are reliable and experienced but they haven't been able to get jobs. What's happened to your husband has happened to most of the Italian farmers in the district. Without a capable person such as yourself in control, those farms will go to wrack and ruin … and so will this boarding house if no-one can pay the rent. Keeping that farm going would do us all a favour.'

'Are the men available now? Could I meet them?'

'Sure. But before I call them down, we'll need to talk a few things through. The size of the job, what you'll pay, things like that.'

'Oh my gosh, I hadn't thought about it. Thanks, Mrs Ross, you're a godsend.'

'This helps me too, don't forget.'

In the half-hour that followed, Edith learnt more about the business of cane growing than she had in four years as Tony's wife. The source of Mrs Ross's knowledge was not disclosed, but she spoke with authority about costs such as labour, fertilizer, pest control, harvesting and the return she could expect from the mill. When they were done, Mrs Ross went upstairs to the rooms.

Shortly afterwards, four burly men followed her into the dining room. All had strong bodies, dark hair, tanned skin, and wild-looking eyes. Had they met on the back streets of Brisbane, she might have feared for her life.

Mrs Ross made the introductions and each fellow made a stiff bow.

The one called Boris assumed the role of spokesman. 'We happy to meet you, Missus. Never before work for lady. You the first. Start tomorrow. Yes?'

Edith said, 'Yes, good. I'll pick you up in the truck at six. Okay?'

They shook hands on the deal and the men sauntered off.

'How can I ever thank you, Mrs Ross?'

'You don't have to, love. Times like this, we women must stick together.'

The planting was finished within a week and Edith duly paid the gang in cash.

Boris said, 'You want good cane workers, Missus? We come back. Yes?'

'Will you stay here in Wooranoora?'

'Yes. We stay boarding house. Missus Ross.'

Goodness, she didn't even know when the crushing season started, let alone the specifics of how to fertilize or when to cut and send the cane to the mill. All this had gone on around her yet she'd always been on the outer edge, watching wide-eyed without understanding what was involved in getting a crop out of the paddock.

What a young fool she'd been. She should have taken more notice; she should have demanded more answers.

Life was full of surprises; you never knew what would happen until it did. Everyone needed a backup. Without actually planning it, over the years Tony had established himself as the backup for his accountancy clients. Due to the language barrier, many had already appointed him power of attorney to act on their behalf. In dealing with the Tax Department, for example, it was easier for him to take immediate action rather than bring the client into town and have to explain everything in Italian.

Tony was an honest man and everyone trusted him.

When war came and so many Italian farmers were arrested, the same powers of attorney allowed Tony to pay his clients' bills, manage their crops, and deposit the mill cheques into their accounts. He'd lived with the business of cane growing for as long as he'd lived with himself. Because it was second nature, he took this knowledge for granted. If Edith ever asked about the farm, he'd brush her questions aside.

Since his departure, the weeks had become a blur. With too many things to think about, Edith had barely slept. Without a hungry man to feed, she'd had all but given up cooking. Bella was content with a sandwich or an egg, while she herself had no appetite whatsoever.

Exhausted she lay on the double bed, listening to the calls of the morning birds while she worried about their future. Although the sun was streaming through the window, her spirit was wallowing in fog. In the next room, Bella was singing to her peg dolly. She should get up, make an effort. But what was the point?

Her eyes closed and she must have drifted off. Tony was beside her, whispering.

She flinched, woke herself up. In the dream what was he saying? It seemed important. From a crevasse of her memory she conjured up a past conversation. In it was the key.

'Growing cane is instinctive, *amore*. You must follow the seasons.'

The season was autumn. That, she knew for a fact.

As for instinct, her impulse was to ask advice from her neighbours who'd been cane farmers for two generations. With renewed energy she got out of bed, put on a clean frock, brushed her hair.

'Come on Bella. Let's visit Mrs Sampson.'

Bella piped, 'Will she have cake?'

'Mrs Sampson always has cake.' For the first time in days she laughed and it lightened the pain in her heart.

Bella was not disappointed. The older woman welcomed them at the door, bustled them into the kitchen—the centre of the house—and cut a big wedge of cake with pink icing.

'Cuppa?' she said to Edith.

'Love one.'

When Mrs Sampson returned with the steaming teapot, she took a long look at Edith and frowned. 'My dear, if you don't mind me saying, you look a bit drained. Are you eating properly?'

'Not as well as I ought to. The thought of food makes me squeamish.'

'How long has this been going on?'

'A few weeks, I suppose. It'll go away.' As if to prove she was healthy, she cut herself a sliver of cake and popped it in her mouth. No sooner had her tongue touched the sickly-sweet icing than her stomach did a backflip. She put her hand over her mouth, raced to the open door and retched over the railing.

Mrs Sampson appeared with a glass of water. In a low voice she said, 'How long since you last bled, my dear?'

She rinsed her mouth before answering. 'It was before Tony went ... maybe two months ago.' Everything had been so chaotic that she couldn't exactly remember.

'You don't think ...?' Edith gasped and pressed her hand to her belly.

Mrs Sampson was beaming. 'That's *exactly* what I think.'

Twelve

In the second week of June 1941, Loveday received the first trainload of prisoners from the internment camp in Hay in New South Wales. The 458 Italians had been held at His Majesty's pleasure since the outbreak of war one year earlier. The next day a second trainload of 502 Italians arrived. They were a more eclectic lot, hailing from various parts of the country—the cities of the east coast and rural centres—but mainly from the cane-growing districts of far north Queensland. In the space of forty-eight hours, the internee population of the Loveday blossomed from nought to nearly one thousand.

In other circumstances, such an influx at short notice might have caused chaos. But Colonel Dean was well prepared. Rosters and schedules had been drawn up ahead of time. Each soldier had been drilled on how to perform their duties. Nothing had been left to chance, yet some things were beyond his control.

For one, the weather was freezing. A bleak wind was blowing in from the west. But by far the biggest problem was food. While potatoes and mutton were in plentiful supply, there were shortfalls in basics such as milk and bread.

At Dean's request, Ted did the rounds of the bakeries in the district to see what could be arranged.

The proprietor of the Barmera bakery summed the situation up nicely with his response. 'Even if I worked all bloody day and all bloody night, me oven's not bloody big enough to make that amount of bread.'

After Ted reported back to Dean, an urgent meeting was convened with the other officers. 'If the local community cannot provide, then we'll have to do it ourselves,' said Dean. 'We cannot let our charges go hungry.'

Discussion followed about how to get the necessary items. On the blackboard in the meeting room, Dean drew up a schedule of tasks. Volunteers were called and names were assigned to the list.

Ted's task was to find out whether any of the internees were bakers. Until then, he had neither met nor spoken to anyone who was Italian. Although the Italian and British armies had fought side-by-side in the Great War, the soldiers themselves had little to do with one another. Most of the battles had raged in the north of Italy, near the foot of the Alps. However, Ted's military career was exclusively in the trenches of France, where his active duty came to an end after he contracted measles and was evacuated.

As he walked toward the gate of the Camp 9 compound, his hands were shaking, not from the cold. Despite the guard towers and the guns, inside that fence he would be outnumbered one thousand to one. What he wouldn't give for a good shot of brandy! Swallowing his fear, he slung his rifle over his shoulder and waited for the guard to open the outside gate of the compound.

'Don't worry, mate. I'll watch your back.' The guard threw him a sympathetic grin.

In no-man's land between the two perimeter fences, Ted waited for the first gate to close before swinging the inner gate open. He thrust out his jaw and adjusted his rifle strap and strode into the inhabited compound for the very first time.

He felt like an intruder on foreign soil.

The Italian internees were standing about in small groups, mumbling in a language he didn't understand. The army had issued them maroon-dyed military uniforms for use both inside and outside the camp, but they'd chosen to wear civvies. The internees from the tropics of Queensland looked out of kilter in heavy woollen jackets or double-breasted suits that would have been at least two decades old.

Most were swarthy and dark-eyed, the stubble on their cheeks so black that the skin appeared to be blue. A more desperate-looking lot he hadn't encountered since the latter days of the Great War. He swallowed the nervous bile that was rising up his throat. He must get a grip or else—one way or another—he might end up dead.

A largish group was sitting on packing cases near the mess hut. In their midst was a distinguished-looking gentleman with silver hair and a goatee. Unlike the others he was wearing a uniform from the Great War—grey jacket, jodhpurs, and puttees—the mark of an officer of the Italian army. As Ted approached, the fellow looked up. Their eyes locked briefly.

Charisma was the word that sprang to mind. He exuded an air of charisma. There was no doubt that he was the one in charge.

Every eye was on Ted. He cleared his throat and said in the simplest English he could think of, 'We need men who can make bread. Do you know of anyone?' He expected them to shake their heads or mumble *no unnerstan'* in thick accents.

To his surprise, the silver-haired gent answered in a perfect British accent. 'How many bakers do you need?'

Ted hadn't been told, so he ad-libbed. 'Why, as many as we can get. At least one should be an actual baker by trade.'

'And will these men receive *payment* for their work?'

That pulled Ted up in his tracks. He had no idea. Soldiers who were held in prisoner of war camps were supposed to be paid a living allowance by their respective countries, however these fellows weren't POWs. They were civilians, captured and held at the will of the nation as a security measure.

'If you give me the names, we'll discuss payment later,' said Ted.

'Perhaps you could raise the matter of payment with the camp commandant first. Then we shall provide the names.' The fellow smiled. 'My name is Alfonso Del Drago. Ask for me when you return.' With that he turned away and resumed his conversation in Italian with the others.

Unofficially dismissed, Ted turned on his heel and walked to the exit gate. He made directly for Colonel Dean's office to report the outcome of his enquiries.

Dean's reaction was most unexpected. Instead of dismissing the suggestion as pure arrogance, he said, 'Del Drago has raised a good point. These men are not soldiers, nor are they criminals. If we want them to work for us, then I believe they are entitled to some sort of payment for their effort. Leave it with me and I'll see what can be done. Until then, we'll all make do on reduced rations of bread. Tell that to Del Drago. Italians love their bread, so I don't think the news will go down well with his supporters. It might be enough to persuade him to find us a baker or two, pending further discussions about payment. In the meantime, get a team together and have them construct a suitable building for a wood-fired oven.'

'Where should it be located?'

Dean considered for a moment. 'Position it beside the roadway and so it can be expanded in the future if necessary. To the north of the recreation hall at General Headquarters is my suggestion. If the building team has a better idea, let me know and we'll discuss.'

'Sir, could I ask a question?'

'Speak.'

'Who is Del Drago?'

'In Italy, he is royalty. In Sydney, he is very high up in the Fascist movement. In the internment camp at Hay, the internees elected him as their leader and spokesman. It seems he has assumed that responsibility in Loveday as well. In short, he is a man of great influence amongst the inmates. Treat him with respect, Lieutenant Long, and you'll get cooperation. Treat him with contempt and he will sabotage us every inch of the way.'

A week later, Prince Del Drago was invited to Dean's office. Ted delivered the written invitation in person. On the spot and without hesitation, Del Drago accepted. Later, at the appointed time, Ted collected him in the truck and drove him to General Headquarters (more commonly referred to as GHQ), which was located outside the barbed wire fence and midway between Camp 9 and the new yet-to-be unoccupied Camp 10.

The two leaders talked one-on-one for an hour behind closed doors. When they were done, Ted drove Del Drago back to the compound. Not another word was spoken.

At sunset, the two hundred officers and soldier-guards were called to the recreation hall at GHQ for an important announcement. Bully-beef sandwiches and tea were provided. When everyone had eaten and settled, Dean stepped onto a chair.

'After representations from the internees, I have put in a request to the head of the Australian Military Forces to provide payment at the rate of one shilling per day to internees who elect to work. This will bring enormous benefit to us all. An active man is a happy man. That is my earnest belief and the basis for this request.

'Payment will encourage the inmates to participate in productive work, which will assist us with the running of this camp and reduce aggression born of idleness and boredom. Under the Geneva Convention, we cannot force a civilian internee to work. That is why if we need their labour, we must provide a suitable incentive. We have already cleared several acres to grow vegetables for consumption within the camp. I intend to explore other cropping options that might give us an income. My ultimate aim is for the internment camps at Loveday to be self-sufficient.

'The means of payment to the inmates will need to be in a currency that cannot be used outside the camp. I have already viewed examples of "paper money" produced by the Hay internment camp and intend to order a supply. In order for this scheme to operate effectively, we shall establish a canteen stocked with items of interest to the men. Cigarettes, sweets, writing paper, fresh fruit, and the like. The canteen will be operated by internees hand-picked by the elected camp leader, Prince Del Drago. He has assured me there are several experienced shopkeepers here who are trustworthy.

'Rationing of bread will continue until our own bakery is completed. Construction is presently underway. I have been given the names of four internees who can make bread. We shall commence operations as soon as possible, using those four bakers on a trial basis. My expectation is that they will train others in the trade. Should our operations be expanded in the future, we shall have sufficient skilled bakers to provide bread for the entire complex.

'Today I received news that four hundred prisoners from Tatura will be arriving within a week. Originally, they were captured in Britain and then shipped to Australia after the fall of France. Most claim to be refugees from the Continent, some are likely to be Jews. This will bring Camp 10 into operation at last.

'Lastly I would like to thank each and every one of you for your hard work over the past six weeks. Building and opening a facility for up to two thousand internees is no mean feat and has not been without its challenges. You have all risen to the occasion. Your work has been first rate.'

As Dean stepped down from the chair, the men applauded. Not the polite applause heard at weddings and school eisteddfods, but a hearty and spontaneous ovation.

With a sense of pride and excitement not felt in years, Ted Long made his way to the old delivery truck, parked by the pegged-out walls of the new bakery, and drove himself home to his dog Bessie. If ever he'd chosen the right pathway in life, this promised to be it.

For the Duration of the War

Thirteen

Brisbane, June 1941

In Brisbane, balmy autumn suddenly snapped into an early winter. At Gaythorne, the tent city had grown with a continuing influx of new internees. Nothing, however, could prevent the westerly winds from seeping through the canvas. Breath came out as fog and toes went into cramps inside thin leather shoes.

For seven months now, Luigi had been in internment. Anger had given way to acceptance as he settled into the daily routine of the military. At dawn, he woke to *Rouse*. The haunting sound of the bugle echoed through the valley, drowning the caw of crows and the warble of magpies.

Half-asleep, he'd pull on his woollen jacket and trudge to the ablutions block where he'd splash his face with water, icy from the corrugated-iron tank and shave with a safety razor. It took twice as long as the cut-throat, which had been confiscated months ago. Perhaps he should grow a beard.

Afterwards he'd join the stampede to the mess-hut for hot lumpy porridge or cold sausages. The rest of the day he'd spend doing nothing.

Tuesday 17 June 1941 began differently. The camp awoke, not to the call of the bugle but the bark of the sergeant's voice.

'Everyone out! Get your kit and line up! Roll call in ten minutes!'

Someone snapped on the electric bulb dangling from the centre of the tent. Its black-out cover—a dark Bakelite dome—directed the light downwards and straight into Luigi's eyes.

'What's the time?' His mouth was sticky with sleep.

'Four-fifteen,' said Vecchio beside him.

Luigi groaned and rolled out of the warm bunk. In a daze, he pulled on his trousers and jacket, stuffed his belongings into the port, and jammed on his hat.

Carlo came into the tent. 'What's happening?'

Luigi shrugged. 'Maybe the war's over and we're going home.'

'Don't even joke about it.' Carlo scowled. '*Bastardi!*'

Outside, two hundred men stamped and blew into their hands. The sky was dark and starless; not yet a glimmer of dawn. The roll was called by torchlight. As usual, everyone was there.

In lines, they marched to the hut at the entrance of the camp. Several army trucks were parked in a semi-circle on the asphalt apron. The inmates climbed in. The vehicles revved through the gate onto South Pine Road.

Where they were going remained a mystery.

Along the deserted thoroughfare they passed through a dim streetscape of timber houses on stilts, picket fences, milk bottles by the door, the nightsoil truck. Near the Roma Street railway yards, fruit and vegetable traders were setting up the daily markets.

The army trucks trundled across a bridge of arches that spanned the broad river. They passed a red-brick building, which looked like a twin of the railway station in Townsville, and stopped a few hundred yards down the tracks.

The cloud cover cracked open and rays of winter sunlight beamed through, yet the cold intensified. A green sign announced they were at the *Southern Brisbane Interstate Station*. A westerly began to wail. The wind lifted hats, flapped trouser legs, filtered through flimsy jackets. Shivering, they grabbed their possessions and rushed into the building. Rust-coloured carriages stretched along the platform beyond.

Vecchio said, 'We're headed south.'

'How do you know?' said Luigi.

'I love everything about trains.' He shrugged as if to apologise. 'This is where the New South Wales standard gauge starts. This line could take us right down to the Victorian border.'

'*Porca miseria!*' said Carlo. 'All that way!'

The men climbed into the carriages. Luigi took a breath and hitched up his pants, which had grown too big for his waist. No-one, not even San Filippo, knew what lay ahead. Already this journey, under custodianship of the army, promised to be more comfortable than the one to Brisbane under police guard. The police, whose job was to wrangle criminals, treated innocent men like *merda*. At least the soldiers, many of whom had fought in the Great War, showed their charges some courtesy.

Vecchio took a window seat; Luigi sat beside him. At each end of the carriage was an armed soldier, both in their middle age and greying at the temples. Apart from the internees from Gaythorne camp, there was no-one else on the train. The locomotive hissed and chugged, the whistle blasted, the carriages inched from the platform. Soon they were rattling through the suburbs, past backyards and factories and paddocks with fat cows. They wound through hills and thick forests, crossed plainlands with wide lazy rivers, crept through sidings and country towns. Late at night and somewhere on the outskirts of Sydney, according to Vecchio, they were transferred to another train.

In the morning, Luigi woke with a stiff neck and pains in his stomach from the doughy sandwiches that they'd been fed along the way. Why the authorities thought men could survive on nothing but white bread and a sugary spread was completely beyond him. He stretched his body and looked out the window at depressing brown plainlands where the grass had been bleached to straw.

At a far-flung siding in a wasteland of spinifex and saltbush, the train stopped. According to Carlo—who was well-informed in all matters of war and politics—this was the town of Hay, site of the largest internment camp in Australia.

Several carriages were shunted onto the rear of the train. Lines of prisoners wearing burgundy-coloured uniforms and lugging bags and boxes and baskets, straggled along the siding. As soon as they boarded, the train ride resumed.

After another day of dust and flies, and another night of discomfort, they crossed a bridge over a broad blue river and entered South Australia. The far north Queenslanders had now travelled two thousand miles from their homes. Apart from the three-month voyage on the steamer to Australia, this was the longest trip Luigi had ever taken.

An hour later the train chugged slowly through a township called Barmera then squealed to a halt in an open field about a mile beyond. Morning fog blanketed the landscape and blocked out the sky. The doors flew open; icy air rushed into the warm carriage. Everyone grabbed their things and jumped to the ground. The stubble was crunchy with frost. Mist swirled around them, cutting visibility to a few yards. Ghostly shapes moved about in the whiteness. They were surrounded by armed soldiers, fifty of them at least. Escape was impossible; there was nowhere to run.

Luigi stretched and inhaled the vaporous air. After countless hours in a stale-smelling carriage, he was fairly drowning in his own phlegm. He coughed and spat, patted his pocket for his tobacco pouch. Alas, it was empty.

For breakfast, they had jam sandwiches and black tea. It had been the same yesterday and the day before. When they'd finished, the guards ordered them to form two lines. On foot, carrying their ports and duffel bags, they set off for the new camp. Vecchio and the other old-timers were given a ride in the back of a truck, but Luigi didn't mind. It felt good to use his legs. The land was flat and the going was easy. By now the fog was lifting, revealing a vast plain dotted with mallee and wattle. The colours were muted: soft and pastel instead of the vibrant clash of the tropics.

After a hike of five miles, they arrived at a prison in the middle of a paddock. Around its perimeter were two runs of barbed-wire fencing about twice the height of a man and a space of about twenty yards between. Four watch towers, bristling with guns and searchlights, overlooked dozens of timber huts set in an arrangement that epitomized military precision. In comparison to the tent city of Gaythorne, the first impression was a no-nonsense fortified gaol. Existing prisoners congregated along the inner fence line, craning their necks to catch glimpses of the newcomers.

Two guards opened the outer gates and the first fifty of the five-hundred strong pack entered no-man's land. The gates shut behind them. The inner gates opened and the new arrivals swarmed into the yard. The process was repeated again and again. Everyone was talking at once as friends and relatives were reunited with those who were already there. Soldiers directed them into a hall with long trestle tables and bench seats. The place was in uproar, everyone shouting over each other to be heard.

A middle-aged officer in army uniform stepped onto a chair and raised his arms. The rabble continued. A guard clanged a metal triangle to shut them up.

Although not a tall man, the officer had the stage presence of Humphrey Bogart. His face was tanned, suggesting a lifetime of outdoor work. In civilian life, he could have been a farmer or a grazier. His hair was dark and cut the regulation short-back-and-sides of the military.

'Please, sit.' His English was slow and clear. 'This is Loveday Internment Camp. I am the camp commandant. My name is Colonel Dean. Please listen closely.'

He paused for an interpreter to translate into Italian.

'Here we shall treat you fairly. Under the Geneva Convention, you have the same rights as other prisoners of war within the British Empire. Take heed: I run a tight camp. You are expected to observe the rules.'

Again, he paused for the interpreter.

'These are the four camp rules that you must obey.

'One. No eating or smoking inside the dormitories.

'Two. Roll-call is at six a.m. and six p.m. sharp. All prisoners are required to report.

'Three. Uniforms must be worn when working outside the compound.

'Four. Any attempts at escape will be dealt with severely.

'Your bags and suitcases will be labelled and put in storage. You may keep civilian clothing, toiletries, and personal effects with you. To pass the time, you are strongly encouraged to work. However, you will not be forced to work if you do not wish to.'

At the end of the speech Luigi joined the queue for uniforms. He was duly issued a pair of second-hand army boots and fatigues the same shade of maroon as worn by the prisoners from Hay. They were kitted out with blankets, palliasses, and pillows, and given their weekly ration of tobacco. For the last small act of kindness, Luigi touched the relic of San Filippo in his pocket and sent him a silent prayer of thanks.

Meanwhile, the guards performed a thorough search of their luggage. All ports, bags, and boxes were upended onto benches. Weapons such as pocket knives and cut-throat razors were confiscated. When Luigi retrieved his port afterwards, he quickly checked the brown-paper lining. Luckily it was still intact.

Dorms were allocated alphabetically, which meant that family members would be housed together. Luigi gathered his things and followed the stream of men to the sleeping huts. Hut W11 was in the last row and close to the perimeter fence. All the huts were identical: sixty feet by eighteen with an iron roof. The timber was so new that it emitted the sweet fragrance of the tree from which it was milled. Inside the hut was a central corridor with a row of double-decker bunks on either side.

Luigi chose a lower bunk. With a sigh, he rolled onto the bare wire base and rested his aching bones. Over the course of the journey he'd had lots of time to think. Coming to terms with internment had been hard, but he'd run out of options. All avenues of appeal had been exhausted. Aside of escaping from this camp—which barbed wire, armed guards, and sheer isolation ruled out—there was no other choice but to survive as best he could. Survive and pray for a quick end to the war.

Exhaustion overcame him. His eyes closed. His muscles relaxed. The babble of the hut faded and he drifted into a peaceful sleep. He woke with someone shaking his arm.

'Hey *paesano*, it's lunch time. We're off to get food.'

The aroma in the mess hall gave a promise of meat stew. After all those jam sandwiches, Luigi didn't care if it was possum or rabbit or mutton or galah. He queued behind a hundred others who jostled and impatiently tapped their plates. At the servery, a baby-faced soldier ladled out brown lumpy ooze with potatoes and a chunk of bread.

In the seven months in custody, it was the best food Luigi had had. With the bread, he mopped up every last trace. Afterwards, he scanned the crowded room. Familiar faces were everywhere: neighbouring farmers, boarders, three brothers from Home Hill who were distant cousins. The joyous rabble of reunion filled the hall.

'*Ciao*, Luigi!' The speaker was one of Renzo's cane-cutting gang who had also been a cabin-mate on the *San Rossore*, the steamer that had brought them from the old country. On arrival he'd gone to Ingham to work on his uncle's cane farm, then he married Rosa and ended up in Wooranoora. Nineteen years in the tropical sun had not been kind. His head was like a speckled egg and his ears were covered in sunspots.

'Gianni Fiumefreddo!' said Luigi.

They embraced and slapped each other on the back.

'What brings you here?' Gianni flashed a set of uneven teeth.

'I'm on vacation, same as you,' said Luigi with a grin.

'Have you seen your brother?'

Luigi frowned. 'I don't know where he is.'

'Come with me.' Gianni beckoned him to the door.

Luigi followed. They passed the kitchen and crossed a broad path. The diamond-shaped compound was actually two triangular segments with a path down the centre. The arrangement of the mess-halls, kitchens, and sleeping huts were mirror-images of each other.

'In here.' Gianni opened the door of another mess-hall.

At exactly the same moment, the brothers spotted one another. Angelo rose from his seat but before he could move, Luigi grabbed him in a hug.

'*O Dio*, they got you too! I prayed you'd be left alone,' said Angelo. In one year the poor fellow seemed to have aged twenty. His skin was sallow and his hair was the sun-bleached colour of cane trash.

'They got me in February. I've been at Gaythorne.' Luigi tried to sound cheerful but his eyes were misting with tears.

Gianni bade them *ciao* and departed.

'When did you get here?' said Luigi.

'Two days ago, they brought us in from Hay. We've been busy setting up the camp; they got us to dig up the irrigation pipes and re-lay them.' Angelo rubbed his lower back. 'I'm too old for pick-and-shovel work.'

'I put in an appeal but it didn't do any good.'

'Me too.' Angelo lowered his voice. 'But I don't care anymore. I'm here amongst friends, fellows I haven't seen in years. And now we are together too.'

Angelo passed his tobacco pouch and Luigi rolled a much-needed cigarette. 'How did they treat you at Hay?' he said through a satisfying cloud of smoke.

'Not too bad. The guards were all right but the place was terrible. Flies like you've never seen, getting in your eyes and up your nose. Sticky bloody things you had to brush off your shirt or they'd get into bed with you. We arrived in mid-winter. My poor bones nearly cracked from the cold. I got sick too, for a long time.'

Luigi and Angelo talked and smoked until the mess hall emptied. Without the warmth of living bodies, the temperature dropped to near freezing.

Angelo was shivering. 'Let's go out in the sun.'

They found a warm spot on the steps of Angelo's hut, out of the grip of the wind. The pale blue of the sky was mottled with wispy cloud. Sparrows bathed in the dust. Being with family and friends would make this barren place easier to bear.

At length Luigi said, 'I tried everything to stay in Wooranoora and look after the farm. Someone must really hate us, that's all I can think.'

'Forget it. There's nothing we can do. Take each day as it comes and make the most of what we've got.'

Days passed with little to do but talk and smoke and play cards. The Fascist leaders and their supporters made it clear they were strongly opposed to Dean's offer of work for no pay. Slogans appeared on the notice boards.

Free labour is slavery.

Australia is our enemy.

Working for enemies destroys our own flesh and blood.

No-one dared contradict the men in power. While the soldiers were their official keepers, the Fascist leaders in the camp decided whether an inmate's life would be tolerable or miserable.

Luigi would rather have done an honest day's work than sit around idle. Soon the cane cutting season would begin. Yet here he was, stuck inside a barbed-wire pen and completely powerless. Years of effort had gone into increasing their cane quota. Back-breaking years of clearing jungle and cultivating the soil. He hoped Tony Zucchero would be able to manage all those farms on his own.

At the end of the second week at Loveday, Colonel Dean announced that the internees could elect a camp leader, a representative who would be involved to some extent in running the camp. That was the trigger for the Fascists to leap into action. The names of a few nominees were bandied around, but all the talk was about the former camp leader of Hay, who was also a member of the royal family of Rome. His name was Prince Alfonso Del Drago.

Against him, all other candidates paled into insignificance. Not only did he carry himself like a nobleman, but he was also educated and eloquent. He promised them paid employment and a workshop where they could make useful things.

One name was submitted to Colonel Dean. It was accepted.

An open meeting was held in the mess hall. Around half the inmates turned up, including Luigi. Standing on a chair in front of his audience, Camp Leader Del Drago began by raising his arm in a Fascist salute. Most of the men in the hall responded.

Viva il Duce!

With a sea of raised arms, it would have been suicide not to conform. Luigi had never been embroiled in politics nor had he ever seen his two beloved countries at loggerheads. Realising he must join the majority or else suffer the consequences, he slowly raised his right arm.

Del Drago held up his palms and the room fell quiet. He addressed them in the king's Italian; his modulated voice was a joy to hear. 'Friends, thank you for your support. I promised to make improvements and I shall not let you down. Already I have spoken with Commandant Dean about our position. From now on, any work done by internee labour will be paid at the rate of one shilling per day.

'In addition, we shall arrange workshops and tuition for anyone who wishes to learn new skills. In our midst are professors, musicians, teachers, craftsmen. If we share our knowledge, we shall all benefit.

'As true patriots, we must remain strong and resilient. We must keep our spirits high until *il Duce* leads our country to glorious victory. *Vive il Duce! Viva l'Italia!*'

Del Drago saluted again by raising his right arm.

'*Viva il Duce! Viva l'Italia!*' echoed the men.

Someone started to sing and others joined in. Soon the mess-hall was ringing to the chorus of the Fascist anthem, *Giovinezza* (Youth).

Fourteen

Loveday, July 1941

The prospect of being productive again raised Luigi's spirits. There was nothing worse than sitting around, wishing the day away. He went to English classes and attended lectures by learned men about astronomy and mechanics and philosophy. Some of the content went right over his head, for his three years of formal education in Sicily had barely covered the basics.

He attended one series of lectures about the progress of the war, delivered in layman's language so anyone could make sense of the chaos. The *professore* from the University of Milano was a thick-set man with a bald patch on top. He wore gold-rimmed pince-nez that balanced precariously on the bridge of his nose. Having devoted a lifetime to the pursuit of learning, he was a man whose opinion was worth hearing.

That the *professore* was a true patriot was obvious from the outset. He spoke passionately about Mussolini's struggle to pull the homeland into prosperity, to expand his control of the Mediterranean, and to return the Italian people to the glory days of the Roman Empire. The war, the *professore* promised, would be over in months. Mussolini's army was outsmarting the Allied Forces in the south of Italy and in the African colonies, while *der Führer* was protecting their northern borders.

'Within this camp we must retain hope and solidarity for *il Duce*. Fascism is the way of the modern world. Soon Italy will be victorious and we shall regain our rightful place as the leaders of all of Europe.'

The more Luigi heard, the more his hope soared. With a renewed spring in his step, he tried to talk his brother into attending. Angelo always demurred, saying he had a headache.

From time to time, Del Drago himself would deliver a speech about the virtues of the Fascist movement and the need for the inmates to put up a unified front. Prisoners who'd been noncommittal about politics began to go to the meetings, for to stay away meant a question mark against their names.

Already Del Drago had established a corps of *carabinieri*—a band of enforcers similar to the Italian military police—who were authorised to do whatever was necessary to unite the inmates against their enemies, to quash dissention amongst the ranks, and to prevent in-fighting within the camp. As this was considered *work*, the *carabinieri* were paid the going rate of one shilling per day for their efforts.

According to Angelo, who'd been at Hay with most of the Camp 9 *carabinieri*, all were avid Fascists and long-time associates of Del Drago.

'Watch what you say,' Angelo warned. 'Anyone could be an informant.'

With the offer of one shilling per day to spend on tobacco or fruit from the camp canteen, Luigi put his name down to work as a cook. Not only did he enjoy kitchen work, but he was also good at it. His self-taught skills had sprung from necessity, and were mainly due to the near-fatal accident he'd had back in 1925.

Three years after coming to Australia, he had been clearing bushland near Wooranoora during the slack season. Working in a gang of five, he was cutting out regrowth and saplings using a cane knife and axe. The vegetation was dense, matted with vines and stinging trees and treacherous prickly lawyer cane. Although it was officially winter, the days were hot and steamy. His skin, beneath the thick woollen singlet that he wore for protection, was covered in nasty scratches. With every swing of the axe, stinging green-ants would shower from the canopy. He'd stamp his feet and brush them off but they'd crawl into his clothing and leave him with itchy red welts.

The foreman called for the gang to take a smoko break. Hungry and longing for a nice cup of tea, Luigi gave the axe one last swing. The tree trunk split in two, held together by a couple of strands of bark. One half of the trunk crashed onto a trampoline of vines. It bounced once then hurtled directly toward him. The jagged end smashed into his gut.

All he remembered was a sickening *THUD*.

Much later he woke up on a soft white cloud and thought he was in Heaven.

According to Angelo, who'd visited him every day in the Wooranoora hospital, the doctor cut off the end of the branch that impaled him and gave him a shot of morphine. To Angelo he said, 'My advice is to pay your respects and call the priest to perform the last rites.'

'Aren't you going to operate?' said Angelo, shocked.

The doctor looked away. 'If he survives the night, I'll consider it. But don't hold your breath.'

Thanks to his brother's prayers, Luigi hung on. After a week of watching and waiting, the doctor performed a patch-up operation, the best he could do in a small country hospital. By some miracle, the branch that had skewered him from front to back had not hit any vital organs.

Many months later, recovered but unfit to work in the cane fields, he took a job as a cook in Mrs Maroney's boarding house.

At that time, the only food he knew was what Mamma cooked. Her recipes had been handed down by word of mouth through generation after generation of womenfolk. Cooking always fascinated him. As a boy, he perched on the table while she chopped and fried and stirred the pot that hung over the fire. The ingredients were simple and seasonal. Tomatoes, onions, peppers, broad beans, garlic, chilli, mushrooms, bitter greens foraged from the fields. Tossed with fresh pasta or sprinkled with olive oil or sharp cheese, each of her creations was *Paradiso* on a plate.

Sadly, most of the items in his mother's Sicilian kitchen were unobtainable in far north Queensland so he needed to substitute or improvise. The first day on the job, Mrs Maroney told him that as well as a hearty breakfast and a hot meal for dinner, the boarders expected puddin'.

'What's *puddin'*?' he said.

Mrs Maroney rolled her eyes. 'You know ... lemon sago, jelly and custard. Something sweet to finish the meal.'

'Okay, *Mississa*.' He had no idea of what she meant. Surely puddin' wouldn't be too hard to make.

In the main street of Wooranoora was a second-hand bookshop. There he found a battered copy of *Mrs Beeton's Cookery Book*. According to the inscription on the inside cover, it had been gifted to Nettie Carver in October 1894. Although it was in English, there were plenty of diagrams.

He found several useful recipes in a section called 'puddings and pastries'. Bread-and-butter pudding, cheese pudding, baked custard pudding, ginger pudding. There was also a handy chapter called 'Australian cookery' with recipes for kangaroo tail soup, roast wallaby, and parrot pie.

For the next two years while his body healed he honed his culinary skills in Mrs Maroney's boarding house kitchen, cooking for up to twenty men each day.

The first time Luigi entered the kitchens of Loveday, he could scarcely believe his eyes. There was not one but four separate food preparation spaces: one for each mess hall. Each had to produce enough food for two hundred and fifty hungry men, three times per day. Breakfast, lunch, and tea. The sheer size of the equipment and quantities of ingredients were beyond his imagination.

The menu, planned by the army, was based on the British palate. For breakfast there was porridge, bread and butter. This was followed by a 'main' course which varied from day to day. It might be sausages or fried eggs or mutton chops with gravy.

The menus for lunch and tea were practically interchangeable. Most days there'd be a broth, followed by some sort of meat with boiled vegetables, and ending with pudding.

Luigi and the other kitchenhands would be working under the direction of an army cook, a nuggetty chap who looked to be on the wrong side of sixty. 'Cookie' was what the men called him behind his back.

'Work fast, work clean' were his welcoming words when they assembled at five-thirty that first morning, ready for the breakfast shift. The crew were arbitrarily allocated tasks. Luigi, who was standing nearest the door, was allocated porridge-making. Disappointed, he sighed. Since his imprisonment, he'd forced himself to eat the lumpy grey stuff to survive. He'd cooked small batches at the boarding house but had no idea how to make a vat full.

In volunteering for kitchen duty, he'd imagined that he might make changes to the food, which would make their lot happier. To an Italian, tasty food was as essential as oxygen. But it seemed he was mistaken. The expectation was that he'd churn out the usual fare. In the process, he'd be criticised by his countrymen for making inedible slop.

The porridge pot was a forty-four-gallon drum cut in half. The sharp edges had been turned to prevent injury. In accordance with the instructions, he measured the rolled oats and mixed them with two-and-a-half times the quantity of cold water. After setting it on the fire, he kept the mixture moving until it bubbled like molten lava. With a spoon the size of a paddle, he stirred until the lumps were out. A small victory. After tasting it, he decided to throw in a handful of salt and some sugar. The closest he got to a compliment was from Vecchio.

'So smooth I could eat it without my false teeth.'

As soon as breakfast was over, the crew began preparing lunch. The barley broth had to be done first, for it took two hours to cook. Mountains of carrots and potatoes had to be peeled using small paring knives. A side of mutton needed to be broken down and the offcuts made into stew. And then there was pudding. Today's was baked rice custard.

By the time tea was finished, Luigi was completely exhausted. Even a day's cane cutting was less strenuous than this. His back was bent and aching; he felt like a man of eighty. In the months of inactivity during internment, he'd lost his fitness. Somehow, he must find the energy to push through, determined as he was to make a difference to the quality of their food.

The opportunity came when Del Drago visited the kitchen a few days later. He swept in like a prince and announced that the suggestion box he'd set up outside his office had yielded dozens of complaints about the food.

'I'll read a selection,' he said in perfectly-modulated Italian.

'Put pasta on the menu.

'Give us more bread.

'Everything tastes like water.

'Less cabbage, more tomatoes.

'Now, comrades, what can we do about this?'

Although Cookie was there, Del Drago didn't bother translating. He folded his arms across his chest and waited for a response.

Gino, a cafe owner from Sydney, was the first to pipe up. 'We don't have any choice but to cook what we're told. All the menus are set and so are the ingredients. Our hands are tied.'

'Really? We'll see about that,' said Del Drago. 'When the stomach is grumbling, so are the men. What if you put your heads together and come up with some alternative menus? Use the same ingredients to make something more palatable. You've got flour, water and eggs. Can any of you make spaghetti from scratch?'

Luigi raised his hand.

A fellow from Turin said, 'There are potatoes. I can make *gnocchi*.'

'But we need olive oil,' said Gino. 'And tomatoes.'

'As we speak, tomato seeds are being planted in the vegetable garden. I'll put in a request for olive oil,' said Del Drago. 'Write down your suggestions for the new menu and I'll take it to the camp commandant tomorrow.'

Everyone in the kitchen was grinning. Everyone except Cookie, who hadn't a clue about what had transpired.

Del Drago was as good as his word. Not a fortnight later, when the supplies arrived from Adelaide, there were a dozen two-gallon tins of olive oil, four boxes of tomato paste, and four extra bags of flour. With the two countries at war, it was surprising that both the oil and the tomato paste had come from Italy.

Gino said, 'They must have done a deal with an importer who had a warehouse full of stock. Maybe he's in Loveday. What a laugh! The Australian army relying on the Italians to get what it needs.' They were speaking the language of the old country. Gino was from a rural district near the foot of the Alps. Not only could he cook, but he also had an eye for presentation.

'I'm thankful we got these things at all,' said Luigi. 'By the way, has anyone told Cookie about the new menu?' He flicked his head to the army cook, who was scribbling a list of next week's camp fare in an exercise book. He could only imagine the look of astonishment when Cookie saw what had been delivered!

'Don't look at me,' said Gino.

'Me neither,' said Luigi. 'Should we ask Del Drago to have a word? After all, it was his idea.'

'No, let it come down through *their* chain of command. It's not Del Drago's place to give orders that should come from a commanding officer. Colonel Dean must have approved the purchase, otherwise it wouldn't have turned up. Let Dean be the one to tell Cookie that the Italians have taken control of the kitchen.'

Until then, Luigi hadn't seen their little victory as a coup. But that's exactly what it was. The thin edge of the wedge. Little by little they could improve their lot and perhaps turn their predicament into something positive. 'So, what do we make for lunch?'

A mischievous grin spread over Gino's face. *'Pasta al pomodoro.* Are you game?'

'Let's do it!'

And so, they set to work making pasta: the traditional dish of *la patria*, the motherland.

Fifteen

Loveday, August 1941

The first Ted heard about the act of internee subversion in Camp 9 was when Sergeant Brian Smithers—also known as Cookie—stormed from the kitchen in such a state of fury that it took half an hour to calm him down.

'I can't bloody work under these conditions! Those bloody ignoramuses have no bloody respect.'

'Whoa! Hold your fire,' said Ted. He led the chief cook through the barbed wire gates to a guard hut outside the compound.

They sat at the table on the porch. Smithers' hands were shaking so hard that Ted offered him one of his cigarettes. The overwrought cook didn't draw back but puffed the smoke out like a steam engine.

'Now, tell me what happened,' said Ted.

'The bloody wogs whinge all the bloody time, then they bloody spring this on me.'

'Exactly what did they do?'

'I'd planned all the bloody menus and done the ordering, then they go ahead—without my authorisation—and make bloody spaghetti for lunch.' Smithers' face was a deep shade of puce. 'In-sub-bloody-ordination, that's what it is.'

'Strictly speaking, they don't report to you. They're civilians, remember?'

'If they can do whatever they bloody well please, how can we keep control of this bloody operation?'

'Through cooperation, negotiation, and reward. Those are Dean's words, not mine. Look, I've never worked like this before either. Certainly not when I was last in the army. Then it was all command and control. Put

107

one foot out of line and you'd be peeling potatoes for a month. No offence, Smithers.'

'In that case, Dean can shove it up his bloody arse.'

'Come on, man. You're a bit hot under the collar now, but it'll blow over. What did you do with the food? Throw it out?'

'Of course not! There's a bloody war going on. There are shortages.'

'So, what was the reaction when the internees got spaghetti? Was there a riot?'

'No. They burst into song!'

'You're kidding!' Ted couldn't help but laugh. 'What did they sing?'

'Some mumbo-jumbo in Italian. They all stood up and raised their arms and sang the song. They had tears in their eyes. Those blokes are bloody crazy, I tell you. And I'm not having any further part of it.'

'You can't quit. You're in the army.'

'I'm sixty-five, Lieutenant. Watch me leave and never come back.' Smithers turned on his heel and exited the hut.

Ted shrugged. He watched the old cook lumber towards the roadway and turn left, heading in the direction of the dorms. There was no doubt in his mind that Smithers would carry out his threat. That very afternoon he'd probably pack his belongings, get a lift to Barmera, and catch the Adelaide train home. Ted picked up the telephone receiver, dialled 1 for GHQ, and asked for Colonel Dean.

'Corporal Brian Smithers, the cook in Camp 9, just walked out.' Ted briefly explained the circumstances, then added that the would-be deserter was beyond the age of retirement.

Dean said, 'Let him go. I'll attend to the necessary paperwork. Do we have a replacement who can handle this sort of work?'

'There's Cooper in Camp 10, but he's got his hands full as it is.'

'Get me Del Drago. I've got an idea.'

Afterwards, Ted Long and the other officers were instructed that, from now on, the internees were responsible for whatever happened inside the compound. That included food, discipline, entertainment, and the allocation of work. The role of the army was to ensure the compound was secure and no-one escaped, and to provide living necessities and medical treatment in the case of serious illness or injury.

'Any requests for expenditure, such as the ordering of food, must come through me. In the first instance, you are to scrutinise the request and note on it whether you consider it reasonable. Are there any questions?'

The instruction was clear enough, but for the old-time army personnel it was hard to imagine how it could ever work. Even Ted, who'd been attracted to Dean's progressive methods, was left scratching his head.

Prisoners running their own prison camp? That was unheard of!

It took a few weeks for the Italian compound to settle into the new way of operating. Del Drago advised Colonel Dean that he'd selected a squad of enforcers to keep the factions under control. He'd also appointed several members of staff to organise work groups, allocate jobs, attend to complaints, and liaise with the Red Cross or the Swiss Consul if necessary.

Part of the deal was that the inmates would grow their own vegetables and the army would provide the seeds. Gardens outside the compound were prepared. Carrots, broad beans, lettuce, tomatoes, and eggplant were sown. When water was added, the soil that appeared dry and barren sprang into life.

Throughout the spring the plants flourished and by early summer the produce was ripe and ready for picking.

One day Del Drago called Ted into his office. He wished to invite Colonel Dean to inspect the gardens on the day of the harvest and dine at his table in the mess hall.

Ted thought the proposition was a bit presumptuous and was coy about putting it to Dean. But to his surprise Dean jumped at the opportunity.

'Stirling effort, Ted. A good working relationship with the internees makes everyone's job easier. This gesture on their behalf proves we are doing it right.'

'But what about safety? It could be a trap. They could slip poison into your food, for example.'

'Ted, you've been watching too many spy movies.'

'If you wake up dead, don't say I didn't warn you.'

'If you're so worried about me, why don't you come as my bodyguard? I'm sure we could wrangle another invitation.'

'And eat wog-food? No thanks!'

'But I insist.'

'Is that an order?'

Dean stroked his chin. 'Yes, Lieutenant. That is an order.'

On the night of the harvest celebration, Dean took three bottles of Barossa wine to share with the prince and his entourage. They sat at a table at the far corner of the mess hall, away from the clatter of the servery.

While all the other prisoners lined up for food, Del Drago's table was waited on as if in a high-class restaurant.

First up was an appetiser of sliced tomatoes, white cheese, green herbs, and crusty bread. Simple and tasty. Next came noodles with red sauce, fried vegetables, and sharp cheese. Third course was slow-cooked mutton, roast carrots and potatoes with garlic and rosemary. The meat was so tender it dissolved in Ted's mouth.

Driving back to GHQ, Dean said, 'What did you think of the wog-food then?'

'All right, I take it back. Best tucker I've had in my life.'

'Ted, I've been thinking. The soil here is far more fertile than I expected. The Italians have proven it with the crops they've grown. The magic ingredient is water. If we put our minds to it, we could turn this place into something wonderful. Make a real impact, if you know what I mean.

'Morphine, for example. Due to the war there is a huge demand for painkillers but the poppy fields of Europe are out of commission. Here at Loveday we are isolated from the rest of the country and also the world. Only *we* know what goes on here. The internees aren't going anywhere and we can trust our men to keep their mouths shut. For obvious reasons, growing opium must be a close-kept secret.

'So, here is my idea. See that long line of trees over there?' Dean indicated a thicket of mallee that screened the back paddock from the road and the river. 'If we could get enough seed, I reckon we could grow a field of poppies in no time. This is an opportunity to make Loveday self-sufficient, which has always been my aim. We would supply a much-needed commodity and, in the process, our inmates would have real work to do instead of pastimes to keep them out of mischief.'

'Wow!' was Ted's immediate response. He needed time to process the idea, which totally opposed his view of what internment should be. As if it weren't enough for the prisoners to run their own show, now it was likely that they'd be asked to collude in an enterprise that necessitated absolute trust.

Sixteen

The state election of March 1941 returned Labor to power with a clear majority. The proportion of primary votes for William Delahunty rose by six percent, testimony to his hard work during the campaign and his ability to gauge the mood of the electorate. However, it had been sheer good fortune that had solved the problem of Italians taking scarce Australian jobs and then sending all their money back home.

The spiralling rate of Italian migration was halted, not by Australia's government, but by Italy's. In the build-up to war in Europe, when countries would need every able-bodied man they could muster, Mussolini was several moves ahead of the British. After his appointment to the top job, he wasted no time in wielding his authority. With one stroke of the pen, all emigration ceased overnight.

Then, after the declaration war in June 1940, thousands of Italian migrants in the electorate of Endeavour were rounded up and despatched to distant internment camps. How this mass movement of humanity might be unwound when the war ended had not been considered. For the moment, they were out of sight, out of mind. There were more pressing issues to address. Of particular importance was the security of far north Queensland, should countries such as Japan enter the war.

Worryingly, Japan's Emperor Hirohito had signed a military pact with the Axis powers of Germany and Italy but was yet to show his hand. Japan was an unknown quantity, a country closed to the British. Who knew what schemes might be brewing. Mainland Australia was within easy striking distance, located a mere hop, step and jump along the islands of the South China Sea, the Dutch East Indies, and New Guinea. As a target, Australia was squarely in the cross-hairs.

In State Parliament, much of the deliberation was about the war. Delahunty argued that, due to the high risk of attack or invasion by Japan—a country that from all accounts had a teeming population and few resources—the far north must be protected.

'For the Japs, far north Queensland would be a gateway to the rest of Australia. I propose that the State provides immediate funds for the construction of fortifications and bunkers in the far north.'

The premier disagreed. 'It is our duty to protect Brisbane first. If our capital cities fall, the enemy will gain control over munitions factories, rail yards, airfields, electricity supply. Our budget is tight. Work should be done in areas of greatest impact.'

The debate went long into the night. Parliament finally approved the construction of public air raid shelters across Brisbane and for brick walls to be built around important buildings such as the State Treasury office, Parliament House, and the Supreme Court.

Delahunty had to settle for a compromise: limited funding for air raid shelters in Cairns and the sugar towns of Gordonvale, Wooranoora, and Innisfail. He viewed this not as a defeat, but the start of a longer-term victory.

In concert with the construction projects, new regulations were passed to safeguard communities from possible attacks. Camouflage was ordered for all public buildings. The cream-coloured twin towers of the Brisbane General Hospital, set high on the hill at Herston, were repainted steel grey to blend into the night sky. Streetlamps were fitted with special shades that deflected light down to the ground. It became mandatory for residents to fit brown-out shades to electric bulbs and block-out curtains to windows.

To help with the war effort, rationing of foodstuffs came into effect. To buy meat, butter, cheese, sugar, coupons were needed in addition to cash. Housewives became masters at substituting coupon-free items for rationed ingredients. Recipes for mock chicken, potato pie, and bean stew abounded. Front-yard flowerbeds were torn up and vegetables were planted in their stead.

At their house in Ashgrove, Delahunty did everything by the book. He had to. These days it was important to show leadership by example. Besides, he'd be politically embarrassed if *The Courier Mail* published photos of his house with roses along the fence and lace curtains in the windows. Recently the Premier had told him in confidence that he would shortly retire. As a senior Cabinet minister, Delahunty intended to put himself forward for the leadership position.

Although it nearly broke Margaret's heart, he stripped the rose garden of its beauty and sowed lettuce, tomatoes, carrots, and peas. Meanwhile Margaret was busy on her Singer treadle machine, turning old blankets into drapes.

Since the move to Brisbane, his relationship with Margaret had improved. She still showed no interest in fulfilling his conjugal rights, but she spoke to him kindly most of the time. As a politician, having a good wife was an asset. His marriage was valuable, something to be protected, if he were to fulfil his ambition to be Premier.

When Parliament went into recess, he took the train north, leaving Margaret to cultivate new friendships in the city. At least once a week they spoke by telephone, more to reassure themselves that the other was still alive than out of affection.

When Parliament was sitting, he'd 'sleep over' at his office in town or arrive home late at night. At least that's what he told Margaret. And, trusting soul that she was, she believed every word that he said.

In reality, Parliament was his alibi.

Amy, his mistress, had been installed in a house at New Farm, close to the branch of the bank where she'd been transferred. New Farm was a workers' suburb of quaint timber cottages constructed at the turn of the century. Although built to a formula—iron roof and curved awnings, veranda at the front, central hallway running between two bedrooms and the kitchen—the outside colours and the garden gave each cottage a unique character. The James Street property that Delahunty rented was no exception. High on the hill, it overlooked the school grounds but was screened from the road by a leafy Moreton Bay fig tree. The location was perfect, especially now that he had a car. In ten minutes, he could walk to his car space near Parliament House, drive along Ann Street to the Valley, and be at their love nest by the time Amy arrived home from work. Sometimes she dropped hints about his impending divorce—it had been impending for more than two years now—but she was always patient and loving.

Amy was the warm antidote to his frigid legal wife.

As far as he knew, Margaret was blissfully unaware of the other woman, and Amy believed that his estranged wife continued to reside in Cairns. In short, life was sweet.

On the last day of Parliament in December 1941, Delahunty sat through hour after hour of tedious debate over amendments to the *Liquor Act*, the most contentious of which was a proposal to increase trading hours by two hours per day. From experience, he knew that the Bill had no chance of being passed before the Christmas recess. Everyone was worn out from a taxing year. The last thing they cared about was whether barflies ought to start swilling beer at nine o'clock in the morning instead of ten.

At last the Speaker checked his timepiece and began the final wrap-up for the year. All the while, Delahunty was wondering whether he should return north to his electorate or remain in Brisbane. With both his women here and the war tipping out of control, he was more conflicted than ever about how to divide his time.

At five-thirty in the evening, the House adjourned. Most of the members were making their way to the Parliamentary bar for a long session of Christmas cheer, but Delahunty was keen to head off. After one round, which he paid for, he made an excuse and left.

Amy was already home when he walked up the back stairs of the cottage. In bare feet she ran to the door to greet him. She looked radiant, her green eyes glistened like cane leaves after rain. How could he leave her here, alone for months, while he attended to his duties a thousand miles away? It would be torture for them both.

'Darling, I have some exciting news.' She took him by the hand and led him inside to the parlour. 'But first can I get you a drink?'

'Whisky would be perfect.'

For several minutes she busied herself in the kitchen. When she reappeared, she had a tray with two drinks and a bowl of peanuts. The whisky she handed to him. The other concoction, which looked remarkably like red cordial, she took herself.

'To us!' he said. They clinked glasses. 'Now, tell me your wonderful news.'

She lowered her eyes and bit her lower lip. The colour of the lipstick reminded him of blood. When she looked up again, her cheeks were shining with tears.

'Darling Amy, what is it? I expected happy news, not this.'

'It *is* happy news. But it's also a bit scary.'

That was when he began to worry.

'You see ...' she took a deep breath. 'We are going to have a baby.'

Delahunty almost fell off the chair. 'But *how*?'

'What we've been doing all these months was bound to lead somewhere.'

'But I *always* took the proper precautions. Oh God, Amy, please don't say there's someone else. That would be the death of me.'

'Sometimes these things happen. Are you very angry?'

He bundled her into his arms, stroked her lustrous hair. 'Of course not, darling. But this changes everything. I need a minute to think it through.'

She got up to leave the room and he let her go. He skolled the whisky and dropped his head into his hands. He was on a knife-edge. Decisions must be made and there wasn't much time to make them.

A baby at his age! He'd never been a father, though once he wanted to be. Although they'd tried, Margaret had been unable to fall pregnant. So, he'd thrown all his energies into work. In his middle age, he expected to meander through the rest of his productive years, fulfilling his political ambitions and leaving a memorable legacy for the people of Queensland. Now it seemed his life would be playing out the wrong way around.

Amy returned, stood over him with her hands on her hips. 'If you don't want to have this baby, I can find someone in Sydney who ...'

'No! How could you even think that? I want this child. It's part of you, part of me. We'll have to figure out a way to make it work.'

'I think it's pretty simple. Divorce your wife and marry me.'

'That's more complicated than you think. When's the little one due?'

'End of April.'

'Jesus! That's four months!' he breathed. 'Why didn't you tell me sooner?'

'I tried. Really, I tried. But I couldn't bring myself to do it.'

He went to the kitchen and poured another shot of whisky. His mind was whirling like the ceiling fan. Whichever way he turned, he was trapped.

If he told Margaret and got a divorce, that would mean bad publicity and backlash from the voters. With all the scandal, he wouldn't stand a chance of being Premier; he might even lose his ministerial portfolio.

If he didn't tell Margaret and continued the pretence, Amy would probably walk out and he'd never see his child.

If he got Amy really offside, she'd probably blab to Margaret out of spite.

The nine-month fuse had been sizzling away under his nose and he hadn't even noticed. Soon her condition would be undeniable. She would be sacked from the bank and then she would have no income at all.

Deep down he loved her; he couldn't let that happen. He must face up to his responsibilities as a father, if not as a lover. At the very least, he must do whatever was necessary to support the child.

Then a lightbulb flashed in his head.

His house in Cairns was empty. Not only was Margaret happy in Brisbane, but she *expected* him to spend half his time up north. If he took

Amy to Cairns with him, he could delay making this delicate situation public and that would buy him time. Perhaps he could persuade Amy to pose as his cousin, or the wife of a dear friend who was fighting the war in Europe.

After all, life was full of little charades.

Amy was less than enamoured with Delahunty's proposition. In fact, she flew into a rage, the likes of which he'd not seen before. The more he tried to calm her through rational argument, the more distressed she became.

Finally, she slapped his face and shouted for all the neighbours to hear. 'If that's how you feel about me, get out of my house now and don't ever come back!'

'This is *my* house,' he said in an even tone. 'If you want this to end, it is *you* who must leave.'

With that, she raced to the bedroom and flung an empty port onto the bed. The wardrobe door banged and wires clattered as she ripped clothing off the hangers. All the while she was sobbing as if her heart would crack.

Delahunty was at a complete loss. Never before had he witnessed such animal fury. Margaret always behaved with dignity and control, even when they fought. He assumed it was the same for all women.

Perhaps this emotional hurricane was due to Amy's condition. Other men had commented that their wives would switch from kind Dr Jekyll to evil Mrs Hyde each time they were expecting. Would these outbursts continue until the baby came?

He remained in the parlour until the emotional tidal wave broke and ebbed away. When she'd fallen quiet, he moved to the bedroom. She was curled up on the covers like a small child. Gently he removed the port full of mangled clothing and sat down on a corner of the bed. 'I didn't mean to upset you. I thought—'

'No, you didn't think at all.' Her voice was like ice.

He hung his head. 'I'm sorry, Amy. Please forgive me.'

She pushed herself up; her emerald-green eyes bored into him. 'William, I want to have your baby and I want us to be together. But Brisbane is where we belong. Cairns is a country town and your wife is there. Even after the divorce, we'd bump into her at the shops or in the street. Everyone's tongues would be wagging. Imagine how embarrassing that would be!'

She had a point. Although people from Sydney called Brisbane 'a big country town', it was large enough to move about incognito. In Cairns, everyone knew everyone's business. That left him with one option.

It was his cue to tell Amy that Margaret no longer lived in Cairns, but he let the opportunity slide. He was already deep in poo and didn't want to risk another explosion. 'Give me a week and I'll sort things out with my wife. I'll call you as soon as I can.' He rose to leave.

'I've put in my resignation to the bank,' she said as if it were an afterthought. 'My last day is Friday.'

Taking his wallet from his pocket, he offered her a five-pound note.

She pushed it away. 'I can manage without your charity, thank you very much.'

'Take it for the baby then.'

She hesitated. Then, without a word, she snatched the banknote and stuffed it into her bra. For one awful moment, she looked like a common prostitute.

'I'll be off then.' Delahunty kissed her forehead. 'I'll call you.'

In the car, he rammed his foot down on the accelerator. God, he needed a drink! The nearest establishment was near the docks, a rundown place frequented by wharfies and thugs. Instead of blending in with the crowd, his suit would make him stand out like dogs' balls. Instead, he swung by the Wickham Hotel's bottle shop and bought a half-bottle of whisky.

Not far from his house in Ashgrove he stopped at a park that had swings and a slippery slide for the kiddies. At this time of night, it was guaranteed to be deserted. He remained in the driver's seat, opened the bottle and downed a shot. The alcohol lubricated his throat and loosened his temper. Ahhhh, now he could think. He must get the story straight before the inevitable showdown with Margaret.

At five a.m. on Monday 8 December, a persistent *ring-ring* woke Delahunty from a deep slumber. He rolled off the daybed in the sleepout and stumbled to the hall to answer the telephone. As he passed the bedroom doorway, he saw Margaret asleep on her stomach. Her hair, once deep chestnut, was now a mousy shade of grey. They had been married for twenty-eight years.

He raced to pick up the receiver before his wife stirred. Rarely did he get calls this early in the day. 'Hello. Delahunty speaking.'

'Delahunty, thank goodness you're home.' It was the Premier. 'I've received urgent news that an American base in Hawaii has been attacked by Japanese bombers. We need to respond immediately. War has come to the Pacific, which means we're in for it. How soon can you get here?'

'Maybe an hour.'

'Good. See you at six sharp.'

DEBBIE TERRANOVA

Delahunty showered and dressed, grabbed a banana and a couple of biscuits from the tin, and left a note on the table for Margaret. At that time of day there was no traffic at all, which meant a quick drive into town.

Already in the cabinet office in George Street were the Premier, his secretary, and three senior ministers.

'Come in Delahunty. Cup of tea?' said the Premier.

Delahunty nodded. 'Are we expecting anyone else?'

'No. Shall we begin?' The Premier gave an outline of the information he'd received. The attack occurred around eight o'clock Sunday morning Hawaiian time and it came without warning or declaration of war. According to initial reports, the Japs used heavy bombers, dive bombers, and submarines in an attempt to destroy the American naval base and airfield. Several US warships were damaged and it was believed that one had sunk.

'For the Japs, the timing was perfect. Sunday morning, everyone would have been relaxed and off guard. That there was no prior declaration of war makes this atrocity all the more despicable. Needless to say, President Roosevelt's response has been swift. Retribution will be forthcoming. Our Prime Minister will make a formal announcement later today. However, he has already informed me of the content.

'Gentlemen, as of now we are at war with Japan. This new enemy poses a formidable threat. They are cunning and ruthless and Australia is right in the firing line. We must urgently review all plans for the safety of the state and do whatever is possible to weather this mighty storm.'

'Hear, hear,' everyone murmured.

Seventeen

For a woman in Edith's advanced state of pregnancy, undertaking a long train journey from Wooranoora to Brisbane with a three-year-old child was pure madness.

Because of the crushing season, she'd delayed the trip for as long as she could. Relying on the know-how of her kind neighbours and the brawn of the Yugoslavs from the boarding house, she'd managed to produce a high-yielding crop. The cane-cutting contractor had arrived on schedule, there'd been no strikes, and the rain had held off until the crop was safely at the mill. She was acutely aware that her success as a farmer was due more to beginner's luck than good management, but nevertheless she'd done it. She'd lived up to Tony's expectations. His words still echoed in her ears.

'Growing cane is instinctive, *amore*. You must follow the seasons.'

Her instinct to get advice from veterans of the industry had served her well. Throughout the season, the Sampsons had taken her under their wing and given as much help as they could, which included minding Bella when she went to town on business.

Not only had she managed to run the farm and contend with all the paperwork that entailed, but she had also brushed aside the pleas of her parents to 'give up and come home'. About the coming baby—their second grandchild—Edith had kept her silence. It was not until her seventh month that she'd worked up the courage to tell them. Her mother had wept. Her father had demanded that she bear the child in a nice clean hospital in a civilised city—meaning Brisbane—and not 'out in the bush like a blackfella'.

Although she'd written to Tony several times about the good news, she had not heard anything back. This added to her mounting concern about his welfare. Surely, wherever he was, his keepers were obliged to tell him about such an important matter. Twice a week she drove to town to pick up the mail. With crossed fingers and tingling hope, she'd wait for the postmaster's wife to thumb methodically through the pile of letters addressed 'c/- Post Office, Wooranoora'. But all she ever received were window-faced envelopes containing farm invoices.

In desperation, she telephoned William Delahunty's electoral office in Cairns. A young male informed her that the Minister was absent in Brisbane due to Parliamentary sittings and could be contacted only in an emergency.

'Try your local police station', he suggested.

Edith strode down Sugarmill Street to the timber cottage with the police sign out the front. Sergeant Pitt was as gruff as usual. Instead of taking her details or offering to locate her husband, Pitt pushed a form across the desk. It was entitled, 'Missing Persons'.

'Is there nothing you can do?' Edith said.

'Internment is out of police hands. If you report him missing, we can make enquiries on your behalf. Can't promise to find him but.'

Edith completed the form and gave it back to the sergeant.

'We'll be in touch in due course,' he said.

As she walked out the door, she heard a tearing sound and a comment muttered beneath the sergeant's breath. 'Got better things to do than play nursemaid to the wife of a bloody dago.'

At the end of November, Edith booked train tickets to Brisbane and packed two ports: one for herself and one for Bella. She tidied the house and arranged for Mr Sampson to drive them to the Wooranoora railway station.

When the *Sunshine Express* arrived at Brisbane's Roma Street Station two days later, Edith's parents were waiting on the platform. Even though she'd paid extra for a sleeping compartment, the trip had been uncomfortable and exhausting. Slumber had been impossible on the hard, narrow bunk. All day, cramps had gripped her belly.

With Bella clinging to her like a strangler vine, Edith stepped from the carriage into the arms of her mother.

'Darling girl! You look dreadful! You should've come home earlier so we could look after you. What were you thinking?'

'Mum, I can look after myself.' She smiled as brightly as she could and lowered the toddler the ground.

Thumb in mouth, Bella hid her face in the folds of her mother's tent-like dress.

'Come and say hello to your Nan and Pop.' Edith tried to coax the little girl out but she stepped backwards, shaking her head.

'She's not used to us. Maybe later,' said Mum. 'Ewan dear, please take us home.'

Ewan Allenby collected his daughter's luggage and laboured over the pedestrian bridge. The car was parked two blocks away. Bella refused to walk and would not allow anyone but her mother to carry her. By the time they reached the car, Edith was out of breath and the abdominal cramps were coming with alarming regularity.

Bella lay across the back seat and rested her head on Edith's lap. 'Ouch!' She sat up. 'Mummy's baby kicked me. Right here.' She rubbed her forehead. 'Bad baby!'

Edith gave her a hug. 'You'll meet your baby brother or sister very soon I think.'

'I told you before, Mummy. I don't want a baby brother.'

'I'm afraid we don't have much choice in the matter, my darling.'

The route to Clayfield took them through the bustling precinct of Fortitude Valley, home to department stores, chain stores, dress shops, butcheries, bakeries, newsagents, chemists, banks, and several pubs. Most of the weekday shoppers were women, dressed in frocks, hats, and gloves. The men were either in military uniforms or business suits. Trams clattering along Ann Street crackled and showered sparks from the gantry of overhead wires. At the corner of Brunswick Street and St Pauls Terrace, the policeman on points-duty waved them through.

The most noticeable change to the city was a plethora of air-raid shelters. More correctly, they were sandbag bunkers with flat concrete rooves, built above ground to accommodate up to fifty people. One was at every tram stop along the way. Edith had seen newsreels about the bombing of London. The attacks had been brutal and relentless. Entire city blocks had been pulverised. Casualties had numbered in the thousands.

Against the might of a squadron of bombers, these flimsy shelters did not offer much protection. Edith chewed her lip. Surely sleepy Brisbane wasn't expecting a *Luftwaffe* attack like London.

Her head hurt from too much thinking, from worrying about Tony and not getting any sleep. Before the new baby was born she should rest. Perhaps now, with her mother there to entertain Bella, she could put up her feet at last.

In Clayfield, her parents' bungalow looked exactly as she remembered. In no time, she was reinstalled in her childhood bedroom. Carved antique duchess, pink hail-spot curtains, wrought-iron single bed made up with crisp white sheets. Her old cot, a solid timber affair, had been set up in one corner. The drop side had been removed to make it look like a proper bed. On the pillowcase was an embroidered heart and a mother's blessing: 'Good night, sleep tight'.

Whether it was relief that she'd reached her destination, or that her parents could lend a hand, or sheer nervous exhaustion, that night Edith slept like a dead woman. But when she woke in the morning, the mattress was drenched. With a disbelieving hand, she touched the sheet, her nightdress, the crotch of her cotton panties. Last time she wet the bed, she was Bella's age. How could this have happened? She eased herself up, tossed off the covers. The white sheets were lolly pink.

The first contraction struck with such force that she crumpled back onto the bed.

Bella burst into the room. 'Mummy! Mummy! There's pancakes for breakfast!' She stopped a few feet away, sensing something was wrong.

Edith gasped, 'Go get Nan. Mummy's not feeling well.'

'Do you have a tummy ache?'

Despite the pain, Edith couldn't help but smile. 'Yes, darling. A big one.'

Four hours later at the Brisbane General Hospital, Edith gave birth to a perfect, wriggling baby boy. His hair was dark like his father's and his skin was rosy like his mother's.

'He's a handsome little man,' pronounced the midwife as she cleaned up the new patient. She swaddled him in a bunny rug and handed him to Edith. His tiny mouth nuzzled her breast and gripped the nipple.

For Edith, it was love at first sight.

If only Tony was there in the waiting room along with the other husbands. Did he even know he was to be a father again? Was he ... the word *alive* skipped briefly across her mind. Her eyes filled with tears. She revised her inner monologue. Was he *happy*?

She glanced at the babe nestled in her arms and kissed his downy head. 'Hello, Anthony Ewan Zucchero. I'm your Mummy.'

Eighteen

Early in the piece, Luigi learnt that the key to survival in Australia was to keep his opinions to himself and drift along with the majority. Unlike others he knew, he couldn't bring himself to bow and scrape to influential men to get favours, nor to speak out against them. Indeed, it was better to go unnoticed, to blend into the landscape, than to stand up for either good or evil.

Lying low was the answer. But he was yet to discover if the strategy would help him survive in a Fascist-dominated internment camp.

Luigi was proud of his adopted country and what it had helped him achieve. But now he was amongst men who harboured animosity towards Australia and demonstrated it every day. At every opportunity, they undermined their captors' well-meaning attempts to make prison life more tolerable.

Luigi had been one of the first to volunteer for paid work in the kitchens. This, he believed, would be good for everyone: himself, his brother, and his fellow inmates who craved home-style food.

The night after their act of defiance—the meal of pasta—he and Gino walked together back to their hut. Although the perimeter fence glowed under the floodlights, deep shadows fell between the huts. The fellow who stopped them was huge; his identity was hidden by a hessian sack that he wore over his head.

'How dare you thumb your nose at the Motherland!'

At first Luigi thought it was a joke. 'Didn't you like the pasta?' he said flippantly.

'Working for the enemy is the same as waging war against our Motherland.'

Gino said, 'But we're trying to make things better. Mutton stew isn't proper food. Real men need pasta.'

The man was unflinching. 'Continue to support the enemy and you will die!' As if to give due emphasis, he spat on the ground. Then he turned away and melted into the night.

Luigi nudged Gino and they broke into a run.

By the time they reached the hut, Luigi's legs were wobbling like jelly. In the safety of the entrance light, he leant breathless against the wall and fumbled in his pocket for a cigarette. His heart was beating fifty to the dozen. He was so unfit, he wondered if he'd ever work his cane farm again. Although not yet fifty, he felt as old as Vecchio.

He struck a wax match on his shoe and lit a cigarette.

Beside him, Gino was doubled over and puffing heavily. 'Do you know who that was?' The way he phrased the question indicated that he already knew.

'*Should* I?'

Gino nodded and lowered his voice. 'One of Piselli's henchmen.'

'Who's Piselli?'

'Shhhh!' Gino leant close. 'The doctor.'

'What are you talking about?' Luigi had been to the camp hospital once: in winter when Angelo had fainted in the mess-hall and was diagnosed with influenza. Angelo had spent three days in isolation before being discharged, weak but recovering. At the time, the doctor seemed perfectly genuine. Later he made follow-up visits to check on Angelo's progress.

'I have it on good authority that Piselli wants to overthrow our camp leader. I know who I'd rather have in charge: Del Drago. He's a man to respect.'

Apart from working in the kitchen together, Luigi barely knew Gino. These matters were dangerous to discuss. For all he knew, Gino himself could be a spy. To disagree or offer an alternative opinion could make him a marked man. He tucked the piece of information about Piselli away and resolved to make his own assessment.

The next morning Luigi was not rostered for work. With time on his hands, he went to the hobbies workshop where the old men congregated to talk or make curios from tree roots or jewellery from silver coins. Conversations were always in olden-day dialects, never in scholarly Italian or English. Most of the regulars hailed from Sicily, from the crumbling towns on the central plateau where Luigi was born, or towns on the slopes of Mount Etna. The workshop was a place of calm and wisdom, where Luigi felt comfortable amongst his countrymen.

From the woodpile, he took a lump of knobby mallee root and set himself up at the workbench beside Vecchio. The woodworking tools were all improvised: the saw was made from a metal packing strap; the chisel was once a spoon; the plane was a piece of glass.

Luigi took up the chisel and began to pick off the spikey bark. His companion had almost finished making a jewellery box, a gift for his niece.

They spoke for a while about the far north and the old country they'd left behind. Both still had family in Sicily but had received no letters for a year. Sometimes it was hard to stay positive when the lack of news made imaginations run wild.

Wistfully, Vecchio said how much he'd enjoyed the pasta the day before. 'When I closed my eyes, I was back home with my Mamma. Mmmmm! Good Italian food made by good Italian cooks, there's no mistaking it.'

Luigi couldn't help but smile, but his instincts warned him to keep his part in it secret. Instead he agreed that the food had indeed improved enormously.

'Whoever had the idea to pay us to work is a genius. The young ones here are starved for activity; they'll make trouble if they're bored. I don't understand why everyone hasn't taken it up.'

'It might not be that simple,' said Luigi.

The old man glanced around the workshop. The others were out of earshot. 'That's true. Some are against it but, believe me, they are in the minority.' He held up his hand. 'I could count them on my fingers.'

'If I wanted to work, should I be scared of the ones who oppose it?'

'Are you a man or a mouse?'

'Then I'll put my trust in Del Drago.' Luigi grinned.

Vecchio returned the smile. *'Molto bene.* Very good. Now, if you've finished with that chisel ...'

Luigi handed him the repurposed spoon and took up a piece of curved glass, which he used to remove the pulp from the mallee root. The last time he'd worked with wood was when they'd bought the farm at Cassowary Valley. With no money, the brothers had made whatever furniture was needed. Beds, table and chairs, shelves, benches were made from scrap from the sawmill. The pieces were rough but serviceable and the farmhouse wallowed in the intoxicating perfume of fresh-cut wood.

In the workshop, Luigi found his rhythm as he scraped the pulp.

Vecchio sat on a stump and lit a smoke. 'You've got a good feel for the wood, *paesano.* Have you ever done any parquetry?'

'Never had time to learn.'

'Well, you've got time now. Come back Thursday and I'll teach you.' Vecchio squatted and reached for something beneath the bench. 'Two hours, sixpence a lesson,' he added cheekily.

'So, this is your contribution to the workforce,' said Luigi lightly, at the same time wondering whether the old man was serious.

The item Vecchio placed on the bench was exquisite: a parquetry case about eighteen inches long and twelve inches wide. It was finished in a herringbone pattern using different colours of wood. In awe, Luigi ran his finger over the surface. It was as smooth as glass.

'You actually *charge* for lessons?'

Vecchio shrugged. 'A man needs money for cigarettes. In case you hadn't noticed, businesses are springing up everywhere. You want a haircut? Go see Lorenzo in Hut E3. You want a winter coat? Giorgio in W10 is a tailor who can turn an army blanket into an overcoat. You want to learn German? See Adolfo in E12. He was a professor of languages at a university in Firenze.'

'How do you know all this?' said Luigi.

'I keep my eyes and ears open.'

Luigi brushed the wood dust off the bench and stowed his partly-finished project on the floor beneath. He hadn't quite decided what it would be, but it was shaping into some sort of trinket box. 'Thanks, Vecchio. See you Thursday morning, eight o'clock.' The lesson would be over by ten and he'd be in time for his lunchtime shift in the kitchen. Pasta was definitely on the menu.

The harassment of Camp 9 workers continued under the cover of darkness. It seemed that the doctor, or whoever else was behind the scheme, was picking them off one by one. From time to time on his way back from evening shift, Luigi would glimpse a man in a hessian sack slipping between the huts.

After the first altercation, Luigi was wary and stuck to the well-lit path. In his pocket he carried a woodworking chisel, which gave him a sense of security.

The scare tactics proved effective. Fewer and fewer of the inmates signed on for work. Then one night in midsummer, everything came to a head. Del Drago's *carabinieri* made their move. The troublesome man with the hessian sack was ambushed. In the scuffle that followed he was knocked out cold. The hood was rudely snatched off and the identity was revealed.

Luigi could scarcely believe his eyes. His would-be assassin was none other than Carlo Monte, the renegade Fascist from Wooranoora.

Luigi helped carry him to the infirmary where they were met by a hard-faced Dr Piselli. The doctor was stumbling around and his breath stank of alcohol. It was clear that he was far from pleased. Instead of rolling up his sleeves and treating the patient, he swore at him then stormed out.

A few days later a new doctor was installed in the infirmary. Carlo was not seen or heard from again.

Without the troublemakers and their ugly threats, Luigi relaxed into a routine that alternated between the kitchen and the workshop.

In autumn 1942, the kitchen took delivery of two live pigs. Where they came from and how they got there was a mystery, but Luigi suspected it was an Easter gift for the men, arranged by Del Drago to thank them for their support.

The first lick of cold weather came without warning. While the days were dry and mild, the nights dropped to near freezing. Rather than cursing the unseasonal weather, the cooks of Camp 9 were overjoyed. Conditions were perfect for *fare miaile* (making the pig).

One of the cooks, a butcher by trade, attended to the slaughter. The other kitchen workers broke down the carcasses. Several pieces were chosen to be salted whole and hung in a corner of the kitchen. In time they would become *prosciutto*, *pancetta* and *capocollo*. The rest would be made into a wonderful array of meat cuts and smallgoods. The head and trotters would be boiled and made into *gelatina* (brawn); the spare ribs would become pasta sauce. Sausages would be made from various offcuts, finely chopped, seasoned and stuffed into casings of cleaned intestine.

The belly pork would be rolled with rosemary and garlic from the garden and slow-roasted for hours. The *porchetta* would be the star of the Easter Sunday feast. Accompanying it would be roasted carrots, potatoes, and pumpkin. Mouths watered in anticipation.

The last time Luigi had eaten pork was more than three years ago, when the brothers acquired a piglet as payment of a debt. When Angelo brought the squealing thing home, wrapped tight in his shirt, Luigi had thrown his hands up in horror.

'Why would you accept a liability instead of cash?'

Angelo said, 'They have no cash to pay. Anyhow, this little fellow will be better than money. You wait and see.'

The first night they had nowhere to keep it and nothing to feed it.

While Angelo built a pen using reclaimed timber, chicken wire and a sheet of corrugated iron, Luigi set to work cooking dinner. Meatballs with boiled potatoes and pumpkin dressed with olive oil, salt and pepper.

By one o'clock, everyone was hungry, including the little pig whose squealing drowned out their conversation.

Angelo shook his head. '*Poverino.*' Poor little thing. He pushed back his chair, picked up his half-eaten plate of food, and took it out to the pig.

A minute later he was back. 'He loves the vegetables. Are there any more?'

The next day, Luigi drove to town and bought a bag of pig feed. In a bucket he mixed the feed with water and made a swill. The animal refused to eat.

Angelo scratched his head. 'Should we try potatoes and pumpkin again?'

'Go right ahead. He's your pig.'

Half an hour later, the meal was ready. Angelo put a chunk of plain boiled potato into the dish, but the pig turned up its snout. 'Do you want oil and pepper, little one?' He tickled its floppy ears.

He brought out the oil tin and the condiments, drizzled golden oil over the vegetables and added seasoning. The dish glistened enticingly in the sun. The piglet took one sniff then gobbled the lot.

Six months later the fully-grown pig, raised entirely on seasoned potatoes and pumpkin, was slaughtered. The pork was sweet and tender, the best they'd ever had.

Easter Sunday lunch at Camp 9 was a triumph. At the end of the meal, the entire mess hall stood and applauded the cooks. *Bravo! Bravo!* they shouted as Luigi, Gino and the others came out and took a bow.

The crowd spontaneously broke into *Giovinezza.* The stirring song, which praised youth, valour, and the greatness of Mussolini, lifted everyone's spirits. The highlight of the day was when Prince Del Drago strode along the line-up of cooks and congratulated each one with a shake of the hand.

Soon the war would end and Italy would have her victory.

Viva il Duce! Viva l'Italia!

Troubles in the East

Nineteen

At Loveday, the news that the Japs had bombed Pearl Harbour was as much of a shock to the guards as it was to the rest of the world. First thing Monday morning, Dean called them all together at GHQ.

'While sudden and appalling, this attack is not completely unexpected. Some time ago the Japanese signed a pact with Germany and Italy, so it was not a matter of *if* but of *when*. However, in taking this action without a declaration of war, Emperor Hirohito has thumbed his nose at international protocol. The American casualties in Hawaii are likely to be horrendous. What this attack shows is that the Japanese are brutal and their *modus operandi* will contravene the rules of engagement that Europeans generally uphold.

'Men, we must prepare ourselves for the inevitable. I expect that within days Adelaide will require us to accommodate Japanese internees or prisoners of war. While we are somewhat familiar with the needs and habits of Germans and Italians, these men will be completely different. To the best of my knowledge, Australia does not have many Japanese civilians. I expect most of our prisoners will come in from overseas.

'There will be challenges ahead. While it's difficult to predict exactly what Hirohito will do next, indications are that he may send his army south through the islands of the Pacific and New Guinea. If that is so, we shall receive prisoners with all manner of tropical diseases. Typhoid, cholera, malaria and the like. Attention to hygiene and isolation facilities for contagious illnesses will be essential.

'I shall keep you informed every step of the way. Commanding officers and engineers, please remain. All others are dismissed.'

Ted and his fellow officers took their places around a large table. Dean set up the chalkboard at one end.

'We must plan for this Japanese influx. When the orders come through, we shall have very little time to act. The new facility must be suitable for up to four thousand prisoners. Your thoughts, gentlemen?'

The site they identified for Camp 14 was the former Barmera aerodrome, half a mile from GHQ and two miles from Camp 9. The design would be completely different from the existing two camps: four times the size and in the shape of a dodecahedron. The twelve-sided complex would be divided into four sections by roads that would cross at the centre. One road would carry foot traffic, while the other would be suitable for heavy vehicles. Guard towers would be strategically placed around the perimeter fence.

Wherever possible the different races would be segregated. Each section would be designated by a letter of the alphabet: 14A for Italians, 14B and 14C for Japanese, 14D for Germans. Inside one of the Japanese sections, a 120-bed hospital with isolation facilities would be built.

As Dean predicted, two days later the orders came to commence construction.

On 5 January 1942, the first group of fifty Japanese—all civilians who had been employed in the Northern Territory pearling industry—walked into camp under guard. Only the barbed wire fence around 14B had been finished. The first night, and for many months to come, the prisoners slept under canvas.

From January until March 1942, the prisoners continued to arrive by the trainload. Most were Japanese ex-patriots captured in the Dutch East Indies or Malaya, but there were also German and Italian internees who'd been arrested in Queensland. To speed up the construction of permanent huts, internees worked alongside soldiers and contracted tradesmen. Progress was painfully slow and tents remained the main shelter for the best part of a year.

In the winter of 1942, Ted Long was told he would be transferred from Camp 9 to the new Italian compound, 14A. He was glad to continue with the Italians, for he'd become accustomed to their quirky ways, the cadence of their language, the aroma of their food. And, at a glance, he could tell when trouble was brewing. In fact, he'd engineered a transfer of one of the major troublemakers in Camp 9 to end a reign of torment and abuse of other inmates.

The internee in question was one Petro Piselli, a medical practitioner who displayed a fanatical affinity to Mussolini. Before his capture, he'd attempted to establish a branch of the Fascist movement in far north Queensland. For various reasons, including his even stronger affinity to the grog, it had never got off the ground.

In Camp 9, he undermined Camp Leader Del Drago's position and generally stirred up unrest. He'd perfected the knack of setting up others to do his dirty work, while keeping himself clean. Surrounded by an entourage of hand-picked thugs, he meted out retribution—usually in the form of a beating—to anyone who dared go against him.

Prisoner transfers were not uncommon and medicos were in high demand. Ted assumed that the not-so-good doctor would have been sent to Hay or Tatura. Without his destructive influence, the compound settled back into a comfortable routine.

When Ted took up his posting at 14A, he was in for a shock. Dr Piselli was there in all his glory. In fact, he was more powerful than before. Not only was he the doctor-in-charge of the infirmary, but he was also the elected camp leader.

Also in 14A was Francesco Fantin, a small man with a big voice, who'd been captured in far north Queensland and had followed the usual route of internment camps, through Gaythorne and Hay, to Loveday. Although Ted could not understand much Italian, Fantin communicated in grand gestures that spoke even louder than his words. He made no secret of his political views—strongly anti-Fascist and leaning towards the far left—and that was what got him into trouble.

Confrontations between the Italian inmates were usually short and sharp. Shouting matches sometimes flared up but soon fizzled out. Physical assaults were rare.

Early in the piece, Francesco Fantin was ambushed outside his tent and received punches to the head and a few kicks to the ribs. His friends lifted him from the ground and carried him, bleeding, to the infirmary. The doctor on duty was Piselli, who had probably engineered the beating in the first place.

Despite this, Fantin was neatly patched up and sent on his way.

It seemed the Hippocratic Oath that Piselli had taken as a physician had precedence over his animosity toward the patient. Perhaps the doctor wasn't so bad after all.

Twenty

The American war machine sprang into action with an immediacy that Delahunty found startling. In retaliation for the Japanese bombing of Pearl Harbour, and the attacks on Malaya and the Philippines that followed soon afterward, President Roosevelt turned his attention from Europe to the new conflict in the Pacific. Of course, the allegiance between the US and Australia would be strengthened. Both countries would rely on each other's military support: one to deliver retribution for a callous and costly attack and the other to prevent invasion by the rice-eaters.

Within a short time, Prime Minister Curtin telephoned the Premier to advise him that certain locations in Queensland were earmarked for US military use. By the time the Premier told Delahunty and the other members of Cabinet, a fleet of American warships was already *en route* to Brisbane.

A few days before Christmas the first convoy, under the protection of the cruiser *USS Pensacola*, entered the Brisbane River. Delahunty was one of the official welcoming party. Crowds of well-wishers and stickybeaks lined the vantage points along the Hamilton reach of the river. The ships docked at Brett's Wharf in Newstead. Cheers and applause rang out as the troops, dressed in smart white uniforms, filed down the gangplanks.

Excitement skyrocketed throughout the female population, who had suffered a man-drought for two years. The Americans were fine-looking fellows who promised to protect Australia from its foes. Rumours abounded that some of the sailors were black. Not even Delahunty had seen a Negro up close before.

If the onlookers expected to see these exotic beings, who by all accounts could sweep a girl off her feet with one sultry look, they were about to be disappointed. Unbeknown to the public at the time, a private war was raging between Prime Minister Curtin and President Roosevelt about what to do with the men of colour.

The White Australia Policy prohibited them from entering the country and Curtin was not about to give up without a fight. He forbade any soldier or sailor whose colour did not conform to Australian law to disembark.

The stalemate continued for weeks before a compromise was struck between the two countries. Roosevelt agreed that he would send black servicemen to Australia only 'in the case of emergency'.

Meanwhile, the white Americans disembarked without mishap and were marched to the nearby Ascot Race Course to set up camp. At the welcome reception for officers that evening, Delahunty sat next to Captain Hank Campbell from the *USS Republic*, where he received an education about America like no other.

'Of course, we must segregate the blacks from the whites,' said Campbell. 'Once we get clearance to disembark the blacks, we'll cordon them off at the present location. This will work as a temporary measure. However, once more vessels are deployed here, the numbers will swell exponentially.'

Delahunty's eyebrows shot up. 'What percentage of the troops is not white?'

'More than half. Mostly they do manual support work for the fighting forces. Building roads and bridges and the like, for which they're ideally suited. The blacks *expect* to be accommodated separately and get mighty agitated if a white man crosses their turf. Where I'm from— Mississippi—*everything* is segregated. Separate churches, separate shops, separate buses, separate schools. Yes sir, if you mix black with white, you get nothing but trouble.'

'Do you know how many troops might come here?'

'Depends on General MacArthur, the man in charge of the Pacific Campaign. At a guess, upward of twenty thousand.'

'Wow!' Delahunty breathed. His mind was reeling. To conceal his dismay, he lifted his beer glass and made a toast to the greatness of America. Both men drank deeply.

A simple calculation set the likely number of Negroes at more than ten thousand. They would need separate *everything* in order to keep them happy. How would a small city like Brisbane handle such an influx? Where could they be accommodated for a start?

'What about entertainment?' said Delahunty. 'How do your men spend their down time?'

'You mean R&R?'

Delahunty scoured his mind for a translation. Rest and recreation. He nodded.

'Same as you guys. Hang out in bars, go to dances, play craps, see the sights, get themselves laid.'

With a sinking heart, Delahunty took another swallow of beer.

When off duty, these fit young men would be out for a good time. Sleepy little Brisbane was simply not equipped for an influx of sex-starved holidaymakers.

Restricted trading hours allowed the pubs to open between eleven in the morning and seven at night. Due to the war, the supply of beer—Australia's national beverage—was also restricted. He knew for a fact that most city hotels had voluntarily reduced trading hours even further in order to eke out scarce stock. The Grosvenor, for example, was down to three hours per day over two swill-sessions: one hour at lunchtime and two hours in the evening from four until six.

As for gambling, placing a bet was legal only at the racetrack, which was now an encampment for American troops. Despite the law, illegal Starting Price (SP) bookmakers persisted—much to the chagrin of the Criminal Investigation Branch of the police force—but even the SP bookies' activities were reduced, for the pubs were their main place of business.

Should he say something to lower Campbell's expectations or talk to his Cabinet colleagues first? He opted for the latter.

'Then we'll work together and make this a success for everyone,' said Delahunty brightly. Pity he didn't feel as confident as he sounded.

The morning before Christmas, Delahunty managed to pin down the Premier for a briefing before he left town for his property near Mackay.

'Be quick, William. The nine o'clock train waits for no man.'

'I'll drive you to the station. We can talk on the way.'

In the car, Delahunty voiced his concerns about the American servicemen and in particular the need for separate lodgings and recreation facilities for the non-whites in order to satisfy the requirements of the US military. 'There'll be trouble ahead if we don't act quickly and decisively. The numbers expected are quite staggering. Far more than I ever imagined.'

'How many?' said the Premier.

'At the welcome dinner, Captain Campbell gave an estimate of twenty thousand troops all up. Half of those are likely to be black.'

The Premier smiled and shook his head. 'Captain Campbell is mistaken, I'm afraid. The Prime Minister telephoned earlier. He's expecting one hundred thousand servicemen to be stationed in Brisbane alone. William, old boy, we are about to experience a friendly invasion. At least I hope it's friendly. Talk to the Chief of Police. Put your heads together. See what solutions you can come up with. Do it now, before Christmas. The second fleet is already on its way.'

'Dear God!' said Delahunty. 'The entire population of this city is less than four hundred thousand. That's one serviceman to every four citizens!'

Straight after Delahunty dropped the Premier at Roma Street Station, he drove to police headquarters. The meeting with the Chief of Police continued for the rest of the day. Senior officers came and went to provide information and clarify procedures. By five o'clock, the most pressing decisions had been made. A plan of action was in place.

In the Premier's absence, it was left to Delahunty to negotiate and finalise arrangements with relevant military leaders and the Lord Mayor of Brisbane.

The plan went something like this. Once the Federal government authorised the coloured troops to disembark, they would be moved directly to South Brisbane, where many of the city's Aboriginal population lived. The area immediately south of the river and extending to Woolloongabba in the east would be designated black. It would be policed to ensure that white servicemen and civilians did not enter, and that black servicemen did not leave after the dusk curfew. In terms of recreational facilities there were sports fields, a dancehall, and several pubs, albeit run-down and shabby. At least ten houses of ill repute operated in the precinct, which police tolerated while nobody caused trouble. While the coloured soldiers would be restricted to living and playing within the designated zone, the white troops had the run of the town.

Young women, hungry for male company, refashioned their frocks and cut their hair in the latest American styles. The US servicemen's uniforms were smart and well-cut; they were generally well-educated and showed nice manners. Better still, they had money to burn on luxuries and items unobtainable anywhere apart from the American Postal Exchange stores. What better way to a girl's heart than a gift of precious nylon stockings?

Christmas morning, the Ascot Race Course was swarming with Brisbane residents of all ages and persuasions, who came with invitations for the soldiers to celebrate yuletide at their private residences. Within an hour, the campsite was vacated.

At Margaret's insistence, Delahunty invited two fresh-faced lads not long out of their teens to their home at Ashgrove. Both were New Yorkers, city raised. Neither had ever camped out until they were drafted into the military.

Margaret greeted them like prodigal sons. She'd roasted a chicken—a rare treat—which she'd bought from a neighbour. Thankfully it had come already plucked and cleaned. To make them feel at home she'd made American brownies. In the process, she'd used up all her coupons so they would have to survive the rest of the month without any sugar.

When they were sitting in the parlour, she said, 'You boys must miss your families.'

'It's sure hard being away from Mom,' said the one called Chuck. He smiled handsomely and made a little show of presenting a gift wrapped in brown-paper. 'A little something from us to thank you for your hospitality. Happy Christmas, Mrs Delahunty.'

She opened the wrapper. Inside was a block of Hershey's milk chocolate. 'Thank you both. You're too kind,' she purred.

During dinner Chuck talked about his home, a two-bedroom apartment in Brooklyn rented by his mother. 'Mom's divorced and works two jobs. My kid sister's still in school. Sometimes finances are tight so I send her my pay-check.'

'What a kind gesture,' said Margaret with sparkles in her eyes.

'What do you think of Australia?' said Delahunty, keen for a more interesting topic of conversation.

'We sure got a hero's welcome coming down the river. All those people on the banks, cheering and waving our flag. I'll never forget it.'

Delahunty said, 'Since that disgraceful attack on Pearl Harbour, we've come to realise that war is right on our doorstep. More than ever, we Allies must stand shoulder to shoulder against the enemy. Your presence gives a lot of comfort and hope that this new phase of the war will be short lived.'

Margaret shot her husband a withering look. 'Dear, let's not ruin today by discussing the war.' To Chuck she said, 'Tell us about Christmas in America.'

He proceeded to describe lashings of snow, pine trees glistening with bright baubles, bell-ringing Santas, candle-light and mistletoe.

'I'd love a white Christmas again,' said Margaret wistfully. 'It's so darn hot here.'

As if to prove a point, she fanned herself with her serviette. The day, which had started mild, had turned into a steam bath. Semicircles of moisture darkened the armholes of her frock. Flies buzzed lazily about the room. One settled on the muslin cloth covering the food and lifted its hind legs to preen. Half-heartedly she shooed it away.

'Sounds wonderful.' Delahunty refilled the boys' glasses with beer. 'Silly that we persist with a hot Christmas dinner when the temperature is in the nineties.' Quickly he added, 'No offence to you, Margaret dear. The meal was truly delicious.'

For the first time in ages, his wife smiled with genuine affection.

Guilt gnawed at his heart, for he still hadn't carried out his promise to Amy. However today was not the day for it. He glanced at his fob watch. Three-thirty. What was she doing right now? Lately he'd been so busy that he hadn't even telephoned to enquire after her health. The longer he left it, the harder it would be. If he weren't careful, he might lose both the loves of his life. Perhaps, when he drove the boys back to camp, he'd make a quick detour to New Farm.

Chuck said, 'If you don't mind, Mr Delahunty, we need to be back at Camp Ascot by four sharp.' He rose and began collecting the dirty dishes.

Margaret took the plates from him. 'No, no, no. I'll do that. Sit down, relax.' She cleared the table and bustled about the kitchen.

'Whenever you're ready I'll run you back,' said Delahunty.

The lads bade Margaret farewell and thanked her again for the dinner.

On the way back to the camp Chuck said, 'We're off duty for the weekend. What does this town offer in entertainment?'

'There are nice beaches on the north and south coasts. In the city, you could go to the botanical gardens or the cinema or a dancehall. The shops are open Saturday mornings. The pubs open for lunch and again in the afternoon. But everything is shut on Sunday.' In the rear vision mirror, Delahunty saw their shocked reaction. He added lamely, 'To a large extent you need to make your own fun.'

'Where can we meet girls?'

'From what I've seen, our girls are crazy for Americans. Wear your uniform in Queen Street. You'll have trouble keeping them away.'

Delahunty dropped the pair at Racecourse Road. Thirty minutes was the limit he set himself for the visit to Amy. If he dallied any longer, he would have to justify his absence to Margaret, and that was a conversation for another day.

As it turned out he needn't have bothered. His knock on the back door resounded through an empty house.

Twenty-one

Brisbane, February 1942

At last Edith received the letter she'd been waiting for. It had travelled a circuitous route from an unknown location to the Wooranoora post office, and then by redirection to her parents' address in Clayfield. The envelope was a deep shade of mustard; her name and the Wooranoora address were type-written.

Barely breathing, she ripped it open and unfolded the single sheet of paper. It was from Tony in his own neat handwriting. Some of the text had been struck out with thick ink, which showed it had already been read by a censor.

> *9 November 1941*
>
> *Amore,*
>
> *I can't begin to tell you how thrilled I am at your wonderful news! If only I could be with you now, and when the little one arrives.*
>
> *As for me, I am as well as can be expected. Most of our friends and neighbours are here at — . I am sharing a dormitory with — and — . We are treated well, have plenty of food, and good clean accommodation. To pass the time, I have been giving lessons to the others in English and bookkeeping.*
>
> *Remember what I said about the stars, amore? When the stars are out, I picture you in the silver light, my beautiful princess. I miss you terribly and can't wait for*

this to be over so I can come home to you and our darling children.

All my love to you and Bella and the little one.

She barely reached the end before a torrent of tears ran down her cheeks and onto the paper. Her emotions were swirling like rapids. Love, relief, disappointment, pride, anger, despair. Back again to love. How cruel this war was! Cruel to innocent men and the women who cared about them.

Immediately, she took pen and ink and began a reply. Every week since baby Anthony's birth she had posted a letter to her husband, care of the Australian Military Forces in Brisbane. Although she doubted he ever received a single one, it was all she could do to keep the candle of hope alive. Now that she knew he was all right, she wrote as if he was sitting at the table instead of locked in a distant prison camp, whose location she was not permitted to know.

27 February 1942

My darling,

Finally, a letter! You wrote in November last and the letter arrived today. I'm so relieved you are well. I'd been worried about you, but now I can relax. What we must do, my love, is survive a few more months and then we shall be together again.

Our sweet little boy, Anthony Ewan Zucchero, is now three months old. He is the spitting image of you, which means he is absolutely gorgeous. I wish you were here with us, to share his smiles and cuddles.

Bella is besotted with her brother and is very possessive. She tickles his tummy and sings him to sleep. They are so cute together you'll weep.

She signed it, sealed it in an envelope, kissed it for luck. Later Bella dropped it into the red post box at the end of the street when they took Anthony for a walk in the pram.

Summer became autumn and the days were growing shorter. Soon it would be Easter and the planting season would begin. Edith worried about how to keep the farm operating until the end of the war. Certainly, she couldn't do it from Brisbane, but her prospects of returning to Wooranoora were slim now that Japan had entered the war.

Troops, recently returned from the battlefields of Europe, were being redeployed to the Pacific. There was speculation that Emperor Hirohito intended to expand his empire to the south, which would put Australia at risk. According to her father, who drank with influential men from the top end of town, the far north was being heavily fortified in case of an attack.

'There is no way I'd allow any daughter of mine to walk into a minefield,' Ewan said. 'Forget the farm. You must stay here with us.'

But she couldn't forget the farm.

The Manor was her home. *Their* home. And sugar was in demand; the price was sky high. Yet, in a move that defied comprehension, the government had locked up the Italians who grew it. Good cane was rotting in the paddocks, all for the lack of labour.

By now some food items—meat, butter, sugar, tea—were expensive and difficult to obtain. When it came to feeding a nation, the military was first on the list. The pick of the produce was shipped to Europe, Africa, the Middle East, or the Pacific for the troops. No-one on the home front minded the shortages or the long queues to buy goods. It was a sacrifice of love, for everyone had at least one friend or relative posted overseas.

To contribute to the war effort and to support themselves and their families, able-bodied women were encouraged to take on 'men's work' in the essential services. Conducting trams, sorting mail, assembling munitions. Women unable to go to work knitted scarves, gloves, and socks to be sent overseas for the freezing northern winters. Everyone was expected to do their bit.

With two young children and an absent husband, Edith searched for a solution to her own predicament. The sooner the wretched war ended, the sooner Tony would come home and their lives would return to normal. In the meantime, new cane had to be planted and the ratoon cultivated and fertilised so that the bank loan could be repaid.

What other choices did she have?

Then it came to her. Until she married and lost her job, she was a qualified teacher. Perhaps, under the circumstances, the Department would agree to reregister her. Perhaps her mother could babysit during school hours. The terms were a mere thirteen weeks long. In the evenings, she could prepare lessons and mark schoolwork. Although teaching was not highly-paid, a full-time job would bring in enough money to make ends meet.

She gathered together all the relevant documents—her Diploma of Teaching from Kelvin Grove College, glowing references from principals of schools where she'd taught, her official service history showing the dates of employment—and made a telephone call to the personnel section of the Department of Education. An appointment was made with the head of personnel the following week. Teachers were in short supply. Due to the war, student teachers, who were bonded to the State for two or three years after graduation, were simply not coming through the system.

Edith was a highly-regarded teacher with several years' experience and had the evidence to prove it. To refuse her request would be a nonsense.

Confidently she strode into the interview room, a spartan wood-panelled cube with a timber table and two chairs. The personnel manager was in his late fifties. Silver hair, double chin, wire-rimmed glasses, and an abundant paunch that strained against the buttons of his white shirt. He rose and introduced himself as Graham Mollicut.

'Please, Miss Allenby, take a seat.'

She corrected him. 'Actually, I'm Edith Zucchero now. All my documents are in my maiden name, which is Allenby.'

'Zucchero is an Italian name, is it not?'

'Yes, but my husband is naturalized and has lived here most of his life.'

'You are still married then?'

'Yes. I've applied for reregistration because my husband is unable to work. I love teaching and we need an income, so I thought ...'

'That the Department would make an *exception* for you?' His face was like a mask.

'Well ... I suppose ... yes.' Her confidence was melting as fast as ice in the noonday sun.

'Tell me, Mrs Zucchero. Why is your husband unable to work?'

Her heart was hammering in her ears and her cheeks were hot. She lowered her eyes. 'It's because of the war. He was interned.'

'Thank you, Mrs Zucchero. Good day.' He stood and motioned for her to leave.

She remained seated. 'What about my application?'

'The Department will contact you in due course.'

'But I'm qualified and ready to work right now. We desperately need the income. Please don't make me beg for my job back.'

'Mrs Zucchero, I'll be frank with you. Firstly, the Department does not employ married women. If we made an exception for you, we would have every married woman on our doorstep wanting to take jobs away from people who are more deserving. Secondly, think of how the school community would react. Your husband is an enemy of this country. That raises suspicions about your allegiance. Would you choose your country over your husband? I think not.'

Tears of fury filled her eyes. 'In other words, I've wasted my time.'

'No, Mrs Zucchero, *you've* wasted *mine*. Now, good day.'

'Good day to you, Mr Mollicut,' she said through her teeth.

As graciously as she could, she grabbed her folder of documents and stalked out of the interview room. In the corridor she made a dash to the ladies' restrooms. Locking herself in a cubicle, she wept until all her tears were spent.

What would she do now? Apart from teaching, the sum of her working experience had been a brief stint as a shop assistant. For six months in high-school, she'd worked at Coles variety store in the Valley on Saturday mornings. The pay was appalling, barely paid the tram fare, and the time commitment played havoc with her studies. It was her father who suggested that she give it away and concentrate on getting a teacher training scholarship instead.

At the hand basin she splashed water on her face, combed her hair and applied fresh lipstick. Her eyes were pink and puffy, suggesting either sticky-eye or insomnia. She opened her compact and daubed around them with powder. The patch-up job went some way towards concealing the evidence of her melt-down.

In the street she waited for a tram. Her thoughts were in a whirl. How could she run the farm without being there? How could she repay the bank without money? How could she get money without a job? Every solution created another problem. Round and round her mind went.

At first, she didn't notice the air-raid siren. It was when the woman beside her said, 'We'd better go, dear,' that she realised what was happening. Vehicles had come to a standstill and people were scurrying into buildings.

Waaaaaaooooooow wailed the siren. Up and down, up and down. An unrelenting rollercoaster of noise.

The nearest shelter was in the basement of McWhirters department store. Policemen and wardens were trying to keep order, directing the mad scramble of pedestrians to the safety of the bunkers. She followed the rush of foot traffic into the store. Panicking people were pushing from behind. An elderly woman toppled down the stairs.

Edith clung to the handrail, counted each step until she reached the bottom. Hundreds of people were already in the shelter. Everyone was jostling for space. She squeezed between bodies to reach a side wall where the sandbags doubled as seats.

'Is this a drill or is it real?' breathed a lass beside her.

'I don't know. This is my first time.'

'Me too.' The girl began to weep. 'I'm really, really scared.'

'Don't worry, we're safe in here.' Yes, thought Edith, *we* might be safe but are my children and their grandparents safe in Clayfield? She began to gnaw her fingernail. And Tony, was he safe too?

The basement hummed with hushed conversations and the soft sound of sobbing. Protocol demanded that noise must be kept down and the lights must be dim. Outside, however, the siren screamed like a banshee.

People were squeezed together shoulder to shoulder, thigh to thigh. Someone started singing *The White Cliffs of Dover*.

The girl sitting beside Edith was shivering.

'Are you cold, honey? You can borrow my cardigan if you like.'

'No, thanks.' She placed her hand protectively over her belly. 'It's just that ...'

'Oh, I see.' Edith touched the girl's wrist, saw there was no ring on her finger. 'I've recently had a baby myself. A sweet little boy. My mother is looking after the two children. I went for an interview to get my old job back, but I don't stand a chance.'

The girl looked up in surprise. Her eyes were the brightest shade of green that Edith had ever seen. 'I had to resign from my job at the bank. No-one knows about the baby, apart from William ... and now you. I haven't even told my brother, and I won't until after we're married.'

'When's the happy day?'

'Soon.' She chewed the corner of her lip. 'Actually, it's a bit complicated.'

Edith had already diagnosed the problem. Although she was not much older than this girl, she knew enough to recognise an affair with a married man. 'Sometimes it's easier to talk to a stranger.'

'Thanks for not judging me.' The girl brightened. 'I'm Amy.'

'Edith.' They smiled at each other.

'Is your husband away?'

'Yes, Tony's down south. He hasn't seen his new son yet.'

'My brother's in the army ... again. He's a lot older than me. He fought in France in the First War and now he's a guard at a prison camp in South Australia. You'd think he'd be sick of fighting wars by now.'

'Where in South Australia?' Edith asked as casually as she could. Her pulse was racing as she held her breath and waited for the reply.

'Not far from Barmera where he lives. I moved to Brisbane after my parents died. Ted was married then so he stayed in South Australia.'

145

Edith chose her words carefully. 'What did Ted tell you about the camp?

'It's called Loveday. The prisoners are all Nazis and Fascists.'

'Not all, surely!'

'Well, they're Germans and Italians any rate. Same thing.'

Edith nodded. 'Gosh, that could be where my husband is. What a coincidence!'

Encouraged, Amy continued. 'Ted's very impressed with his boss, which is saying a lot. Nothing much impresses him these days. The camp is clean and well-run.'

'Do they treat the prisoners well?'

'As far as I know. But who cares about enemy prisoners?'

'They're human beings,' said Edith gently.

Amy sniffed. 'When you hear what happens to *our* soldiers who are taken prisoner in other countries, these blokes have got it made.'

The all-clear siren sounded and a cheer rang through the shelter. People scrambled to their feet and queued at the foot of the staircase to be let out.

'It's been nice talking to you,' said Edith. 'All the best for the little one.'

'Wait! What's your last name? When I write to my brother, I'll ask him about Tony.'

Without batting an eyelid Edith said *Allenby*. After this morning's harsh lesson in the personnel office, she would henceforth avoid her husband's name. 'We're in the telephone book at Clayfield,' she added.

'I'll call you. Cheerio.'

The 'Friendly Invasion'

Twenty-two

Cairns, 27 July 1942

For Delahunty, the end of July meant he would soon leave the tropics where he'd been for the mid-year recess and return to a cool winter in Brisbane. Parliament would reconvene in two weeks, so there was ample time to finalise his affairs before making the two-day journey south.

He had been in his electorate alone. Margaret had refused to endure another hot stinking rainy season in the far north and Amy had given him the cold shoulder. Of course, he'd felt an enormous sense of responsibility toward her, the mother of his newborn child. He'd continued to provide her accommodation and a weekly allowance for food, and he'd talked to her on the telephone a few times, in particular around the time of the birth in April, but she'd rebuffed his pleas for her to join him in Cairns. Perhaps she didn't want to be with him anymore and was too timid to end it.

In an odd sort of way, he felt relieved. It was one thing to have a fling with a pretty young thing, but quite another to be in a serious relationship with two women at the same time. At his age, it was downright exhausting.

Since going to live in the city, Margaret had become her old self again. The blanket of depression that had smothered her in the tropics seemed to have fallen away. City life suited her. The shops, the cinemas, the theatre, the galleries. Not that Brisbane was as bright a light as Sydney or Melbourne. And, in comparison to the razzle-dazzle of New York, it was barely a candle. But the 'big country town', now brimming with US servicemen, was vibrating with a buzz never experienced before.

According to Margaret's letters, which she posted every week without fail, she'd made new friends and was 'painting the town red' in the nicest of ways. They'd been to the modern American diners that had

149

sprung up in the Valley, feasted on hamburgers with mustard and ketchup, crunched on French fries, drunk gallons of syrupy Coca-Cola.

At the Trocadero she'd watched the young ones turn the dance-floor upside-down. A shocking new dance craze called the Jitterbug had swept everyone off their feet. What fun she'd had learning the steps! And at her age! Apart from the sandbags and air-raid shelters that had taken over the streets, it was hard to believe there was a war on, she wrote.

In one way, Delahunty was pleased but a part of him was also envious. Who were these new friends anyway? Was Margaret up to something?

In the Cairns house, he made himself breakfast, a soft-boiled egg with buttered toast and black tea, and took the tray onto the back verandah. He sat in the cane armchair with the Saturday edition of *The Cairns Post* open across the occasional table. Cutting the top off the egg, he found it had gone hard so he scooped it out and mashed it onto the toast. After all this time, his culinary skills hadn't improved one iota. Margaret, on the other hand, was a wonderful cook.

The front page of the newspaper reported his visit to Innisfail the week before, when he'd met with cane farmers and the manager of the sugar mill. Lack of man-power was proving to be a big problem. Farmers told him that the bulk of the previous season's harvest had been done by the growers themselves because so few men were available. Even then, much of the crop had been left to stand over and rot in the paddock.

'What is the government doing about the labour shortage?' they demanded.

Delahunty had no immediate answers, but he promised to raise their concerns when he returned to Brisbane. A few solutions were rattling about in his head but none were clean and simple.

Prison labour. He recalled his last visit to Stewart's Creek Gaol in Townsville. No, that would never do. Drunks, lunatics and wild-men, the lot of them. Using prisoners would create more problems than it would solve.

Internees. He thought about the Italian canecutters, who were locked up in internment camps down south. He remembered a long-ago conversation with a pair of women pleading for a husband to be freed. A big internment camp was at Gaythorne in Brisbane. If the internees were hand-picked and guarded by police or soldiers, would that work? Again, he shook his head. More trouble than it was worth. Besides, he'd promised his constituents that he'd rid the far north of Italian parasites. The proposal would be certain to lose him votes.

Female labour. The newly-formed Women's Land Army was touting for business, its volunteers keen to support the war effort. The thought was discounted before it fully formed. No woman could perform the strenuous work of cutting cane and certainly not in fierce tropical heat.

The best idea was to use the men already in the district. Soldiers. At that time Cairns was practically overrun with Australian servicemen who'd been deployed there to protect the north from Japanese invasion. Since the Japs' bombing attack on Darwin Harbour in February—which had been largely hushed-up to prevent national hysteria—the government had crammed forces into far north Queensland.

So far, nothing had happened. The soldiers stationed there were engaged in nothing but patrols and drills. In his opinion, it was activity for activity's sake. Surely some of those fit young men could be reassigned to help out an industry that relied on manual labour. He made a mental note to contact the federal minister responsible for the military first thing on Monday morning.

After brushing the crumbs from his shirt, he drained his cup. The tea was cold and bitter. Damn, why couldn't he make breakfast like Margaret? Although he would never admit it, he was missing her. Without her chatter and bustle, the house felt empty and soulless. It was as if someone had broken in and stolen his favourite armchair or all the books in his library. Whatever made this house a home, was gone. Perhaps he should telephone his wife. Her reassuring voice might be enough to fill the void. He eased out of the armchair—the gammy knee was playing up again—and limped to the hallstand. There sat the telephone in a black Bakelite tuxedo with silver trim.

As he reached for the receiver, the phone began to ring. Delahunty picked up the receiver, answered *hello* in his usual modulated tone. The operator announced a trunk call from Brisbane and asked if he wished to proceed.

'Go ahead.'

It was the Premier. 'William, there's been another air attack by the Japs. On Townsville this time. No damage reported, thank God. One enemy flying boat. The ordnance landed in the harbour. All of Queensland is now on high alert. I'm convening an urgent Cabinet meeting early next week. How soon can you get here?'

'By train, Wednesday evening at a guess.'

'Do whatever it takes. I need you here right now. General MacArthur is setting up a US command centre in Brisbane. We must work with him to shore up the State. In the meantime, treat this information as top secret.

The press must not get their hands on it. We need to prevent hysteria and maintain order and control.'

'This is most concerning indeed. I'll call you back when I make the necessary travel arrangements.'

Rubbing his chin, Delahunty laid the receiver on its cradle and checked his fob watch. Ten fifteen. On Saturdays all businesses shut at noon. There was no time to waste. He jumped in his car and drove to the Abbott Street address of the local booking agents. There he was informed that, due to the war, all flying boat services to Brisbane were cancelled as of last February. In fact, all the flying boats had been commandeered by the Air Force. The few small planes that remained in commercial service were doing charter work for the military.

To drive one thousand miles in two days was unthinkable. The car was temperamental and the road was mostly unsealed. In the wet it became impassable and earlier flooding had left a catastrophe of wrecked bridges. The *Sunshine Express* was the best option after all. He made a reservation on the next available train, due to depart Cairns on Sunday morning and arrive in Brisbane forty-eight hours later.

For the rest of the day he rushed around, meeting his secretary at the electoral office to make arrangements for his absence. Finally, he packed his port and gathered all the papers and files he'd need in Brisbane. A stickler for routine, he hated having his well-planned schedules disrupted. The attack on Townsville sounded like a rogue pilot who sought fame for single-handedly conquering Australia. Either that or he had a death-wish. With the Japs, you could never tell.

By evening Delahunty was tired and agitated. For dinner he ate the remaining food in the house: a tin of bully beef, scrambled eggs and toast. It wasn't brilliant, but he'd cooked worse. He switched on the wireless. Thankfully the attack on Townsville was not mentioned on the ABC news. There were reports of a successful campaign against Rommel in El Alamein and a RAF incendiary attack on Hamburg. Slowly but surely, the Allies were gaining control over the Axis nations. The Japanese would stand no chance against the might of the United States.

Bored with British war propaganda, he tuned into shortwave. The wireless made a hissing sound, interspersed by a few sharp crackles. He moved the needle slowly from one side of the band spectrum to the other, pausing whenever he got a signal. He stopped at Radio Tokyo.

The sing-song voice of the female announcer was so warm it could melt hearts. Her English, spoken with a light American accent, was impeccable.

'Hello, dear friends ... I mean, dear *enemies*. This is Rose, bringing you sweet music to remind you of home. Don't you miss the smell of your mom's apple pie, or your comfy armchair by the fire, or the sound of your child's laughter? You could have all this tomorrow if you treated our country with respect. That's not so difficult, is it?

'Anyway, here's a lovely song to remind you of home.'

Danny Boy. The lyrics were gut-wrenching, bringing tears even to Delahunty's hard eyes.

'There, dear enemies. I hope that soothes your homesickness. Now for the news. First up, Australia. I am happy to report that this morning your military installations were smashed by our air units in two separate raids on Townsville. In the first, our pilots destroyed your airfields, oil tanks, shipping, and supply dumps. In the second, the remaining military installations were bombed. The attack on Townsville is one of the heaviest since the fall of Singapore. Do not underestimate us, dear enemies. We do not give up. Go home to your families now before it is too late.'

Delahunty snapped off the wireless. He'd heard enough to realise how much damage broadcasts like this would do to morale. His government had done the right thing to ban the use of shortwave for the general population. Whether it was enforced was hard to know. The police sergeant in Cairns swore that all shortwave wirelesses in town had been confiscated. Except Delahunty's. As a Cabinet Minister, he had reason to get news of the world and was therefore exempt.

Tuesday morning, Delahunty went directly from Roma Street Station to the Cabinet room at Parliament House. There was no doubt about it: the war was changing Brisbane.

General MacArthur and his entourage were already in town, staying at an 'unknown and secret location', according to the newspapers. But blind Freddy could see the heavy security measures around Lennons Hotel.

MacArthur's office accommodation, two blocks away, was in the process of being fitted out. The Romanesque sandstone building would become the nerve centre for US forces in Australia; his chambers would be where offensives against the Imperial Japanese Army would be planned and controlled.

Directly opposite the General's office was the American Postal Exchange store, where US servicemen could purchase practically anything they wanted—Oreo biscuits, chocolate bars, waistband elastic, Coca-Cola, peanut butter—when Australians had to rely on ration books or the black market.

Already the unfair availability of life's luxuries was causing tensions between soldiers of the two nations. Fuelled by copious quantities of beer, swilled as fast as humanly possible in limited trading hours, skirmishes regularly broke out. Pubs now operated for just one hour per day. Hoteliers in the inner city were in collusion. The opening times were staggered to maximise profits. As one establishment closed, all the barflies would lurch down the street to the next. So far, both the US Military Police and the Queensland Police had kept their own in check, but there needed to be an overall plan in case things got out of hand.

South-east along Edward Street toward the river was the infamous green door. The unobtrusive entry was actually a small workman's access within the larger door of a workshop. Day and night, soldiers from both sides of the Pacific could be seen loitering outside. As one exited, another entered. Unknown to the office girls who walked past in droves—to get lunch or the mail or to do the banking—this unassuming place was Brisbane's busiest brothel. For the clients, timing was critical. Sometimes schoolboys would keep places in queue while intending clients went to the nearest open bar for Dutch courage. The queue-keepers were tipped handsomely. In one day, an enterprising young lad could earn enough to keep himself and his mates in cigarettes for a week. Brothels in Queensland were illegal, yet they were expected and necessary with so many men in town. Should measures be taken to intervene? Or should they legalise the oldest profession? No. That would never fly with the teetotallers and wowsers. It was easier to let sleeping dogs lie.

Then there was the problem of the black servicemen who were confined within the boundaries of South Brisbane. From all reports, the handsome dark-skinned GIs were a hit with the ladies. In South Brisbane, women were free to come and go as they pleased. And rather a lot of women were very pleased to do exactly that.

Mixed-race dating was considered scandalous but mixed-race marriages flew in the face of the White Australia Policy. As the law stood, it was impossible for a man of colour to take an Australian wife and remain in this country.

The first Cabinet meeting ran all day and into the night. A multitude of issues was debated, in particular the sudden influx of Americans. The general conclusion was that whatever General MacArthur needed to run his war and keep his troops happy, he could have in the public interest. The door was open and so too was the chequebook.

On Wednesday the unthinkable happened. A second Japanese air strike was made on Queensland. Eight bombs were dropped at night on farmland not far from Cairns. Only one exploded, damaging a family home and injuring a little girl. Again, the attack was hushed-up by the Australian government. Delahunty later learnt that the Jap bomber was not part of a squadron but operating in isolation and the shells were released in error.

It was too close for comfort. Delahunty ordered the Cairns police to evacuate everyone who was neither in the military nor involved in the production of food. Women and children were packed off to the Atherton Tablelands, which was considered safe. They would be billeted with friends or relatives or complete strangers. As usual in the far north, when the chips were down, everyone worked together.

The round of Cabinet meetings continued throughout the week. On Friday night, the last exhausting meeting finished at seven. Instead of going to Ashgrove, Delahunty caught a tram to New Farm. He hadn't spoken to Amy in months and hadn't yet seen his own child. His letters had gone unanswered and she was never home when he telephoned.

The tram dropped him outside the Brunswick Hotel, a short walk from the cottage he rented as their love nest. The house itself was in darkness. A knock at the door confirmed that nobody was home. He cupped his hands and peered through the glass. The furniture was intact and dishes were draining on the sink.

Where would a young mother go at night?

He slipped a note under the door and went home to his wife.

*

It was September 1942. With the focus of wartime attention now on Brisbane, the job of a state minister ramped up from busy to totally frantic. New demands piled in every day. What made it so tricky was that state laws often conflicted with the requirements of the US Supreme Commander of the Southwest Pacific, General MacArthur. Debates raged in the House. Parliamentary sittings ran through the night.

On the domestic front, Margaret supported Delahunty through it all. Always dinner would be ready when he came home exhausted from battles with his peers and the Opposition. No matter how late he arrived, his wife would be either reading in the living room or making biscuits in the kitchen. In a city dimmed by fear, she was his beacon of light.

On the other hand, Amy had practically slid off the radar. After several more unsuccessful attempts at getting her on the telephone, Delahunty decided to go to the New Farm house again in person.

It was Wednesday night, the first week of September. All day he'd been fielding questions and criticisms from the press that the government had sold out to the Yanks. Citizens who'd been initially welcoming of the friendly invasion from across the Pacific, were complaining that Queensland had become the forty-ninth state of America. It was easy to see why, when every decision that he and his colleagues made was biased towards the American allies, who were also the chief protectors of Australian soil. It was a classic case of 'damned if you do and damned if you don't'.

He cleared his desk, switched off the light, and caught the tram to New Farm. As he walked up James Street he saw Amy ahead of him. Surprisingly she was alone, no baby in sight. He picked up pace but before he could catch her, she turned and entered a neighbouring cottage.

Should he follow or wait at her place?

He decided on the latter. To avoid snoopy neighbours, he went around the back. The door was locked so he sat on the top step. It wasn't long before he heard a key rattling the front door lock. A door squeaked. Shoes clicked on the floorboards. Water gushed in the sink. There were muffled voices: male and female. The woman didn't sound like Amy.

Standing, he peered through the window glass. In the kitchen, a man in US army uniform was sitting at the little table. His back was towards the window. A red-haired woman was pouring two glasses of beer. At that moment, she glanced up and saw him. She put her hands on her hips and stormed towards the back door.

Delahunty stood his ground. After all, this was his house; he had a right to be there.

'What do you want?' Her lips and her nails were fire-engine red.

'Where's Amy?'

'There's nobody here by that name, mister. Sure you've got the right address?'

'Absolutely. I pay the rent. Who are you?'

The redhead took a step back and turned to the soldier. 'Honey, come here please.'

A chair scraped back. 'What's up, buddy?' His voice was like silk; the accent was Texan. The man came and stood behind the woman. He was a good six foot four tall and built like the proverbial brick shithouse.

Delahunty straightened his stance; compared to the other man he felt like a midget. 'Who are you and what are you doing here?'

'None of your goddam business,' said the soldier. 'Get out before I call the cops.'

'Listen here, my good man. I am the one who should be calling the police. Unless you explain your presence in my house, I can only conclude that you are trespassing.'

The pair looked quizzically at each other.

The woman chewed on her lower lip. 'A friend of ours said we could stay. We've got nowhere else to go.'

'Is your friend a young woman with a baby?'

'She's young but there's no baby.'

'What's her name then?'

'Mrs Long.'

Delahunty pursed his lips. His blood pressure was rising; his face was on fire. 'Does she live in James Street?'

The woman answered. 'Yes. Number forty-three.'

Delahunty turned to leave then thought better of it. 'How much rent do you pay?'

'That's rather personal,' said the soldier. 'Don't say anything, angel.'

'Go drink your beer while it's cold. I'll handle this.' The redhead flicked her hair and watched him walk to the kitchen. In a low voice she said to Delahunty, 'Three pounds a week. Mister, if this really is your house, please let us stay.'

Delahunty mumbled something unintelligible about needing to sort out this mess, then stomped down the stairs. Behind him, raised voices drifted out of the house. He didn't care. His attention was on Amy and this outrageous turn of events.

Brimming with fury, he stormed along the footpath to number forty-three, threw open the gate and thundered up the steps. He raised his fist and slammed it on the open door. Amy poked her head into the hallway. Quick as a flash she disappeared again. Uninvited he strode into the house and up the hall. He found her in a back room, cowering behind a double bed.

'Don't you come near me, William Delahunty. Not in that mood.'

'I'll do whatever I bloody well like.' He took a solid step into the room. 'What's going on, Amy? This had better be good!'

She stood up and squared her shoulders. 'It's over between us.'

For a heartbeat Delahunty was speechless. 'Ungrateful cow!' he spat. 'After all I've done for you!'

'You've done nothing, William. You messed up my life then shot through to your precious electorate, leaving me here to fend for myself. Well, that's not what I want. So, I've made some changes.'

'Including subletting my house and pocketing the money?'

She shrugged. 'A girl's got to live.'

157

'Where's the baby? Where's my son?'

She averted her eyes and twirled a lock of hair around her finger.

'Well? Where is he?'

Her gaze slid to a black-and-white snapshot on the dresser. Tears trickled down her cheeks. 'I had no choice.'

Delahunty's heart leapt into his mouth. 'What have you done with him?'

'He's at St Vincent's at Nudgee.'

'You put our son in an orphanage!' He raised his fist, slammed it down on the bed. 'How *could* you! This is how you treat your own flesh and blood?'

'William, I had to. I couldn't manage. You don't know how hard it's been. When my life is in order, I'll get him back.'

Delahunty dropped himself onto the bed. 'You had a place to live. If you wanted money, you should have asked. Only a monster gives up her new baby.'

'I miss him every day, but this is for the best.' She folded her hands over her heart. On her finger was a gold band.

He reached across the bed and grabbed her left wrist, twisted it around so that the wedding ring was under her nose. 'What else haven't you told me, Amy?'

With all the dignity of a diva, she drew herself up to full height. Gently she removed her hand from his grip. 'Like I said before, it's over between us.'

Twenty-three

By spring, Ted had been at Camp 14A for three months. While the Fantin factor seemed to have settled through the cold months, unseasonal heat was stirring up old dust.

Hot winds from Central Australia blew in great clouds of black cattle flies that numbered in the millions. Like freckles they stuck to the backs of shirts; crawled into eyes and nostrils; and licked the sweat off bare skin. Eating became a health hazard, for each mouthful was peppered with flies. Even the walls of the newly-completed permanent huts did little to stop the invasion. The persistent little buggers were enough to drive some men crazy.

Francesco Fantin was one. Sick of flies crawling all over his head, he sewed hankies onto his hat. The pieces of cloth draped from the hat-brim to his shoulders, enclosing his face in a veil. This was fuel for the rabble-rousers, who began a jovial assault on his manhood.

The breaking point came when one called him '*finocchio*' (faggot). Although half the bully's size, Fantin swung a wild punch that connected with the other man's temple and he dropped like a sack of potatoes. Panicking, Fantin raced towards his sleeping hut. Two of Piselli's henchmen gave chase and tackled him to the ground. Fantin fell hard, the wind knocked out of his sails.

While all this was going on, Ted was watching from the guard tower. He was reluctant to intervene in internee disputes. Dean had made it clear that they were perfectly capable of fighting and resolving their own battles. But this was shaping up to be more serious than a tiff. He rested his hand on the telephone, ready to call for reinforcements if the situation worsened.

Fantin and his tormentor were dusted off and taken to the infirmary. Instinct told Ted that the altercation was not over. Although he relaxed the grip on his rifle, he continued to watch the compound with the eyes of a hawk.

Half an hour later, Fantin re-emerged from the infirmary minus the hat with the veil. He spat on the ground and lit a smoke.

Later in the shade outside his hut he played cards with his comrades. Everyone was talking and joking; their laughter sounded raucous and slightly insane. From time to time they refilled their pannikins from a brown-glass container.

With his own eyes, Ted had seen the still set up in one of the huts. A triumph of ingenuity, it was made from forty-four-gallon drums that had been cut and joined together. Copper-pipe offcuts curled from the top of the apparatus into a separate collection chamber. The ingredients were grapes, sugar, water. *Grappa*, the liquor it produced, was so strong it could have been used to fuel rockets.

Like all the guards, Ted turned a blind eye to the illicit activity. Providing the alcohol caused no trouble, it would have been folly to have taken it away. Even so, the inmates were coy about the still's existence and wore a smirk of collusion whenever it was mentioned. The odd-shaped device was codenamed 'the polenta pot'.

The game of cards outside Fantin's hut went on until the bell sounded for tea. The players packed up their things and wandered to the mess hall. Even when the various cliques converged near the entrance, there was not a word, not a shove, not a jostle.

For the rest of the week, all was quiet.

No, it wasn't quiet. It was *too* quiet.

Something was simmering … and it sure as hell wasn't *grappa*.

Late in October, a large contingent of Italian internees arrived from Western Australia. From the police reports, they were all highly active in the Fascist movement and therefore dangerous men. The police descriptions—*extreme Fascist, fanatical Fascist,* or even *rabid Fascist*— were universal, for the police used emotive shorthand expressions to describe anyone they thought worthy of arrest.

Ted was on duty at compound 14A on the day the Western Australians arrived. They were allocated the newly-completed compound 14D, which was adjacent. Two barbed wire fences and a walkway separated them from the east coasters. Although physical contact was not possible, they could see and call to each other across no-man's land.

To welcome them, the inmates of 14A struck up the Fascist song, *Giovinezza*. In typical style, Francesco Fantin mocked the impromptu performance by laughing and making rude signs. Dropping a hand grenade would not have caused a bigger reaction.

One of the Fascist mob delivered a swift back-hander to Fantin's face. He fell to the ground and curled up in the foetal position. His cronies spirited him away.

Camp Leader Piselli called out to Ted in the guard tower. 'Hey you! We want a prisoner swap. Western Australians in exchange for these bloody Redshirts. Tell the commandant to come straight away or else there'll be a riot.'

Another guard took Ted's place as he hurried off in search of Colonel Dean. Dean's jeep was parked near the guard hut at 14D. It was lucky he'd not yet returned to GHQ after receiving the new inmates. Ted bounded into the hut but no-one was there.

Outside again, he turned this way and that, squinting against the glare. In the distance was a small contingent of men in khaki. He trotted around the outer perimeter fence, found Dean and two senior officers inspecting freshly-dug rabbit holes.

'Those little bastards will make a right mess of our vegetables,' said Dean, kicking the dry earth. 'And it's spring: breeding season. We'd better put out the traps.'

Ted saluted. 'Sir, there's trouble afoot in 14A. Piselli wants a prisoner swap.' He went on to explain what had happened.

Dean sucked on his pipe. 'What do you know about these fellows?'

'If you want names and backgrounds, I can look up their records.'

'That's not what I mean. What's the cause of this continuing conflict?'

Ted thought for a moment. 'Some are from the north of Italy and some are from the south. I've observed that, in general, the northerners behave like they own the place and treat the southerners as second-rate citizens.'

'Where's this Fantin fellow from?' said Dean.

'The north.'

'And his assailant?'

'Also from the north.'

'Hmmm. It must be something else. Piselli said "Redshirts". What are Redshirts exactly?'

Ted shrugged.

'See what you can find out and report back after lunch.'

'Consider it done.' Ted walked away with a spring in his step.

He knew exactly the man to speak to. His name was Tony Zucchero and he was a cane farmer cum accountant from far north Queensland. An educated fellow, he knew what was going on and supported neither faction in the camp. He'd arrived with the last lot from Hay. The official reason for his arrest was 'collusion with the enemy'. In reality, his clients had given him power of attorney over dozens of farms and businesses around Wooranoora. Judging by the number of internees from Wooranoora, the police there must have rounded up every Italian in the district. Ted was certain that Tony Zucchero was as straight as the barbed-wire perimeter fence.

As per the protocol, Ted went directly to the camp leader's office and spoke to Piselli. 'Before Colonel Dean considers your request, he needs more information. In particular, what are your reasons?'

'The trouble-makers in here make it hard for everyone. We must keep the peace.'

'Anything else?'

The camp leader shook his head.

'Can I talk to the internees?'

'Who in particular?'

Ted named a few, taking care to include some of Piselli's *carabinieri* corps as well as Tony Zucchero. He was careful to avoid mention of Fantin and his supporters, which was sure to meet opposition.

'No problem. I'll get them straight away. You want an interpreter?'

'Yes, good idea.' For once the doctor seemed cooperative.

One by one in alphabetical order, Ted interviewed the men in a closed office. The *carabinieri* told the same story as their leader. 'Keep the peace' was something of a Party line. They were tight-lipped about everything else and Ted obtained no new information. He timed each interview: ten minutes. That way he'd not appear to play favourites.

He expected that Tony Zucchero would be a different matter entirely. Although there was a lot of ground to cover, Ted allocated the same amount of time. He dismissed the interpreter, for the accountant's English was better than his own.

The meeting began with a shake of hands. Without the usual pleasantries, Ted began. 'I'll be straight with you, Mr Zucchero. Your camp leader has requested a prisoner swap: Western Australians in 14D for Redshirts in 14A. Do you know why?'

The other man glanced around the office. Satisfied they were completely alone, he answered in a quiet and even voice. 'Then I'll be straight with you, Lieutenant. This compound is run by the Fascists. The camp leader and his police are all fanatics. Anyone who doesn't support

Mussolini doesn't stand a chance. Fantin and his friends are Redshirts. Communists, if you like. They oppose everything Fascism stands for. Most of the inmates here are moderates. They'll go along with anything just to keep the peace.'

Keep the peace. There was that phrase again.

Tony Zucchero continued. 'Others couldn't give a rat's arse. However, everyone here is at risk. Going against the powerbrokers means your life isn't worth living. That said, a prisoner swap will add more Fascists to an already strong power base. You may be playing right into their hands. Perfect conditions for an uprising or breakout. If I were Colonel Dean, I'd be extremely cautious.'

'Thank you, I'll let him know. Any other suggestions?'

'Watch Fantin. He's your canary in the coalmine.'

'Thanks again. If there's anything I can do ...'

'There is something. I've written dozens of letters to my wife but haven't heard back. Could you make contact with her? Find out if she and my children are okay?'

He helped himself to a piece of writing paper on the desk, scribbled Edith's name and the address, care of the Wooranoora Post Office.

'I'll see what I can do.'

After Ted reported his findings to Colonel Dean, a meeting of all the commanding officers in the camp was called. Dean outlined the problem, which he called 'factional unrest', and allowed ample time for discussion about how best to handle it. Each officer put forward his own views and gave anecdotes to back them up.

The officer in charge of Camp 9 said, 'If this prisoner exchange were to proceed, it would create a precedent which could compromise the security of the entire camp. The Fascists would have us eating out of their hands. Such a move would prove that the power belongs to Mussolini and not to the Australian military. By all means, we must keep the peace, but on *our* terms, not theirs.'

The Camp 10 commanding officer said, 'If their request, which seems reasonable, is denied and a riot or other calamity results, the blame will rest squarely on us.'

The more they spoke, the more obvious it became that the mixed compounds should be reviewed and some of the various nationalities and persuasions should be segregated. The minute-keeper recorded that the Germans were 'arrogant, appreciated strict discipline and firm control'.

The Italians were 'naturally temperamental, needed firm handling, but once shown who was in control had to be led like a schoolboy'.

The Japanese were 'subservient, model prisoners'. Their fanatical desire to maintain 'face' made them easy to handle in their eagerness to obey all orders and instructions to the letter.

Dean called the meeting back to order and summarised what had been said. He added, 'Lieutenant Long has done some excellent research which has shed light on possible motives for this prisoner swap request. In my opinion, they are entirely political. While we have encouraged the internees to take control within the compounds, we must not allow them to control us or undermine our decisions.

'For that reason, I shall ask the camp leader of 14A to make his request through the usual channels. That means lodging a formal application with the Swiss Consul, which will go through the diplomatic process. As camp commandant, I shall contribute my recommendations before a formal response is made.'

In awe, Ted shook his head at the cleverness of the approach. In effect, it meant the decision could be delayed without bringing his integrity into question. In the meantime, the guards would be on high alert, in particular in 14A, in order to prevent further violence between inmates who supported opposing ideologies.

For reasons of his own, Francesco Fantin seemed determined to continue his personal war against the Fascists. Apparently, his next big idea came from a visit to the latrines. He emerged with a mischievous grin and a square of newspaper in his hand.

On that scrap of paper was an advertisement asking people to support the Russian allies, whose soldiers faced a freezing winter fighting the Nazis in northern Europe. The appeal was for sheepskins to be sent from Australia to Stalin's troops. Donations were sought and an address was given.

In secret, Fantin went to work within the compound, collecting as much cash as the inmates could spare. A smart man, he would have carefully picked his marks, for the consequences of being discovered by Piselli and his henchmen would have been dire.

The objective was duly achieved and without interference. On 14 November 1942, a short piece appeared on page five of an Adelaide newspaper.

Support for an Allied victory and admiration for Russia have been expressed by anti-Fascist aliens in a South Australian internment camp. The group set up a collection amongst inmates and as a result have sent a

significant donation to the 'Sheepskins for Russia'
appeal.

Like wildfire, the treason against Italy's alliance with Germany spread throughout Camp 14A. The day after the newspaper article, 'Fantin stinks of death' was written in blood across the wall of his hut. It was only a matter of time before someone acted.

16 November 1942 was a shocker of a day: ninety-eight in the shade and not a breath of breeze. Flies buzz-dived the compound, settled on anything that offered moisture. Blowflies droned inside the huts and loitered in the latrines. Despite the best efforts of the cleaning crews, the rubbish drums seethed with maggots.

At six-thirty in the evening, the sun finally dipped beneath the red ribbon of the horizon, bringing slight relief from the heat. From the guard tower, Ted scanned the compound. Something was up; he could sense it. He brushed the flies off his sleeves and tugged at his sweat-soaked collar. Not six inches away, his rifle was propped up against the wall. His nerves were jumpy; his fingers were itchy.

Then he heard it. A commotion near the infirmary.

One of the *carabinieri* ran out towards him, shouting and waving his hands. 'Hey mister! We got a very sick man. We must get him to the hospital quick.'

Ted made the call for backup then entered the compound.

Inside the infirmary, Francesco Fantin lay unconscious on the bed. Blood was bubbling from his mouth. Piselli explained that in the heat the patient had fainted and struck his head on a piece of wood, or maybe the water tap.

'He's in a bad way. I need better equipment to treat him.'

'Put him on a stretcher. We'll carry him to the hospital,' said Ted.

The camp hospital was in the adjoining compound, which was in the precinct set aside for the Japanese. It was run by a surgeon from the north of Italy who'd arrived in Australia as a political refugee in 1939. Sadly, poor timing and an even poorer choice of associates had landed him in trouble. He'd been arrested and interned, along with his medical practice partner, at the very start of the war.

Ted and another guard lifted the stretcher. The load was light, for Fantin was a slightly-built man. Not once in that hundred-yard journey did he move. Not a groan, not a wince.

In the hospital, the surgeon took one look at the patient and stepped back shaking his head. 'This man is dead. His skull is fractured, his neck is broken, his ribs are smashed.'

'I was told he fainted and hit his head,' said Ted.

The surgeon stroked his chin. 'These injuries are not consistent with a fall. He has been assaulted and has died as a result.'

The police investigation of Fantin's death was a brief but tricky affair. No internee would admit to having seen or heard anything. Everyone, including members of Fantin's clique, had an alibi to prove they were not in the vicinity when he met his end.

But Ted had heard the threats with his own ears.

'Those who speak will die.'

'One Fantin a day from now on.'

Two days later, one of Piselli's men was identified as the alleged perpetrator. However, it remained unclear whether his intention was to kill, or if he was acting in self-defence, or if someone else was behind the attack.

As a result of the death, Commandant Dean ordered an immediate review of the accommodation arrangements within all six Loveday compounds. It was decided that the safety of the internees would take priority over concerns about possible breakouts.

Fascists and Nazis would be held in Camps 14A and 14D respectively. Italian anti-Fascists and neutral long-term residents of Australia would be moved to Camp 9.

Greater security measures and extra guards would be added to the high-risk cluster of compounds at Camp 14. Conversely, the security at the other two camps would become more relaxed.

Ted applied for and was granted two weeks' furlough in order to visit his sister in Brisbane. For once, he was glad to be out of the place.

Twenty-four

Brisbane, 26 November 1942

At three o'clock Thursday afternoon, Edith finished her shift at the munitions factory in Salisbury and caught the train to Central Station. She'd arranged to meet Amy and her brother, an officer at the Loveday internment camp, who was on short leave in Brisbane. By now Edith had received several one-page letters from her husband but none had been particularly informative. The censorship of important bits persisted and she wondered if the same had happened to the letters she'd written to him. She hoped that meeting Amy's brother would bring her some peace of mind and confirm that he was indeed as healthy and well-accommodated as he claimed.

She left the station by way of 'the clocks', a row of ten timepieces set in a sandstone wall. Each face showed the time in the famous cities of the world. London, New York, San Francisco, Colombo, Singapore, Hong Kong. She walked down the staircase, bypassed the row of sandbagged air-raid shelters built down the middle of Ann Street, and stepped over the pipe carrying water from the river, a firefighting provision in case of an attack.

Gnawing on the inside of her mouth, she trudged down the Edward Street hill towards the cafe where they'd arranged to meet. She would have to come clean about her name. All this time, ever since the unlikely friendship that had sprung up with Amy in the air-raid shelter, Edith had been using her maiden name.

The name Allenby had been good to her. It had gained her a job and a regular income. Without it she never would have started the tutoring business, which she ran in the afternoons on the verandah of her parents' home.

In Brisbane, the name Zucchero—the Italian word for *sugar*—would have been poison. Everyone distanced themselves from the Italians. Even women like her, who'd married an Italian, were shunned. As Zucchero, Edith would have lived under a cloud. Parents would not have trusted her to teach their children. The munitions factory, whose existence and location were top secret, would never have considered her for the job.

In order get information from Amy's brother, she would have to admit to the lie. She wondered how Amy would react. But more importantly she worried whether it was such a good idea to divulge her identity to a soldier who might have authority over her husband's welfare. At the time, when Amy suggested the meeting, Edith had jumped at the invitation. Who wouldn't have? But would her deception turn them both against her?

Outside the American Postal Exchange store a crowd had gathered. This was the largest of the PX stores in Brisbane and was off-limits to Australian servicemen and civilians, who had to rely on making-do, home-made, or rations. Some enterprising young women had taken advantage of the situation by becoming friendly with GIs in exchange for scarce commodities which were easily converted to black-market cash.

Edith waited for the policeman on points duty to wave them across. Two GIs were standing on the corner. One was bemoaning the fact that he'd walked the streets and couldn't find anywhere that served meals of roasted turkey.

As a meat, turkey was unheard of in Brisbane. It was hard enough to get chicken. Dressed poultry was not available in shops. People raised their own in backyard pens. A chicken dinner was an all-day affair. It meant killing, plucking, and gutting the bird. A messy, smelly, unpleasant task that was guaranteed to turn a meat-lover into a vegetarian.

'Ha! *Turkey* for a mob of *turkeys*.' The flippant remark was made by a passing Australian soldier.

'It's Thanksgiving Day, man. Show some respect,' said the GI.

It was unclear exactly what happened next, but within seconds the pair came to blows. Edith scooted across the road into the safety of the cafe.

For weeks, tensions between the troops had been mounting. The newspapers had picked up on it and sided with the locals. Many of the disputes were due to jealousy and it was easy to see why. The well-dressed, well-mannered, well-heeled Yanks had no trouble attracting girls while the Aussie diggers were missing out.

'Overpaid, oversexed and over here' screamed the headlines. This threw even more fuel on the fire.

The Shingle Inn was packed. Every booth of the wood-panelled cafe was occupied. There were chattering friends, mothers with children, couples on an afternoon date. Black-uniformed waitresses scurried between tables, bearing large trays of teapots, cups, scones and sandwiches. Edith scanned the faces.

At the back, Amy was waving. Sitting beside her was an older man in army uniform.

The women kissed cheeks.

'Edith, this is my brother, Lieutenant Ted Long.'

Ted made an awkward grin, an indication he was shy with women. 'Pleased to meet you, Mrs Allenby. I've heard a lot about you.'

'All good, I hope.' Edith's palms were moist with sweat.

Amy said, 'Of course, silly. Now, I've already taken the liberty of ordering tea and scones. Otherwise we'll never get served.'

After the preliminary chit-chat—the unseasonal hot weather, the chaotic state of the city battened down for war—Edith had the opportunity to ask the question that had been burning her lips all day. 'I understand you live in South Australia, Lieutenant.'

'Yes, Barmera in the Riverland district. I'm stationed at Loveday.'

'I think my husband Tony might be there. Perhaps you know him?'

'Amy asked me. I'm afraid not.'

Edith dropped her eyes and fidgeted with her serviette.

A waitress came and dealt out the food and tea-things from a tray.

'Sorry, Mrs Allenby. You must miss him a lot.' Looking completely out of his depth, Ted tugged at his shirt collar.

Edith glanced around the room; it was blurry through her tears. She reached across the table and squeezed her friend's wrist. 'Please forgive me, Amy. I haven't been entirely honest with you.'

'Whatever about?'

'Allenby is my maiden name. I use it because of the war.'

Edith lowered her voice to barely a whisper. 'My husband is Antonio Zucchero. He was taken prisoner for no reason other than his Italian ancestry. He's not a Fascist and he's done nothing wrong. I believe he's in an internment camp somewhere in South Australia. I haven't heard from him in weeks; I'm desperate to know if he's all right.'

Amy's mouth half-opened in surprise. Then she clasped Edith's hand, gave it a squeeze, and murmured into her ear. 'You never judged me about *you-know-what*, and I won't judge you either.'

Ted seemed lost in thought. Presently he said, 'Zucchero. Yes, I *do* know him. He's a good man. Don't worry, he is fine. He teaches English and bookkeeping and works in the gardens. He's well-liked by everyone, prisoners and guards alike.'

Edith's cheeks were running with tears. 'Thank you, Lieutenant Long. I can't tell you how much this means to me. To know he is well is beyond words. Please, could you give him this?' She rummaged in her handbag for an envelope. 'It's not sealed. You may read what's inside if you wish. I understand about wartime security and all that.'

Ted took the envelope and folded it into his pocket. 'There's no need for me to read it, Mrs Zucchero. I'll hand-deliver your letter as soon as I return.'

By the time they finished afternoon tea, it was going on four o'clock. Down the street outside the PX store, an agitated crowd of servicemen from both sides of the Pacific was milling about. The rabble could be heard blocks away. Tension crackled like a bushfire. The men spilled out across the footpath and onto Adelaide Street. US Military Police blew whistles and drew guns. The mob surged forward. The MPs were outnumbered fifty to one.

'It'll be hot in the old town tonight,' said Ted, steering the women in the opposite direction.

Amy hugged her chest. 'Edith, we'll walk you to the tram stop.'

They hurried up the hill. From behind came the sound of breaking glass and sirens. A megaphone voice ordered civilians to clear the streets.

The melee continued, on and off, for two days and two nights.

The front page of *The Courier Mail* reported a Russian victory over Germany with six thousand Axis troops killed. The rather less-bloody 'Battle of Brisbane' received coverage on page three. By the end of the riot, six servicemen had been shot, one fatally, and three other people had been injured.

The clergy had a field day, blaming liquor and the decline of Faith as reasons for 'the degeneration of today's youth'. Although a public enquiry was called for, the event was largely hushed-up in order to prevent bad blood between soldiers who were supposed to be Allies.

After the conversation with Ted about Loveday, Edith's mind was set at ease. Although she missed her husband terribly, she was no longer worried that his treatment was like the ugly reports of prisoner-of-war camps in Nazi Germany.

With sufficient income flowing from her munitions job and the tutoring work, it was a welcome bonus when the cheque arrived from the mill at the end of the crushing season. Her neighbours, the Sampsons, had been managing the farm in her absence and Edith paid them for their trouble. The mill cheque also covered the overdraft repayments and gave her a buffer for the following year.

When it seemed her fortune had turned a corner, the unexpected happened.

After morning smoko, the forewoman called Edith off the factory floor. 'Telephone call for you. Take it upstairs.'

As Edith raced up the metal staircase to the spartan office on the mezzanine, her blood was running cold. Was there an accident? Was her father sick? What about the children? In the space of two minutes her imagination played out a series of equally awful scenarios.

Puffing, she picked up the receiver and held it to her ear. 'Hello?'

'Darling. Before you get anxious, everyone here is fine.' It was her mother's no-nonsense voice. 'A telegram came for you. Should I open it?'

Edith didn't know whether to feel relieved or more worried. Had something happened to her husband?

'Please open it.'

'Oh my dear, I'm afraid the news is not good.'

In Edith's experience, telegrams *never* brought good news. 'So ...?'

Her mother read out the message. '*Oscar Sampson has passed away. Call me ASAP re your farm.* It's signed Sergeant Pitt, Wooranoora Police.'

Tears sprang to Edith's eyes. 'He was such a dear man. Nothing was too much trouble. Poor Mrs Sampson! What will she do now? They didn't have any children and treated me like their daughter. I must go and pay my respects. I'll call Sergeant Pitt from a payphone later.'

'Do whatever you think is best. We'll talk it through when you get home.'

Edith replaced the receiver, plodded slowly down the stairs, and took her place in the line of women who assembled hand grenades and shells for a living.

Two days later, Edith caught the Cairns-bound train, leaving the children in the care of their grandparents. At sixty-three, her mother was an active and capable woman and she loved the kids as her own. Less could be said of her father, who had been forced out of the stockbroking firm due to the legacy of the Great Depression and a longer-than-expected war. Lately he'd turned to his cellar of wines and spirits—collected over a lifetime of easy money—in the hope of finding comfort.

Never before had Edith been away from her babies; an indefinite absence weighed on her conscience.

After disembarking in Wooranoora, she carried her port the short distance to the Italian Boarding House, hoping to leave it with Mrs Ross until she sorted out the police paperwork and arranged transport to the farm.

The front door of the boarding house was shut. Surprising. Usually that door remained open day and night, and had done so ever since she moved to Wooranoora. She raised her hand and knocked, but she could already feel the emptiness. In front, the grass was long and straggly. The ashes of hundreds of cane fires were like a carpet on the verandah. Window panes were smashed, glass littered the ground. As if in a dream she left her port by the door and wandered down the side of the building.

The backyard was a jungle; creepers clambered over one another and completely overran the outhouses. The clothes line—a set of wires strung between posts on either side of the yard—had become a trellis for vines. In the banana grove, overripe bunches had been molested by flying foxes.

It was obvious that no-one had lived there for some time.

At the police station, Sergeant Pitt explained that Oscar Sampson's funeral had taken place a week earlier. His widow had gone south to stay with her sister until the end of the war.

'So, nobody is managing either my farm or the Sampsons?'

'Correct. I presume the farm is in your husband's name.'

'I guess so. He owned it before we were married.'

The sergeant reached beneath the desk for a form. 'The amount of cane grown here has taken a terrible dive but the mill must continue to operate. If there are no other options, I have the authority to appoint the Public Curator to operate the farm on your husband's behalf. Even if you don't agree, I am *obliged* to appoint the Public Curator so that the supply of sugar is not jeopardised.'

'What if I were to employ a manager?'

Pitt laughed mockingly. 'And where, Mrs Zucchero, would you find a man capable of managing a cane farm? In case you hadn't noticed, all the Italians have gone and the military has appropriated the machinery from abandoned farms for the war effort. Even if, by some miracle, you found such a person, he'd be lucky to harvest a crop.'

'We'll soon see about that!' She turned on her heel to leave.

'Okay, I'll play your silly game. You have one week to find a farm manager. If I don't get a name by then, it's the Public Curator.'

'You'll have a name. That, I promise you.' Already a plan was forming. All she needed was the courage to carry it out.

Twenty-five

With a port in his hand and a blanket-roll under his arm, Tony Zucchero stood at the door of Luigi's hut. His expectant grin ran from ear to ear.

As soon as they saw him, the inmates from the far north pumped his hand and bundled him into the hut. They regaled him with cigarettes and pieces of precious chocolate. He'd always been a popular fellow who involved himself in every sporting event, social occasion, and fundraiser in Wooranoora.

Although Luigi was delighted to see Tony, part of him was gutted. The arrangements he'd made for the farm and boarding house had now come unstuck. What would become of their properties now that both brothers, and also their appointed administrator, were all behind a barbed wire fence?

Tony Zucchero was never supposed to be interned. He'd been in the country since he was a kid; his wife Edith was British-Australian. As well as that he was the best cane farmer in the district and the most honest person Luigi knew.

Surrounded by the welcoming party, Tony told them about the Fantin murder, which he thought had been a catalyst in the prisoner reshuffle.

'*Mamma mia!* There's been nothing as bad as that here,' said Angelo sitting on the edge of the bed.

'It's certainly good to be amongst friends again,' Tony added. 'And a relief to be out of that rats' nest in 14A.'

A bottle of camp-made wine was opened and someone made a toast.

'To victory!'

'No,' said Tony. 'To our release.'

They raised their tin pannikins and quaffed the young red wine.

Later, when Tony and Luigi were alone in the hut, Tony spoke about the day of the murder and how no-one dared to speak up. 'In my opinion, they got the wrong man.'

Luigi raised his eyebrows, thick as two black caterpillars.

Sotto voce, Tony said, 'The man who swung the weapon might have done the fatal deed but in my opinion the doctor was behind it.'

'Piselli?' breathed Luigi.

Tony nodded.

'He was sent away from this camp because he made a lot of trouble,' said Luigi.

'Always watch your back. People aren't what they seem.'

'Well, we don't need to worry about Piselli anymore. While Del Drago is our leader, he'll never return to this camp.'

In silence, they smoked. The last shards of daylight were cutting patterns on the hut wall. There was no need to rush; the hands of time moved slowly.

Tony lay back on the bed, folded his arms behind his head and sighed. 'I owe you an apology, my friend.'

'What for?'

'I promised to look after your affairs but I've failed. I promised to look after lots of other people's too. That's probably why I was arrested. Too much control. Someone wanted to get me. But the person they are really punishing is my dear Edith.' His eyes misted. 'She was expecting another child when I was arrested, but I didn't know until after he was born. Baby Anthony arrived last November.'

'What wonderful news! Congratulations!'

'Two weeks ago he turned one. One whole year and I haven't seen a photo.'

Luigi didn't know what to say.

'I was arrested just after you. Edith and the little ones have been staying with the in-laws in Brisbane, so I suppose our farms have gone to ruin.' Tony sighed again. 'This bloody war! It goes on and on.'

'It's not so bad. We have our health; there's plenty to eat here. Edith and your children are safe. Our land is still there; a bit of work and the cane will be growing again.'

Tony sat up and slapped him on the back. 'You're right, Luigi. I must stop feeling sorry for myself. The most important things are family and friends.'

'Come with me and I'll show you around.'

Doing the rounds of the huts, Tony was greeted by scores of men from the far north. Everywhere he went, they came to shake his hand and ask where he'd been and what he'd been doing. The centre of attention, he was right in his element. The frown lines melted and he looked like the young man he was.

Luigi kept the best part of the tour until last. Gino, who had just started his shift, let them into the kitchen and took over the commentary. He showed Tony the long strands of fresh pasta, looped over broom handles. The prosciutto made in autumn was now as dry as wood. Gino shaved off a few pieces for them to sample. It was satisfyingly chewy and had the perfect amount of salt.

Gino said, 'Next year there'll be lots more of this wonderful stuff.'

He told them of a scheme to build a piggery. The Germans in Camp 10 had complained about the never-ending supply of mutton and had put in a request for more pork. According to Gino's sources, Dean had taken the idea on board and would let them know in a few weeks.

Tony shook his head in disbelief. 'Everything here is so organised and controlled. In 14A, we were living under a perpetual cloud. Hatchet-men and spies everywhere. Whatever suggestions we made were completely ignored.'

Gino shrugged. 'Del Drago's a good leader. He works *with* our captors, not against them.'

'There's plenty of paid work and lots of activities,' Luigi added.

Tony said, 'In 14A, we weren't allowed to work. Anyone who did was punished. It was awfully boring and there were fights every day. To keep myself occupied, I gave English classes for free. But Piselli frowned upon that too. "When we win the war, we won't need English. We will all speak Italian," he used to say.'

Luigi had heard that sentiment before. He remembered Carlo Monte, the crazy Fascist from Wooranoora and his rage against everything this country held dear. Perhaps he, too, had fallen under Piselli's spell.

Gino glanced at his wristwatch. 'Sorry, I've got to get cracking. Can't keep hungry men waiting.'

Luigi and Tony strolled down the central path away from the kitchen. They passed the canteen with its display of temptations: stone fruit, boiled lollies, cigarettes. Continuing, they passed the hospital and camp leader's hut. Del Drago would be in his office, talking to inmates about problems or disputes. His secretary would be planning next week's work roster or tallying up payments for the previous week.

Further down the path were the latrines, the ablutions block, and the laundry. Three men with towels tied around their waists were at the concrete washtubs, dipping and scrubbing. Clothes, pegged to lines strung between the huts, flapped like bunting.

A good distance beyond was the hobbies workshop. The door was open so they went in. As usual, it was a buzz of activity. It was Thursday: parquetry day. Various wooden shapes were sorted into piles on the bench. Half a dozen internees were sawing or sanding or gluing the pieces under the guidance of the master artisan, Vecchio.

Proudly, Luigi lifted his half-finished box from beneath the bench. The pattern was herringbone, dark wood alternating with blond. Each slat, half an inch wide, perfectly abutted its neighbour. 'I've always wanted to learn. This is my first attempt.'

'Why, it's beautiful!' Tony skipped his fingers across the lid.

'Every day there are classes. You can learn a language, or European history, or how to make a pair of boots. There's also a theatre troupe that puts on plays and musicals.'

'What about paid work?' said Tony.

'As you know, I'm a cook. Angelo does farm work. Every day he goes out on the truck. I don't know exactly what they grow. Some special crop. He's a bit tight-lipped about it.

'You can do woodcutting, or cleaning, or construction work. Mostly you get a flat rate of pay: one shilling per day. Some fellows run classes and charge sixpence a lesson. The sky's the limit if you're smart.'

Tony's eyes were sparkling. 'That's fantastic! I could teach English and bookkeeping and law. Time passes quicker when you're busy.'

A Turning Point

Twenty-six

Loveday, March 1943

Time passed quickly indeed. Before Luigi knew it, the dry heat of summer was over and it was autumn. The tides of war in Europe had apparently turned in favour of the Allies. News of Allied victories, no matter how small, was communicated to the internees as if to prove resistance was futile. Although he kept his thoughts to himself, Luigi celebrated their every success. Every battle won was one step closer to the end. And the sooner the bloody war was over, the sooner they'd be going home to their farms.

Now the most feared enemy was not the Axis forces but the Japs, who were playing by their own set of rules and pushing south through the islands of Malaya and the East Indies. Darwin had been bombed the year before; Aussie diggers were slogging it out in the jungles of New Guinea.

In Camp 9, life went on unchanged. One day after another, the same as the one before. Same faces, same activities, same routines.

Cold winds brought in rain. Not the heavy deluge that made Wooranoora famous as one of the wettest towns in the country, but a constant dreary drizzle that left a moist film over the landscape.

Luigi was in the kitchen, warmed by the wood-fired ovens and the rush of activity. It was mid-morning. He was chopping vegetables for minestrone, hurrying to get everything done in time for lunch at noon.

The door flew open and Tony Zucchero dashed in.

'It's Angelo,' he puffed. 'Come quick.'

Luigi dropped the knife and raced past Tony to the door. The open truck that transported the work crews had stopped outside the camp

179

hospital. Several men in maroon uniform were milling about; some were carrying a stretcher.

With a sinking heart, he ran towards them.

Angelo's face was ashen; his pallor was accentuated by the dirty-beetroot colour of his work uniform. His eyes were shut but he was not asleep. His chest rose and fell in an alarming manner. It was clear he was fighting for breath.

The doctor came out, stethoscope in hand, and told the stretcher-bearers to hurry the patient inside. Luigi remained where he was, preferring to leave the professionals to attend his brother rather than get in the way.

Instead he turned to the work crew. 'What happened?'

'One minute he was working and the next he was lying on the ground.'

'So, he just fainted?'

'I dunno. I suppose. He sort-of fell down and didn't get up.'

Luigi felt an ache in his gut. This fainting thing had happened before. Last time, he'd been diagnosed with influenza. Although Angelo remained ill for a long time, he appeared to have made a complete recovery.

The night before, Angelo had been in fine form. In fact, as they lay in their adjoining bunks he'd said, 'I haven't felt this good in years.'

Outside the hospital Luigi leant on the railing and lit a smoke. The workmates who'd carried the stretcher came out, muttering and shaking their heads.

'Were you there? Did you see what happened?' Luigi said.

They could shed no new light but everyone agreed that Angelo was in a bad way.

Luigi took a deep breath and entered the hospital. In the examination room, the doctor and an assistant were attaching a drip to the patient's arm. Angelo remained unconscious, his weather-beaten face as white as paper.

The doctor glanced up and gave a tight smile. 'You're his brother?'

'*Si*. How is he?'

'He's had quite a turn. We're trying to stabilise him. He may need to be transferred to the larger hospital in Camp 14 where there's better equipment.'

'What's wrong with him?'

'We need to do tests but I think it's his heart.'

'*O Dio!*' Luigi took a shocked step backwards. Angelo was more than a brother; he was a best friend and a lifelong companion. A strong, patient man who always put others before himself. Although the age difference was not great, to Luigi he'd been a second father. He was the voice of reason whenever the world went mad. To lose him now …

'It's Luigi,' he whispered into Angelo's ear. 'You must get through this.'

The form on the bed lay still. Then, with an effort, a forefinger lifted from the bed.

'Look! He can hear me!'

'That's promising,' said the doctor. 'For now, he needs rest. I'll let you know if there's any change.'

Luigi plodded down the steps. He lit another cigarette, said a prayer to San Filippo on his brother's behalf, and debated what he should do. After ten minutes of wandering around in circles, he headed back to the kitchen. Activity was an antidote: it would help him forget his troubles.

He weighed the cook's knife in his hand. For a moment, he gazed at the long broad blade and wondered if he could continue. Then he remembered the men who depended on him for their midday meal. He took a peeled carrot, pressed the knife against its middle, felt the crisp crack against the board, smelt the sweet juice. He took another and another until he was back in the rhythm.

Soon the pot was bubbling on the burner; the hearty aroma of the minestrone drifted into his nostrils. Wholesome and comforting.

Gino came in with a bunch of big round seedpods. He shook the pods and they rattled like castanets. 'Who likes poppy seed cake?'

'Where'd you get those?' said Luigi.

'The work crew on the truck brought them back.'

'You mean, the truck that's outside the hospital?'

'*Si.* They were harvesting opium. Some of the seedpods were dry, so they picked them.'

Despite his worries, Luigi began to chuckle. 'You mean to say that my brother has been growing *opium* poppies and this is the first I've heard of it?'

'It's all legit,' said Gino. 'Done under CSIRO supervision to make painkillers.'

'How do you know these things?'

Gino tapped his nose. 'I have my sources.'

'Okay, let's do it for Angelo.'

After lunch, Luigi was told that his brother had been transferred to the hospital at Camp 14. He was also told that the doctor-in-charge was a highly-regarded surgeon who had worked in the best hospitals in Italy. Angelo could not have been in more capable hands.

181

In Luigi's pocket was the little pouch with the relic of his saint. He ran his fingers over it and sent up a prayer. Whether it was love, or faith, or friendship, or poppy seed cake, a feeling of well-being flowed through his body. Hope replaced despair.

Twenty-seven

Loveday, March 1943

Because Ted had given evidence at the inquest into Fantin's death and in the resultant civil court case, Colonel Dean offered him a transfer out of 14A. 'Might be safer all round' were Dean's exact words.

To be honest, Ted was most relieved. He had no wish to be associated with men who held grudges. Dr Piselli had been cleared of any wrongdoing in the Fantin case. However, Ted believed he was on the doctor's hitlist for retribution.

Ted assumed he'd go back to Camp 9 with the Italians from far north Queensland. But to his surprise and dismay, he was allocated Camp 10 instead.

Camp 10 had the reputation of being a snake-pit of different nationalities, ethnicities, religions, ideologies, classes, and political beliefs. Nearly all had German or Italian origins. Even so, there was layer upon layer of complexity. Most were civilians who had been captured overseas, specifically in Great Britain, Iran, or Palestine. A few had been living in Australia. There was also a handful of Finnish resistance fighters who'd been captured by the Russians in northern Europe.

The guards classified the Germans into five groups. The largest—inmates who railed against Australia and the Allied war effort—were labelled 'Nazis'. Anti-Nazis, Stalinists, Jews, and general dissidents were lumped together under the label 'communists'. Well-to-do gentry and noblemen were called 'Junkers', after a German honorific title with no English translation. Ex-patriot businessmen and company executives arrested in Europe, Asia, or the Middle East were nicknamed 'commercial mafia'. Lastly, those who showed no allegiance to anything at all were called 'moderates'. What made the camp infamous was the propensity of certain groups to attempt escape.

Around the time Ted took up his new post, the German internees of Camp 10 asked permission to build a European-style coffee house to remind them of home. The structure was to be light and airy with large windows and a high sloping roof. Around it would be a brushwood fence and herb gardens. The crowning glory, right at the centre of the building, would be an open fireplace with a brick chimney. An artist's impression was supplied, along with a draftsman's drawings which showed the dimensions and positioning of the coffee house within the compound. The plan was for the internees to build the main structure using timber and to manufacture the chimney bricks from clay mined within the compound boundaries.

Colonel Dean asked the guards if they had any objections. From the information supplied it seemed like a good idea. Until then the German camp leader had been vehemently opposed to inmates doing any sort of paid work because it would 'help the Allied war effort'. This proposal was a turnabout of sorts. It stood to benefit not only the men who built the coffee house but also other inmates who would have a nice new venue in which to socialise or attend classes.

The sole objection was whether the fireplace would be used to make illicit liquor, but the guard who raised it was quickly shut down by the major in charge.

'The benefits far outweigh the risks.'

Dean called for a vote. Everyone in the room raised his hand and so the request was unanimously approved.

Construction began immediately. The positions of the building and the new gardens were marked out with pegs and string. One of the internees, a geologist, pronounced that the best place for the clay pit was near Hut 44. Topsoil was removed and placed in the garden beds. Rectangular brick moulds were fashioned out of wood. A kiln was built. The area around Hut 44 was alive with activity. Every day, the site crawled with willing workers and a vocal audience gathered to praise or criticise or offer improvements to the design.

From his vantage point in the guard tower, Ted watched the progress of construction. The marked-out site for the cafe building was practically under his nose but his vision of the clay pit was partially obscured by a corner of Hut 44.

Over the course of three weeks the foundations were laid, and the timber frame was put together. All the timbers used on the project were felled and milled by internees at Moorook woodcutting camp situated near the River Murray about half-an-hour's drive from Loveday. The timber was fresh and incredibly hard. The army provided them with the necessary hand-tools to cut, drill, and nail the pieces of the puzzle together.

Other workers began on the fireplace. According to the blueprints, around ten thousand bricks would be required. Clay was plentiful, dug from a wide shallow pit within the barbed wire fence. One by one the moulds were filled with wet clay and lined up to dry. When leather-dry, the bricks were de-moulded and left for a week in the sun before being baked in the kiln. Progress was slow, but the process of brickmaking seemed to give the workers a sense of pride and satisfaction.

The mood in the compound was calm and organised, a far cry from Ted's concerns about trouble-making, escapes, and mutiny. So much so that he wondered why Camp 10 had such a bad reputation. In comparison to the travails of Camp 14A, this was like taking a vacation.

Ted set down his rifle on the guard-tower floor and lit a cigarette. The day was warm, the sky was clear. Nothing much was happening. A blessing, he knew, but it gave him precious little to do but sit and watch. Every day was the same. He found himself wishing for something out-of-the-ordinary to happen to break the boredom.

The thirty or so internee workmen were wearing their maroon fatigues. The attire was always worn outside Loveday, where it was mandatory, but it was usually shunned inside the compounds.

Mentally Ted shrugged. There was no fathoming these German chaps; it seemed their mission in life was to be contrary.

From a distance it was hard to distinguish one man from another; in maroon they all looked the same. One exception was a tall fellow who wore a white neckerchief. The others moved about like red-backed ants, busily following the same paths. Everyone carried buckets, presumably full of clay or water or rubble from the pit. The scrap of white cloth set the tall one apart and made him easy to track. What he did was most peculiar. He moved constantly between the pit and Hut 44. He didn't dig or fill moulds or set out bricks to dry. And he went nowhere near the construction site. It seemed he was doing nothing much at all, apart from wearing out his boots.

Ted unhooked the binoculars from the nail. He honed in on the maroon brigade milling about the pit. Another worker was as bald as an egg. Ted leant his elbows on the railing and focussed in. He too was moving between the pit and the Hut 44. For half hour Ted followed various workers through the binoculars. Eventually he had to put the glasses away; the constant refocussing and jiggling was making him motion sick. But he had seen enough to be on sure ground.

Reaching for the telephone, he called the major. 'Sir, I wish to report unusual activity in the vicinity of the construction site.'

'Go on, Lieutenant.' By the tone of his voice, the major was keenly interested. Perhaps he knew their *modus operandi* better than anyone. From all accounts there had been an overly long period of docility and compliance in the camp. Was this the calm in the eye of the cyclone or was it part of a grand plan?

Ted recounted what he'd seen at the clay pit.

'I'll alert the other guards. Remain at your post and carry on as usual. At the change of shift, come to my office.'

'Yes, sir.' Ted hung up the receiver, wiped sweaty palms on his trousers, and checked his wristwatch. It was going on eleven-thirty. Shift change was at twelve-fifteen, when the internees would be safely inside the mess hall for lunch. He gripped his rifle and, for the next thirty minutes until the lunch bell rang, he continued to watch the workmen swarm around the pit. Nothing else happened at all.

At twelve-thirty, the five duty guards gathered in the major's office. No-one else had noticed anything untoward in the compound.

Thoughtfully the major stroked his jaw and turned to Ted. 'On a scale of one to ten, how confident are you that these *unusual activities* indicate subversion?'

Put on the spot and feeling alone, Ted wavered. 'About a six, sir. The evidence, admittedly, is flimsy. However, I've seen desperate men before and know what they are capable of. Better safe than sorry.'

'Fair enough, Lieutenant Long. You and I shall pay a visit while the inmates are eating lunch. One way or another, this mystery will be solved.'

Inside the perimeter fence of Camp 10, the pair walked directly to the clay pit. It was broader and shallower than it appeared from the guard tower. All those bricks had used up a surprisingly small amount of clay. Ted retraced the footsteps of the white-neckerchief man, which led to Hut 44. The hut sat on stumps; the floorboards were a foot off the ground. Two steps up and they were inside.

The dormitory was neat and tidy and the floorboards had been freshly swept. All the bunks were made in the precision style of the military: sheets tucked in as tight as drums and blankets folded on top. Shelves ran along the walls and luggage racks jutted out overhead. Each inmate had ample space to stow his stuff. Books were plentiful; the shelves were full of them. Ted strolled the length of the central aisle, casting his eyes from one side to the other. Everything was in order, nothing was out of place.

The two officers looked quizzically at each other.

Ted shrugged. 'Sorry, sir. It seems I was mistaken.'

'Let's look outside,' said the major. 'We'll split up and see what we can find.'

Ted began walking clockwise around the exterior of Hut 44 and his commanding officer went the other way.

On the northern side of the building was a herb garden with a newly-laid brick edge. In the middle of the garden was a large clay pot which held a massive rosemary bush. The pot, the same colour as Loveday clay, sat on a slab of wood about eighteen inches square. Around it was crumbled clay, an indication it had been recently moved.

Ted stepped into the garden bed. Breathing the fragrance of bruised rosemary, he clasped the pot and heaved with all his might. It lifted easily. Too easily. A pot that size and full of soil should have weighed around sixty pounds. He lifted the lower branches of the rosemary bush and found it had not been planted in the pot *per se*, but in a one-gallon container placed inside the empty pot.

Furthermore, the soil around the wooden slab showed signs of having been disturbed. He stamped on the slab with his boot; it echoed like an empty box.

By this time, the major had arrived. 'What is it, Lieutenant?'

'Sir, can you give me a hand?'

Together they lifted the slab. Beneath it was a hole large enough for a man.

Ted eased himself in. Wooden wedges had been driven into the sides as footholds. The drop to the bottom was around six feet. Then there was a ninety-degree turn and the hole became a tunnel.

The tunnel was fifty yards long. It commenced at Hut 44, ran beneath the inner perimeter fence and continued into no-man's land. Another week and it would have been through to freedom.

The ploy used by the Nazis to disguise the rubble was immediately obvious. Waste from the tunnel was transferred to the clay pit where it was used to make bricks. That explained the never-ending supply of clay and the over-abundance of bricks.

The tunnel was promptly demolished but the coffee house was allowed to continue to completion. The German internees ousted the existing camp leader and elected one of the moderates in his stead. There were no further attempts at escape.

Twenty-eight

Wooranoora, March 1943

As promised, by the end of the week Edith gave Sergeant Pitt the name of a manager for her husband's cane farm.

If Pitt was surprised, he took pains not to show it. Instead, he calmly opened a notebook and licked the end of an indelible pencil. 'Mr Ewan Allenby,' he said as he wrote the name. 'Postal address and telephone?'

'Care of the post office at Wooranoora. No telephone.'

'I do hope Mr Allenby is suitably qualified for the position.'

'His references are impeccable.' Edith smiled to herself. It had not been easy to tell such a lie, but she was desperate. It was imperative that she keep control of the farm. She resolved to not discuss it with her father, who'd been pleading with her to return to Brisbane. The less he knew about the deception, the better.

When Edith looked around Wooranoora all she could see was evidence that the Public Curator, so far removed from the rural north, had neither the skill nor the manpower to operate a multitude of abandoned cane farms. Scores of once-productive properties were now overrun with weeds. By the end of next season, it would be a miracle if there'd be enough cane for the mill to process.

'I look forward to meeting your manager then,' said the sergeant. 'When does he start?'

Behind her back, she crossed her fingers. 'Oh, he's already started,' she said airily.

After departing the police station, Edith bought supplies from the Chinaman's store and drove herself to *The Manor* in the old Ford truck. Luckily the farmhouse was separated from most others in the district. Unless you were a local or knew where the property was, it would be easy to miss the turnoff. So far this had worked in her favour. The military had not touched any of the vehicles, equipment, or machinery. The house was exactly as she'd left it, save for a forest of shoulder-high grass.

The wet season was drawing to an end, but the ground was still boggy. Soon she'd need to attend to the planting. In the past she'd relied on the Yugoslavs from the boarding house, but that avenue was now closed. Instead of the bustle of seasonal workers, now there were red-eyed wives who struggled to survive on their own and squadrons of soldiers moving equipment and troop carriers between towns. Air-raid shelters had been built along Sugarmill Street and a brown-out, the same as Brisbane, was in force.

In the cane fields, the ratoon was growing nicely. The back paddock had been ploughed, thanks to the Sampsons. Without their help, the farm would have been in the same dreadful state as all the other Italian farms that had been forcibly vacated without notice. Poor Mr Sampson. She made herself a promise to visit the cemetery on the northern outskirts of town and pay her respects. As for Mrs Sampson, Edith had written her a letter of condolence, which she'd left with the postmaster for forwarding. It would have been nice to have returned the favour by planting the Sampson's property too. But, as it was, Edith already had her work cut out.

As soon as the rain clouds lifted, Edith took her husband's cane knife and hacked a path to the machinery shed. The two tractors were parked side by side: an old blue Fordson and a yellow Caterpillar crawler. The implements—plough, scarifier, disc harrow—were rust red, despite being stored under cover. On the southern end of the shed were three drums used to store fuel: one for diesel, one for kerosene, one for petrol. Fuel was nigh-on impossible to buy, for the military had first call. She held her breath and tapped the drums with the edge of the cane-knife.

Tong. The deep resonating tone indicated they were practically full.

She placed the cane knife on a fuel drum and walked over to the Fordson. Although she'd never driven a tractor, she'd watched Tony often enough to know that the engine could be a mongrel to start. Gingerly she hauled herself up onto the bum-shaped driver's seat, wiggled the levers, and examined the workings.

She remembered a long-ago explanation of Tony's that there were two fuel tanks: petrol and kero. Somewhere along the side of the machine were the on-off taps and a glass fuel bowl; the crank handle was right at the front. Things had to be done in the right order, otherwise the engine wouldn't start and that would be the end of that.

With hands on hips she circumnavigated the tractor, pausing to poke at the various levers and switches in the hope of finding inspiration. To be perfectly honest, she was scared of it. If only she could ask someone for instructions.

But there was no-one to ask. If she wanted to clear around the house to control snakes and vermin, she must do it herself. She needed to take stock so she went back to the house for a good strong cup of tea and a biscuit. And to give herself a stern talking-to.

Later, in a more positive frame of mind, she filled the Fordson's fuel tanks, turned on the petrol tap and checked that the bowl was pink. She heaved on the crank handle, got the engine to fire and let it idle a while. Then came the moment of truth. Nervously holding her breath, she switched over from petrol to kero. The engine spluttered once then roared.

Woo-hoooooooo! She squealed like a kid on a fairground ride.

She reversed the tractor out of the shed, made a turn, and backed up close to the disc harrow. Climbing down, she hitched the implement in place and dropped in the pin. Back in the driver's seat, she pushed the gear lever to forward and took a practice run across the yard. Once she got a feel for it, the job was easy. In an hour the long grass was reduced to mulch and the ibis moved in for a feast. After returning the machinery to the shed, she disconnected the disc harrow and shut off the fuel.

Perhaps she *could* manage on her own. Today she'd proven to herself that she could handle a tractor. With the Fordson, she could plough and drill and fertilize. If she could hire a couple of workers, she could have the back paddock planted by May. But where would she find able bodies in a town that was deserted of men?

A brilliant idea burst into her head. If men weren't available, she'd hire *women*. A few months earlier, the Australian Women's Land Army (AWLA) had become a national service. To help with the war effort, city women were recruited to work in rural areas. The newspapers had already reported a number of successes. In Stanthorpe, the AWLA had harvested stone fruit that would have otherwise been left to rot on the trees. On the Darling Downs they'd ploughed wheat fields, planted cotton, and cared for orphan lambs. While there had been a bit of pushback from staunch unionists, the farmers welcomed them with open arms. That their pay was a fraction of a man's wage was an added bonus. City women wouldn't be skilled in cane farming, but Edith knew they'd learn fast and work hard. All she had to do was make a phone call.

Three weeks later, a team of five young women arrived on the train. They'd come all the way from Sydney, their fares paid by the government. In preparation, Edith had cleaned the canecutters' barracks, white-washed the walls, made curtains from two old dresses, and filled a vase with canna lilies cut from the garden. The place looked bright and welcoming.

She drove to the station to pick them up. They were dressed for action in overalls, sandshoes, and broad-brimmed hats. In turn they shook her hand as if she were a man and introduced themselves.

Betty, Grace, Elsie, Violet, Dot.

'No *Miss* or *Mrs* formalities for us,' said Dot. 'Using Christian names is the latest thing in Sydney.'

Edith smiled. 'Welcome to Wooranoora, ladies. People are a little old-fashioned here. In town I'm *Mrs Zucchero* but you can call me *Edith*.'

The *girls*, as they preferred to be called, climbed into the tray of the truck. At *The Manor* they exclaimed in delight at their surroundings. Not only the neat accommodation, which they applauded, but also the emerald cane fields, the broad indigo sky, the riot of birds.

At daybreak next morning, the girls went to work. Edith showed them how lay the stalks of green cane along the drills, and chop them into foot-long lengths before covering them with soil. The six women worked shoulder-to-shoulder for seven days straight: four hours in the morning and four in the afternoon with a long rest break in the middle to avoid the heat of the sun.

Not once did anyone swear or complain. The girls were quick, neat, and efficient, and completely different to the swaggering Yugoslavs, who liked to drink slivovitz at sundown and sing long into the night.

Starved for female company, Edith had taken to eating her meals in the barracks with the girls. While she supplied the ingredients, they all shared the cooking. Dinner, the main meal of the day, was served at noon. Usually there would be damper and a salad of fresh vegetables from the garden. The main dish would be all-in stew or *meat surprise*—so named because it contained no meat at all, hence the surprise—or fried fish, which they trapped in the nearby Russell River.

The girls regaled her with stories of Sydney. Dancehalls, dress shops, picnics by the Harbour, backyard parties on Saturday nights. All single and in aged their twenties, their lives sounded carefree and uncomplicated in comparison to Edith's. It was hard not to envy them. For the first time in years, she began to relax and enjoy herself.

At the end of the week, Constable Moody paid them a visit. It seemed that the Wooranoora police were also the agency for Manpower, the federal government body that arranged work for the AWLA. All the women were sitting on the verandah of the cookhouse. They'd just finished dinner. Betty was clearing the dirty dishes and Violet was pouring cups of tea.

'Good afternoon, ladies. I'm looking for the manager, Mr Allenby.'

Edith scrambled to her feet. 'He's gone to Cairns on business. I'm his daughter. Can I help?' She gave him her most dazzling smile.

'I wanted to check that the work he ordered through the Women's Land Army has been done to his satisfaction.'

'Absolutely! The planting will be finished today. The girls have done a great job.'

'Good. It seems word travels fast. Other farmers in the district are clamouring to engage their services.' He took a small notebook from his shirt pocket. 'One of the names on the list is Sampson. Your neighbour, I believe.'

Edith nodded. 'Mrs Sampson is recently widowed. She's staying with her sister down south.'

'She telephoned yesterday. She's returning to Wooranoora soon and intends to operate the farm until she can sell it. Her main concern is the planting. If the women of the Land Army are finished here, would Mr Allenby release them to the Sampson farm? Perhaps he could supervise them too.'

'I'm sure he'd be happy to.' Edith turned to the women. 'When can you start, girls?'

Dot, the unofficial spokeswoman, piped up. 'Day after tomorrow?' The others nodded in agreement.

'Excellent! I'll come back at the end of the week and see how it's progressing. There are already four other farms on the list. At this rate, I'd better get more gangs quick-smart. Thank you, ladies.'

When he'd gone, Edith explained to the girls that her father was nominated as the manager so that she wouldn't lose the farm. She also told them about the wonderful help she'd received from her neighbour the previous year.

'Good for you, Edith!' said Dot. 'Damn men think women are stupid. But we know better, don't we girls? We'll do our best for Mrs Sampson too.'

'If you like, you can stay in the barracks here.'

'Oh, Edith. We'd love to!' said Violet. 'More tea anyone?'

Twenty-nine

Over time, the hobbies workshop at Camp 9 became a hub and meeting place for the Sicilian internees. The regulars produced beautiful woodwork, carvings, and sculptures from clay and scrap metal. From time to time they'd put on an exhibition which Colonel Dean and the officers would attend.

Tools were improvised and they used whatever materials were on hand. Occasionally a saw or a hammer or a piece of wire would 'fall off the back of a truck'. Pilfering from their captors was rife, but seldom was the perpetrator caught or punished. And so it happened that the men of the hobbies workshop made a shortwave wireless set.

Saturday nights, Luigi and Angelo would join their comrades in the workshop to listen to the Italian news. The time difference between Italy and South Australia was eight-and-a-half hours; six o'clock in the evening in Rome was two-thirty a.m. the next day in Loveday. On weekends, no-one got much sleep. It was worth it to hear *la verità* (the truth) about the war.

The hobbies workshop was situated directly beneath the southernmost guard tower but that section of the fence was never patrolled. There was no need. No-one in Camp 9 ever attempted escape. The guards were relaxed about their middle-of-the-night activities and left them to their own devices.

Other nights, the men would tune in to the British shortwave broadcasts to get another version of the war. All countries broadcast propaganda, so hearing different reports of the same story went some way toward finding a realistic middle ground.

It was midwinter. White frost crusted the ground as ten men, wrapped in blankets, huddled inside the workshop. At the centre of the hut, they'd built a firepit with a domed roof and a chimney pipe. It doubled as a pizza oven.

The shortwave wireless was tuned to Great Britain. The announcer was speaking in a toff accent about battles raging in the south of Italy.

> *Today we announce the capture of two key towns in the campaign for Sicily. Nicosia and Agira, which were in German hands, have been captured by the Americans and the Canadians respectively.*
>
> *The Allied forces made a swift overnight advance and, after several hours of fierce fighting, took a key road junction. The German Mount Etna Line has been smashed and their communications systems are in chaos. The Fifteenth Armoured Division is retreating to the north.*
>
> *The Allies have taken some 75,000 prisoners in Sicily alone. The American Secretary for War has advised that the campaign is in its final phase and a successful conclusion is expected within days.*

In the workshop, a mighty cheer rang out.

According to earlier Italian reports, the Nazis had entered Italy to protect the country from Allied invasion. However, the people of Italy would have considered that the Germans were the real invaders.

Sicily, in particular, was no stranger to foreign invasion. Throughout history, the island had been occupied or controlled by Greeks, Carthaginians, Byzantines, Arabs, Normans, Bourbons, and the Spanish. In all cases, the dominating forces took scarce food, plundered and destroyed homes, raped womenfolk, suppressed religion.

While it was good that the Germans were on the run, Luigi dared not imagine the devastation their defeat would have caused.

Seventy-five thousand prisoners of war, the number quoted in the report, was truly staggering. The entire population of Agira was less than nine thousand. It was hard to imagine their hilltop town being blasted by bombers and tanks. What had happened to Mamma, his brothers and their families?

He dropped his head into his hands and sobbed. '*O Dio! O Dio!*'

A sick feeling came over him. His chest became tight and there was no air in the workshop.

Beside him, Angelo had tears running down his cheeks. 'What hope would they have against tanks and machine guns?'

Vecchio said, 'Our houses are like fortresses. Sicilians are tough: they've weathered centuries of battles and earthquakes. A few stray bullets won't make much difference.'

Luigi rubbed his chest. 'Mamma should have been here, safe in Australia. We wanted to bring her out before the war but they wouldn't let us. I feel so bloody helpless.'

On the 17 August 1943, British shortwave reported that Messina, the last German stronghold in Sicily, had fallen. The Allied campaign was over. The liberation of the island had taken thirty-eight days. The Germans retreated across the Straits of Messina to the mainland, pursued by Allied warships, which gave them a one-thousand-shell send-off as they reached the coast of Calabria.

Hitler's army had its tail firmly between its legs.

The next night, the Sicilians held a commemoration to mark the end of war in their island state and also to mourn the dead. In the piazza near the workshop they laid out a feast cooked by Luigi and some of his countrymen. There were *sfinciuni* (pizza bread with tomato topping), *arancini* (stuffed rice balls), roasted *carciofi* (artichokes), sweet deep-fried *crostoli* pastries, camp-made wine and *grappa*.

Before the meal they said prayers to the patron saints of their towns in Sicily. Next came food and drink, which was consumed with gusto. Praise was lavished on the cooks.

Later a three-piece band consisting of squeezebox, guitar, and tambourine struck up the folk-tune, *la Tarantella*. The men linked hands and moved in a circle, weaving and turning. For a few precious hours there was no war, no killing, and no barbed wire fences.

Weeks later, they learnt that King Vittorio Emanuele had ousted Mussolini and appointed Marshal Badoglio as Prime Minister in his place. Then, on 13 October 1943, Badoglio did an amazing thing.

Open-mouthed, Luigi listened to the shortwave broadcast in the middle of a windswept night. In the workshop, the fire was crackling and so was the static of the wireless. He pulled an army blanket around him and lit a smoke.

The voice of Badoglio came across strong and clear. He spoke with the assurance of a military leader and condemned the atrocities done by the Germans against Italy. Then he said what no-one expected to hear.

'Every German must be driven from Italian soil. From this day forward, Italy will march shoulder to shoulder with the United Nations'.

It took a few minutes for the import of these two short sentences to sink in. If Italy had now turned against her former Axis partner and sided with the British, did that mean he and his fellow Italians were no longer enemies of Australia?

A bubble of hope rose in Luigi's throat. He glanced around the room. The others were also digesting the remarkable announcement.

It was Vecchio who broke the silence. '*Paesani*, that means we are free!'

For a moment there was confusion, then everyone broke into whoops of delight.

Viva l'Italia! Viva l'Australia!

'There's no reason for us to be held here anymore! Let's go get Del Drago!' Although it was nearly three in the morning, Vecchio strode out of the workshop. A dozen others followed, wearing blankets as protection from the cold.

Luigi trailed a little behind the pack. Up ahead, Vecchio was rapping on the door of the camp leader's hut. The door flew open; there was a terse exchange.

Vecchio returned, wearing an ear-to-ear grin. 'Del Drago said it can wait until morning.'

'But it *is* morning,' said Luigi.

Vecchio laughed. 'So it is, my friend. So it is.'

Some of the men began to sing; their accompaniment was the rhythm of their boots. They kicked the dust, slapped their thighs. Others joined in and a celebration began.

Inmates from nearby huts came to see what the fuss was about. As word spread, the assembly swelled. Soon it became a full-blown party that went on until dawn.

On 22 October 1943, Angelo walked free. Due to his health, he was in the first group of internees to be released. He would not be alone, for Vecchio would be travelling with him.

The day they departed on the truck, Angelo wore his old civilian suit and carried a brown port of belongings. On his finger was a memento of

Loveday: a florin ring engraved with a lucky horseshoe. It was a gift from Luigi to wish him *buon viaggio*.

As the truck rumbled toward the gate, Luigi called out. 'Take care, brother. When you get home, be sure to dig the vegetable patch.'

Angelo waved. The truck turned onto the road to Barmera and disappeared into a cloud of dust.

Thirty

Barmera, July 1943

Not long after the tunnel incident, Ted Long received an unexpected visitor. More accurately, there were two. A young woman and a baby. Unannounced they arrived on his doorstep one Thursday evening.

'Oh my Lord!' said Ted when he opened the door.

In truth it had taken him a moment to recognise his own sister. Amy seemed to have shrunk since he'd last seen her. Her blue floral dress, once her Sunday best, now fitted like a hessian sack. Her hair was greasy, as if it hadn't been washed in weeks. Without makeup she seemed younger than her twenty-nine years. The baby was fussing. Snot oozed from his nose. On the path beside her was an ancient perambulator stacked with ports, no doubt containing enough clothing for a very long stay.

'Why didn't you tell me you were coming?' he said.

'I wrote but you never answered. Please, Ted, can you put us up for a few weeks?'

'How could I refuse my little sister? Come in out of the cold.'

She stepped over the threshold into the warmth of the tiny parlour. 'Mmmm. Nice and cosy. Exactly what we need. Poor little Bobby has been out of sorts.' With a grubby cloth she wiped the baby's face. 'Bobby, say hello to your Uncle Ted.'

The infant gurgled then sneezed.

'*Uncle* Ted? When did I become an uncle?'

'About a year ago. It's a long story.'

Ted scratched his head. Ever since she was a child, she never ceased to amaze him. Just as well he was a patient man, for trying to prise out the truth would shut her up as tight as a clam. 'Cup of tea?'

'Have you got any food? And milk for the baby?'

In a cupboard, he found a packet of arrowroot biscuits and a wedge of cheese. The milk was the powdered variety in a tin. He put it all on the table, along with a glass of water and a spoon, and set the kettle on the stove.

While he rattled about the kitchen, Amy recounted the long trip. From Brisbane, they'd caught four trains over as many days. With no money for accommodation, they'd slept overnight on wooden benches at railway stations and used public facilities to wash.

'You're lucky I was home,' he said. 'If I was on late shift, you could have spent another night out in the cold.'

'I've never been much good at planning things.' She looked up and shrugged. 'But it always seems to work out in the end.'

He gave her a wry smile and brought the brown teapot to the table. Bobby had settled in a bunny rug in the crook of Amy's arm and was slurping milk. His eyelids were fluttering closed. The poor little mite had a rash all over his arms and face. Some of the spots had festered and were oozing.

As if she could read his mind, Amy explained. 'Mosquito bites.'

'Are you sure?' Ted poured two cups of tea. 'I'm no doctor, but I know the measles when I see it.'

She put her hand to her mouth. 'Couldn't be! He's just a baby.'

'Do you mind if I take a closer look?' He unfolded the bunny rug and pulled up the vest. The infant's chest was covered in red splotches. 'How long has he been like this?'

'I ... I hadn't noticed until now. Honest. On the journey he was a bit feverish, then he got this awful runny nose.'

'Give him a feed, then put him to bed. He needs to be kept away from light. Measles can send a person blind, you know. If he gets any worse, there's a hospital in Barmera.'

'Oh Ted, I must be a terrible mother. I just got him back.' She began to cry.

'Got him back? Where from?'

She blushed and hung her head.

As gently as he could, he said, 'Do you know who the father is?'

Amy nodded.

'And he's married?'

Again, she nodded.

'But he won't leave his wife or take responsibility for the baby?'

'Oh Ted, it was awful! I had to put poor Bobby in an orphanage! I had no choice. It was impossible on my own. Then I got evicted and had nowhere to live. That's why I came here. Please, Ted, don't turn us out.'

Ted put his arms around her. Her tears moistened his shirt. 'It's okay, petal.' He stroked her hair the way he'd stroke his dog Bessie. 'We all make mistakes.'

Tears tumbled down his cheeks as his mind slid back into the past. Mistakes! He'd lost count of the terrible things he'd done. On the battlefields of France and then back home, where he'd taken it all out on his long-suffering wife. Correction: *ex*-wife.

If only he could replay his life!

The first thing he'd reverse would be a hasty decision made by a sixteen-year-old lad—his kid brother, Fred—who'd lied about his age and signed up for the adventure of a lifetime. Ted who was ten years older and wiser, hadn't tried to talk him out of it. How bloody thoughtless! Under his watch, Fred had fought and died in the trenches of France. By some cruel twist of fate, the life of Lieutenant Ted Long had been spared. Not by valour but an attack of the measles.

Ted slept on the couch while Amy and Bobby took his double bed. His shift at Loveday began at five. He woke at four and quietly made himself breakfast: two boiled eggs, toast, and a pot of tea.

Before leaving, he poked his head into the bedroom. Both his visitors were sleeping like the dead. His eyes misted. Amy's small frame made her seem all the more vulnerable. He cursed that married man, whoever he was, for taking advantage of his little sister. Lying beside her, the baby was curled up with a thumb in his rosebud mouth.

As the guards used to say, 'at Loveday there's never a dull moment'. The day after Amy arrived, the not-dull moment was a brutal assault in the German section of Camp 10. Ted was given the task to investigate. He didn't have much to go on, except that one of the parties had seemed intoxicated and an empty Renmano wine bottle—probably the weapon that was used—had been found at the scene.

Wine and spirits were not permitted in the camp, not that the rule had ever been policed. All the guards knew about the Italians' so-called 'polenta pot' for making *grappa*. As long as everyone behaved themselves, it was easier to ignore it.

Ted started the investigation, not with the guards but the German internees. Most spoke passable English, so there was no need for an interpreter. He asked them one question. 'How could a bottle of commercial wine be brought in?'

All fingers pointed to a fellow called Günter Herzfeld, the 'go-to' man of the compound. For a small fee he could source almost anything. While the canteen stocked a small range of common items, it certainly did not sell liquor.

Strict security also surrounded currency. Internees were not permitted to have any silver coins of the realm and could keep only a shilling-worth of pennies. Specially-minted tokens were used for all transactions within the camp. The internment coins were made of copper and had a hole punched in the centre. On one side they were marked *Internment Camps*; the value of the coin was marked on the other. In the outside world they were worthless.

These measures were meant to discourage escape. In reality, they created new avenues for enterprising men like Herzfeld.

Ted tried to locate Herzfeld, only to discover he was out at Moorook and would be back in the late afternoon. Undeterred, Ted found an informant in a crusty old fellow called Fritz Meier.

'Herzfeld can get anything,' said Meier.

'Yes, so I'm told. How does he get the money ... or are you saying he's a thief?'

'No, not a thief. A businessman. He does deals when we're out.'

At the time, Germans were working at a woodcutting camp on the far side of the River Murray. Moorook was two miles from Loveday as the crow flies and six miles by road. The shortest route was to go to the northern bank of the river, row a boat across, then walk five minutes through bushland to the camp. Every day, eighteen internees and five guards went to Moorook by road. On the way there, the truck would stop at a certain farmhouse for the men to buy fruit for lunch.

'How did you pay for it?' Ted asked.

'Herzfeld would collect a bit of tobacco from each of us, then he'd give the tobacco to the truck driver, who'd pay for the fruit in cash.'

While the practice was slightly dodgy, Ted didn't see much harm in it. Certainly, it was not enough to make a fuss. 'Did he buy anything other than fruit?'

Meier looked down and examined his palms. The skin was ragged from handling rough lumber. 'Don't rightly know.'

No further information was forthcoming so Ted ended the interview.

Other inmates gave similar responses. The only thing for it was to wait until five o'clock, when the army truck returned. Then he could interview the legendary Herzfeld.

The note Ted had left Amy on the kitchen table said he'd be home by three. Now he'd be lucky to get away before seven. The commandant wanted answers, and he wanted them today. Because the victim had been hospitalised, the assault was reportable to the big brass in Adelaide and would likely end up as a police matter.

Ted was obliged to obey commands. He hoped Amy would understand and that little Bobby had not taken a turn for the worse.

On the stroke of five, the army truck roared through the gates of the compound. Twenty-three tired, hungry men disembarked.

'Which one is Herzfeld?' Ted asked no-one in particular.

An escort guard indicated a muscular man, six-foot tall and broad-shouldered, who'd jumped down from the truck.

Ted addressed the man-mountain. 'Herzfeld?'

'*Ja?*'

'You speak English?'

'*Ja,*' said the man again. 'I speak good English.'

Ted said, 'I'm investigating an incident and need to ask you a few questions. Please come with me to the camp leader's hut.'

'As you wish.' Herzfeld walked calmly beside Ted and made no attempt at conversation.

Inside the hut, they were shown to a partitioned office. They sat one on either side of a desk. Ted gave a brief outline of the incident.

'That fight had nothing to do with me.' A red flush crept up Herzfeld's neck. Despite the coolness of the afternoon, his forehead was beaded in sweat.

'You aren't in any trouble. The culprit has already been caught.'

'I don't want to make trouble for others either,' said Herzfeld.

'I have one question. How did a bottle of wine find its way into the compound?'

Herzfeld glared at Ted, the sort of look that could drill through steel. His eyes were ice-blue. They were alone in the cubicle. Ted swallowed. He could feel his Adam's apple move against the collar of his shirt.

'Very well,' the big man said at length. 'The wine came from Edwards' store at Moorook. We got a tin boat and rowed across the river to get it.'

'What did you use for money?'

'I gave my friend tobacco and he gave the shopkeeper cash.'

'How much did it cost?

'Seven shillings and sixpence.'

'For how many bottles?'

'Four. I put them in a sugarbag to carry them back. I sold one and we drank the rest in the hut. It was Easter. Germans celebrate Easter Sunday with a nice meal and some wine. I know wine is *verboten*, but I thought a little would do no harm.'

'Have you bought wine like this before?'

'Maybe a bottle or two.'

'Is your friend an internee?'

'No.'

'Is he a guard then?'

'Yes, but I will not say his name.'

'Okay, I'm done. You can go. I have to report this to Commandant Dean, but I promise you have nothing to fear.' *Unlike others*, Ted muttered beneath his breath.

Outside, the night was dark and chilly. Ted drove his truck a few hundred yards from Camp 10 to GHQ.

In the colonel's office, Dean listened intently. 'Tomorrow, interview all the guards. This rogue must be identified and held to account. He has crossed the line between respect for the inmates and mateship. I shall not tolerate Army officers colluding with their charges.'

'Is that all, sir?'

'Yes, Lieutenant Long. You've done well.' He saluted.

Ted returned the salute then raced to his truck. He should have been home hours ago. What would he find? Would Amy and the baby still be there? The day before, she'd been in a dangerous mood, the sort that might lead anywhere. The closer he got to the cottage, the tighter he clenched the wheel.

Thankfully a weak cone of light was glowing in the kitchen. He parked the truck in the driveway and quickly went inside. To his surprise, Amy was not only still there but she'd also cooked him dinner.

*

Three months passed. Having little Bobby in the house gave Ted a whole new lease on life. In the evenings and on days off, he'd take the little chap out to play. Ted made him a hobby-horse from a broom-handle and a wooden offcut for a face. He also commissioned a German internee to make a miniature train, for which he paid in forbidden cash.

The train consisted of a red engine, three carriages, two wagons, and a guard's van. There was even a miniature driver, and six tiny passengers. It was an enormous hit with Bobby, but Amy frowned and quickly confiscated the figurines.

'It's beautiful, Ted, but he's way too young for it. If he put one of those little people in his mouth, he could choke.'

'Then put it away until he's older. The fellow who made it is a master woodcarver from Bavaria. The craftsmanship is superb, don't you think?'

'Yes, lovely. Now why don't you take Bobby outside? I'll finish up here.' To Bobby she said, 'Be good for Uncle Ted.'

An hour later, when Ted and his nephew returned, there was no sign of the toy train. On the table was a packet of jelly snakes and a cake with white icing. The little boy made straight for the lollies, stuffing them in his mouth two at a time. Due to rationing, sweets were practically impossible to buy. Ted wondered what Amy had done to get her hands on all that sugar. Although he had his suspicions, he didn't want to cause an upset by asking.

By then, the truce between big brother and little sister was beginning to wear thin. One week later, Amy announced that she missed the city and wanted to return to Brisbane. Not one for indecision or lingering farewells, she bought a train ticket and packed the very next day.

Ted drove them to Barmera station. 'What will you do now? Won't it be as hard as before?'

'I've got a plan.' She flicked her hair back and gave him a cryptic grin.

'Will you share it with your favourite brother?'

'You're the *only* brother I've ever known.' Amy laughed. 'But it's a secret plan.'

No matter how hard he tried to wheedle it out, her lips remained sealed.

Finally, he shrugged. 'You're all grown up and can look after yourself. Right?'

'You betcha!' She hugged him, swung the toddler onto her hip, and stepped onto the train. Through the carriage window, Bobby waggled his little hands. Not once did Amy looked down at the platform or see Ted waving them goodbye. It was as if she'd already blocked out one part of her life and was keen to get on with the next.

Having a young child in the house had not been easy, for Bobby continued to sleep fitfully by night and was tired and cranky by day. Tea had to be eaten before six o'clock, for shortly afterwards was the witching hour when he'd howl until he fell sleep.

But without him, Ted's cottage was as empty as a hollow log.

Thirty-one

The momentous day that Italy swapped sides went almost unnoticed in Delahunty's tunnel-vision world of domestic politics.

The Courier Mail seemed slightly bored by the event, as if the war in Europe was old news and nothing mattered now except the unfolding events in the Pacific. In reporting Italy's about-turn, the paper did not pretend to have its own sources and deferred instead to a report in the *New York Times*.

In it, the quality of Badoglio's troops was described as 'questionable' because of their 'singularly unimpressive military record'. It was suggested that Badoglio himself had 'no political future and no political ambitions' and that his time in power would be short-lived. The sentiment was typical of the war-weariness that had befallen the populace.

In Queensland, all eyes were on New Guinea, a short boat ride from mainland Australia, where battles were raging against the Japanese invaders. General MacArthur's troops were right in the thick of it and so were the Australians. Several months earlier, the Japanese had mounted a campaign to take Port Moresby. They had come within thirty miles of their objective when the Aussies pushed back through mountains and jungles along a rough track called Kokoda. It was a costly battle for both sides, with many hundreds of casualties. But it meant that far north Queensland had been given a reprieve from invasion by the island-hopping enemy.

Of greater concern to Delahunty was the Brisbane Line, the 'defence plan of last resort'. It could better be described as a line of retreat should the Japanese succeed in conquering the north. The phrase had been first coined by the Labor Party as a scaremongering tactic for the 1942 federal election. It worked: Labor won the election.

The plan was simple. In the case of Japanese invasion, Australian defence forces would to fall back to a line somewhere near Brisbane. South of that line would be defended, north of it would be relinquished to the Japs. Various locations of the elusive line were bandied around in conversation. For some, the line was south of Rockhampton; others said it was on the northern outskirts of Brisbane; yet others said that all of Queensland would go to the Japs and only the southern states would be defended. Whether the Brisbane Line was fact or legend was never confirmed, but talk of it crept into common parlance. Even MacArthur himself used the term. Perhaps he liked the idea and intended to put it into action if the campaign in New Guinea failed.

Ever since the rumours about the Brisbane Line got out, Delahunty's phone had been running hot. Constituents from towns in the far north asked if they should evacuate. His staff had been instructed to assure them there was no such plan. Anything to prevent him being swamped with troublesome phone calls. He already had enough to deal with; a new crisis cropped up every day. Even so, the most persistent citizens still managed to track him down.

Of course MacArthur is up to the job, he'd tell them. 'The Allies are certain to win the war.' Under the circumstances, he could do no more. But the confidence of his responses concealed a gnawing doubt in his heart.

Was far north Queensland really out of firing range? He thought not.

He was acutely aware that politicians in the federal arena, even members of his beloved Labor Party, couldn't give a shite about Queensland. They barely knew where Brisbane was, let alone Cairns. To them, the northern state was a wasteland of sugar cane farms, crocodile-infested rivers, and sparsely-populated bushland dotted with unremarkable towns that caused more trouble than they were worth. According to the southerners, Queenslanders had no culture and even less education; the downfall of the state would be no great loss to the nation. Quite the reverse.

Thank God he'd bought the house in Ashgrove and his wife was happy there. At least they had somewhere safe to live. Cairns was getting too hot for comfort, in more ways than one.

His relationship with Margaret had taken a turn for the better. Sometimes it was like the early days when they were newlyweds. Like a pair of comfy old slippers, they'd become an easy fit. Weeknights, he'd get away from the office by six so they could dine together. The range of ingredients was somewhat limited due to rationing, but Delahunty had a substantial cellar of wine, thanks to the passing of a long-time friend who'd bequeathed him an entire collection of exotic reds on one condition: that he promised to drink the lot before he died. Even mock brains with boiled cabbage and mashed potato tasted respectable when accompanied by a bottle of aged Bordeaux.

More than a year had passed since Amy had shown him the door. Sometimes he wondered what had happened to his son, the poor child abandoned by both parents. Sometimes he felt guilty. Once he took a drive to the orphanage at Nudgee and sat in the car outside the gate, gazing at children running about in the yard. The little boy would be barely out of nappies; it was unlikely he'd be out there amongst the bare-foot urchins in hand-me-down clothes. One day he'd work up the courage to visit. Perhaps he'd take him a tin toy to show he was a father who cared.

Many times, he'd tried to tell Margaret what had happened. But his home life was running so smoothly that he didn't dare rock the boat. For all he knew, Amy and her alleged *husband* might have moved back to Adelaide. Two thousand miles apart, it was unlikely he'd ever see her again.

No, it would be kinder all round if this little secret were taken to his grave.

So, with the turnabout of Italy barely registering, Delahunty drove home to a loving wife in a nice middle-class suburb of Brisbane. As he walked up the stairs, the delicious aroma of home cooking enveloped him and lifted his mood. His stomach rumbled as he inhaled the smell of rabbit stew with celery and tomatoes. The rabbit-o always came around on a Friday, hawking meat that had been killed across the border in New South Wales. The creatures were gamey and full of buckshot. But the way Margaret cooked them, rabbit tasted as succulent and sweet as chicken. All you had to do was go softly, so as not to crack a tooth on a lead pellet.

Thankfully in the Delahunty household, Fridays were not restricted to fish. He detested fish. The fish-o sold oily stinking mullet, caught in the muddy Brisbane River. A thoroughly nasty culinary experience. He'd rather eat bread and jam.

Chatter wafted out through the open front door. The voices were as familiar as the freckles on his arms, yet he never expected to hear them together. With his back to the night and his face lit by the dim brown-out lamp, he stopped dead in his tracks.

Margaret sounded a little tipsy. 'What a darling little man. You are so lucky. When I was younger, I would have given anything to have had a baby.'

A young child giggled.

'Thank you for inviting us. I don't know what we would've done without you.'

No, it couldn't be!

Delahunty shut his eyes. Was he dreaming? He blinked twice and scanned the surroundings. The house looked as spick and span as usual. There were no things of nightmares: no ghouls, assassins, man-eating monsters. Everything seemed completely normal.

'You must promise to stay until you find a nice place to live,' said Margaret.

'Mrs Delahunty, you're too kind.'

Oh God! That voice!

'Please dear, call me Margaret.' A spoon clanked against a saucepan. 'Hmmm, needs more salt.' Another clank of the spoon. 'I don't know what's keeping my husband. He should be home by now.'

Delahunty felt sick to the stomach. For a brief moment he considered making a hasty exit. As MacArthur would say, 'There is no shame in a strategic retreat.' But Margaret had already said that the visitor could stay indefinitely, so the battle was lost before it began.

Prepared or not, it was time to own up to his crime. In his mind, he'd pictured this moment but he'd never imagined his emotions would be running wild. His chest was so tight he could scarcely breathe and his heart was thumping like a steam pump. He gathered his courage and took a step over the threshold, acutely aware that he might be about to meet his maker.

With a face of granite, he strode into the kitchen as if he'd just arrived home.

At the stove Margaret spun around. She was wearing her best frilled apron, the one for Sunday visitors. 'Hello dear, you're home at last. I'd like you to meet a friend of mine. This is Amy and her little boy, Bobby.'

Delahunty turned to the mother and child at the table. Perched on his mother's knee, Bobby was chewing a crust of bread.

'Hello Amy. It's been quite a while.'

'Yes, it has.' Amy smiled politely. 'Margaret and I met at the Red Cross tea rooms this afternoon. I'm back in Brisbane and didn't have anywhere to go. Honestly, renting a flat these days is like finding a gold nugget in Queen Street. Anyway, your wife is very kind. She's asked us to stay.'

The little boy dropped the crust and wriggled to get down.

'You already *know* each other?' Margaret took a swallow of red wine.

Delahunty studied the geometric pattern on the linoleum. He glanced at Amy. Her green eyes sparked with challenge. She might as well have shouted out to the neighbourhood. *If you won't tell her, then I shall.*

'Yes, we know each other rather well in fact.'

'I'm surprised Amy didn't mention it.' The serving spoon was poised above the steaming pot. 'Shall I dish up?'

With the utmost self-control he said, 'Margaret, put down the spoon and come here please.' He moved a chair out from under the table so she could sit.

'William, you're making me nervous.' Biting her lip, she obeyed.

He cleared his throat. 'Margaret, these past few years ... Amy and I ...' He choked on the sentence. This was going to be harder than expected. He looked into his wife's glistening eyes and in that moment realised there was only one woman for him. She meant more than anything else in this world. And now he stood to lose her.

'Please, tell me so I can stop worrying,' she murmured.

'Yes, William. Go on, tell her.' This was Amy.

There was no other way but to blurt it out. 'Once we were lovers but now it's over.'

Margaret's mouth opened and closed but her tears refused to fall.

A look of triumph lit Amy's face. Meanwhile Bobby scrabbled about on the floor, his pink tongue licking the lino.

'And ...' Amy was urging him on.

Delahunty hung his head. 'Bobby is my son.'

Margaret was shaking; she looked as if she might faint.

'Please forgive me, Margaret. This will never happen again, I promise.'

His wife folded her arms and glared at him. 'So, a confession at last!' Colour returned to her face; she became red and blotchy. Was it the change-of-life hot flushes or was she about to blow a gasket?

'Do you think I'm blind as well as stupid?' she hissed. 'How many years have we been married?'

'Twenty-nine.'

'And you think I don't know about your little dalliances?'

Now it was Amy's turn to look shocked. 'But, William, you said ...'

He ignored the interruption. 'None of those girls meant anything to me. Mere comfort when I couldn't have you.'

'I honestly don't care what you do while you're away. Just tell me. I don't want to make a fool of myself by asking your girlfriend to stay.'

Amy reached for her handbag. 'We'd better be going.'

'No. We are reasonable adults here. The offer of a room still stands. Only a cold-hearted witch would throw a mother and baby out on the street.' Margaret's voice softened. 'I mean it, Amy. Think of your child.'

'Amy also needs to confess. The place at Nudgee?' Delahunty prompted.

Sheepishly Amy told her about the orphanage, then admitted subletting the cottage in James Street that Delahunty had rented for her. 'What I did was wrong, but what choice did I have? William told me that his marriage—*your* marriage—was over. I suppose I lived in the hope that he would keep supporting us.'

'But you wore a ring that day. I couldn't continue the arrangement if you had a husband,' said Delahunty.

'Men are so dumb! I pretended to be married. I had to. Single mothers are treated like dirt. Luckily my brother Ted came to the rescue. I've spent the last three months with him in South Australia. The reason I came back is that a boy needs his father.'

'Oh my Lord!' groaned Delahunty. 'What an unholy bloody mess!'

'William, language!' Margaret nodded at the little boy. 'Now, if we all put our heads together, I'm sure we can work this out.'

While Delahunty's life had just caved in, Margaret seemed calm and in control. If he didn't know her so well, he might have concluded that she'd planned the entire setup.

For once, he was utterly in awe of her.

The End and the Beginning

Thirty-two

Wooranoora, December 1943

When Australia's war with Italy ended, Edith had expected Tony to come home straight away. But it was not to be. As she discovered, the wheels of government turned very slowly indeed.

Her enquiries through the Wooranoora police led nowhere, so she wrote to the Australian Military Forces at their headquarters in Brisbane asking for information about the return of Italian internees. When weeks later she received a one-line response—*your enquiry will be dealt with in due course*—she wrote to the most powerful man in the far north, William Delahunty.

By return mail she was advised, 'Repatriation of displaced persons could take between six months and a year'. While Delahunty's response was not particularly enlightening, at last she could put a time-frame on her expectations. Meanwhile—however long that might be—she would have to keep muddling through. She missed her husband and she missed her children who remained out of harm's way in Brisbane. For all their differences in opinion, she also missed her fusspot parents, in particular her mother. Letters arrived twice a week and they usually included black-and-white snapshots of a pair of happy kids. The photographs went some way toward satisfying the craving she felt. But a photo was a mere scrap of paper; what she really needed was their affection.

With the 1943 crushing season over and still no sign of Tony, she'd telephoned her parents from the post office and asked if they'd bring the children to Wooranoora by train. First class and all expenses paid, she promised. Neither of her parents had ever travelled north of Maryborough, so a change of scenery would do them all good.

'But it's such a long way,' complained her father. 'The children are at a difficult age and your mother and I aren't getting any younger.'

'Then I'll come and collect them myself,' she huffed.

'Perfect. Let us know when you've made the arrangements. Don't rush back north either. We'd love you to stay a while.'

Before she knew it, she'd agreed to something she hadn't intended. She hung the earpiece on the hook and paid the clerk for the trunk-line call.

Outside, she mentally kicked herself for allowing her father to corner her yet again. For several minutes she fumed and paced up and down the pavement. Calmer, she began to work it through. The harvest was over; there was not much to do on the farm for a few months. The mill cheque was in the bank; money was not an issue. Tony had written from some far-flung place where he was obliged to do farm work until the authorities allowed him to come home. At this rate, she could see her way clear for three weeks, maybe four, until the growing cycle started over.

No time like the present.

With intent, she walked past the shopfronts of Sugarmill Street to the bank and withdrew enough cash for a return train ticket to Brisbane. On the way to the railway station, she passed the drapery store. In the window was a roll of fabric, blue as the sky with a pattern of white hail-spots. It had been years since she'd had anything new. Throughout the war, clothing was rationed, as was the fabric to make it. Worse, it seemed that cheerful colours had been banned. Everything was austerity brown or battleship grey or army khaki. It was time to put colour back in her life.

She went in and used all her coupons (and a goodly amount of cash) to purchase three yards, enough to make a dress. If she put her mind to it, she'd be able to run it up on the treadle machine in a day or two. With the brown-paper parcel tucked under her arm, she crossed the tracks to the railway ticket office.

'Next train to Brisbane is Friday,' said the stationmaster. 'There's one sleeping compartment left. Would you like me to book it?'

Edith paid for return tickets for herself and a concession single from Brisbane for Bella. In the process, she discovered that her younger child could travel for free.

In Brisbane, her father picked her up from Roma Street Station. He came alone. She felt a pang of disappointment that her children were not there to meet her.

'You look nice and bright,' he said. 'I'm sick of seeing pretty women in drab dresses.'

'Thanks, Dad.' She twirled around and the skirt billowed around her legs. 'How are Bella and Anthony? I thought you might have brought them.'

'When I left for the station, they were still asleep and your mother had one of her headaches.'

'Oh.' The reality of dealing with mundane family matters came flooding back. For nearly two years she'd lived independently, making her own decisions, following her own set of rules. Being in charge was a wonderful feeling. Sometimes she wondered how she would adjust when her husband returned. Would she continue to manage their affairs or would he seize the reins?

At her parents' home in Clayfield, the children—now bathed and dressed in clean clothing—raced out squealing. Her mother, in dark sunglasses, trailed behind. Edith bent down and scooped her babies into her arms. Tears of joy rolled unchecked down her cheeks. She'd been so busy keeping their business together that she'd had to push these two little angels from her mind.

How much they'd grown! What milestones had she missed? The little one, Anthony, was putting on a brave face. Now two-and-a-half years old, he was seeing his mother as if for the first time. He regarded her through deep brown eyes, sizing her up, assessing if she deserved to be called *Mummy*.

Being older, Bella remembered her from before. Desperately she clung to Edith's neck and whispered in her ear. 'Promise you won't ever leave us again.'

That was when Edith's heart shattered. She sobbed into her daughter's soft chestnut hair. 'I promise, darling.'

'Never ever?' persisted the girl.

'Never ever again,' said Edith emphatically.

Bella squeezed Edith harder, taking her breath away. She planted wet kisses all over her face, then wriggled to the ground and ran off. Edith was left holding Anthony, who'd decided he preferred his grandmother to the new lady in the sky-blue dress. He began to wail. Nan came to the rescue and carried him inside.

'Now see what all that gallivanting has done!' said her father. 'You've been gone so long, your own son doesn't know you.'

She gave her father a withering look and went to pick up her bags.

'It's about time you realised what's important in this life, my girl. I don't know what they put in the water up there, but it's given you some crazy ideas. Your place is at home raising your children, not pretending to be a man with a cane farm.'

She bit back tears. 'I didn't have a choice.'

'Everyone has choices,' he spat. 'Your mistake was marrying that—'

'Why don't you say it? Why don't you say *wog* and be done with it?'

'As you wish. If you'd married someone *sensible*—one of our *own* like your mother—this never would have happened.'

'Pity help me if I'd married someone like you!' As she stalked off toward the house, she threw the last grenade over her shoulder. 'I'm going to pack the children's things and we'll leave today.'

'Wait, Edith! I didn't mean it like that.'

She pretended not to have heard and continued into the kitchen where she found both children clinging to their grandmother.

'Edith dear, please put on the kettle.' Her mother's voice was as gentle and patient as ever. 'I think we all need to calm down and talk.'

As Ewan entered the room, she shot a glance like a dagger across the kitchen. 'More importantly, your father owes you an apology. Don't you, dear?'

Edith spun around. Her father avoided her eyes and lowered himself into a chair.

The kettle was forgotten; Edith folded her arms across her chest. 'I'm listening.'

Her father looked the epitome of wretched. He fiddled with the edge of the tablecloth and pressed his lips into a thin line.

'What I did was for your own good. Please remember that …' His voice faltered.

'What exactly did you do, Dad?'

'You needed to be here where it's safe. But you were so pigheaded … it was the only way I think of …' Again, he faded into silence.

Edith glared at her father. 'What are you talking about?' She already suspected the answer, yet her heart refused to believe that he could do such an abominable deed.

'Just spit it out, Ewan. Put the poor girl out of her misery.'

He took a breath and looked Edith straight in the eye. 'It was me who arranged the internment of your husband. For your own safety, I telephoned my friend, William Delahunty, and explained the situation. He did the rest. My dearest Edith, please accept my deepest and sincerest apologies.'

Completely speechless, Edith steadied herself on the counter. At that moment, she could have killed him with her bare hands. Tears of fury welled and her lip began to quiver. Just then, she felt a gentle tug on her skirt. She looked down into Bella's enormous brown eyes.

'Don't be sad, Mummy.'

Thirty-three

Twenty men with bloodshot eyes and aching bones disembarked the train at Wooranoora Station. Amongst them was Luigi. Apart from one night when they'd slept under canvas at a staging camp in Brisbane, they had travelled non-stop for six days and five nights. All the men were suffering the effects of too little sleep and too much heat. Yet they couldn't wipe the grins off their faces.

On Christmas Day, they'd celebrated their freedom with an impromptu feast: sandwiches from a station cafe in Woop Woop, a bag of plums, bottles of unchilled beer. They had music too: a mouth organ and a tin whistle. It was the best Christmas ever, for the dark days were finally over.

On the platform at Wooranoora was a welcoming party of wives and children, jiggling with excitement. But, as expected, there was nobody waiting for Luigi. Bottled-up emotions brought tears to his eyes. He turned away from the joyful reunions and concentrated instead on gathering his possessions before the train chugged out of the station and continued towards Cairns.

Ever since his release, he had both yearned for and dreaded this moment. Through the trees he caught glimpses of the boarding house and the nearby shed, which was used as a mechanic's workshop. Nightmares of fires and cyclones had plagued him and he'd wake in a cold sweat, hoping none of it was true.

From where he was standing, everything looked exactly as he'd left it.

Loaded to the eyeballs with ports and boxes, he headed for the boarding house. But the closer he got, the more he realised that three

217

years' neglect had taken its toll. The paint was peeling like onion skin; most of the windows were smashed; a spidery black swastika had been painted across an entire wall. Some ignorant *stronzo* must have thought they were colluding with the Nazis. Ha! The thought was almost enough to make him sick.

The front door was shut. As Luigi put his hand on the knob, it creaked open. 'Anyone there?' he shouted down the hall.

No-one replied. Instead of the aroma of Mrs Ross's baking, the building was ripe with foul odours.

He wandered down the hallway, the thud of his shoes echoing in the emptiness. The dining room was depleted of chairs. Thieving *bastardi*! Glasses and dirty china had been left on the tables. Pieces of broken crockery lay all over the floor. A large puddle indicated a serious leak in the roof or the guttering of the second storey.

Continuing on, he reached the cookhouse at the rear. Here the stench was unbelievable. Dishes, thick with mould, filled the sink. In one corner was the main culprit: an oozing sack of rotten potatoes.

A wave of nausea washed over him and he made a dash outside.

Recovering his composure, Luigi spoke aloud as if to reassure himself. 'Nothing a clean and a lick of paint won't fix.' But he knew it would take weeks of work to make the place habitable again.

At the workshop, he peered through the mud-splattered window, hoping to get a glimpse of the pickup which he'd left in the care of Tom the mechanic. Except for a bare workbench and several sheets of metal propped against the wall, the shed was completely empty.

Perhaps Angelo had retrieved the vehicle and taken it to the farm. Because the telephone was not connected, there was no way of asking. Luigi would have to find his own way out to Cassowary Valley.

The open-sided shed behind the boarding house stored a vast array of stuff that might come in handy one day. Mattresses, corrugated iron, rope, engine parts, timber, packing cases, broken chairs, empty drums. Luigi ventured in, stepping between the tightly packed items. Beside a crate of rags and partly hidden by a sheet of plywood was a bicycle. It was dirty and rusty and sticky with cobwebs.

He dragged it onto the grass and wiped it down with a rag. Returning to the shed, he opened the wonky old dresser and rummaged about amongst tins of paint, jars of rat poison, bottles of weed-killer. The oil can was right at the back.

When he'd finished, he prodded the tyres. They were flat and the rubber was cracked. He found the hand-pump and filled them with air.

Luckily there seemed to be no punctures. Finally, he tied his belongings on with rope and mounted the bike.

As he pedalled out to the road, he remembered the restriction order, a condition of his release. Before he could go home, he was required to report his whereabouts to the police.

With a burning face, he relived the last time he was at the police station. That day he was paraded through the town in handcuffs and unceremoniously shoved aboard the southbound train. He remembered the smirking face of Sergeant Pitt, the crash of the wagon door, its wood splintered by nails, and the choking odour of dust and sweaty men. But the shame was the worst. The shame of being imprisoned with no chance of proving his innocence.

At the Wooranoora police station, the constable at the counter was courteous. The badge read *Constable Jackson*. Sergeant Pitt was nowhere to be seen.

Jackson crossed Luigi's name off a list and stamped his identity card. When he was done he said casually, 'Is Angelo Innocenti a relation of yours?'

'Yes, my brother. He was sent home early because he wasn't well.'

'He's due to report next week. I can mark him off and save him the trouble.'

Luigi could scarcely believe his ears. 'Thanks. By the way, have you seen our Terraplane pickup? I left it at Tom's Garage for safekeeping but it isn't there now.'

The constable shook his head. 'Let me know if you can't find it.'

The road to Cassowary Valley was more potholed and treacherous than before. Steering a loaded bicycle was tricky work. Luigi had to re-tie the load and nearly took a tumble near the creek. At last he sped down the home slope and pulled up at the farm gate.

On the verandah of the farmhouse sat Angelo with a teacup in his hand. In two months he had aged ten years. His hair was practically white and he was as hunched as Vecchio. He waved, put down the cup, and limped down the steps. 'Welcome home, brother!'

Luigi pushed the bicycle up the slope to the house. As if in a dream, he gazed around their beloved farm. It was completely different from when he'd left.

What used to be lawn was now head-high weeds. Stinking Roger, giant sensitive weed, wild raspberry, lantana. Vines snaked through the grass. Rotted watermelon and pumpkin carcasses lay about the yard.

Beyond the house, the cane fields were in a terrible state. Flattened by rain, wind and neglect, they were probably ridden with vermin. Whoever in the Public Curator's office was supposed to be running the place hadn't done their job.

Luigi untied the luggage and laid his bike on the ground. He was dog-tired. What he really needed was a cigarette, a good feed, and his comfy old bed.

Over a hastily-prepared meal of spaghetti with oil, garlic, pepper, and cheese, Angelo gave a brief rundown of his return trip. Except for dark circles around his eyes, his face was as white as the pasta.

'First they sent me to work on a pineapple farm. Summerlands was the name; it was somewhere outside of Brisbane. I got real sick. The owner wrote the army a letter, saying I couldn't work there anymore. Then he drove me to a boarding house in Spring Hill where I stayed a couple of days. Finally, I caught a train home.'

'Did you drive the pickup from the station?' said Luigi hopefully.

Angelo shook his head. 'That nice new constable brought me home. I've stayed here ever since.'

'The pickup is missing but it can wait. I'll have a proper look around tomorrow.'

At dawn Luigi woke to the joyous screech of the mountain lorikeets. Refreshed and keen to assess the condition of the farm, he pulled on his old shorts and retrieved his cane knife from under the bed.

Through the towering weeds, he hacked a path to the machinery shed. He was in for a shock. The shed was completely empty. Gone were the yellow Caterpillar, the chaff cutter, the harnesses, the plough, the other farm implements, and all of his tools.

'*Porca miseria!*'

In the shade of the corrugated iron roof, he squatted and rolled a smoke. Without machinery, they couldn't operate. He hawked and spat. A gob of wrath and despair.

The weed forest extended from the house to the cane fields. At the creek-end, native jungle had reclaimed the land they'd cleared all those years ago.

With the cane knife he continued hacking his way parallel to the creek. Lawyer cane prickles caught him and ripped his flesh like fish-hooks.

His sandshoe trod on something smooth in the undergrowth. It flinched beneath his foot. He leapt aside, took quick aim. Coppery scales flashed in the sun. *Swish* went the cane knife.

Swish. Swish.

The only good snake is a dead snake. He was terrified of the things.

Stomping the trash to scare off any others, he paced the northern boundary of their land. One hundred yards to the east, morning sunlight reflected off the iron roof of the barracks. He proceeded along the creek, then cut across the overgrown firebreak. At the canecutters barracks he opened each of the four doors. Wads of mattress fibre were scattered over the floorboards and the rooms smelt of rat pee. Thankfully the roof and beams remained sound. All it needed was a clean.

When Luigi returned to the farmhouse, Angelo was in the kitchen drinking tea. On the table the enamel teapot was puffing out steam. Angelo liked to make the tea so it was ready to serve. As well as tea leaves and boiling water, he'd put in several spoons of sugar and milk.

Luigi poured himself a pannikin full and lit a smoke before relating the bad news. 'The cane is a total write-off and all our machinery is gone. Where do we start?'

Angelo said, 'That fellow Vecchio said compensation was paid after the Great War. We should write to the government.'

'Australia is still *at* war, remember?'

'Hmmm. Can we get a loan and buy new equipment?'

Luigi rolled his eyes. Everything cost money and they hadn't received a mill cheque in two years. There was twenty pounds still in the lining of his port, so they wouldn't starve. But twenty pounds was nowhere near the amount needed to replace a tractor.

Angelo said, 'There's nothing in our bank account and two shillings in the house.'

'Did you find the tin?' said Luigi.

Angelo shrugged. 'What tin?'

'When you left Loveday, I said *be sure to dig the vegetable patch.*'

'I don't remember.'

'Come with me.' With renewed energy Luigi rummaged in the cutlery drawer for the big serving spoon and headed out the back door. Angelo followed.

The vegetable patch was in some semblance of order. Angelo had cleared the worst of the weeds so parsley, bitter lettuce, and carrots were struggling through. In the far corner, Luigi squatted and pushed the spoon into the ground. About six inches down, it hit metal. He dug around the treacle tin, levered it out and brushed the soil off the lid. Inside were the banknotes he'd withdrawn shortly before he was captured.

'Get your bicycle, Angelo. We're going to town to see what we can buy.'

The going was slow, for Angelo needed to stop frequently to catch his breath. In town they left their bicycles in the driveway between the boarding house and the mechanic's workshop. As Luigi walked the boundary, he tried to ignore the ugly swastika. A wild raspberry vine had invaded the yard around the workshop. He peered into the prickly maze and spotted something metallic and black.

'Angelo, it's here! The Terraplane is here!'

'*Mamma mia!*'

They pulled away the prickly vine. The pickup was covered in dirt and rotted plant matter. The axles were up on blocks. The bonnet was open but there was not much inside. The main components—carburettor, distributor, pump, generator, battery—had been pilfered. Luigi retrieved his bicycle and set off for the police station down the road. Angelo followed not far behind.

Behind the counter, Sergeant Pitt was wearing his usual belligerent expression.

'We've found our pickup,' Luigi announced.

'Congratulations,' said Pitt.

'But half of it is missing. The engine and the wheels are gone.'

Pitt opened his notebook. 'Describe the vehicle.'

'Terraplane, 1934 model.'

'You mean the one near the garage?'

'Yes.'

'Ha! There's a war on you know. Shortages and all. The way that vehicle was left, you were practically asking someone to come along and take whatever he needed.'

'So, there's nothing you'll do to help us?'

'Not much we can do. I recorded it as *abandoned* months ago.'

Angelo muttered to Luigi in Sicilian. 'Let's get out of here.'

Outside, they wheeled the bikes down Sugarmill Street towards the general store. As they went to enter, the door slammed in their faces.

The warning on the glass said it all. *No Dagos.*

Luigi swore and slapped his hand on the door. Despite all they'd been through, they were still being punished. Perhaps they ought to leave this town. Maybe they should go somewhere new and start over. He thought about Gino, his restaurateur friend from Sydney. Maybe he could start a cafe of his own. Gino said there was good money in food. Surely the work would be easier than growing cane. But at this point Luigi had no choice. They had to rebuild the farm first, otherwise they'd get nothing for it.

'We'll go to the Chinaman's. He won't lock us out,' said Angelo.

They continued along Sugarmill Street to Tiy Lee's overstocked store. There they bought a hammer, a saw, an axe, a brush hook, a shovel, and a garden fork.

By the time Luigi tied the implements to the cross-bars, sweat was trickling down his back. Dark clouds loomed above the mountains; the air was humid and dense.

After the wet season they'd make a start on repairing the cane fields. The bulk of the work could be done in a few weeks. In the meantime, they'd try to recover their machinery and farm implements from the government, or whoever else had taken them.

A month passed. The tractor and the implements were still missing. If they'd have been borrowed by a farmer, they would have come back by now. Without machinery there was no farm. The brothers made a formal complaint to the police.

Young Constable Jackson was on duty, a good sign. He checked their identity cards, and crossed their names off the list of released internees.

Is that all?'

'When we were down south, our machinery disappeared. We need it back urgently,' said Luigi.

Jackson went to the filing cabinet, flicked through a few dozen manila folders, removed one marked with their surname. He opened it and leafed through. 'Aha, here it is. Everything was put into the custodianship of the Public Curator. They have impounded your machinery for safe-keeping. You should write to their office in Cairns.'

'We also want to ask about compensation for the boarding house. It's in a dreadful state and we haven't received any rent in a year.'

'Public Curator.'

'One other thing. We found our car on blocks with the wheels and half the engine missing. Would the Public Curator have those things too?' said Angelo.

Luigi whispered to him in Sicilian, 'Enough. You'll make more trouble for us.'

Meanwhile Constable Jackson had been flipping through the pages of their file. 'There's something here about a Terraplane pickup. In

September last, the Public Curator reported the theft of some parts. It seems they haven't shown up yet.'

'Obviously,' Angelo mumbled as they walked outside.

Later at the farm, Luigi put pen to paper. For an hour he slaved over the wording.

'There, that should do it.' He passed the finished letter to Angelo.

'Read it to me.'

Luigi cleared his throat and began.

> *Dear Sir,*
>
> *I am writing to you about our farm property at Wooranoora. Both my brother and I were lately released from internment. But when we returned, we found our farm in a terrible state and all our machinery gone. Both myself and my brother are now idle and cannot do anything on the farm. Would you be good enough to locate our belongings so we can get back to work? As time goes on it will be too late to do the necessary work for the sugar cane season. Whatever you have of ours, kindly send it back as soon as possible.*
>
> *I await an early reply.*

'Perfect,' said Angelo.

Luigi folded the paper and stuffed it into an envelope.

The letter produced a response of sorts. The Caterpillar tractor was returned from its holding pen. However, the Public Curator provided no information about the whereabouts of their implements.

Later Luigi went to see Tony Zucchero, hoping to borrow a plough and disc harrow. Because Edith had operated the farm while he was in internment, nothing had been lost or confiscated. Tony was as generous as always, offering whatever was needed in exchange for help with the planting in April. A fair deal. Luigi agreed without hesitation.

On the last day of January, the brothers made the hard decision. With no financial help forthcoming from the government, they needed to put the past behind them and prepare their land for the next crop.

Luigi filled the long-spouted can with kerosene and poured a line around the edge of the cane field. Angelo followed with a burning torch. The fire caught quickly. Tongues of flame lapped the darkening sky. Black smoke blocked out the sunset.

They retreated upwind to watch the cremation. Flickers of orange lit their sweaty faces. The fire marked the lowest point. Ahead lay a lot of backbreaking work.

But then, a new beginning.

Thirty-four

Wooranoora, January 1944

The four weeks in Brisbane quickly passed. Before Edith could fully take stock of her redefined relationship with her parents, she was back on the train north. This time she had two infants to amuse and stop from annoying the other passengers. The two-day trip passed in a blur of nursery rhymes and silly games designed to keep them quiet. By the time she stepped onto the platform at Wooranoora railway station, she felt as if she'd been through a cyclone. To her surprise, Mrs Sampson was waiting there with the truck.

'Welcome home, honey.' The older woman threw her arms around Edith. 'Thank you for everything you've done.'

'No, it's me who should be thanking you.' She returned the hug. 'I'm so sorry about Mr Sampson. He was a lovely man. I took some flowers to him, up on the hill.'

'Thank you. Yes, he was a good man and a good husband.' Mrs Sampson brushed away a tear. 'Now, let's get these two cherubs home, shall we?'

Edith stowed the ports and bags in the back of the truck and lifted the children into the cab. Lastly, she climbed up herself. She placed Bella in the middle and Anthony on her lap. The fit was tight, especially with Mrs Sampson's ample posterior. There was barely enough room to move the gearstick.

'Oh, I almost forgot,' said Mrs Sampson. 'Sergeant Pitt came sniffing around your place this morning. He said you should contact him as soon as you're back. Do you want to go there now or later?'

'Now, please. There might be news about Tony.'

226

The truck rattled across the railway tracks onto Sugarmill Street and stopped outside the police station. 'You go in, love. I'll stay here and ...'

Edith was gone before the sentence ended.

She walked up to the counter. Sergeant Pitt was writing notes at his desk. He looked up and made a grimace, which others might have described as a smile. It was the first time she'd seen his teeth, brown from nicotine. The word *pleasant* was not in his vocabulary.

'Ah, Mrs Zucchero. How kind of you to pay us a visit.' His greeting rang false.

'I heard you were looking for me this morning.'

'I was actually looking for Mr Allenby, your farm manager. You see, we've been informed that your husband is shortly to be returned to Wooranoora. As I've never had the pleasure of meeting Mr Allenby, I thought I would inform him in person that his services will no longer be necessary. You see, one of the conditions of your husband's release is that he must return to work on his own property. That is wherein the problem lies.'

Edith's blood pressure was starting to rise. Valiantly, she held her tongue.

'This morning I ascertained there is no such person as Ewan Allenby in Wooranoora. What do you say to that, Mrs Zucchero?' He bared his teeth again; triumph was written all over his ugly dial.

Edith threw her hands up in surrender. 'All right, I admit a little white lie. I don't actually have a man running the farm, but you must agree that the place has been properly managed. If you don't believe me, ask the chairman of the mill. We cut our quota of cane and got it in on schedule. This morning did you see any infestations of weeds? Does the place look run down? No. All that is because a *woman* worked damn hard during her husband's unforeseen absence. Correction: his unjust imprisonment. My husband's only crime was to help hardworking migrants keep their businesses afloat. Now, what do you say to *that*, Sergeant Pitt?'

'I could have you arrested for abusing a police officer.'

At that moment, Edith noticed a third person in the room: a fresh-faced constable who was trying to conceal his large frame behind a filing cabinet.

'Constable, did you witness any abuse? Did I swear? Did I threaten anyone?'

Sheepishly the young man shook his head. 'No, ma'am.'

Pitt's face went a deep shade of red. He looked as if he might explode.

Edith softened her voice. 'You said there was news about my husband. Do you know when he'll be coming home?'

The constable piped up before his boss could answer. 'We received the list this morning. Antonio Zucchero is due to be repatriated from the Chermside Staging Camp in Brisbane on 24 January.'

'That's tomorrow!' Edith could have kissed the lad. 'What wonderful news! Thank you, Constable. Thank you from the bottom of my heart!'

She skipped down the steps and danced back to the truck. 'Tony will be here by the end of the week!' she sang.

'Why are you crying again, Mummy?' said Bella.

Edith laughed, a little hysterically. 'These are happy tears, my sweet. Your Daddy is coming home.'

The train from Brisbane arrived on schedule. Edith and the children were on the platform as Tony and a handful of others disembarked. When the hugs and kisses and tears of reunion were through, they walked together across the tracks to the police station to have his whereabouts recorded. The formalities over, they returned to the truck.

With his port and belongings stowed in the tray, Tony climbed into the driver's seat as he always did. The children snuggled into their mother's lap. The truck roared from the station and turned into Russell River Road, the shortest route to the farm. The sun was shining and the paddocks were sprouting green shoots of cane.

Whether the war in Europe and the Pacific was over was of no importance to Edith.

All that mattered was the family was together again.

Thirty-five

The end of the war was nigh. According to Army sources and also the press, it was now certain that the Allies would be victorious over Nazi Germany.

At Loveday Internment Camp, each new twist had brought its challenges. But now there was no doubt about the outcome. Colonel Dean had made the momentous decision to allow the internees full access to the *Adelaide Advertiser*. Previously, newspapers were supplied in six-inch squares for use in the latrines.

At the end of December 1944, the headlines crowed about American-British triumphs in Europe as Hitler's forces were pushed back from the countries they'd invaded. The Germans were retreating back to the Fatherland where they belonged. Soon the fighting would be over and everyone could begin to rebuild the lives they'd had to abandon.

The sooner the better was Ted's opinion.

A year had passed since the Italian internees had been released and Camp 9 had been closed. Now Loveday was preparing to divest itself of the German contingent as well. Although it seemed that surrender was imminent, the German inmates were still officially enemies and therefore could not yet be released into the community. In winding down the number and size of internment camps in Australia, the Army decreed that all German prisoners would be transferred to a camp at Tatura in Victoria, leaving only Japanese at Loveday. That also meant the closure of Camp 10 and the Moorook woodcutting camp.

The transfers would create a mountain of paperwork for Ted. Arranging the transportation of five hundred-odd men under guard to a different military area would be no simple task. Thankfully it was scheduled for early January, leaving Ted free to have a week's furlough and a jolly good rest over Christmas.

What a year it had been!

In the office at GHQ, Ted dipped the pen nib into ink and made a start on entries to the German internees' record cards. He needed to make sure they were all correct and up-to-date before writing the same entry—Transferred to Tatura—six hundred times. It was worse than writing out lines in detention at school, for each word had to be legible and the card inkblot free.

With the European internees now either released or transferred to camps elsewhere in Australia, the attention of the guards turned to the Japanese. Two compounds remained in operation: Camps 14B and 14C. The war in the Pacific became the focus of all Australia's military effort, for the Japanese Imperial Army had proved to be a formidable opponent. The Japs were clever, unpredictable and prepared to make the ultimate sacrifice for their Emperor. In the islands to the north of Australia, kamikaze pilots had taken out munitions plants, bridges, and airfields with utmost accuracy and maximum destruction.

The greatest shame of a Japanese soldier was to be captured by the enemy rather than killed in action. The shame was worse than death. Yet, despite their best efforts, becoming a prisoner of war was exactly what happened to many thousands of Japanese Imperial servicemen. In the New South Wales internment camp at Cowra, the Jap POWs staged a suicide breakout, which resulted in more than two hundred men dead. This, along with military action taken by the Americans against their homeland, sparked fears that a similar event might happen at Loveday.

Although the guards carried rifles while on duty, an audit of the camp had revealed that most didn't know how to properly use or maintain the things. In the two decades between wars, the ageing soldiers had either forgotten how or had never been taught. That aside, there'd been a general she'll-be-right attitude in the European-dominated compounds. Rifles were considered unnecessary: weapons of last resort.

But the Japanese were a different matter entirely. Stricter security was needed, and with urgency. Dean ordered all the guard towers from the vacated camps to be dismantled and reassembled a mile down the road at Camp 14. The guards were issued with automatic weapons, and this time he made sure they were properly trained.

Ted, finally released from clerical duties, was one of the soldiers responsible for keeping the Japanese prisoners in check. He had not been in Camp 14 since 1942, so when he first climbed into the guard tower overlooking 14B, his eyes grew wide in amazement. In those two years, the compound had been completely transformed.

A bare brown canvas had turned into a Japanese watercolour. There were stone shrines, ordered gardens of bamboo and spiky grasses, dry riverbeds of raked pebbles, ornamental bridges over ponds, waterlilies.

Every nook of the man-made landscape was moving with human activity. Here was a troupe of acrobats, practicing their craft. There was a group of old men, moving slowly and in perfect harmony through an exercise routine. Around a shrine was a congregation of worshippers, bowing and murmuring prayers. Beneath a bamboo shelter sat a semicircle of scholars with their teacher. Others were tending the gardens or whittling lengths of bamboo or sweeping the gravel paths with bundles of sticks. The inmates wore coolie hats and baggy trousers. Although he'd never been to Japan, the scene in front of him was exactly as he pictured life there: serene yet disciplined. Everyone had a purpose and everyone was busy in his own quiet way.

Later Colonel Dean explained to the guards who were new to the Japanese compounds that first impressions could be misleading.

'What they choose to reveal is but a veneer. While the surface may be smooth, treacherous waters may lie beneath. Japs are inscrutable by nature. You cannot tell what they are thinking or what they will do next.'

Dean went on to give an account of the Cowra breakout in the August past. It had been triggered by a naïve decision of the army to transfer all the Japanese prisoners to the internment camp at Hay at short notice.

'The evening after the inmates were informed, they stormed the perimeter fence armed with crude weapons: baseball bats, bits of jagged metal and the like. The first wave flung themselves against the barbed wire with only blankets for protection. They sacrificed themselves as human ladders for those coming behind.

'The uprising took everyone by surprise. Terrible loss of life. Four soldiers and more than two hundred Japs, not to mention dozens wounded. Under the circumstances the guards did a mighty job, but they were not properly prepared. That will not happen at Loveday. Not on my watch.

'These people are supremely loyal to their Emperor and consider it their duty to die for their country. I suspect that as the war in the Pacific draws to its inevitable close, the reaction here may be catastrophic.

'Men, we must be ever vigilant. The mood can change fast. Any deviation from the day-to-day routine must be reported immediately, no matter how insignificant it might seem. We must remain calm and in control.'

Ted had not yet had much contact with the slightly-built prisoners. In particular communication was difficult. Although he'd never studied Italian or German, he found the cadence of their speech similar to English. Like English, many words were derived from Latin, Greek, or Nordic roots. Once his ear was attuned to the accent, he could grasp a broad understanding of what was being said. Perhaps he had an ear for languages. Or perhaps, during the last war in Europe, he'd absorbed more than he realised.

The Japanese language was entirely different from anything he'd ever known. When he gave an instruction, the Japs would stare at him with blank faces. If he used his hands—an international sign language that usually worked with Europeans—they still didn't understand. And if they spoke to him in their sing-song dialects, he was at a complete loss. It was as if they'd come from another galaxy.

According to the records, all the inmates had been civilians. Most were family men who'd gone to the Dutch East Indies or Malaya for work. A smaller group hailed from the pearling centres of Darwin or Broome or were descended from Japanese miners who'd come to the gold rush towns in the mid eighteen-hundreds. Despite being born in Australia, none had citizenship because Orientals were not considered white.

It was a third-generation Japanese-Australian—a shearers' cook— who took Ted most by surprise. The poor fellow could barely speak a word of Japanese, so he took every opportunity to have a chin-wag with the guards. His name was Albert. Despite his struggle with the dominant language in the compound, he seemed to know everything that went on. This made him a useful contact for a guard. In return for information, Ted would give him a tin of bully beef or a wad of tobacco. In a court of law, this would probably be construed as collusion, but Ted preferred to call it 'a reciprocal arrangement'. Everyone was a winner.

As American warships closed in on the island Okinawa, tensions in Camp 14 rose, exactly as Colonel Dean predicted. In May 1945, a letter written by the camp leader of 14C was intercepted and translated. The implication was that an Allied invasion of the southernmost island of Japan would trigger an uprising.

Security at Loveday was stepped up. The number of duty guards was doubled.

The morning that Albert appeared beneath the guard tower, the first frost of winter dusted the grass. His arms were raised above his head in the manner of a human starfish and he began to wave them vigorously. It was clear the matter was urgent. In accordance with security procedures, Ted called for backup before climbing down the ladder.

Albert pointed to the entry gates. The pair walked in parallel along the fence lines, one on the inside and one on the outside, with no-man's land in the middle. Ted opened the external entry gate and strode across the bare ground to the internal gate.

'What's up, mate?'

Albert looked agitated. 'Okinawa. If it falls, there's talk of a mass suicide.'

Ted's mouth opened but no words came out. Didn't they have wives and families in Japan? Why would a man throw his life away for nothing?

Although his gut reaction was to ask why, it was more important to get reliable information. He remembered Dean's speech, gathered his wits, and instead asked *how*.

'They're cutting blankets into strips,' said Albert.

'Do you think they'll attempt a break out?'

'Probably not. No, I think they'll end it quietly.'

Ted thanked his informant and promised a reward for his trouble. He set his jaw and proceeded directly to the commandant's office.

If Dean was surprised, he didn't show it. 'I knew there was trouble brewing. Another guard received a tip-off that the mainland Japanese were planning to break out and kill as many soldiers as they could in the process. Failing that, they will probably commit suicide rather than be sent back to Japan.'

This time Ted couldn't hold back. 'Sir, why would they do such a thing?'

'It's their culture. Soldier or civilian. To not die for their country during war is a cause of great shame. In their villages they would be spat on, beaten or shunned. But to sacrifice their lives for the glory of Japan brings honour to their families.'

'Is there nothing we can do to prevent it? Albert says they're going to hang themselves with ropes made of blanket. But with winter coming in, we can't confiscate their blankets, can we?'

'If they choose to do this, they'll find a way,' said Dean evenly.

'I still don't get it. How does hanging yourself in an Australian internment camp count as sacrificing your life for the Emperor?'

'Who would ever know the truth? In Japan, these men are already revered as fallen heroes. Ceremonies would have been held to honour them. To show up hale and hearty three years later would be like returning from the dead.'

Slowly Ted shook his head. 'I'll never understand them, I'm afraid.'

'You don't have to. Keep your eyes open and your back covered.'

Ted saluted and turned on his heel to leave.

'Wait! There *is* something we can do. The atmosphere here is so tense you could cut it with a knife. A diversion might work. Baseball is popular, I understand.'

Ted grinned. 'I believe you're right. I'll have a word to Albert.'

It was 10 June 1945, the start of winter proper. The two Japanese compounds were dressed up like a holiday. Scores of paper kites flew above the huts, dipping and swooping like colourful birds of prey. In the afternoon, the inaugural baseball match would be played. 14B versus 14C. The field would be the roadway down the centre of the complex, allowing supporters from both sides to get a good view without leaving their respective compounds. While baseball had become a popular pastime, this was the first time that Colonel Dean had approved an inter-compound match. If today went well, Ted knew the intention was to continue.

When the mess bell sounded to announce the commencement of the match, five hundred internees from both camps had gathered at the wire to watch. Ted and his fellow guards stood inside the inner wire fence, along the boundaries of the baseball field.

The umpire was a guard who'd lived for a time in Boston and knew the rules. The teams had made coloured bibs to wear over their maroon uniforms. Red for 14B and blue for 14C. The toss was won by the Reds. They chose to field.

The teams were evenly matched. Despite erratic pitching, several batters hit home runs, which set the crowd on fire. All focus was on the plate or the pitcher as he wound up to hurl the ball. As the game came into the ninth inning, the scores were dead even. The excitement in both camps was palpable.

The Blues made three runs. Now the pressure was on the Reds.

The first two batters were struck out without a swing. Two down, one to go. It seemed the Reds had given up without a fight. Albert was next up. After a few practice swings, he stepped into the box. He tapped the bat on the plate and raised it to his shoulder. Whether he cast an evil eye or whispered an old shearer's curse, no-one would never know, but at that moment the pitcher lost concentration. Four wild balls later, Albert walked to first base. The next batter belted the ball to shortstop who fumbled, then overthrew. The two ran hard between bases. The next hit got the man safely to first.

Final inning, two men out, loaded bases. Now it was all or nothing.

The crowd was going crazy; each side was shouting in Japanese and waving paper flags the colour of its team.

The fourth batter stepped up. He spat on his palms, settled his feet, steadied the bat at waist height. The first pitch. With all his might, he swung.

The ball found the sweet-spot. A satisfying crack. It whizzed over high over heads towards centre field. The fielder was running backwards, his glove over his head. He jumped, missed, stumbled, fell. The ball hurtled along the ground, two other fielders sprinting after it. Meanwhile the runners scooted around the bases and the crowd roared.

One home, two home, three home.

The batter came charging around as the ball sailed into the infield. The catcher dropped his glove. The batter took a dive.

'Safe!' yelled the umpire.

The final score was twenty-two to twenty-one. The Reds supporters were dancing with joy.

'Best thing we ever did,' said Colonel Dean afterwards. 'A good time was had by all.'

The baseball matches continued on a weekly basis for the next two months. No breakouts were attempted and no-one took his own life.

On 15 August 1945, shortly after America dropped atomic bombs on the cities of Nagasaki and Hiroshima, Emperor Hirohito announced an unconditional surrender by Japan. The guards were told within fifteen minutes of Colonel Dean receiving the news from Adelaide. They cheered and slapped each other's backs. At last it was over.

Although Ted cheered with his workmates, he had mixed feelings. Soon he'd be out of work and bumbling around the house without a purpose. He shook everyone's hand and joined in with the back-slapping but his heart wasn't in the celebration.

When they'd quietened down, Dean said, 'We'd better break the news to the inmates. I don't think they'll be happy. We'll call in the camp leaders and let them listen to the Emperor's speech in their own language. They can convey the message to the men.'

As predicted, the reaction in the compounds was of shock and disbelief. Even with the recording of Hirohito's speech playing over the PA system, some refused to believe it.

'It's a trick.'

'That isn't Hirohito; it's an impersonator.'

'Japan would never surrender.'

Thirty-six

The war with Japan ended as suddenly and as spectacularly as it began. Less than a week after America's second atomic bomb obliterated the city of Nagasaki instantly killing countless thousands, Japan surrendered.

The Telegraph, Brisbane's afternoon paper, was first to break the news.

PEACE! shouted the front page in four-inch bold letters. The accompanying photograph showed crowds who'd flowed out of the shops and office buildings into Queen Street. People of all ages were dancing through knee-deep ticker-tape, riding on the bonnets of cars, and kissing perfect strangers.

As a senior politician, William Delahunty was there, not dancing or riding about on cars, but celebrating in the way he knew how: with cigars and lots of handshakes. In particular he shook the hand of every serviceman he encountered. American and Australian, white and black. Yes, he even ventured across the Victoria Bridge and into notorious South Brisbane, where the servicemen of colour were based. He thanked them profusely and in person for their help in bringing victory to the Pacific.

At the Doctor Carver Club on Grey Street, the party was well under way. Delahunty—the only white man there—was received as an honoured guest. The four-piece band was playing improvised jazz. Coca-Cola was flowing as fast as the Brisbane River in flood. Everyone was dancing. If his gammy leg hadn't been playing up, he probably would have joined them. For now, he was content to sit near the servery and watch their lithe bodies bounding and twisting and throwing each other into spins.

One good thing the Americans had brought to this country was a new way to dance that was active and joyous and came straight from the heart.

236

Unlike ballroom, there were no restraints. The Pride of Erin, Viennese Waltz, and Gypsy Tap demanded set moves and perfect coordination. But the Jitterbug and the Jive gave the dancers complete freedom to move how they pleased. How he wished he was young again!

The band stepped up the tempo. The floor was packed and the dancers were on fire. The centre opened up to allow an enthusiastic pair some elbowroom. They flung each other around like acrobats: the black soldier in US uniform and the white woman in a red dress. He tossed her into the air, swung her between his legs, slid her along the floor. She did somersaults right over his back and landed square on her feet. Not once did they miss a beat of the music. The others formed a circle around them and clapped.

Enjoying their unbounded energy, Delahunty sipped his soda. He would have liked something stronger, but the place was run by Red Cross volunteers and hard liquor was forbidden. Instead he lit a cigar and added more smoke to the cigarette haze.

The band swept into a crescendo, then banged out the finale of the set. The couple took a bow and then strolled hand-in-hand to the refreshments bar. That was when Delahunty's eyes nearly popped out of their sockets.

One of the dancers was Amy.

'Hello, William,' she said casually as if expecting to see him there. She leant over and kissed him chastely on the cheek. She was still holding the hand of her dance partner. 'I'd like you to meet Eugene, my fiancé.'

Delahunty grasped the other man's outstretched hand and gave it a hearty shake. 'Congratulations.' Surprisingly his voice was steady. He put it down to years of practice, saying what he didn't believe in the interests of the common good. Inside, every cell of his body was screaming with anger and astonishment.

'After we're married, we're going to Chicago to live.' On Amy's face was a look of triumph, as if this dusky young man was the answer to her cesspit of woes. 'I've come to the conclusion that Brisbane is a bit of a dump, isn't it Eugene?'

'I wouldn't say that, babe. It's a small town with a big heart.'

'Anyway, it's got nothing on Chicago. Right?'

Eugene's eyes lit up. 'Yeah, babe. There's no place like home.'

How prosaic! The comment was straight out of *The Wizard of Oz*. Did people in America actually talk like that?

'So, when's the big day?'

'Saturday next week. As soon I heard the news that the war was over, I got straight on the telephone. Seems like every other girl in town had the same idea. You wouldn't believe how many calls it took to get a church and a hall for the reception.' She went on to give details of the places and times. 'Of course, you and Margaret are invited.'

Delahunty dropped his head. It was something that he'd rather not do. In fact, the very idea was a bit bizarre: taking your long-standing wife to your ex-lover's wedding. 'Thanks. I'll talk to Margaret and let you know.'

'After everything you've both done to help me, it's the least I can do.' She wore that sweet yet seductive smile that had lured him in the first place. 'I mean it, William.'

His heart did a backflip and he found himself unexpectedly simmering with desire. After all her antics, why couldn't he blot her out of his mind?

But there was more to it than that. He envied her young beau for his vitality and good looks, attributes he'd once had, now eroded by the passage of time. It was hard to admit that he was yesterday's man, a shadow of his former self. Getting older wasn't easy. Even in the Party meetings, when he looked around the table, he was the most senior by several years. Now, thanks to Amy and the kindness of his wife, he had a reason to get on with the business of living, whatever that entailed.

A sudden heatwave flowed through his body; sweat was trickling down his back and his shirt collar was strangling him. The room began to slowly spin. If he didn't get some fresh air, he'd be lying on the floor. He made an excuse and hastened outside.

On Grey Street, a crowd of coloured servicemen was waiting to get into the club. Some were with girlfriends, some were with pals in jovial groups. Everyone was jiving to an inner beat. He walked slowly toward the iron structure of the Victoria Bridge. Trams full of revellers were rattling across from the central city. At the southern entrance to the bridge he leant on a railing and rested. The cold whip of an August westerly snapped him back to reality. He rubbed his eyes, gazed down into the brown swirl of the river.

Now that the war was over, the world would inevitably change. It had taken two atomic bombs to convince the Japanese to say *enough*. Two cities had been destroyed; entire families were dead. He thought about the closing stages of the war in Europe: the incineration of Dresden and the destruction of Berlin. Residences, civic buildings, palaces, cathedrals, museums. All gone to rubble.

Destroying life and property was not exclusive to invading Axis forces led by power-hungry despots. The Allies had done untold damage to cities and towns right across Europe. All that devastation had been engineered in the name of Peace. Apart from the loss of thousands of troops and the enormous financial cost, the nations of America, Canada, Australia, New Zealand had come out virtually unscarred. While Darwin had copped a few bombs from the Japs and midget submarines had fired a couple of torpedoes in Sydney Harbour, the remainder of the continent was intact.

How would destroyed countries ever recover?

For six years now, Delahunty had focussed on managing the next crisis. Navigating unchartered political territory had had its appeal. Being one of the decision-makers for a war had been challenging and a little dangerous, even though Australia had been lucky enough to stay mostly out of harm's way.

Now the government would need to focus on unwinding all the measures introduced in the name of national security. Military personnel would return home. Ex-soldiers would need to find jobs, marry, buy houses, raise families. Women who'd been doing the work of men would have to step aside and return to their rightful place in the home. Land and machinery that had been appropriated by the military would need to be returned to its owners. Army installations and internment camps would need to be shut down, the equipment liquidated. There was so much to be done that his head hurt.

He continued walking across the bridge. Back in Queen Street, the victory party was just getting started. As residents switched on their wirelesses and heard the good news, they flocked into town to celebrate. Even the policemen had joined in, kissing and hugging and dancing with anyone within reach.

Delahunty caught the next tram to Ashgrove.

One week later, Delahunty and Margaret, together with their little boy Bobby, attended the wedding of Amy and Eugene at St Mary's church, followed by a modest reception at McWhirter's cafeteria in the Valley.

As expected, Amy looked radiant in a borrowed gown: a powderpuff of white satin and chiffon with a beaded bodice and a long veil. The groom was neat in US military dress uniform. They were a fine-looking couple, once you got used to the idea of a mixed-race union. There could be no debate about where to live, for Eugene was not able to remain in the country.

On the dancefloor, Amy told Delahunty that her husband was due to depart for San Francisco aboard the *USS Navigator* first thing on Monday morning. Through a friend of a friend—and also the provision of a substantial financial incentive—she had managed to secure a berth on a 'bride ship' the following week. Apparently, this was the war bride's equivalent of winning the lottery.

'You have no idea how many women are queueing up to follow their husbands overseas,' she said. 'At this stage, I won't be back. I wanted to say that you're a good man, William. I couldn't think of a better father and role model for our son.'

He gave her a squeeze and a peck on the cheek. 'We'll love him and look after him, Amy. When we get back to Cairns, we'll say he was a late but wonderful surprise for a long-married couple. No-one but us three will ever know the truth.'

*

The little boy, christened Robert William Delahunty, went on to be raised by loving parents—his natural father and his adoptive mother—in far north Queensland.

Twenty-five years later he would enter state politics, following a course set by his father and mentor, Sir William James Delahunty.

Thirty-seven

Loveday, February 1946

Although the war was officially over, the logistics of getting everyone home was another matter. Transport was impossible to get; all shipping was in military service and a long way from Australia. The first priority was to bring the Australian troops back, in particular the sick and wounded.

At Loveday some eighteen hundred Japanese remained in the two compounds. There was plenty for them to do. Internee labour was used to dismantle Camps 9 and 10. The salvage was auctioned off to local farmers and businesses. The crops were harvested and the pigs were sent to slaughter.

On 20 February 1946, the Japanese internees boarded express trains bound for Melbourne where they would embark on the *Koei Maru* for the return voyage to Japan.

The war machine was gradually being unwound. With space now available, Loveday received their first prisoners of war, two and a half thousand Italians and three hundred Germans. These were fighting men who had been captured on the battlefields of Europe or North Africa and held in other POW camps within Australia.

In November and December 1946, the Italian soldiers were repatriated in three separate ships back to their homeland. The German POWs, the last prisoners ever held at Loveday, departed in January 1947.

On the final day, when what was left of Loveday was deserted and the offices at GHQ were packed up, Dean put his hand on Ted's shoulder. 'Thanks, mate, for all your good work. I couldn't have managed without you.'

Ted felt his face getting hot. It wasn't easy to receive compliments. 'Arrh, it was nothing. But thanks for talking me into it. Without you and Loveday I would have been a lost man.'

'I know, mate. I've seen it before. The world wasn't meant to be seen through the bottom of an empty glass. So, what will you do now?'

Ted shrugged. 'Between you and me, I'm a bit scared about the future.'

'I've been meaning to talk to you. Since our soldiers have gone back to being civilians, everyone's been busy getting married and setting up house. I know this fellow in Adelaide who has a furniture workshop. He can't keep up with the demand. Perhaps you'd like to meet him?'

A smile crept across Ted's face. Not many like him were handed a second chance on a silver platter. The opportunity to start life afresh in a new city wasn't something he should pass up. Before he could think of a hundred excuses to knock it back, he shook Dean's hand.

'Thanks mate, I'd love to.'

Thirty-eight

Wooranoora, 1948

It took four years for the Innocenti Brothers to recover from their internment. By the end of 1948 they'd added two more properties—rundown houses in far-flung places—to a growing list of assets. Both were acquired in exchange for rent that was owing. Having received no compensation from the government for their losses, they relied on barter and the generosity of neighbours until they could buy the necessary farm implements. The wrecked Terraplane pickup was replaced with a black sedan of the same make.

Angelo announced he wanted a place of his own. Until then, the unwritten agreement between them had been to split their assets and income equally. Before he could buy a property, he would have to go through the naturalization process and renounce his Italian citizenship.

Constable Jackson helped Angelo fill out the application form. A notice of intention was published in *The Cairns Post*. No objections were received. The police report stated that he was 'of good character and repute'. Two months later, he became a British subject.

Angelo bought a bush block from the council. Bordered by the Russell River, the land was flat and heavily wooded. Although it would take a huge effort to clear, it was perfect for growing sugar cane using machinery rather than horses. He named the property *Sixty-Seven* after its section number on the cadastral map.

Now aged in his late fifties, Angelo struggled with the heavy work. Often he'd need to take a rest break when he'd sit on a log, have a smoke, and sip sweet tea laced with vermouth. Working slowly and methodically, he and Luigi cleared enough land in a month to plant a crop.

When their brother Tano wrote asking them to sponsor his family—himself, his wife, and five children—to migrate, the brothers leapt at the opportunity. They'd tried twice before: once during the Great Depression and again just before the war. Now Australia had opened its arms to refugees and migrants from Europe and there was a good chance of success.

Luigi said, 'Perhaps I should go to Sicily and bring them back.'

'What for?' said Angelo.

'I want to get married.'

'Who to?' Angelo's eyes went as wide as saucers.

'I don't know yet. I'll find a nice woman.'

Angelo was gawking at him as if he had two heads, then he broke into a sly grin. 'Would you find someone for me too?'

'No problem.' Luigi laughed.

'Are you *serious*?'

'Are *you*?' Luigi lifted his brows.

'When would you go?' said Angelo.

'After the planting and I'll stay as long as it takes.'

Since returning from Loveday, he'd had been toying with the idea. He yearned to be like Tony Zucchero, happy and contented with a loving wife and young brood.

Last birthday, Luigi had turned fifty-four. For most of his life he'd toiled to make a home for himself and the family he always intended to have. As it was, he was increasingly likely to see out his days as a bachelor. If he delayed even one more year, he'd be getting too old to carry out the plan.

Expecting a long and difficult process through government channels, he applied for a passport. Just four weeks later a navy-blue booklet, stamped with the British crown and the Australian coat of arms, arrived in the mail. Straight away he booked a berth on a steamer bound for Napoli.

In April 1949, Angelo drove him to the Wooranoora railway station, from where he'd take the southbound train to Brisbane. With him was a trunk full of clothing, gifts for the relations, and a folding Brownie camera. For the first time in years he had a spring in his step, and hope in his heart that he would not return alone.

* * *

Thank you for reading my novel.

For indie authors like me, reviews are like gold.

If you enjoyed the read, please take a minute to leave a review
on the website of your favourite bookseller or
a reader review site such as Goodreads.

Thank you again and happy reading.
Debbie Terranova

References and Acknowledgements

Australian War Memorial: Information about World War 2 accessed through the website http://www.awm.gov.au.

Local Historical Societies and Libraries: Paper records and information accessed in the offices of the Cairns Historical Society, Gordonvale Historical Society, Babinda Library, Cobdogla Irrigation Museum, the MacArthur Museum Brisbane.

National Archives of Australia: Files (paper and digitised) relating to Luigi and other internees, and the Loveday Internment Camps. Accessed in the National Archives offices in Brisbane, Adelaide, Sydney, and Canberra. Electronic access to digitised files through the website http://www.naa.gov.au.

Newspapers: *The Advertiser, The Cairns Post, The Telegraph, The Courier Mail*. Editions from 1939 to 1945 accessed electronically through http://www.trove.nla.gov.au.

State Libraries: Printed and archival material about internment in Australia accessed in the State Library of Queensland, State Library of New South Wales.

Individuals: Sam Terranova, for sharing Luigi's amazing story and memories of growing up in the sugar cane town of Babinda. Sam also took on the mammoth task of helping to edit the manuscript.

The late Max Scholz of Barmera for imparting first-hand knowledge of the Loveday Internment Camps and sharing his collection of World War Two and internment camp memorabilia.

Beta readers Davide Cottone and Elise Terranova for insights, encouragement, and invaluable feedback.

Fellow author Ruth Bonetti who has accompanied me on this long but rewarding writing journey.

Elise Terranova for her beautiful cover design.

Selected Bibliography

Austral Archaeology. *Loveday Internment Camp Archaeological Report.* Adelaide 1992. Report commissioned by the State Heritage Branch, Department of Environment and Planning, South Australia.

Dean, Edwin Thayer. *Internment in South Australia.* 1946. Report published by the authority of the Committee appointed to record the History of Internment in South Australia, Adelaide.

Dignan, Don. *Chiaffredo Venerano Fraire, 1952—1931.* In *The Queensland Experience*, by Maximilian Brändle (ed). Phoenix Publications, Indooroopilly, Brisbane. 1991.

Morton, Clive. *Francesco Fantin, Wartime Murder and Cover Up.* Journal of the Royal Historical Society of Queensland, Vol. 18, No. 6, May 2003: 256-272.

Noyce, Pat. *Bert's Story.* Barmera District War Memorial Community Centre, S.A. 1994.

Scholz, Max. *As I Remember: The Loveday Internment Camps.* Max Scholz, Barmera, S.A. 2004.

About the author

Debbie Terranova is a prize-winning author of historical fiction and crime mysteries with a conscience. She has been writing creatively for more than ten years and has published novels, novellas, and short stories.

Enemies within these Shores, historical fiction about life, love, and internment in Australia during World War Two, is her third novel.

Crime mystery novels, *Baby Farm* and *The Scarlet Key* are gripping romps in and around Brisbane, featuring a dynamic duo of journalist super-sleuths, Seth VerBeek and Cate Bradshaw.

Mowbray Bathers, a heart-warming story about coming of age and brotherly love, was a winner of *One Book Many Brisbanes* in 2011.

Connect with Debbie Terranova

Website: terranovapublications.com
Email: terranovapublications@gmail.com
Facebook: Terranova Books

Other titles by Debbie Terranova

The Scarlet Key, crime mystery novel
When an envelope containing a shiny red key lands on his newsroom desk, reporter Seth VerBeek is thrust into a thrilling crime adventure. On investigation he discovers the corpse of a tattooed woman.

Who is she? Why and how did she die?

The cast of flawed but unforgettable characters includes a socialite, a psychic tattooist, a female greyhound trainer, a retired art teacher, and a 'personal handyman' who specialises in matters of the heart. Each character's story unfolds like a slow striptease. One by one, layers of subterfuge are peeled off until all is laid bare.

The Scarlet Key is a page-turner that tackles ageing, finding love again, healing, forgiveness, and the choices to be made near the end of life.

Baby Farm, crime mystery novel
How much is a baby worth?

Politician Vann Willis is on track to find out when a blast rips through her electoral office. Her Inquiry into forced adoptions and surrogacy has uncovered crooked deals so she forms an unlikely partnership with investigative reporter, Seth VerBeek.

Together, they explore the seamy side of Maidenhead, a gothic homestead that was once a hideaway for pregnant teens. Now, its electrified fence suggests the enterprise is far more sinister.

Dark secrets emerge. Vann's life is under threat. One relationship ends while another blossoms. At the heart of it all is the baby farm.

Mowbray Brothers, short fiction
Saturday night, summer of 1920. Mowbray Park is where the local lads go for a laugh, a beer, and a smoke. Eight-year-old Lucky sneaks out of bed to discover his brother and hero has taken a dare that could cost much more than his one shilling bet.

Mowbray Brothers is set in world that no longer exists. An era of gaslight, rattling trams, Saturday night sing-songs, and a sand-bottomed river with a bathing enclosure at its edge. Inspiration came from the author's father and his stories of growing up in Brisbane in the 1920s.

www.ingramcontent.com/pod-product-compliance
Lightning Source LLC
Chambersburg PA
CBHW021004120726

47905CB00009B/2848